The Rembrandt Affair

Daniel Silva is the number one *New York Times* bestselling author of *The Unlikely Spy, The Mark of the Assassin, The Marching Season, The Kill Artist, The English Assassin, The Confessor, A Death in Vienna, Prince of Fire, The Messenger, The Secret Servant, Moscow Rules* and *The Defector*. He is married to NBC News *Today* correspondent Jamie Gangel. They have two children, Lily and Nicholas. In 2009, Silva was appointed to the United States Holocaust Memorial Museum Council.

Visit the author's website at: www.danielsilvabooks.com

Also by Daniel Silva

The Defector

Moscow Rules

The Secret Servant

The Messenger

Prince of Fire

A Death in Vienna

The Confessor

The English Assassin

The Kill Artist

The Marching Season

The Mark of the Assassin

The Unlikely Spy

The Rembrandt Affair

DANIEL SILVA

MICHAEL JOSEPH
an imprint of
PENGUIN BOOKS

MICHAEL JOSEPH

Published by the Penguin Group
Penguin Books Ltd, 80 Strand, London WC2R 0RL, England
Penguin Group (USA) Inc., 375 Hudson Street, New York, New York 10014, USA
Penguin Group (Canada), 90 Eglinton Avenue East, Suite 700, Toronto, Ontario, Canada M4P 2Y3
(a division of Pearson Penguin Canada Inc.)
Penguin Ireland, 25 St Stephen's Green, Dublin 2, Ireland (a division of Penguin Books Ltd)
Penguin Group (Australia), 250 Camberwell Road,
Camberwell, Victoria 3124, Australia (a division of Pearson Australia Group Pty Ltd)
Penguin Books India Pvt Ltd, 11 Community Centre,
Panchsheel Park, New Delhi – 110 017, India
Penguin Group (NZ), 67 Apollo Drive, Rosedale, North Shore 0632, New Zealand
(a division of Pearson New Zealand Ltd)
Penguin Books (South Africa) (Pty) Ltd, 24 Sturdee Avenue,
Rosebank, Johannesburg 2196, South Africa

Penguin Books Ltd, Registered Offices: 80 Strand, London WC2R 0RL, England

www.penguin.com

First published in the USA by G. P. Putnam's Sons 2010
First published in Great Britain by Michael Joseph 2010
3

Printed in Great Britain by Clays Ltd, St Ives plc

A CIP catalogue record for this book is available from the British Library

HARDBACK ISBN: 978-0-718-15528-5

TRADE PAPERBACK ISBN: 978-0-718-15529-2

www.greenpenguin.co.uk

Penguin Books is committed to a sustainable future for our business, our readers and our planet. The book in your hands is made from paper certified by the Forest Stewardship Council.

For Jeff Zucker,
for friendship, support, and personal courage.

And, as always, for my wife, Jamie, and
my children, Lily and Nicholas.

Behind every great fortune lies a great crime.

—HONORÉ DE BALZAC

PROLOGUE

PORT NAVAS, CORNWALL

By coincidence it was Timothy Peel who first learned that the stranger had returned to Cornwall. He made the discovery shortly before midnight on a rain-swept Wednesday in mid-September. And only because he had politely declined the persistent entreaties from the boys at work to attend the midweek bash at the Godolphin Arms up in Marazion.

It was a mystery to Peel why they still bothered to invite him. Truth be told, he had never cared much for the company of drinkers. And these days, whenever he set foot in a pub, there was at least one intoxicated soul who would try to badger him into talking about "little Adam Hathaway." Six months earlier, in one of the most dramatic rescues in the history of the Royal National Lifeboat Institution, Peel had plucked the six-year-old boy from the treacherous surf off Sennen Cove. The newspapers had crowned Peel a national hero but were then dumbfounded when the broad-shouldered twenty-two-year-old with movie-idol looks refused to grant a single interview. Peel's silence privately annoyed his colleagues, any one of whom would have leapt at the chance for a few moments of celebrity, even if it meant reciting the old clichés about "the importance of teamwork" and "the proud traditions of a proud service." Nor did it sit well with the beleaguered residents of West Cornwall, who were always looking for a good reason to boast about a local boy and stick it to the English snobs from "up-country." From Falmouth Bay to Land's End, the mere mention of Peel's name invariably provoked a puzzled shake of the head. A bit odd, they would say. Always was. Must have been the divorce. Never knew his real father. And that mother! Always took up with the wrong sort. Remember Derek, the whiskey-soaked playwright? Heard he used to beat the lad. At least that was the rumor in Port Navas.

It was true about the divorce. And even the beatings. In fact, most of the idle gossip about Peel had a ring of accuracy. But none of it had anything to do with his refusal to accept his role as hero. Peel's silence was a tribute to a man he had known only briefly, a long time ago. A man who had lived just up Port Navas Quay in the old foreman's cottage near the oyster farm. A man who had taught him how to sail and how to repair old motorcars; who had taught him about the power of loyalty and the beauty of opera. A man who had taught him there was no reason to boast simply for doing one's job.

The man had a poetic foreign-sounding name, but Peel had always thought of him only as the stranger. He had been Peel's accomplice, Peel's guardian angel. And even though he had been gone from Cornwall for many years now, Peel occasionally still watched for him, just as he had when he was a boy of eleven. Peel still had the dog-eared logbook he had kept of the stranger's erratic comings and goings, and the photos of the eerie white lights that used to glow in the stranger's cottage at night. And even now, Peel could picture the stranger at the wheel of his beloved wooden ketch, coming up the Helford Passage after a long night alone on the sea. Peel would always be waiting in his bedroom window, his arm raised in a silent salute. And the stranger, when he spotted him, would always flash his running lights twice in response.

There were few reminders of those days left in Port Navas. Peel's mother had moved to the Algarve coast of Portugal with her new lover. Derek the drunken playwright was rumored to be living in a beachfront hut in Wales. And the old foreman's cottage had been completely renovated and was now owned by posh weekenders from London who threw loud parties and were forever yelling at their spoiled children. All that remained of the stranger was his ketch, which he had bequeathed to Peel the night he fled Cornwall for parts unknown.

On that rainy evening in mid-September, the boat was bobbing at its mooring in the tidal creek, waves nudging gently against its hull, when an unfamiliar engine note lifted Peel from his bed and carried him back to his familiar outpost in the window. There, peering into the wet gloom, he spotted a metallic gray Range Rover making its way slowly along the road. It came to a stop outside the old foreman's cottage and idled a moment, headlamps doused, wipers beating a steady rhythm. Then the driver's-side door suddenly swung open, and a figure emerged wearing a dark green Barbour raincoat and a waterproof flat cap pulled low over his brow. Even from a distance, Peel knew instantly it was the stranger. It was the walk that betrayed him—the confident, purposeful stride that seemed to propel him effortlessly toward the edge of the quay. He paused there briefly, carefully avoiding the pool of light from the single lamp, and stared at the ketch. Then he quickly descended the flight of stone steps to the river and disappeared from view.

At first, Peel wondered whether the stranger had come back to lay claim to the boat. But that fear receded when he suddenly reappeared, clutching a small parcel in his left hand. It was about the size of a hardcover book and appeared to be wrapped in plastic. Judging from the coat of slime on the surface, the package had been concealed for a long time. Peel had once imagined the stranger to be a smuggler. Perhaps he had been right after all.

It was then Peel noticed that the stranger was not alone. Someone was waiting for him in the front seat of the Rover. Peel couldn't quite make out the face, only a silhouette and a halo of riotous hair. He smiled for the first time. It seemed the stranger finally had a woman in his life.

Peel heard the muffled thump of a door closing and saw the Rover lurch instantly forward. If he hurried, there was just enough time to intercept it. Instead, in the grips of a feeling he had not known since childhood, he stood motionless in the window, arm raised in a silent salute. The Rover gathered speed and for an instant Peel feared the stranger had not seen the signal. Then it slowed suddenly and the headlamps flashed twice before passing beneath Peel's window and vanishing into the night.

Peel remained at his post a moment longer, listening as the

sound of the engine faded into silence. Then he climbed back into bed and pulled his blankets beneath his chin. His mother was gone, Derek was in Wales, and the old foreman's cottage was under foreign occupation. But for now, Peel was not alone. The stranger had returned to Cornwall.

PART ONE

PROVENANCE

I

GLASTONBURY, ENGLAND

Though the stranger did not know it, two disparate series of events were by that night already conspiring to lure him back onto the field of battle. One was being played out behind the locked doors of the world's secret intelligence services while the other was the subject of a global media frenzy. The newspapers had dubbed it "the summer of theft," the worst epidemic of art heists to sweep Europe in a generation. Across the Continent, priceless paintings were disappearing like postcards plucked from the rack of a sidewalk kiosk. The anguished masters of the art universe had professed shock over the rash of robberies, though the true professionals inside law enforcement admitted it was small wonder there were any paintings left to steal. "If you nail a hundred million dollars to a poorly guarded wall," said one beleaguered official from Interpol, "it's only a matter of time before a determined thief will try to walk away with it."

The brazenness of the criminals was matched only by their competence. That they were skilled was beyond question. But what the police admired most about their opponents was their iron discipline. There were no leaks, no signs of internal intrigue, and not a single demand for ransom—at least not a real one. The thieves stole often but selectively, never taking more than a single painting at a time. These were not amateurs looking for quick scores or organized crime figures looking for a source of underworld cash. These were *art* thieves in the purest sense. One weary detective predicted that in all likelihood the paintings taken that long, hot summer would be missing for years, if not decades. In fact, he added morosely, chances were extremely good they would find their way into the Museum of the Missing and never be seen by the public again.

Even the police marveled at the variety of the thieves' game. It was a bit like watching a great tennis player who could win on clay one week and grass the next. In June, the thieves recruited a disgruntled security guard at the Kunsthistorisches Museum in Vienna and carried out an overnight theft of Caravaggio's *David with the Head of Goliath*. In July, they opted for a daring commando-style raid in Barcelona and relieved the Museu Picasso of *Portrait of Señora Canals*. Just one week later, the lovely *Maisons à Fenouillet* vanished so quietly from the walls of the Matisse Museum in Nice that bewildered French police wondered whether it had grown a pair of legs and walked out on its own. And then, on the last day of August, there was the textbook smash-and-grab job at the Courtauld Gallery in London that netted *Self-Portrait with Bandaged Ear* by Vincent van Gogh. Total time of the operation was a stunning ninety-seven seconds—even more impressive given the fact that one of the thieves had paused on the way out a second-floor window to make an obscene gesture toward Modigliani's luscious *Female Nude*. By that evening, the surveillance video was required viewing on the Internet. It was, said the Courtauld's distraught director, a fitting end to a perfectly dreadful summer.

The thefts prompted a predictable round of finger-pointing over lax security at the world's museums. The *Times* reported that a recent internal review at the Courtauld had strongly recommended moving the Van Gogh to a more secure location. The findings had been rejected, however, because the gallery's director liked the painting exactly where it was. Not to be outdone, the *Telegraph* weighed in with an authoritative series on the financial woes affecting Britain's great museums. It pointed out that the National Gallery and the Tate didn't even bother to insure their collections, relying instead on security cameras and poorly paid guards to keep them safe. "We shouldn't be asking ourselves how it is great works of art disappear from museum walls," the renowned London art dealer Julian Isherwood told the newspaper. "Instead, we should be asking ourselves why it doesn't happen more often. Little by little, our cultural heritage is being plundered."

The handful of museums with the resources to increase security rapidly did so while those living hand to mouth could only bar their doors and pray they were not next on the thieves' list. But when September passed without another robbery, the art world breathed a collective sigh of relief and blithely reassured itself the worst had passed. As for the world of mere mortals, it had already moved on to weightier matters. With wars still raging in Iraq and Afghanistan, and the global economy still teetering on the edge of the abyss, few could muster a great deal of moral outrage over the loss of four rectangles of canvas covered in paint.

The head of one international-aid organization estimated that the combined value of the missing works could feed the hungry in Africa for years to come. Would it not be better, she asked, if the rich did something more useful with their excess millions than line their walls and fill their secret bank vaults with art?

Such words were heresy to Julian Isherwood and his brethren, who depended on the avarice of the rich for their living. But they did find a receptive audience in Glastonbury, the ancient city of pilgrimage located west of London in the Somerset Levels. In the Middle Ages, the Christian faithful had flocked to Glastonbury to see its famous abbey and to stand beneath the Holy Thorn tree, said to have sprouted when Joseph of Arimathea, disciple of Jesus, laid his walking stick upon the ground in the Year of Our Lord 63. Now, two millennia later, the abbey was but a glorious ruin, the remnants of its once-soaring nave standing forlornly in an emerald parkland like gravestones to a dead faith. The new pilgrims to Glastonbury rarely bothered to visit, preferring instead to traipse up the slopes of the mystical hill known as the Tor or to shuffle past the New Age paraphernalia shops lining the High Street. Some came in search of themselves; others, for a hand to guide them. And a few actually still came in search of God. Or at least a reasonable facsimile of God.

Christopher Liddell had come for none of these reasons. He had come for a woman and stayed for a child. He was not a pilgrim. He was a prisoner.

It was Hester who had dragged him here—Hester, his greatest love, his worst mistake. Five years earlier, she had demanded they leave Notting Hill so she could find herself in Glastonbury. But in finding herself, Hester discovered the key to her happiness lay in shedding Liddell. Another man might have been tempted to leave. But while Liddell could live without Hester, he could not contemplate life without Emily. Better to stay in Glastonbury and suffer the pagans and druids than return to London and become a faded memory in the mind of his only child. And so Liddell buried his sorrow and his anger and soldiered on. That was Liddell's approach to all things. He was reliable. In his opinion, there was no better thing a man could be.

Glastonbury was not entirely without its charms. One was the Hundred Monkeys café, purveyor of vegan and environmentally friendly cuisine since 2005, and Liddell's favorite haunt. Liddell sat at his usual table, a copy of the *Evening Standard* spread protectively before him. At an adjacent table, a woman of late middle age was reading a book entitled *Adult Children: The Secret Dysfunction*. In the far back corner, a bald prophet in flowing white pajamas was lecturing six rapt pupils about something to do with Zen spiritualism. And at the table nearest the door, hands bunched contemplatively beneath an unshaved chin, was a man in his thirties. His eyes were flickering over the bulletin board. It was filled with the usual rubbish—an invitation to join the Glastonbury Positive Living Group, a free seminar on owl pellet dissection, an advertisement for Tibetan pulsing healing sessions—but the man appeared to be scrutinizing it with an unusual devotion. A cup of coffee stood before him, untouched, next to an open notebook, also untouched. A poet searching for the inspiration, thought Liddell. A polemicist waiting for the rage.

Liddell examined him with a practiced eye. He was dressed in tattered denim and flannel, the Glastonbury uniform. His hair was dark and pulled back into a stubby ponytail, his eyes were nearly black and slightly glazed. On the right wrist was a watch with a thick leather band. On the left were several cheap silver bracelets. Liddell searched the hands and forearms for evidence of tattoos but found none. Odd, he thought, for in Glastonbury even grandmothers proudly sported their ink. Pristine skin, like sun in winter, was rarely seen.

The waitress appeared and flirtatiously placed a check in the center of Liddell's newspaper. She was a tall creature, quite pretty, with pale hair parted in the center and a tag on her snug-fitting sweater that read GRACE. Whether it was her name or the state of her soul, Liddell did not know. Since Hester's departure, he had lost the capacity to converse with strange women. Besides, there was someone else in his life now. She was a quiet girl, forgiving of his failings, grateful for his affections. And most of all, she needed him as much he needed her. She was the perfect lover. The perfect mistress. And she was Christopher Liddell's secret.

He paid the bill in cash—he was at war with Hester over credit cards, along with nearly everything else—and made for the door. The poet-polemicist was scribbling furiously on his pad. Liddell slipped past and stepped into the street. A prickly mist was falling, and from somewhere in the distance he could hear the beating of drums. Then he remembered it was a Thursday, which meant it was shamanic drum therapy night at the Assembly Rooms.

He crossed to the opposite pavement and made his way along the edge of St. John's Church, past the parish preschool. Tomorrow afternoon at one o'clock, Liddell would be standing there among the mothers and the nannies to greet Emily as she emerged. By judicial fiat he had been rendered little more than a babysitter. Two hours a day was his allotted time, scarcely enough for more than a spin on the merry-go-round and a bun in the sweets shop. Hester's revenge.

He turned into Church Lane. It was a narrow alleyway bordered on both sides by high stone walls the color of flint. As usual, the only lamp was out, and the street was black as pitch. Liddell had been meaning to buy a small torch, like the ones his grandparents had carried during the war. He thought he heard footfalls behind him and peered over his shoulder into the gloom. It was nothing, he decided, just his mind playing tricks. *Silly you, Christopher*, he could hear Hester saying. *Silly, silly you.*

At the end of the lane was a residential district of terraced cottages and semidetached houses. Henley Close lay at the northernmost edge, overlooking a sporting field. Its four cottages were a bit larger than most in the neighborhood and were fronted by walled gardens. In Hester's absence, the garden at No. 8 had taken on a melancholy air of neglect that was beginning to earn Liddell nasty looks from the couple next door. He inserted his key and turned the latch. Stepping into the entrance hall, he was greeted by the chirping of the security alarm. He entered the disarm code into the keypad—an eight-digit numeric version of Emily's birth date—and climbed the stairs to the top floor. The girl waited there, cloaked in darkness. Liddell switched on a lamp.

She was seated in a wooden chair, a wrap of jeweled silk draped over her shoulders. Pearl earrings dangled at the sides of her neck; a gold chain lay against the pale skin of her breasts. Liddell reached out and gently stroked her cheek. The years had lined her face with cracks and creases and yellowed her alabaster skin. It was no matter; Liddell possessed the power to heal her. In a glass beaker, he prepared a colorless potion—two parts acetone, one part methyl proxitol, and ten parts mineral spirits—and moistened the tip of a cotton-wool swab. As he twirled it over the curve of her breast, he looked directly into her eyes. The girl stared back at him, her gaze seductive, her lips set in a playful half smile.

Liddell dropped the swab to the floor and fashioned a new one. It was then he heard a noise downstairs that sounded like the snap of a lock. He sat motionless for a moment, then tilted his face toward the ceiling and called, "Hester? Is that you?" Receiving no reply, he dipped the fresh swab in the clear potion and once again twirled it carefully over the skin of the girl's breast. A few seconds later came another sound, closer than the last, and distinct enough for Liddell to realize he was no longer alone.

Rotating his body quickly atop the stool, he glimpsed a shadowed figure on the landing. The figure took two steps forward and calmly entered Liddell's studio. Flannel and denim, dark hair pulled into a stubby ponytail, dark eyes—the man from the Hundred Monkeys. It was clear he was neither a poet nor a polemicist. He had a gun in his hand, and it was pointed directly at Liddell's heart. Liddell reached for the flask of solvent. He was reliable. And for that he would soon be dead.

2

ST. JAMES'S, LONDON

The first indication of trouble occurred the following afternoon when Emily Liddell, age four years seven months, emerged from St. John's parish preschool to find no one waiting to take her home. The body was discovered a short time later, and by early that evening Liddell's death was officially declared a homicide. BBC Somerset's initial bulletin included the victim's name but made no mention of his occupation or any possible motive for the killing. Radio 4 chose to ignore the story, as did the so-called quality national papers. Only the *Daily Mail* carried an account of the murder, a small item buried among a litany of other sordid news from around the country.

As a result, Christopher Liddell's death might have gone unnoticed by London's art world since few of its lofty citizens ever soiled their fingers with the *Mail*. But that was not true of tubby Oliver Dimbleby, a lecherous dealer from Bury Street who had never been shy about wearing his working-class roots on his well-tailored sleeve. Dimbleby read of the Glastonbury murder over his midmorning coffee and by that evening was blaring the news to anyone who would listen at the bar of Green's Restaurant, a local watering hole in Duke Street where dealers gathered to celebrate their triumphs or lick their wounds.

One of the people Dimbleby cornered was none other than Julian Isherwood, owner and sole proprietor of the sometimes solvent but never boring Isherwood Fine Arts, 7-8 Mason's Yard, St. James's, London. He was "Julie" to his friends, "Juicy Julie" to his partners in the occasional crime of drink. He was a man of contradictions. Shrewd but reckless. Brilliant but naïve. Secretive as a spy but trusting to a fault. Mostly, though, he was entertaining. Indeed, among the denizens of the London art world, Isherwood Fine Arts had always been regarded as rather good theater. It had enjoyed stunning highs and bottomless lows, and there was always a hint of conspiracy lurking somewhere beneath the shimmering surface. The roots of Isherwood's constant turmoil lay in his simple and oft-stated operating creed: "Paintings first, business second," or PFBS for short. Isherwood's misplaced faith in PFBS had occasionally led him to the edge of ruin. In fact, his financial straits had become so harrowing a few years back that Dimbleby himself had made a boorish attempt to buy Isherwood out. It was one of many incidents the men preferred to pretend had never happened.

But even Dimbleby was surprised by the shocked expression that came over Isherwood's face the instant he learned about the death in Glastonbury. Isherwood quickly managed to compose himself. Then, after muttering something preposterous about having to visit a sick aunt, he threw back his gin and tonic and made for the door at flank speed.

Isherwood immediately returned to his gallery and placed a frantic call to a trusted contact on the Art and Antiques Squad at Scotland Yard. Ninety minutes later, the contact called back. The news was even worse than Isherwood expected. The Art Squad pledged to do its utmost, but as Isherwood stared into the yawning chasm of his ledger books, he concluded he had no choice but to take matters into his own hands. Yes, there had been crises before, he thought gravely, but this was the real thing. He could lose it all, everything he had worked for, and innocent bystanders would pay a high price for his folly. It was no way to end a career—not after everything he had accomplished. And certainly not after everything his poor old father had done to ensure Julian's very survival.

It was this wholly unexpected memory of his father that caused Isherwood to once again reach for his phone. He started to dial a number but stopped. Better not to give him advance warning, he thought. Better to show up on his doorstep, cap in hand.

He replaced the receiver and checked his calendar for the following day. Just three unpromising appointments, nothing that couldn't be moved to another time. Isherwood drew a heavy line through each entry and at the top of the page scribbled a single biblical name. He stared at it for a moment, then, realizing his mistake, obliterated it with a few firm strokes of his pen. *Pull yourself together,* he thought. *What were you thinking, Julie? What on earth were you thinking?*

3

THE LIZARD PENINSULA, CORNWALL

The stranger settled not in his old haunt along the Helford Passage but in a small cottage atop the cliffs on the western edge of the Lizard Peninsula. He had seen it for the first time from the deck of his ketch, a mile out to sea. It stood at the farthest end of Gunwalloe Cove, surrounded by purple thrift and red fescue. Behind it rose a sloping field crisscrossed by hedgerows; to the right stretched a crescent beach where an old shipwreck lay sleeping just beneath the treacherous surf. Far too dangerous for bathing, the cove attracted few visitors other than the occasional hiker or the local fishermen who came when the sea bass were running. The stranger remembered this. He also recalled that the beach and the cottage bore an uncanny resemblance to a pair of paintings executed by Monet in the French coastal town of Pourville, one of which had been stolen from a museum in Poland and was missing to this day.

The inhabitants of Gunwalloe were aware of none of this, of course. They knew only that the stranger had taken the cottage under highly unusual circumstances—a twelve-month lease, paid in full, no muss, no fuss, all details handled by a lawyer in Hamburg no one had ever heard of. Even more perplexing was the parade of strange cars that appeared in the village soon after the transaction. The flashy black sedans with diplomatic plates. The cruisers from the local constabulary. The anonymous Vauxhalls from London filled with gray men in matching gray suits. Duncan Reynolds, thirty years retired from the railroad and regarded as the most worldly of Gunwalloe's citizenry, had observed the men giving the property a hasty final inspection the evening of the stranger's arrival. "These lads weren't your basic ready-to-wear security men," he reported. "They were the real thing. *Professionals,* if you happen to get my meaning."

The stranger was clearly a man on a mission, though for the life of them no one in Gunwalloe had a clue what it was. Their impressions were formed during his brief daily forays into the village for supplies. A few of the older ones thought they recognized a bit of the soldier in him while the younger women admitted to finding him attractive—so attractive, in fact, that some of their menfolk began to dislike him intensely. The daft ones boasted about having a go at him, but the wiser ones preached caution. Despite the stranger's somewhat small stature, it was obvious he knew how to handle himself if things got rough. Pick a fight with him, they warned, and chances were good that bones would get broken. And not his.

His exotic-looking companion, however, was another story. She was warmth to his frost, sunlight to his gray clouds. Her exceptional beauty added a touch of class to the village streets, along with a hint of foreign intrigue. When the woman's mood was upbeat, her eyes actually seemed to emit a light of their own. But at times there was also a discernible sadness. Dottie Cox from the village store speculated that the woman had lost someone close to her recently. "She tries to hide it," said Dottie, "but the poor lamb's obviously still in mourning."

That the couple was not British was beyond dispute. Their credit cards were issued in the name Rossi, and they were often overheard murmuring to one another in Italian. When Vera Hobbs at the bakery finally worked up the nerve to ask where they were from, the woman replied evasively, "London, mostly." The man, however, had maintained a granite silence. "He's either desperately shy or he's hiding something," Vera concluded. "I'd wager my money on number two."

If there was one opinion of the stranger shared by everyone in the village, it was that he was extremely protective of his wife. Perhaps, they ventured, a bit *too* protective. For the first few weeks after their arrival, he never seemed to stray more than a few inches from her side. But by early October, there were small signs that the woman was growing weary of his constant presence. And by the middle of the month, she was regularly making trips to the village unescorted. As for the stranger, it seemed to one observer that he had been sentenced by some internal tribunal to forever walk the cliffs of the Lizard alone.

At first, his excursions were short. But gradually he began taking long forced marches that kept him away for several hours at a time. Cloaked in his dark green Barbour coat with a flat cap pulled low over his brow, he would troop south along the cliffs to Kynance Cove and Lizard Point, or north past the Loe to Porthleven. There were times when he would appear lost in thought and times when he adopted the wariness of a scout on a reconnaissance mission. Vera Hobbs reckoned he was trying to remember something, a theory Dottie Cox found laughable. "It's obvious as the nose on your face, Vera, you old fool. The poor dear isn't trying to remember anything. He's doing his very best to forget."

Two matters served to raise the level of intrigue in Gunwalloe still higher. The first concerned the men who always seemed to be fishing in the cove whenever the stranger was away on one of his walks. Everyone in Gunwalloe agreed they were the worst fishermen anyone had ever seen—in fact, most assumed they were not fishermen at all. And then there was the couple's only visitor, a broad-shouldered Cornish boy with movie-idol good looks. After much speculation, it was Malcolm Braithwaite, a retired lobsterman who smelled perpetually of the sea, who correctly identified the lad as the Peel boy. "The one who rescued little Adam Hathaway at Sennen Cove but refused to say a word about it," Malcolm reminded them. "The odd one from Port Navas. Mother used to beat the daylights out of him. Or was it the boyfriend?"

The appearance of Timothy Peel ignited a round of intense speculation about the stranger's true identity, most of which was conducted under the influence at the Lamb and Flag pub. Malcolm Braithwaite decreed he was an informant hiding out in Cornwall under police protection, while Duncan Reynolds somehow got it into his head that the stranger was a Russian defector. "Like that bloke Bulganov," he insisted. "The poor sod they found dead in the Docklands a few months ago. Our new friend better watch his step or he might meet the same fate."

But it was Teddy Sinclair, owner of a rather good pizzeria in Helston, who came up with the most controversial theory. While trolling the Internet one day for God knows what, he stumbled upon an old article in the *Times* about Elizabeth Halton, the daughter of the former American ambassador, who had been kidnapped by terrorists while jogging in Hyde Park. With great fanfare, Sinclair produced the article, along with an out-of-focus snapshot of the two men who had carried out her dramatic Christmas-morning rescue at Westminster Abbey. At the time, Scotland Yard had claimed that the heroes were officers of the SO19 special operations division. The *Times*, however, reported that they were actually agents of Israeli intelligence—and that the older of the two, the one with dark hair and gray temples, was none other than the notorious Israeli spy and assassin Gabriel Allon. "Look at him carefully. It's *him*, I tell you. The man now living in Gunwalloe Cove is none other than Gabriel Allon."

This prompted the most uproarious outburst of laughter at the Lamb and Flag since a drunken Malcolm Braithwaite had dropped to one knee and declared his undying love for Vera Hobbs. When order was finally restored, a humiliated Teddy Sinclair wadded the article into a ball and tossed it into the fire. And though he would never know it, his theory about the man from the far end of the cove was altogether and entirely correct.

IF THE STRANGER was aware of the scrutiny, he gave no sign of it. He watched over the beautiful woman and hiked the windswept cliffs, sometimes looking as if he were trying to remember, sometimes as though he were trying to forget. On the second Tuesday of November, while nearing the southern end of Kynance Cove, he spotted a tall, gray-haired man standing precariously on the terrace of the Polpeor Café at Lizard Point. Even from a long way off, he could tell the man was watching him. Gabriel stopped and reached into his coat pocket, wrapping his hand around the comforting shape of a Beretta 9mm pistol. Just then, the man began to flail his arms as though he were drowning. Gabriel released his grip on the gun and walked on, the sea wind roaring in his ears, his heart pounding like a kettledrum.

4

LIZARD POINT, CORNWALL

How did you find me, Julian?"

"Chiara told me you were headed this way."

Gabriel stared incredulously at Isherwood.

"How do you think I found you, petal?"

"Either you pried it out of the director-general of MI5 or Shamron told you. I'm betting it was Shamron."

"You always were a clever boy."

Isherwood added milk to his tea. He was dressed for the country in tweeds and wool, and his long gray locks appeared to have been recently trimmed, a sure sign he was involved with a new woman. Gabriel couldn't help but smile. He had always been amazed by Isherwood's capacity for love. It was matched only by his desire to find and acquire paintings.

"They say there's a lost land out there somewhere," Isherwood said, nodding toward the window. "Apparently, it stretches from here to the Isles of Scilly. They say that when the wind is right you can hear the tolling of church bells."

"It's known as Lyonesse, the City of Lions, and it's nothing but a local legend."

"Like the one about an archangel living atop the cliffs of Gunwalloe Cove?"

"Let's not get carried away with the biblical allusions, Julian."

"I'm a dealer of Italian and Dutch Old Master art. Biblical allusions are my stock-in-trade. Besides, it's hard not to get carried away in a place like this. It's all a bit isolated for my taste, but I can understand why you've always been drawn to it." Isherwood loosened the buttons of his overcoat. "I remember that lovely cottage you had over in Port Navas. And that dreadful little toad who used to watch over it when you weren't around. Remind me of the lad's name."

"Peel," said Gabriel.

"Ah, yes, young Master Peel. He was like you. A natural spy, that one. Gave me a devil of a time when I came looking for that painting I'd placed in your care." Isherwood made a show of thought. "Vecellio, wasn't it?"

Gabriel nodded. "*Adoration of the Shepherds*."

"Gorgeous picture," said Isherwood, his eyes glistening. "My business was hanging by the thinnest of threads. That Vecellio was the coup that was going to keep me in clover for a few more years, and you were supposed to be restoring it. But you'd disappeared from the face of the earth, hadn't you? Vanished without a trace." Isherwood frowned. "I was a fool to ever throw in my lot with you and your friends from Tel Aviv. You use people like me. And when you're done, you throw us to the wolves."

Isherwood warmed his hands against the tarnished aluminum

teapot. His backbone-of-England surname and English scale concealed the fact that he was not, at least technically, English at all. British by nationality and passport, yes, but German by birth, French by upbringing, and Jewish by religion. Only a handful of trusted friends knew that Isherwood had staggered into London as a child refugee in 1942 after being carried across the snowbound Pyrenees by a pair of Basque shepherds. Or that his father, the renowned Paris art dealer Samuel Isakowitz, had been murdered at the Sobibor death camp along with Isherwood's mother. Though Isherwood had carefully guarded the secrets of his past, the story of his dramatic escape from Nazi-occupied Europe had managed to reach the ears of the legendary Israeli spymaster Ari Shamron. And in the mid-1970s, during a wave of Palestinian terrorist attacks against Israeli targets in Europe, Shamron had recruited Isherwood as a *sayan,* a volunteer helper. Isherwood had but one assignment—to assist in building and maintaining the operational cover of a young art restorer and assassin named Gabriel Allon.

"When did you speak with him?" Gabriel asked.

"Shamron?" Isherwood gave an ambiguous shrug of his shoulders. "I bumped into him in Paris a few weeks ago."

Gabriel, by his expression, made it clear he found Isherwood's account less than credible. No one bumped into Ari Shamron. And those who did rarely lived to recall the experience.

"Where in Paris?"

"We had dinner in his suite at the Ritz. Just the two of us."

"How romantic."

"Actually, we weren't completely alone. His bodyguard was there, too. Poor Shamron. He's as old as the Judean Hills, but even now his enemies are ruthlessly stalking him."

"It comes with the territory, Julian."

"I suppose it does." Isherwood looked at Gabriel and smiled sadly. "He's as stubborn as a mule and about as charming. But a part of me is glad he's still there. And another part lives in fear of the day he finally dies. Israel will never be quite the same. And neither will King Saul Boulevard."

King Saul Boulevard was the address of Israel's foreign intelligence service. It had a long and deliberately misleading name that had very little to do with the true nature of its work. Those who worked there referred to it as the Office and nothing else.

"Shamron will never die, Julian. Shamron is eternal."

"I wouldn't be so sure, petal. He didn't look well to me."

Gabriel sipped his tea. It had been nearly a decade since Shamron had done his last tour as chief, and yet he still meddled in the affairs of the Office as though it were his private fiefdom. Its ranks were filled with officers who had been recruited and groomed by Shamron—officers who operated by a creed, even spoke a language, written by him. Though he no longer had a formal position or title, Shamron remained the hidden hand that guided Israel's security policies. Within the corridors of the Israeli security establishment, he was known only as the *Memuneh,* the one in charge. For many years, he had devoted his formidable power to a single mission—persuading Gabriel, whom he regarded as a wayward son, to assume his rightful place in the director's suite of King Saul Boulevard. Gabriel had always resisted; and after his last operation, Shamron had finally granted him permission to leave the organization he had served since his youth.

"Why are you here, Julian? We had an arrangement. When I was ready to work, I would make contact with *you*, not the other way around."

Isherwood leaned forward and placed a hand on Gabriel's arm. "Shamron told me about what happened in Russia," he said softly. "Heaven knows I'm no expert, but I doubt even you have the power to erase a memory like that."

Gabriel watched the seagulls floating like kites above the tip of Lizard Point. His thoughts, however, were of a birch forest east of Moscow. He was standing next to Chiara at the edge of a freshly dug grave, his hands bound behind his back, his eyes fixed on the barrel of a large-caliber pistol. At the other end of the gun was Ivan Kharkov, Russian oligarch, international financier, arms dealer, and murderer. *Enjoy watching your wife die, Allon.* Gabriel blinked and the vision was gone.

"How much did Shamron tell you?"

"Enough to know that you and Chiara have every right to lock yourselves away in that cottage and never come out again." Isherwood was silent for a moment. "Is it true she was pregnant when she was taken from that road in Umbria?"

Gabriel closed his eyes and nodded. "Ivan's kidnappers gave her several doses of sedative while they were moving her from Italy to Russia. She lost the baby while she was in captivity."

"How is she now?"

"Like a newly restored painting. On the surface, she looks wonderful. But underneath . . ." Gabriel's voice trailed off. "She has losses, Julian."

"How extensive?"

"There are good days and bad."

"I read about Ivan's murder in the newspapers. The French police seem convinced he was killed on orders from the Kremlin or by an angry business rival. But it was you, wasn't it, Gabriel?

You were the one who killed Ivan outside that posh restaurant in Saint-Tropez."

"Just because I'm officially retired now doesn't mean the rules have changed, Julian."

Isherwood replenished his teacup and picked reflectively at the corner of his napkin. "You did the world a favor by killing him," he said quietly. "Now you have to do one for yourself and that gorgeous wife of yours. It's time for you and Chiara to rejoin the living."

"We are living, Julian. Quite well, actually."

"No, you're not. You're in mourning. You're sitting an extended *shivah* for the child you lost in Russia. But you can walk the cliffs from here to Land's End, Gabriel, and it will never bring that baby back. Chiara knows it. And it's time for you to start thinking about something other than a Russian oligarch named Ivan Kharkov."

"Something like a painting?"

"Exactly."

Gabriel exhaled heavily. "Who's the artist?"

"Rembrandt."

"What condition is it in?"

"Hard to say."

"Why is that?"

"Because at the moment, it's missing."

"How can I restore a missing painting?"

"Perhaps I'm not making myself clear. I don't need you to *restore* a painting, Gabriel. I need you to *find* one."

5

LIZARD POINT, CORNWALL

They walked along the cliffs toward Lizard Light, a study in contrasts, figures from different paintings. Isherwood's hands were shoved into the pockets of his tweed country coat, the ends of his woolen scarf fluttering like warning flags in the raw wind. Paradoxically, he was speaking of summer—a sultry afternoon in July when he had visited a château in the Loire Valley to pick over the collection of its deceased owner, one of the more ghoulish aspects of an art dealer's dubious existence.

"There were one or two paintings that were mildly interesting, but the rest was complete crap. As I was leaving, my mobile rang. It was none other than David Cavendish, art adviser to the vastly rich, and a rather shady character, to put it mildly."

"What did he want?"

"He had a proposition for me. The kind that couldn't be discussed over the phone. Insisted I come see him right away. He was staying at a borrowed villa on Sardinia. That's Cavendish's way. He's a houseguest of a man. Never pays for anything. But he promised the trip would be well worth my time. He also hinted that the house was filled with pretty girls and a great deal of excellent wine."

"So you caught the next plane?"

"What choice did I have?"

"And the proposition?"

"He had a client who wanted to dispose of a major portrait. A Rembrandt. Quite a prize. Never been seen in public. Said his client was disinclined to use one of the big auction houses. Wanted the matter handled privately. He also said the client wished to see the painting hanging in a museum. Cavendish tried to portray him as some sort of humanitarian. More likely, he just couldn't bear the thought of it hanging on the wall of another collector."

"Why you?"

"Because by the rather low standards of the art world, I'm considered a paragon of virtue. And despite my many stumbles over the years, I've somehow managed to maintain an excellent reputation among the museums."

"If they only knew." Gabriel shook his head slowly. "Did Cavendish ever tell you the seller's name?"

"He spun some nonsense about faded nobility from an Eastern land, but I didn't believe a word of it."

"Why a private sale?"

"Haven't you heard? In these uncertain times, they're all the rage. First and foremost, they ensure the seller total anonymity. Remember, darling, one normally doesn't part with a Rembrandt because one is tired of looking at it. One parts with it because one needs money. And the last thing a rich person wants is to tell the world that he's not so rich anymore. Besides, taking a painting to auction is always risky. Doubly so in a climate like this."

"So you agreed to handle the sale."

"Obviously."

"What was your take?"

"Ten percent commission, split down the middle with Cavendish."

"That's not terribly ethical, Julian."

"We do what we have to do. My phone stopped ringing the day the Dow went below seven thousand. And I'm not alone. Every dealer in St. James's is feeling the pinch. Everyone but Giles Pittaway, of course. Somehow, Giles always manages to weather all storms."

"I assume you got a second opinion on the canvas before taking it to market?"

"Immediately," said Isherwood. "After all, I had to make sure the painting in question was actually a Rembrandt and not a Studio of Rembrandt, a School of Rembrandt, a Follower of Rembrandt, or, heaven forbid, in the Manner of Rembrandt."

"Who did the authentication for you?"

"Who do you think?"

"Van Berkel?"

"But of course."

Dr. Gustaaf van Berkel was widely acknowledged to be the world's foremost authority on Rembrandt. He also served as director and chief inquisitor of the Rembrandt Committee, a group of art historians, scientists, and researchers whose lifework was ensuring that every painting attributed to Rembrandt was in fact a Rembrandt.

"Van Berkel was predictably dubious," Isherwood said. "But

after looking at my photographs, he agreed to drop everything and come to London to see the painting himself. The flushed expression on his face told me everything I needed to know. But I still had to wait two agonizing weeks for Van Berkel and his star chamber to hand down their verdict. They decreed that the painting was authentic and could be sold as such. I swore Van Berkel to secrecy. Even made him sign a confidentiality agreement. Then I boarded the next plane to Washington."

"Why Washington?"

"Because the National Gallery was in the final stages of assembling a major Rembrandt exhibit. A number of prominent American and European museums had agreed to lend their own Rembrandts, but I'd heard rumors about a pot of money that had been set aside for a new acquisition. I'd also heard they wanted something that could generate a few headlines. Something sexy that could turn out a crowd."

"And your newly discovered Rembrandt fit that description."

"Like one of my tailor-made suits, petal. In fact, we were able to reach a deal very quickly. I was to deliver the painting to Washington, fully restored, in six months' time. Then the director of the National Gallery would unveil his prize to the world."

"You didn't mention the sale price."

"You didn't ask."

"I'm asking."

"Forty-five million. I initialed a draft agreement of the deal in Washington and treated myself to a few days with a special friend at the Eden Rock Hotel in Saint Barths. Then I returned to London and started looking for a restorer. I needed someone good. Someone with a bit of natural discretion. Which is why I went to Paris to see Shamron."

Isherwood looked to Gabriel for a response. Greeted by silence, he slowed to a stop and watched the waves crashing against the rocks at Lizard Point.

"When Shamron told me that you still weren't ready to work, I reluctantly settled on another restorer. Someone who would jump at the chance to clean a long-lost Rembrandt. A former staff conservator from the Tate who'd gone into private practice. Not quite as elegant as my first choice but solid and much less complicated. No issues with terrorists or Russian arms dealers. Never asked me to keep a defector's cat for the weekend. And no dead bodies turning up. Except now." Isherwood turned to Gabriel. "Unless you've given up watching the news, I'm sure you can finish the rest of the story."

"You hired Christopher Liddell."

Isherwood nodded slowly and gazed at the darkening sea. "It's a shame you didn't take the job, Gabriel. The only person to die would have been the thief. And I'd still have my Rembrandt."

6

THE LIZARD PENINSULA, CORNWALL

Hedgerows lined the narrow track leading north from Lizard Point, blocking all views of the surrounding countryside. Isherwood drove at a snail's pace, his long body hunched over the wheel, while Gabriel stared silently out the window.

"You knew him, didn't you?"

Gabriel nodded absently. "We apprenticed together in Venice under Umberto Conti. Liddell never cared for me."

"That's understandable. He must have been envious. Liddell was gifted, but he wasn't in your league. You were the star, and everyone knew it."

It was true, thought Gabriel. By the time Christopher Liddell arrived in Venice he was already a skilled craftsman—more skilled, even, than Gabriel—but he had never been able to win Umberto's approval. Liddell's work was methodical and thorough but lacked the invisible fire Umberto saw each time Gabriel's brush touched a canvas. Umberto had a magic ring of keys that could open any door in Venice. Late at night he would drag Gabriel from his room to study the city's masterpieces. Liddell became angry when he learned of the nocturnal tutorials and asked for an invitation. Umberto refused. Liddell's instruction would be limited to daylight hours. The nights belonged to Gabriel.

"It's not every day an art restorer is brutally murdered in the United Kingdom," Isherwood said. "Given your circumstances, it must have come as something of a shock."

"Let's just say I read the stories this morning with more than a passing interest. And none mentioned a missing Rembrandt, newly discovered or otherwise."

"That's because on the advice of the Art and Antiques Squad at Scotland Yard, the local police have agreed to keep the theft a secret, at least for the time being. Undue publicity only makes recovery more difficult since it tends to invite contact from people who don't actually have possession of the painting. As far as the public is concerned, the motive for Liddell's murder remains a mystery."

"As it should be," said Gabriel. "Besides, the last thing we need to advertise is that private restorers keep extremely valuable paintings under less than secure circumstances."

It was one of the art world's many dirty secrets. Gabriel had always worked in isolation. But in New York and London, it was not unusual to enter the studio of an elite restorer to find tens of millions of dollars' worth of paintings. If the auction season was approaching, the value of the inventory could be stratospheric.

"Tell me more about the painting, Julian."

Isherwood glanced at Gabriel expectantly. "Does that mean you'll do it?"

"No, Julian. It just means I want to know more about the picture."

"Where would you like me to begin?"

"The dimensions."

"One hundred four by eighty-six centimeters."

"Date?"

"Sixteen fifty-four."

"Panel or canvas?"

"Canvas. The thread count is consistent with canvases Rembrandt was using at the time."

"When was the last restoration?"

"Hard to say. A hundred years ago . . . maybe longer. The paint was quite worn in some places. Liddell believed it would require a substantial amount of inpainting to knock it into shape. He was worried about whether he would be able to finish it in time."

Gabriel asked about the composition.

"Stylistically, it's similar to his other three-quarter-length portraits from the period. The model is a young woman in her late twenties or early thirties. Attractive. She's wearing a wrap of jeweled silk and little else. There's something intimate about it. She clearly managed to get under Rembrandt's skin. He worked with a heavily loaded brush and at considerable speed. In places, it appears he was painting *alla prima,* wet into wet."

"Do we know who she is?"

"There's nothing to identify her specifically, but the Rembrandt Committee and I both concur it's Rembrandt's mistress."

"Hendrickje Stoffels?"

Isherwood nodded. "The date of the painting is significant because it was the same year Hendrickje gave birth to Rembrandt's child. The Dutch Church didn't look kindly on that, of course. She was put on trial and condemned for living with Rembrandt like a whore. Rembrandt, archcad that he was, never married her."

Isherwood seemed genuinely disturbed by this. Gabriel smiled.

"If I didn't know better, Julian, I'd think you were jealous."

"Wait until you see her."

The two men lapsed into silence as Isherwood guided the car into Lizard village. In summer, it would be filled with tourists. Now, with its shuttered souvenir stands and darkened ice-cream parlors, it had the sadness of a fête in the rain.

"What's the provenance like?"

"Thin but clean."

"Meaning?"

"There are gaps here and there. Rather like yours," Isherwood added with a confiding glance. "But there are no claims against it. I had the Art Loss Register run a quiet search just to be certain."

"The London office?"

Isherwood nodded.

"So they know about the picture, too?"

"The Art Loss Register is dedicated to finding paintings, darling, not stealing them."

"Go on, Julian."

"It's believed the painting remained in Rembrandt's personal collection until his death, whereupon it was sold off by the bankruptcy court to help pay his debts. From there, it floated around The Hague for a century or so, made a brief foray to Italy, and returned to the Netherlands in the early nineteenth century. The current owner purchased it in 1964 from the Hoffmann Gallery of Lucerne. That beautiful young woman has been in hiding her entire life."

They entered a tunnel of trees dripping with ivy and headed downward into a deep storybook hollow with an ancient stone church at its base.

"Who else knew the painting was in Glastonbury?"

Isherwood made a show of thought. "The director of the National Gallery of Art in Washington and my shipping company." He hesitated, then added, "And I suppose it's possible I may have mentioned it to Van Berkel."

"Did Liddell have any other paintings in his studio?"

"Four," replied Isherwood. "A Rubens he'd just finished for Christie's, something that may or may not have been a Titian, a landscape by Cézanne—quite a good one, actually—and some *hideously* expensive water lilies by Monet."

"I assume those were stolen as well?"

Isherwood shook his head. "Only my Rembrandt."

"No other paintings? You're sure?"

"Trust me, darling. I'm sure."

They emerged from the hollow into the open terrain. In the distance, a pair of massive Sea King helicopters floated like zeppelins over the naval air station. Gabriel's thoughts, however, were focused on a single question. Why would a thief in a hurry grab a large Rembrandt portrait rather than a smaller Cézanne or Monet?

"Do the police have a theory?"

"They suspect Liddell must have surprised the thieves in the middle of the robbery. When it went bad, they killed him and grabbed the closest painting, which happened to be mine. After this summer, Scotland Yard is quite pessimistic about the chances for recovery. And Liddell's death makes it more complicated. This is now first and foremost a murder investigation."

"How long until your insurance company pays out?"

Isherwood frowned and drummed one finger nervously on the wheel. "I'm afraid you've just hit upon my dilemma."

"What dilemma?"

"As of this moment, the rightful owner of the Rembrandt is still the unnamed client of David Cavendish. But when I took possession of the painting, it was supposed to come under my insurance policy."

Isherwood's voice trailed off. It contained a melancholy note Gabriel had heard many times before. Sometimes it appeared when Isherwood's heart had been broken or when he had been forced to sell a cherished painting. But usually it meant he was in financial trouble. Again.

"What have you done now, Julian?"

"Well, it's been a rough year, hasn't it, petal? Stock market declines. Real estate crashes. Falling sales for luxury items. What's a small independent dealer like me supposed to do?"

"You didn't tell your insurance company about the painting, did you?"

"The premiums are so bloody expensive. And those brokers are such leeches. Do you know how much it would have cost me? I thought I could—"

"Cut a corner?"

"Something like that." Isherwood fell silent. When he spoke again, there was a note of desperation in his voice that had not been present before. "I need your help, Gabriel. I am personally on the hook for forty-five *million* dollars."

"This isn't what I do, Julian. I'm a—"

"Restorer?" Isherwood gave Gabriel a skeptical glance. "As we both know, you're not exactly an ordinary art restorer. You also happen to be very good at finding things. And in all the time I've known you, I've never asked you for a favor." Isherwood paused. "There's no one else I can turn to. Unless you help me, I'm ruined."

Gabriel rapped his knuckle lightly on his window to warn Isherwood that they were approaching the poorly marked turnoff for Gunwalloe. He had to admit he was moved by Isherwood's appeal. The little he knew about the case suggested it was no ordinary art theft. He also was suffering from a nagging guilt over Liddell's death. Like Shamron, Gabriel had been cursed with an exaggerated sense of right and wrong. His greatest professional triumphs as an intelligence officer had not come by way of the gun but through his unyielding will to expose past wrongs and make them right. He was a restorer in the truest sense of the word. For Gabriel, the case was like a damaged painting. To leave it in its current state, darkened by yellowed varnish and scarred by time, was not possible. Isherwood knew this, of course. He also knew he had a powerful ally. The Rembrandt was pleading his case for him.

A medieval darkness had fallen over the Cornish coast by the time they arrived in Gunwalloe. Isherwood said nothing more as he piloted his Jaguar along the single street of the village and headed down to the little cottage at the far end of the cove. As they turned into the drive, a dozen security lamps came instantly to life, flooding the landscape with searing white light. Standing on the terrace of the cottage, her dark hair twisting in the wind, was Chiara. Isherwood watched her for a moment, then made a show of surveying the landscape.

"Has anyone ever told you this place looks exactly like the *Customs Officer's Cabin at Pourville*?"

"The girl from the Royal Mail might have mentioned it." Gabriel stared at Chiara. "I'd like to help you, Julian . . ."

"But?"

"I'm not ready." Gabriel paused. "And neither is she."

"I wouldn't be so sure about the last part."

Chiara disappeared into the cottage. Isherwood handed Gabriel a large manila envelope.

"At least have a look at these. If you still don't want to do it, I'll find a nice picture for you to clean. Something challenging, like a fourteenth-century Italian panel with severe convex warping and enough losses to keep those magical hands of yours occupied for several months."

"Restoring a painting like that would be easier than finding your Rembrandt."

"Yes," said Isherwood. "But nowhere near as interesting."

7

GUNWALLOE COVE, CORNWALL

The envelope contained ten photographs in all—one depiction of the entire canvas along with nine close-up detail images. Gabriel laid them out in a row on the kitchen counter and examined each with a magnifying glass.

"What are you looking at?" Chiara asked.

"The way he loaded his brush."

"And?"

"Julian was right. He painted it very quickly and with great passion. But I doubt he was working *alla prima*. I can see places where he laid the shadows in first and allowed them to dry."

"So it's definitely a Rembrandt?"

"Without question."

"How can you be so certain just by looking at a photograph?"

"I've been around paintings for a hundred thousand years. I

know it when I see it. This is not only a Rembrandt but a great Rembrandt. And it's two and a half centuries ahead of its time."

"How so?"

"Look at the brushwork. Rembrandt was an Impressionist before anyone had ever heard the term. It's proof of his genius."

Chiara picked up one of the photos, a detail image of the woman's face.

"Pretty girl. Rembrandt's mistress?"

Gabriel raised one eyebrow in surprise.

"I grew up in Venice and have a master's degree in the history of the Roman Empire. I do know something about art." Chiara looked at the photograph again and shook her head slowly. "He treated her shabbily. He should have married her."

"You sound like Julian."

"Julian is right."

"Rembrandt's life was complicated."

"Where have I heard that one before?"

Chiara gave a puckish smile and returned the photograph to its place on the counter. The Cornish winter had softened the tone of her olive skin while the moist sea air had added curls and ringlets to her hair. It was held in place by a clasp at the nape of her neck and hung between her shoulder blades in a great cloud of auburn and copper highlights. She was taller than Gabriel by an inch and blessed with the square shoulders, narrow waist, and long legs of a natural athlete. Had she been raised somewhere other than Venice, she might very well have become a star swimmer or tennis player. But like most Venetians, Chiara regarded sporting contests as something to be viewed over coffee or a good meal. When one required exercise, one made love or strolled down to the Zattere for a gelato. Only the Americans exercised with compulsion, she argued, and look what it had wrought—an epidemic of heart disease and children prone to obesity. The descendant of Spanish Jews who fled to Venice in the fifteenth century, Chiara believed there was no malady that could not be cured by a bit of mineral water or a glass of good red wine.

She opened the stainless steel door of the oven and from inside removed a large orange pot. As she lifted the lid there arose a warm rush of steam that filled the entire room with the savor of roasting veal, shallots, fennel, and sweet Tuscan dessert wine. She inhaled deeply, poked at the surface of the meat with her fingertip, and gave a contented smile. Chiara's disdain for physical exertion was matched only by her passion for cooking. And now that she was officially retired from the Office, she had little to do other than read books and prepare extravagant meals. All that was expected of Gabriel was an appropriate display of appreciation and undivided attention. Chiara believed that food hastily consumed was food wasted. She ate in the same manner in which she made love, slowly and by the flickering glow of candles. Now she licked the tip of her finger and replaced the cover on the pot. Closing the door, she turned and noticed Gabriel staring at her.

"Why are you looking at me like that?"

"I'm just looking."

"Is there a problem?"

He smiled. "None at all."

She furrowed her brow. "You need something else to occupy your thoughts other than my body."

"Easier said than done. How long before dinner?"

"Not long enough for that, Gabriel."

"I wasn't suggesting *that*."

"You weren't?" She pouted playfully. "I'm disappointed."

She opened a bottle of Chianti, poured two glasses, and pushed one toward Gabriel. "Who steals paintings?"

"Thieves steal paintings, Chiara."

"I guess you don't want any of the veal."

"Allow me to rephrase. What I was trying to say is that it really doesn't matter who steals paintings. The simple truth is, they're stolen every day. Literally. And the losses are huge. According to Interpol, between four and six billion dollars a year. After drug trafficking, money laundering, and arms dealing, art theft is the most lucrative criminal enterprise. The Museum of the Missing is one of the greatest in the world. Everyone is there—Titian, Rubens, Leonardo, Caravaggio, Raphael, Van Gogh, Monet, Renoir, Degas. *Everyone*. Thieves have pillaged some of man's most beautiful creations. And for the most part, we've done nothing to stop it."

"And the thieves themselves?"

"Some are bumblers and adventurers looking for a thrill. Some are ordinary criminals trying to make a name for themselves by stealing something extraordinary. But unfortunately a few are real pros. And from their perspective, the risk-reward ratio is weighted heavily in their favor."

"High rewards, low risks?"

"Extremely low risks," Gabriel said. "A security guard might shoot a thief during a bank robbery, but to the best of my knowledge no one has ever been shot trying to steal a painting. In fact, we make it rather easy for them."

"Easy?"

"In 1998, a thief walked into Room Sixty-seven of the Louvre, sliced Corot's *Le Chemin de Sèvres* from its frame, and walked out again. An hour elapsed before anyone even realized the painting was missing. And why was that? Because Room Sixty-seven had no security camera. The official postmortem proved more embarrassing. Louvre officials couldn't produce a complete list of employees or even an accurate accounting of the museum's inventory. The official review concluded that it would be harder for a thief to rob the average Paris department store than the most famous museum on earth."

Chiara shook her head in amazement. "What happens to the art after it's stolen?"

"That depends on the motive. Some thieves are just out to make a quick score. And the quickest way to convert a painting into cash is by handing it over in exchange for a reward. In reality, it's ransom. But since it's almost always a small fraction of the painting's true value, the museums and the insurance companies are only too happy to play the game. And the thieves know it."

"And if it's not a ransom job?"

"There's a debate within the art world and law enforcement over that. Some paintings end up being used as a sort of underworld currency. A Vermeer stolen from a museum in Amsterdam, for example, might fall into the hands of a drug gang in Belgium or France, which in turn might use it as collateral or a down payment on a shipment of heroin from Turkey. A single painting might circulate for years in this manner, passing from one criminal to the next, until someone decides to cash in. Meanwhile, the painting itself suffers terribly. Four-hundred-year-old Vermeers are delicate objects. They don't like being stuffed into suitcases or buried in holes."

"Do you accept that theory?"

"In some cases, it's indisputable. In others . . ." Gabriel shrugged. "Let's just say I've never met a drug dealer who preferred a painting to cold hard cash."

"So what's the other theory?"

"That stolen paintings end up hanging on the walls of very rich men."

"Do they?"

Gabriel peered thoughtfully into his wineglass. "About ten years ago, Julian was putting the finishing touches on a deal with a Japanese billionaire at his mansion outside Tokyo. At one point during the meeting, the collector excused himself to take a call. Julian being Julian, he got out of his seat and had a look around. At the far end of a hallway he saw a painting that looked shockingly familiar. To this day, he swears it was *Chez Tortoni*."

"The Manet stolen in the Gardner heist? Why would a billionaire take such a risk?"

"Because you can't buy what's not for sale. Remember, the vast majority of the world's masterpieces will never come on the market. And for some collectors—men used to always getting what they want—the unobtainable can become an obsession."

"And if someone like that has Julian's Rembrandt? What are the chances of finding it?"

"One in ten, at best. And the odds of recovery drop precipitously if it isn't recovered quickly. People have been searching for that Manet for two decades."

"Maybe they should try looking in Japan."

"That's not a bad idea. Any others?"

"Not an idea," Chiara said carefully. "Just a suggestion."

"What's that?"

"Your friend Julian needs you, Gabriel." Chiara pointed to the photographs spread along the countertop. "And so does she."

Gabriel was silent. Chiara picked up the photograph showing the canvas in full.

"When did he paint it?"

"Sixteen fifty-four."

"The same year Hendrickje gave birth to Cornelia?"

Gabriel nodded.

"I think she looks pregnant."

"It's possible."

Chiara scrutinized the image carefully for a moment. "Do you know what else I think? She's keeping a secret. She knows she's pregnant but hasn't worked up the courage to tell him." Chiara glanced up at Gabriel. "Does that sound familiar to you?"

"I think you would have made a good art historian, Chiara."

"I grew up in Venice. I *am* an art historian." She looked down at the photo again. "I can't leave a pregnant woman buried in a hole, Gabriel. And neither can you."

Gabriel flipped open his mobile phone. As he entered Isherwood's number, he could hear Chiara singing softly to herself. Chiara always sang when she was happy. It was the first time Gabriel had heard her sing in more than a year.

8

RUE DE MIROMESNIL, PARIS

The sign in the shop window read ANTIQUITÉS SCIENTIFIQUES. Beneath it stood row upon row of meticulously arranged antique microscopes, cameras, barometers, telescopes, surveyors, and spectacles. Usually, Maurice Durand would spend a moment or two inspecting the display for the slightest flaw before opening the shop. But not that morning. Durand's well-ordered little world was beset by a problem, a crisis of profound magnitude for a man whose every waking moment was devoted to avoiding them.

He unlocked the door, switched the sign in the door from FERMÉ to OUVERT, and retreated to his office at the back of the shop. Like Durand himself, it was small and tidy and lacking in even the slightest trace of flair. After hanging his overcoat carefully on its hook, he rubbed an island of chronic pain at the base of his spine before sitting down to check his e-mail. He did so with little enthusiasm. Maurice Durand was a bit of an antique himself. Trapped by circumstance in an age without grace, he had surrounded himself with symbols of enlightenment. He regarded electronic correspondence as a disagreeable but obligatory nuisance. He preferred pen and paper to the ethereal mist of the Internet and consumed his news by reading several papers over coffee in his favorite café. In Durand's quietly held opinion, the Internet was a plague that killed everything it touched. Eventually, he feared, it would destroy Antiquités Scientifiques.

Durand spent the better part of the next hour slowly working his way through a long queue of orders and inquiries from around the world. Most of the clients were well established; some, relatively new. Invariably, when Durand read their addresses, his mind drifted to other matters. For example, when responding to an e-mail from an old client who lived on P Street in the Georgetown section of Washington, he couldn't help but think of the small museum located a few blocks away. He had once entertained a lucrative proposal to relieve the gallery of its signature painting: *Luncheon of the Boating Party* by Renoir. But after a thorough review—Durand was always thorough—he had declined. The painting was far too large, and the chances for success far too small. Only adventurers and mafiosi stole large paintings, and Durand was neither. He was a professional. And a true professional never accepted a commission he could not fulfill. That's how clients became disappointed. And Maurice Durand made it his business never to disappoint a client.

Which explained his anxious mood that morning and his preoccupation with the copy of *Le Figaro* lying on his desk. No matter how many times he read the article surrounded by a perfect red triangle, the details did not change.

Well-known British art restorer . . . shot twice in his Glastonbury residence . . . motive for murder unclear . . . nothing missing . . .

It was the last part—the part about nothing being missing—that troubled Durand most. He scanned the article again, then reached for his phone and dialed. Same result. Ten times he had called the same number. Ten times he had been condemned to the purgatory of voice mail.

Durand replaced the receiver and stared at the newspaper. *Nothing missing* . . . He wasn't sure he believed it. But given the circumstances, he had no choice but to investigate personally. Unfortunately, that would require him to close the shop and travel to a city that was an affront to all things he held sacred. He picked up the phone again and this time dialed a new number. A computer answered. But of course. Durand rolled his eyes and asked the machine for a first-class ticket on the morning TGV to Marseilles.

9

GUNWALLOE COVE, CORNWALL

In the aftermath of the affair, all those involved agreed that no quest for a stolen masterpiece had ever begun in quite the same way. Because within minutes of accepting the assignment, Gabriel Allon, the retired Israeli assassin and spy, placed a quiet call to none other than Graham Seymour, deputy director of the British Security Service, MI5. Upon hearing Gabriel's request, Seymour contacted the Home Secretary, who in turn contacted the chief constable of the Avon and Somerset Police, headquartered in Portishead. There the request encountered its first resistance, which crumbled when the chief constable received yet another call, this one from Downing Street. By late that evening, Gabriel had notched a small but significant victory—an invitation to view the home and studio of his old colleague from Venice, Christopher Liddell.

He woke the following morning to find the other side of the bed empty—unusual, since he was nearly always the first to rise. He lay there for a moment listening to the splashing of water in the shower, then headed into the kitchen. After preparing a large bowl of café au lait, he switched on his laptop and skimmed the news. Out of habit, he read the dispatches from the Middle East first. A sixteen-year-old girl had carried out a suicide bombing in a crowded market in Afghanistan, a mysterious explosion in a remote corner of Yemen had claimed the lives of three senior al-Qaeda leaders, and Iran's always-entertaining president had made yet another incendiary speech about wiping Israel from the face of the earth. Led by the new administration in Washington, the civilized world was murmuring veiled threats about sanctions while in Jerusalem the Israeli prime minister warned that with each turn of the centrifuges the Iranians were moving closer to a nuclear weapon.

Gabriel read these accounts with an odd sense of dislocation. He had given more than thirty years of his life to protecting the State of Israel and by extension its Western allies. But now, having finally convinced the Office to release him, he could only wonder at the truth behind the headlines. Any regrets about retirement, however, quickly evaporated when Chiara entered the room, her hair still damp, her skin luminous. Gabriel peered at her over the top of the computer and smiled. For the moment, at least, he was more than willing to leave the problems of Iran and Islamic terrorism to other men.

It was 9:15 when Gabriel and Chiara climbed into the Range Rover and departed Gunwalloe Cove. The traffic was moderate; the weather, volatile: brilliant sun one minute, biblical rain the next. They reached Truro by ten, Exeter by eleven, and by noon were approaching Glastonbury's southwestern flank. At first glance it appeared to be nothing more than a prosperous and slightly dull English market town. Only when they reached Magdalene Street did the true character of modern Glastonbury reveal itself.

"Where in God's name are we?" asked Chiara.

"Venus," said Gabriel.

He eased into Henley Close and switched off the engine. Waiting outside the house at No. 8 was Detective Inspector Ronald Harkness of the Avon and Somerset Constabulary's Criminal Investigation Department. He had a ruddy, outdoor complexion and wore a blazer that had seen better days. Judging by his expression, he was not pleased to be there, which was understandable. Higher Authority had conspired against Harkness. It had instructed him to open his active crime scene to a pair of art investigators named Rossi. Higher Authority had also ordered Harkness to cooperate fully, to answer all questions to the best of his ability, and to give the art investigators a wide berth. What's more, it had been suggested to Harkness that he might recognize Mr. Rossi. And if that turned out to be the case, Harkness was to keep his trap shut and his eyes on the ground.

After a round of judicious handshakes, Harkness gave them each a pair of gloves and shoe covers and led them across the unkempt garden. Attached to the front door was a lime green notice forbidding all unauthorized visitors. Gabriel searched the jamb in vain for evidence of forcible entry, then, stepping into the foyer, was greeted by a vague scent he recognized as acetone. Harkness closed the door. Gabriel looked at the security keypad mounted on the wall.

"It's a high-quality system," Harkness said, taking note of Gabriel's interest. "The last activity occurred at six fifty-three p.m. the evening of the murder. We believe it was the victim returning from dinner. After triggering the front-door sensor, he immediately entered the correct code to disarm. Unfortunately, he didn't reset the system once inside the house. According to the security company, he rarely did. We believe the thief knew this."

"Thief?"

The detective nodded. "We have an initial suspect. It appears he spent at least three days in Glastonbury surveilling both the property and the victim before making his move. In fact, he and Mr. Liddell had dinner together the night of the murder." Harkness caught himself. "Well, not exactly together. Have a look at these."

He produced a pair of CCTV still photos from his coat pocket and handed them over to Gabriel. The first showed Christopher Liddell departing a café called the Hundred Monkeys at 6:32 p.m. on the evening of his murder. The second showed a man with a stubby ponytail, dressed in denim and flannel, leaving the same café just three minutes later.

"We have a couple more that were shot alongside St. John's Church and near the preschool. That's where Liddell's daughter is a student. A pity. She's a lovely child."

"But none of the killer near the house?"

"Unfortunately, the area of CCTV coverage ends a few streets from here." The detective examined Gabriel carefully. "But I suspect you noticed that on the way in, didn't you, Mr. . . ."

"Rossi," said Gabriel. He examined the face of the suspect, then handed the photographs to Chiara.

"Is he British?" she asked the detective.

"We don't think so. He stayed with a group of New Age squatters in an empty field a couple of miles outside town. They say he spoke English with a pronounced French accent and rode a motorcycle. Called himself Lucien. The girls liked him."

"And I assume he hasn't appeared in any more CCTV images since the murder?" she asked.

"Not so much as a glimmer." The detective accepted the photographs from Chiara and looked at Gabriel. "Where would you like to start?"

"His studio."

"It's in the attic."

The detective led them up a flight of narrow stairs, then paused on the landing at the foot of the next flight. It was littered with yellow evidence markers and covered by a great deal of dried blood. Gabriel cast a glance at Chiara. Her face was expressionless.

"This is where Liddell's body was found," Harkness said. "The studio is one more flight up."

The detective stepped carefully over the evidence markers and started up the stairs. Gabriel entered the studio last and waited patiently for the detective to switch on the halogen work lamps. The harsh white glow was hauntingly familiar, as was everything else about the room. Indeed, with a few minor changes, Gabriel might well have mistaken the studio for his own. In the center stood a tripod with a Nikon camera pointed toward a now-empty easel. To the right of the easel was a small trolley cluttered with bottles of medium, pigment, and Series 7 sable brushes by Winsor & Newton. The Series 7 was Umberto Conti's favorite. Umberto always said a skilled restorer could do anything with a good Series 7.

Gabriel picked up one of the bottles of pigment—Alizarin Orange, once manufactured by Britain's Imperial Chemical Industries, now nearly impossible to find. Mixed with transparent blacks, it produced a glaze unique in its richness. Gabriel's own supply was running dangerously low. The restorer in him wanted to slip the bottle in his pocket. Instead, he returned the bottle to its place and studied the floor. Scattered around the base of the trolley were several more evidence markers.

"We found broken glass there along with two small wads of

cotton wool. We also found the residue of a liquid chemical mixture of some sort. The lab is still working on the analysis."

"Tell your lab it's a mixture of acetone, methyl proxitol, and mineral spirits."

"You sound fairly sure of yourself."

"I am."

"Anything else I should know?"

It was Chiara who answered. "In all likelihood, your lab technicians will discover that the proportions of the solution were two parts acetone, one part methyl proxitol, and ten parts mineral spirits."

The detective gave her a nod of professional respect. Clearly, he was beginning to wonder about the true identities of the two "art investigators" with friends at MI5 and Downing Street.

"And the cotton wool?" he asked.

Gabriel lifted a pencil-sized wooden dowel from the trolley to demonstrate. "Liddell had begun removing the dirty varnish from the painting. He would have wound the cotton around the end of this and twirled it gently over the surface. When it became soiled, he would have dropped it on the floor and made a new one. He must have been working when the thief entered the house."

"How can you be sure?"

"Because a good restorer always cleans up his studio at the end of a session. And Christopher Liddell was a good restorer."

Gabriel looked at the camera. It was attached by a cable to a large-screen iMac computer, which stood at one end of an antique library table with leather inlay. Next to the computer was a stack of monographs dealing with Rembrandt's life and work, including Gustaaf van Berkel's indispensable *Rembrandt: The Complete Paintings*.

"I'd like to see the photographs he made of the canvas."

Harkness appeared to search his mind for a reason to object, but could find none. With Chiara peering over his shoulder, Gabriel powered on the computer and clicked on a folder labeled REMBRANDT, PORTRAIT OF A YOUNG WOMAN. Inside were eighteen photos, including several that had been taken after Liddell had begun the process of removing the varnish. Three of the shots seemed to focus on a pair of thin lines—one perfectly vertical, the other perfectly horizontal—that converged a few centimeters from Hendrickje's left shoulder. Gabriel had encountered many types of surface creasing during his long career, but these were unusual in both their faintness and regularity. It was obvious the lines had intrigued Liddell as well.

There was one more thing Gabriel needed from the computer. It was the duty of every restorer to keep a record of the procedures carried out on a painting, especially one as important as a newly discovered Rembrandt. Though Liddell was still early in the restoration process at the time of his death, it was possible he had recorded some of his initial observations. Without asking for permission, Gabriel started the word-processing program and opened the most recent document. It was two pages in length and written in Liddell's precise, scholarly prose. Gabriel read it quickly, his face an inscrutable mask. Resisting the impulse to click PRINT, he closed the document, along with the photo folder.

"Anything unusual?" the detective asked.

"No," said Gabriel, "nothing at all."

"Is there anything else you would like to see?"

Gabriel switched off the computer and said, "Just one more thing."

10

GLASTONBURY, ENGLAND

They stood shoulder to shoulder at the edge of the landing and stared silently down at the dried blood. "I have photographs," said the detective, "but I'm afraid they're not for the squeamish."

Gabriel wordlessly held out his hand and accepted a stack of eight-by-ten prints—Christopher Liddell, eyes frozen wide in death, a gaping exit wound at the base of his throat, a small entry wound in the center of his forehead. Again, Harkness watched Gabriel intently, plainly intrigued by his failure to register even a hint of revulsion at the sight of a brutally murdered corpse. Gabriel handed the photos to Chiara, who examined them with a similar dispassion before returning them to the detective.

"As you can see," he said, "Liddell was shot twice. Both rounds exited the victim and were recovered. One from the wall, the other from the floor."

Gabriel examined the wall first. The bullet hole was located approximately three feet above the floor, opposite the flight of stairs descending from the studio.

"I assume this is the neck shot?"

"That's correct."

"Nine millimeter?"

"You obviously know your weaponry, Mr. Rossi."

Gabriel looked up toward the third-floor studio. "So the killer fired from the top of the stairs?"

"We don't have a final report yet, but the angle of the wound, combined with the angle that the round entered the wall, would suggest that. The medical examiner says the shot struck the victim in the back of the neck, shattering the fourth cervical vertebra and severing the spinal cord."

Gabriel looked at the crime-scene photographs again. "Judging from the powder burns on Liddell's forehead, the second shot was fired at close range."

"A few inches," Harkness agreed. Then he looked at Gabriel and added provocatively, "I suppose a professional assassin might refer to that one as the control shot."

Gabriel ignored the remark and asked whether any of the neighbors had reported hearing gunshots. Harkness shook his head.

"So the gunman used a suppressor?"

"That would appear to be the case."

Gabriel crouched and, tilting his head to one side, examined the surface of the landing. Just beneath the bullet hole in the wall were several tiny flakes of plaster. *And something else as well . . .* He remained on his haunches a moment longer, imagining Liddell's death as though it had been painted by the hand of Rembrandt, then announced he had seen enough. The detective switched off the crime-scene lamp, at which point Gabriel reached down and carefully dragged the tip of his gloved finger across the landing. Five minutes later, when he climbed into the Rover with Chiara, the glove was safely in his coat pocket, inside out.

"You've just committed a very serious crime," Chiara said as Gabriel started the engine.

"I'm sure it won't be the last."

"I hope it was worth it."

"It was."

HARKNESS STOOD on the doorstep like a soldier at ease, hands clasped behind his back, eyes following the Rover as it proceeded out of Henley Close at an altogether unacceptable rate of speed. *Rossi* . . . Harkness had known it was a lie the instant the angel descended from his chariot. It was the eyes that had given him away, those restless green torches that always seemed to be looking right through you. *And that walk* . . . Walked as though he were leaving the scene of a crime, thought Harkness, or as if he were about to commit one. But what on earth was the angel doing in Glastonbury? And why was he inquiring into the whereabouts of a missing painting? Higher Authority had decreed there would be no such questions. But at least Harkness could wonder. And perhaps one day he might tell his colleagues that he had actually shaken the hand of the legend. He even had a souvenir of the occasion, the gloves worn by the angel and his beautiful wife.

Harkness removed them now from his coat pocket. Strange, but there were only three. Where was the fourth? By the time the taillights of the Rover disappeared around the corner, Harkness had his answer. But what to do? Run after him? Demand it back? Couldn't possibly do that. Higher Authority had spoken. Higher Authority had instructed Harkness to give the angel a wide berth. And so he stood there, trap shut, eyes on the ground, wondering what the angel had hidden in that damn glove.

II

SOMERSET, ENGLAND

Gabriel peered at the tip of his left forefinger.

"What is it?" asked Chiara.

"Lead white, vermilion, and perhaps a touch of natural azurite."

"Flakes of paint?"

"And I can see fabric fibers as well."

"What kind of fabric?"

"Ticking, the kind of heavy cotton or linen that was used for mattress covers and sails in seventeenth-century Holland. Rembrandt used it to fashion his canvases."

"What does the presence of paint flakes and fibers on the landing mean?"

"If I'm correct, it means we're looking for a Rembrandt with a bullet hole in it."

Gabriel blew the material from his fingertip. They were heading westward along a two-lane road through the Polden Hills. Directly ahead, a bright orange sun hung low above the horizon suspended between two thin strata of cloud.

"You're suggesting Liddell fought back?"

Gabriel nodded. "The evidence was all there in his studio."

"Such as?"

"The broken glass and chemical residue, for starters."

"You think it was spilled during a physical struggle?"

"Unlikely. Liddell was smart enough to know not to get into a wrestling match with a well-armed thief. I think he used his solvent as a weapon."

"How?"

"Based on the residue on the floor, I'm guessing Liddell threw it in the thief's face. It would have burned his eyes badly and left him blinded for several seconds—enough time for Liddell to run. But he made one mistake. He took *her* with him."

"The Rembrandt?"

Gabriel nodded. "It's too big to hold with one hand, which means he would have had to grasp it by both vertical lengths of the stretcher." Gabriel demonstrated by gripping the steering wheel at the three o'clock and nine o'clock positions. "It must have been awkward trying to carry it down that narrow staircase, but Liddell almost made it. He was just a couple of steps from the landing when the first shot hit him. That shot exited the front of Liddell's neck and, if I'm correct, pierced the painting before entering the wall. Judging from the composition and color tone of the paint flakes, I'd say the bullet passed through the right side of her face."

"Can a bullet hole be repaired?"

"No problem. You'd be surprised at the idiotic things people do to paintings." Gabriel paused. "Or *for* paintings."

"What does that mean?"

"Christopher was a romantic. When we were in Venice together, he was always falling in love. And invariably he would end up with a broken heart."

"What does that have to do with the Rembrandt?"

"It's all in his restoration notes," Gabriel said. "They're a love letter. Christopher had finally fallen for a woman who wouldn't hurt him. He was obsessed with the girl in that painting. And I believe he died because he wouldn't let her go."

"There's just one thing I don't understand," Chiara said. "Why didn't the thief take any of the other paintings, like the Monet or the Cézanne?"

"Because he was a professional. He came there for the Rembrandt. And he left with it."

"So what do we do now?"

"Sometimes the best way to find a painting is to discover where it's been."

"Where do we start?"

"At the beginning," said Gabriel. "In Amsterdam."

12

MARSEILLES

If Maurice Durand were inclined toward introspection, which he was not, he might have concluded that the course of his life was determined the day he first heard the story of Vincenzo Peruggia.

A carpenter from northern Italy, Peruggia entered the Louvre on the afternoon of Sunday, August 20, 1911, and concealed himself in a storage closet. He emerged early the following morning dressed in a workman's white smock and strode into the Salon Carré. He knew the room well; several months earlier, he had helped to construct a special protective case over its most famous attraction, the *Mona Lisa*. Because it was a Monday, the day the Louvre was closed to the public, he had the salon to himself, and it took only a few seconds to lift Leonardo's small panel from the wall and carry it to a nearby stairwell. A few moments later, with the painting concealed beneath his smock, Peruggia walked past an unmanned guard post and struck out across the Louvre's vast center courtyard. And with that the world's most famous work of art vanished into the Paris morning.

Even more remarkable, twenty-four hours would elapse before anyone noticed the picture was missing. When the alert finally went out, the French police launched a massive if somewhat farcical search. Among their first suspects was an avant-garde painter named Pablo Picasso, who was arrested at his Montmartre apartment despite the fact he had been hundreds of miles from Paris at the time of the actual theft.

Eventually, the gendarmes managed to track down Peruggia but quickly cleared him of any suspicion. Had they bothered to look inside the large trunk in his bedroom, the search for the *Mona Lisa* would have ended. Instead, the painting remained hidden there for two years, until Peruggia foolishly tried to sell it to a well-known dealer in Florence. Peruggia was arrested but spent just seven months in jail. Years later, he was actually permitted to return to France. Oddly enough, the man who carried out the greatest art crime in history then opened a paint store in the Haute-Savoie and lived there quietly until his death.

Maurice Durand learned several important lessons from the strange case of Peruggia. He learned that stealing great paintings was not as difficult as one might think, that the authorities were largely indifferent to art crime, and that the penalties generally were light. But the story of Peruggia also whet Durand's appetite. Antique scientific instruments were his birthright—the shop had belonged to his father, and his grandfather before that—but art had always been his great passion. And while it was true there were worse places to spend one's day than the first arrondissement of Paris, the shop was not a particularly exciting way to earn a living. There were times when Durand felt a bit like the trinkets lining his little display window—polished and reasonably attractive but ultimately good for little more than gathering dust.

It was this combination of factors, twenty-five years earlier, that had compelled Durand to steal his first painting from the Musée des Beaux-Arts in Strasbourg—a small still life by Jean-Baptiste-Siméon Chardin that hung in a corner rarely visited by guards or patrons. Using an old-fashioned razor, Durand sliced the painting from its frame and slipped it into his attaché case. Later, during the train ride back to Paris, he attempted to recall his emotions at the moment of the crime and realized he had felt nothing other than contentment. It was then that Maurice Durand knew he possessed the qualities of a perfect thief.

Like Peruggia before him, Durand kept his trophy in his Paris apartment, not for two years but for two days. Unlike the Italian, Durand already had a buyer waiting, a disreputable collector who happened to be in the market for a Chardin and wasn't worried about messy details like provenance. Durand was well paid, the client was happy, and a career was born.

It was a career characterized by discipline. Durand never stole paintings to acquire ransom or reward money, only to provide inventory. At first he left the masterpieces to the dreamers and fools, focusing instead on midlevel paintings by quality artists or works that might reasonably be confused for pictures with no problem of provenance. And while Durand occasionally stole from small museums and galleries, he did most of his hunting in private villas and châteaux, which were poorly protected and filled to the roof with valuables.

From his base of operations in Paris he built a far-flung network of contacts, selling to dealers as far away as Hong Kong,

New York, Dubai, and Tokyo. Gradually, he set his sights on bigger game—the museum-quality masterpieces valued at tens of millions, or in some cases hundreds of millions, of dollars. But he always operated by a simple rule. No painting was ever stolen unless a buyer was waiting, and he only did business with people he knew. Van Gogh's *Self-Portrait with Bandaged Ear* was now hanging in the palace of a Saudi sheikh who had a penchant for violence involving knives. The Caravaggio had found its way to a factory owner in Shanghai while the Picasso was in the hands of a Mexican billionaire with uncomfortably close ties to the country's drug cartels. All three paintings had one thing in common. They would never be seen again by the public.

Needless to say, it had been many years since Maurice Durand had personally stolen a painting. It was a young man's profession, and he had retired after a skylight assault on a small gallery in Austria resulted in a back injury that left him in constant pain. Ever since then he had been forced to utilize the services of hired professionals. The arrangement was less than ideal for all the obvious reasons, but Durand treated his fieldmen fairly and paid them exceedingly well. As a result, he had never had a single unpleasant complication. Until now.

It was the south that produced the finest wines in France and, in Durand's estimation, its best thieves as well. Nowhere was that more true than the ancient port of Marseilles. Stepping from the Gare de Marseille Saint-Charles, Durand was pleased to find the temperature several degrees warmer than it had been in Paris. He walked quickly through the brilliant sunshine along the Boulevard d'Athènes, then turned to the right and headed down to the Old Port. It was approaching midday. The fishing boats had returned from their morning runs and atop the steel tables lining the port's eastern flank were arrayed all manner of hideous-looking sea creatures, soon to be turned into bouillabaisse by the city's chefs. Normally, Durand would have stopped to survey the contents of each with an appreciation only a Frenchman could manage, but today he headed straight for the table of a gray-haired man dressed in a tattered wool sweater and a rubber apron. By all appearances, he was a fisherman who scrounged a respectable living from a sea now empty of fish. But Pascal Rameau was anything but respectable. And he didn't seem surprised to see Maurice Durand.

"How was the catch, Pascal?"

"*Merde,*" Rameau muttered. "It seems like we get a little less every day. Soon . . ." He pulled his lips downward into a Gallic expression of disgust. "There'll be nothing left but garbage."

"It's the Italians' fault," said Durand.

"Everything is the Italians' fault," Rameau said. "How's your back?"

Durand frowned. "As ever, Pascal."

Rameau made an empathetic face. "Mine, too. I'm not sure how much longer I can work the boat."

"You're the richest man in Marseilles. Why do you still go to sea every morning?"

"I'm *one* of the richest. And I go out for the same reason you go to your shop." Rameau smiled and looked at Durand's attaché case. "You brought the money?"

Durand nodded.

"It's not wise to carry large amounts of cash in Marseilles. Haven't you heard, Maurice? This town is full of thieves."

"Very good thieves," Durand agreed. "At least, they used to be."

"A business like ours can be unpredictable."

"Weren't you the one who always told me that blood is bad for business, Pascal?"

"That's true. But sometimes it's unavoidable."

"Where is he?"

Rameau tilted his head to the right. Durand walked along the Quai de Rive Neuve toward the mouth of the harbor. About halfway down the marina was a motor yacht called *Mistral.* Seated on the aft deck, feet propped on the gunwale, eyes concealed by dark glasses, was a man with shoulder-length dark hair pulled into a stubby ponytail. His name was René Monjean, among the most gifted of Durand's thieves and usually the most dependable.

"What happened in England, René?"

"There were complications."

"What kind of complications?"

Monjean removed the sunglasses and stared at Durand with a pair of bloodred eyes.

"Where's my painting?"

"Where's my money?"

Durand held up the attaché case. Monjean put on the glasses and got to his feet.

13

MARSEILLES

"You really should see a doctor, René. Acetone can cause permanent damage to the cornea."

"And when the doctor asks how the acetone got in my eyes?"

"Your doctor wouldn't dare ask."

Monjean opened the door of the small fridge in the galley and took out two bottles of Kronenbourg.

"It's a bit early for me, René."

Monjean put one bottle back and shrugged—*Northerners*. Durand sat down at the small table.

"Was there really no other way to deal with the situation?"

"I suppose I could have let him escape so he could telephone the police. But that didn't seem like such a good idea." He paused, then added, "For either one of us."

"Couldn't you have just disabled him a little?"

"I'm surprised I actually managed to hit him. I really couldn't see much at all when I pulled the trigger." Monjean pried the top from the bottle of beer. "You've never—"

"Shot someone?" Durand shook his head. "I've never even carried a gun."

"The world has changed, Maurice." Monjean looked at the attaché case. "You have something in there for me?"

Durand popped open the locks and removed several bundles of hundred-euro notes.

"Your turn, René."

Monjean opened an overhead locker and removed a cardboard tube, roughly five inches in diameter and three feet in length. He pried off the aluminum top and shook the tube several times until three inches of canvas was protruding from the end.

"Be careful, René. You'll damage it."

"I'm afraid it's a bit late to worry about that."

Monjean unfurled the painting across the tabletop. Durand stared in horror. Just above the right eye of the woman was a perforation that looked as if it could have been made by a pencil. Her silk wrap was stained with something dark, as were her breasts.

"Tell me that isn't blood."

"I could," Monjean said, "but it wouldn't be the truth."

"Who did it belong to?"

"Who do you think?" Monjean took a long pull at his beer and explained.

"Too bad you didn't take more careful aim," Durand said. "You might have actually hit her right between the eyes."

He probed at the hole, then licked the tip of his finger and scrubbed at the surface of the painting until he smeared a small patch of the blood.

"Looks like it will come right off," Monjean said.

"It should."

"What about the bullet hole?"

"I know a man in Paris who might be able to repair it."

"What kind of man?"

"The kind who produces forgeries."

"You need a restorer, Maurice. A very good one."

"At the core of every good restorer lies a forger."

Monjean didn't appear convinced. "May I give you a piece of advice, Maurice?"

"You just shot a Rembrandt worth forty-five million dollars. But please, René, feel free."

"This painting is trouble. Burn it and forget about it. Besides, we can always steal another one."

"I'm tempted."

"But?"

"I have a client waiting. And my clients expect me to deliver. Besides, René, I didn't get into this business to destroy paintings. Especially not one as beautiful as this."

14

AMSTERDAM

In the cutthroat world of the art trade, there was one principle that was supposed to be sacrosanct. Provenance, the written record of a painting's chain of ownership, was everything. Theoretically, dealers did not sell paintings without a proper provenance, collectors did not buy them, and no decent restorer would ever lay hands on a picture without knowing where it had been and under what conditions it had hung. But after many years of conducting provenance research, Gabriel had learned never to be shocked by the secret lives led by some of the world's most sought-after works of art. He knew that paintings, like people, sometimes lied about their pasts. And he knew that, often, those lies revealed more than the so-called truths contained in their printed pedigrees. All of which explained his interest in De Vries Fine Arts, purveyors of quality Dutch and Flemish Old Master paintings since 1882.

Occupying a stately if somewhat sullen building overlooking Amsterdam's Herengracht canal, the gallery had always presented itself as the very picture of stability and good manners, though a brief glimpse into the darkest chambers of its past would tell a markedly different story. Regrettably, none was darker than its conduct during the Second World War. Within weeks of Holland's capitulation, Amsterdam was inundated by a wave of Germans looking for Dutch paintings. Prices soared so quickly that ordinary citizens were soon scouring their closets for anything that might be regarded as an Old Master. The De Vries gallery welcomed the Germans with open arms. Its best customer was none other than Hermann Göring, who purchased more than a dozen paintings from the gallery between 1940 and 1942. The staff found Göring to be a shrewd negotiator and secretly enjoyed his roguish charm. For his part, Göring would tell colleagues in Berlin that no shopping spree in Amsterdam was complete without a stop at the exquisite gallery along the Herengracht.

The gallery had also played a prominent role in the history of Rembrandt's *Portrait of a Young Woman.* Of the three known times that the painting changed hands in the twentieth century, two of the sales had been conducted under the auspices of De Vries Fine Arts. The first sale had occurred in 1919, the second in 1936. Both had been private, meaning that the identity of buyer and seller were known only to the gallery itself. Under the rules of the art trade, such transactions were to remain confidential for all eternity. But in some circumstances—with the passage of enough time or for the right amount of money—a dealer could be cajoled into opening his books.

Gabriel entrusted that delicate task to Julian Isherwood, who had always enjoyed a cordial professional relationship with the De

Vries gallery despite its questionable past. It took several hours of heated telephone negotiations, but Isherwood finally convinced Geert de Vries, great-grandson of the founder, to surrender the records. Isherwood would never tell Gabriel the exact price he had paid for the documents, only that it had been steep. "Remember one thing about art dealers," he said. "They are the lowest of God's creatures. And economic times like these bring out the worst in them."

Gabriel and Chiara monitored the final stages of the negotiations from a charming suite at the Ambassade Hotel. After receiving word that the deal had been finalized, they left the hotel a few minutes apart and made the short walk along the Herengracht to the gallery, Chiara on one side of the canal, Gabriel on the other. Geert de Vries had left photocopies of the records at the front desk in a buff envelope marked ROSSI. Gabriel slipped it into his bag and bade the receptionist a pleasant afternoon in Italian-accented English. Stepping outside, he saw Chiara leaning against a lamppost on the opposite bank of the canal. Her scarf was knotted in a way that meant she had not noticed surveillance of any sort. She followed him to a café in the Bloemenmarkt and drank hot chocolate while he worked his way laboriously through the documents.

"There's a reason why the Dutch speak so many languages. Their own is impenetrable."

"Can you make it out?"

"Most of it. The person who bought the painting in 1919 was a banker named Andries van Gelder. He must have been hit hard by the Great Depression. When he sold it in 1936, he did so at a considerable loss."

"And the next owner?"

"A man named Jacob Herzfeld."

"Are Dutch boys ever named Jacob?"

"They're usually called Jacobus."

"So he was Jewish?"

"Probably."

"When was the next sale?"

"Nineteen sixty-four at the Hoffmann Gallery of Lucerne."

"Switzerland? Why would Jacob Herzfeld sell his painting there?"

"I'm betting it wasn't him."

"Why?"

"Because unless Jacob Herzfeld was extremely lucky, he probably wasn't alive in 1964. Which means it's quite possible we've just discovered a very large hole in the painting's provenance."

"So what are we going to do now?"

Gabriel shoved the documents back into the envelope.

"Find out what happened to him."

15

AMSTERDAM

Portrait of a Young Woman, oil on canvas, 104 by 86 centimeters, was painted in a large house just west of Amsterdam's old center. Rembrandt purchased the property in 1639 for the price of thirteen thousand guilders, an enormous sum even for a painter of his stature and one that would eventually lead to his financial undoing. At the time, the street was known as Sint Antonisbreestraat. Later, due to a change in the neighborhood's demographics, it would be renamed Jodenbreestraat, or Jewish Broad Street. Why Rembrandt chose to live in such a place has long been a matter of debate. Was it because he harbored a secret affinity for Judaism? Or did he choose to reside in the district because it was home to many other painters and collectors? Whatever the case, one thing is beyond dispute. The greatest painter of Holland's Golden Age lived and worked among Amsterdam's Jews.

Shortly after Rembrandt's death, a number of large synagogues were constructed near the opposite end of Jodenbreestraat around the Visserplein and Meijerplein. The redbrick buildings somehow managed to survive the Nazi occupation of the Netherlands, though most of the people who prayed there did not. Nestled within a complex of four old Ashkenazi synagogues is the primary keeper of this terrible memory, the Jewish Historical Museum. After passing through the magnetometer at the front entrance, Gabriel asked for the research facility and was directed to the lowest level. It was a modern space, clean and brightly lit, with long worktables and an internal spiral staircase leading to the upper stacks. Given the lateness of the hour, it was empty except for a single archivist, a tall man in his early forties with reddish blond hair.

Without going into specifics, Gabriel said he was looking for information about a man named Jacob Herzfeld. The archivist asked for the correct spelling, then walked over to a computer terminal. A click of the mouse brought up a page for a database search engine. He entered Herzfeld's first and last name and clicked again.

"This could be him. Jacob Herzfeld, born in Amsterdam in March 1896, died at Auschwitz in March 1943. His wife and daughter were murdered at the same time. The child was only nine years old." The archivist glanced over his shoulder at Gabriel. "They must have been rather well-to-do. They lived at a good address on Plantage Middenlaan. It's quite close to here, just on the other side of Wertheim Park."

"Is there a way to tell if any members of the family survived?"

"Not using this database, but let me check our files."

The archivist disappeared through a doorway. Chiara roamed the stacks while Gabriel sat down at the computer and scrolled through the names of the dead. *Salomon Wass, born in Amsterdam, 31 May 1932, murdered at Sobibor, 14 May 1943 . . . Alida Spier, born Rotterdam, 20 September 1915, murdered at Auschwitz, 30 September 1942 . . . Sara da Silva Rosa, born Amsterdam, 8 April 1930, murdered at Auschwitz, 15 October 1942 . . .* They were but three of the 110,000 Dutch Jews who had been sealed into freight cars and dispatched eastward for murder and cremation. Only one-fifth of Holland's Jews survived the war, the lowest percentage of any Western country occupied by the Germans. Several factors contributed to the lethality of the Holocaust in Holland, not least of which was the enthusiastic support given the project by many elements of Dutch society. Indeed, from the Dutch police officers who arrested Jews to the Dutch rail workers who transported them to their deaths, Dutch citizens were active at nearly every stage of the process. Adolf Eichmann, the managing director of the Final Solution, would later say of his local helpers, "It was a pleasure to work with them."

The archivist reappeared, holding a single sheet of paper. "I thought I recognized the name and address. There was another child who survived. But I don't think she'll talk."

"Why not?" Gabriel asked.

"We have an annual conference here in Amsterdam that focuses on the children who were hidden during the Holocaust. Last year, I handled the registration." He held up the sheet of paper. "Lena Herzfeld attended the first session but left almost immediately."

"What happened?"

"When we asked her to write down her memories of the war

for our archives, she became very agitated and angry. She said it had been a mistake to come. After that, we never saw her again."

"A reaction like that isn't uncommon," Gabriel said. "It took years for some survivors to talk about their experiences. And some never have."

"That's true," the archivist agreed. "But the hidden children are among the least understood victims of the Holocaust. Their experience has its own special tragedy. In most cases, they were handed over to complete strangers. Their parents were simply trying to save them, but what child can truly comprehend being left behind?"

"I understand," said Gabriel. "But it's important that I see her."

The archivist searched Gabriel's face and seemed to recognize something he had seen before. Then he smiled sadly and handed over the slip of paper.

"Don't tell her where you got the address. And be sure to treat her gently. She's fragile. They're all a bit fragile."

16

AMSTERDAM

The archivist told Gabriel and Chiara everything else he knew. Lena Herzfeld had worked as a teacher in the Dutch state school system, had never married, and, as it turned out, lived just around the corner from her old family home. It was a small street with a leafy green park on one side and a terrace of gabled houses on the other. Hers was a narrow little house with a narrow black door at street level. Gabriel reached for the bell but hesitated. *She became very agitated and angry . . . After that, we never saw her again.* Perhaps it was better to leave her undisturbed, he thought. He knew from personal experience that coaxing memory from a survivor could be a bit like crossing a frozen lake. One wrong step and the entire surface could crack with disastrous results.

"What's wrong?" Chiara asked.

"I don't want to put her through it. Besides, she probably doesn't remember."

"She was nine when the Germans came. She remembers."

Gabriel made no movement. Chiara pressed the bell for him.

"Why did you do that?"

"She came to that conference for a reason. She wants to talk."

"Then why did she get so upset when they asked her about the war?"

"They probably didn't ask her the right way."

"And you think *I* can?"

"I know you can."

Chiara reached for the bell again but stopped at the sound of footfalls in the entrance hall. An exterior light came on, and the door retreated a few inches, revealing a small, spare woman dressed entirely in black. Her pewter-colored hair was carefully brushed, and her blue eyes appeared clear and alert. She regarded the two visitors curiously, then, sensing they were not Dutch, addressed them in flawless English.

"May I help you?"

"We're looking for Lena Herzfeld," said Gabriel.

"I'm Lena Herzfeld," she replied calmly.

"We were wondering whether we might speak with you."

"About?"

"Your father." Gabriel paused, then added, "And about the war."

She was silent for a moment. "My father has been dead for more than sixty years," she said firmly. "As for the war, there is nothing to discuss."

Gabriel shot a glance at Chiara, who ignored him and quietly asked, "Will you tell us about the painting, then?"

Lena Herzfeld seemed startled but quickly regained her composure. "What painting is that?"

"The Rembrandt your father owned before the war."

"I'm afraid you have me confused with someone else. My father never owned a Rembrandt."

"But that's not true," Gabriel interjected. "Your father did indeed own a Rembrandt. He purchased it from De Vries Fine Arts on the Herengracht in 1936. I have a copy of the bill of sale if you would like to see it."

"I have no wish to see it. Now if you'll excuse me, I—"

"Then will you at least have a look at this?"

Without waiting for an answer, Gabriel pressed a photograph of the painting into her hands. For several seconds, Lena Herzfeld's face betrayed no emotion other than mild curiosity. Then, bit by bit, the ice began to crack, and tears spilled down both cheeks.

"Do you remember it now, Miss Herzfeld?"

"It's been a very long time, but, yes, I remember." She brushed a tear from her cheek. "Where did you get this?"

"Perhaps it would be better if we spoke inside."

"How did you find me?" she asked fearfully, her gaze still fixed on the photograph. "Who betrayed me?"

Gabriel felt as if a stone had been laid over his heart.

"No one betrayed you, Miss Herzfeld," he said softly. "We're friends. You can trust us."

"I learned when I was a child to trust no one." She looked up from the photograph. "What do you want from me?"

"Only your memory."

"It was a long time ago."

"Someone died because of this painting, Miss Herzfeld."

"Yes," she said. "I know."

She returned the photograph to Gabriel's hand. For an instant, he feared he had pushed too far. Then the door opened a few inches wider and Lena Herzfeld stepped to one side.

Treat her gently, Gabriel reminded himself. *She's fragile. They're all a bit fragile.*

17

AMSTERDAM

Gabriel knew the instant he entered Lena Herzfeld's house that she was suffering from a kind of madness. It was neat, orderly, and sterile, but a madness nonetheless. The first evidence of her disorder was the condition of her sitting room. Like most Dutch parlors, it had the compactness of a Vermeer. Yet through her industrious arrangement of the furnishings and careful choice of color—a glaring, clinical white—she had managed to avoid the impression of clutter or claustrophobia. There were no pieces of decorative glass, no bowls of hard candy, no mementos, and not a single photograph. It was as if Lena Herzfeld had been dropped into this place alone, without parentage, without ancestry, without a past. Her home was not truly a home, thought Gabriel, but a hospital ward into which she had checked herself for a permanent stay.

She insisted on making tea. It came, not surprisingly, in a white pot and was served in white cups. She insisted, too, that Gabriel and Chiara refer to her only as Lena. She explained that she had worked as a teacher at a state school and for thirty-seven years had been called only Miss Herzfeld by students and colleagues alike. Upon retirement, she had discovered that she wanted her given name back. Gabriel acceded to her wishes, though from time to time, out of courtesy or deference, he sought refuge behind the formality of her family name. When it came to identifying himself and the attractive young woman at his side, he decided it was not possible to reciprocate Lena Herzfeld's intimacy. And so he plucked an old alias from his pocket and concocted a hasty cover to go with it. Tonight he was Gideon Argov, employee of a small, privately funded organization that carried out investigations of financial and other property-related questions arising from the Holocaust. Given the sensitive nature of these investigations, and the security problems arising from them, it was not possible to go into greater detail.

"You're from Israel, Mr. Argov?"

"I was born there. I live mainly in Europe now."

"Where in Europe, Mr. Argov?"

"Given the nature of my work, my home is a suitcase."

"And your assistant?"

"We spend so much time together her husband is convinced we're lovers."

"Are you?"

"Lovers? No such luck, Miss Herzfeld."

"It's Lena, Mr. Argov. Please call me Lena."

The secrets of survivors are not easily surrendered. They are locked away behind barricaded doors and accessed at great risk to those who possess them. It meant the evening's proceedings would be an interrogation of sorts. Gabriel knew from experience that the surest route to failure was the application of too much pressure. He began with what appeared to be an offhand remark about how much the city had changed since his last visit. Lena Herzfeld responded by telling him about Amsterdam before the war.

Her ancestors had come to the Netherlands in the middle of the seventeenth century to escape the murderous pogroms being carried out by Cossacks in eastern Poland. While it was true that Holland was generally tolerant of the new arrivals, Jews were excluded from most segments of the Dutch economy and forced to become traders and merchants. The majority of Amsterdam's Jews were lower middle class and quite poor. The Herzfelds worked as peddlers and shopkeepers until the late nineteenth century, when Abraham Herzfeld entered the diamond trade. He passed the business on to his son, Jacob, who undertook a rapid and highly successful expansion. Jacob married a woman named Susannah Arons in 1927 and moved from a cramped apartment off the Jodenbreestraat to the grand house on Plantage Middenlaan. Four years later, Susannah gave birth to the couple's first child, Lena. Two years after that came another daughter, Rachel.

"While we regarded ourselves as Jews, we were rather well assimilated and not terribly religious. We lit candles on Shabbat but generally went to synagogue only on holidays. My father didn't wear a beard or a *kippah,* and our kitchen wasn't kosher. My sister and I attended an ordinary Dutch school. Many of our classmates didn't even realize we were Jewish. That was especially true of me. You see, Mr. Argov, when I was young, my hair was blond."

"And your sister?"

"She had brown eyes and beautiful dark hair. Like hers," she added, glancing at Chiara. "My sister and I could have been twins, except for the color of our hair and eyes."

Lena Herzfeld's face settled into an expression of bereavement. Gabriel was tempted to pursue the matter further. He knew, however, it would be a mistake. So instead he asked Lena Herzfeld to describe her family's home on Plantage Middenlaan.

"We were comfortable," she replied, seemingly grateful for the change of subject. "Some might say rich. But my father never liked to talk about money. He said it wasn't important. And, truthfully, he permitted himself only one luxury. My father adored paintings. Our house was filled with art."

"Do you remember the Rembrandt?"

She hesitated, then nodded. "It was my father's first major acquisition. He hung it in the drawing room. Every evening he would sit in his chair admiring it. My parents were devoted to each other, but my father loved that painting so much that sometimes my mother would pretend to be jealous." Lena Herzfeld gave a fleeting smile. "The painting made us all very happy. But not long after it entered our home, things started to go wrong in the world around us. Kristallnacht, Austria, Poland. Then, finally . . . *us*."

For many residents of Amsterdam, she continued, the German invasion of May 10, 1940, came as a shock, since Hitler had promised to spare Holland so long as it remained neutral. In the chaotic days that followed, the Herzfelds made a desperate bid to flee, first by boat, then by road to Belgium. They failed, of course, and by the night of the fifteenth, they were back in their home on Plantage Middenlaan.

"We were trapped," said Lena Herzfeld, "along with one hundred and forty thousand other Dutch Jews."

Unlike France and Belgium, which were placed under German military control, Hitler decided that the Netherlands would be run by a civilian administration. He gave the job to Reichskommissar Arthur Seyss-Inquart, a fanatical anti-Semite who had presided over Austria after the Anschluss in 1938. Within days, the decrees began. At first, a benign-sounding order forbade Jews from serving as air-raid wardens. Then Jews were ordered to leave The Hague, Holland's capital, and to move from sensitive coastal areas. In September, all Jewish newspapers were banned. In November, all Jews employed by the Dutch civil service, including those who worked in the educational and telephone systems, were summarily dismissed. Then, in January 1941, came the most ominous Nazi decree to date. All Jews residing in Holland were given four weeks to register with the Dutch census office. Those who refused were threatened with prison and faced confiscation of their property.

"The census provided the Germans with a map showing the name, address, age, and sex of nearly every Jew in Holland. We foolishly gave them the keys to our destruction."

"Did your father register?"

"He considered ignoring the order, but in the end decided he had no choice but to comply. We lived at a prominent address in the most visible Jewish neighborhood in the city."

The census was followed by a cascade of new decrees that served to further isolate, humiliate, and impoverish the Jews of Holland. Jews were forbidden to donate blood. Jews were forbidden to enter hotels or eat in restaurants. Jews were forbidden to attend the theater, visit public libraries, or view art exhibits. Jews were forbidden to serve on the stock exchange. Jews could no longer own pigeons. Jewish children were barred from "Aryan" schools. Jews were required to sell their businesses to non-Jews. Jews were required to surrender art collections and all jewelry except for wedding bands and pocket watches. And Jews were required to deposit all savings in Lippmann, Rosenthal & Company, or LiRo, a formerly Jewish-owned bank that had been taken over by the Nazis.

The most draconian of the orders was Decree 13, issued on April 29, 1942, requiring Jews over the age of six to wear a yellow Star of David at all times while in public. The badge had to be sewn—not pinned but *sewn*—above the left breast of the outer garment. In a further insult, Jews were required to surrender four Dutch cents for each of the stars along with a precious clothing ration.

"My mother tried to make a game out of it in order not to alarm us. When we wore them around the neighborhood, we pretended to be very proud. I wasn't fooled, of course. I'd just turned eleven, and even though I didn't know what was coming, I knew we were in danger. But I pretended for the sake of my sister. Rachel was young enough to be deceived. She loved her yellow star. She used to say that she could feel God's eyes upon her when she wore it."

"Did your father comply with the order to surrender his paintings?"

"Everything but the Rembrandt. He removed it from its stretcher and hid it in a crawl space in the attic, along with a sack of diamonds he'd kept after selling his business to a Dutch competitor. My mother wept as our family heirlooms left the house. But my father said not to worry. I'll never forget his words. 'They're just objects,' he said. 'What's important is that we have each other. And no one can take that away.'"

And still the decrees kept coming. Jews were forbidden to leave their homes at night. Jews were forbidden to enter the homes of non-Jews. Jews were forbidden to use public telephones. Jews were forbidden to ride on trains or streetcars. Then, on July 5, 1942, Adolf Eichmann's Central Office for Jewish Emigration dispatched notices to four thousand Jews informing them that they had been selected for "labor service" in Germany. It was a lie, of course. The deportations had begun.

"Did your family receive an order to report?"

"Not right away. The first names selected were primarily German Jews who had taken refuge in Holland after 1933. Ours didn't come until the second week of September. We were told to report to Amsterdam's Centraal Station and given very specific instructions on what to pack. I remember my father's face. He knew it was a death sentence."

"What did he do?"

"He went up to the attic to retrieve the Rembrandt and the bag of diamonds."

"And then?"

"We tore the stars from our clothing and went into hiding."

18

AMSTERDAM

Chiara had been right about Lena Herzfeld. After years of silence, she was finally ready to speak about the war. She did not rush headlong toward the terrible secret that lay buried in her past. She worked her way there slowly, methodically, a schoolteacher with a difficult lesson to impart. Gabriel and Chiara, trained observers of human emotion, made no attempt to force the proceedings. Instead, they sat silently on Lena's snow-white couch, hands folded in their laps, like a pair of rapt pupils.

"Are you familiar with the Dutch word *verzuiling*?" Lena asked.

"I'm afraid not," replied Gabriel.

It was, she said, a uniquely Dutch concept that had helped to preserve social harmony in a country sharply divided along Catholic and Protestant lines. Peace had been maintained not through interaction but strict separation. If one were a Calvinist, for example, one read a Calvinist newspaper, shopped at a Calvinist butcher, cheered for Calvinist sporting clubs, and sent one's children to a Calvinist school. The same was true for Roman Catholics and Jews. Close friendships between Catholics and Calvinists were unusual. Friendships between Jews and Christians of any sort were virtually unheard of. *Verzuiling* was the main reason why so few Jews were able to hide from the Germans for any length of time once the roundups and deportations began. Most had no one to turn to for help.

"But that wasn't true of my father. Before the war, he made a number of friends outside the Jewish community through his business dealings. There was one man in particular, a Roman Catholic gentleman named Nikolaas de Graaf. He lived with his wife and four children in a house near the Vondelpark. I assume my father paid him a substantial amount of money, but neither of them spoke of such things. We entered the de Graaf house shortly before midnight on the ninth of September, one by one, so that the neighbors wouldn't notice us. We were each wearing three sets of clothing because we didn't dare move about the city with suitcases. A hiding place had been prepared for us in the attic. We climbed the ladder and the door was closed. After that . . . it was permanent night."

The attic had no amenities other than a few old blankets that had been laid upon the floor. Each morning, Mrs. de Graaf provided a basin of fresh water for rudimentary washing. The toilet was one floor below; for reasons of security, the de Graafs requested its use be limited to two visits per family member each day. Talking above a whisper was forbidden, and there was to be no verbal communication whatsoever at night. Clean clothing was provided once a week, and food was limited to whatever the de Graafs could spare from their own rations. The attic had no window. Lights or candles were not permitted, even on Shabbat. Before long, the entire Herzfeld family was suffering from malnutrition and the psychological effects of prolonged exposure to darkness.

"We were white as ghosts and very thin. When Mrs. de Graaf was cooking, the smell would rise up to the attic. After the family had eaten, she would bring us our portion. It was never enough. But, of course, we didn't complain. I always had the impression that Mrs. de Graaf was very frightened about our presence. She barely looked at us, and our trips downstairs made her edgy. For us, they were the only break from the darkness and the silence. We couldn't read because there was no light. We couldn't listen to the radio or speak because noise was forbidden. At night, we listened to the German *razzias* and trembled with fear."

The Germans did not conduct the raids alone. They were assisted by special units of the Dutch police known as Schalkhaarders and by a German-created force known as the Voluntary Auxiliary Police. Regarded as fanatical Jew hunters who would stop at nothing to fill their nightly quotas, the Auxiliary officers were primarily members of the Dutch SS and Dutch Nazi party. Early in the deportation process, they were paid seven and a half guilders for each Jew they arrested. But as the deportations steadily drained Holland of its Jews and prey became harder to find, the bounty was increased to forty guilders. In a time of war and economic privation, it was a substantial sum of money, one that led many Dutch citizens to supply information about Jews in hiding for a few pieces of silver.

"It was our greatest fear. The fear that we would be betrayed. Not by the de Graafs but by a neighbor or an acquaintance who knew of our presence. My father was most concerned about the de Graaf children. Three were teenagers, but the youngest boy was my age. My father feared the boy might accidentally tell one of his schoolmates. You know how children can be. They say things to impress their friends without fully understanding the consequences."

"Is that what happened?"

"No," she said, shaking her head emphatically. "As it turned out, the de Graaf children never breathed a word about our presence. It was one of the neighbors who did us in. A woman who lived next door."

"She heard you through the attic?"

Lena's eyes rose toward the ceiling, and her gaze grew fearful. "No," she said finally. "She saw me."

"Where?"

"In the garden."

"The garden? What were you doing in the garden, Lena?"

She started to answer, then buried her face in her hands and wept. Gabriel held her tightly, struck by her complete silence. Lena Herzfeld, the child of darkness, the child of the attic, could still cry without making a sound.

19

AMSTERDAM

What followed was the confession of Lena Herzfeld. Her transgression had started as a minor act of disobedience committed by a desperate child who simply wanted to touch the snow. She had not planned the adventure. In fact, to this day she did not know what woke her in the early-morning hours of February 12, 1943, or what prompted her to rise quietly from her bed and descend the ladder from the attic. She remembered the hall had been in complete darkness. Even so, she had no trouble finding her way to the bathroom. She had taken those same seven steps, twice each day, for the past five months. Those seven steps had constituted her only form of exercise. Her only break from the monotony of the attic. And her only chance to see the outside world.

"There was a window next to the basin. It was small and round and overlooked the rear garden. Mrs. de Graaf insisted the curtain be kept closed whenever we entered."

"But you opened it against her wishes?"

"From time to time." A pause, then, "I was only a child."

"I know, Lena," Gabriel said, his tone forgiving. "Tell me what you saw."

"I saw fresh snow glowing in the moonlight. I saw the stars." She looked at Gabriel. "I'm sure it seems terribly ordinary to you now, but to a child who had been locked in an attic for five months it was . . ."

"Irresistible?"

"It seemed like heaven. A small corner of heaven, but heaven nonetheless. I wanted to touch the snow. I wanted to see the stars. And part of me wanted to look God directly in the eye and ask Him why He had done this to us."

She scrutinized Gabriel as if calculating whether this stranger who had appeared on her doorstep was truly a worthy recipient of such a memory.

"You were born in Israel?" she asked.

He answered not as Gideon Argov but as himself.

"I was born in an agricultural settlement in the Valley of Jezreel."

"And your parents?"

"My father's family came from Munich. My mother was born in Berlin. She was deported to Auschwitz in 1942. Her parents were gassed upon arrival, but she managed to survive until the end. She was marched out in January 1945."

"The Death March? My God, but she must have been a remarkable woman to survive such an ordeal." She looked at him for a moment, then asked, "What did she tell you?"

"My mother never spoke of it, not even to me."

Lena gave a perceptive nod. Then, after another long pause,

she described how she stole silently down the stairs of the de Graaf house and slipped outside into the garden. She was wearing no shoes, and the snow was very cold against her stockinged feet. It didn't matter; it felt wonderful. She grabbed snow by the handful and breathed deeply of the freezing air until her throat began to burn. She spread her arms wide and began to twirl, so that the stars and the sky moved like a kaleidoscope. She twirled and twirled until her head began to spin.

"It was then I noticed the face in the window of the house next door. She looked frightened—truly frightened. I can only imagine how I must have looked to her. Like a pale gray ghost. Like a creature from another world. I obeyed my first instinct, which was to run back inside. But I'm afraid that probably compounded my mistake. If I'd managed to react calmly, it's possible she might have thought I was one of the de Graaf children. But by running, I betrayed myself and the rest of my family. It was like shouting at the top of my lungs that I was a Jew in hiding. I might as well have been wearing my yellow star."

"Did you tell your parents what had happened?"

"I wanted to, but I was too afraid. I just lay on my blanket and waited. After a few hours, Mrs. de Graaf brought us our basin of fresh water, and I knew we had survived the night."

The remainder of the day proceeded much like the one hundred and fifty-five that had come before it. They washed to the best of their ability. They were given a bit of food to eat. They made two trips each to the toilet. On her second trip, Lena was tempted to peer out the window into the garden to see if her footprints were still visible in the snow. Instead, she walked the seven steps back to the ladder and returned to the darkness.

That night was Shabbat. Speaking in whispers, the Herzfeld

family recited the three blessings—even though they had no candles, no bread, and no wine—and prayed that God would protect them for another week. A few minutes later, the *razzias* started up: German boots on cobblestone streets, Schalkhaarders shouting out commands in Dutch.

"Usually, the raiding parties would pass us by, and the sound would grow fainter. But not that night. On that night the sound grew louder and louder until the entire house began to shake. I knew they were coming for us. I was the only one who knew."

20

AMSTERDAM

Lena Herzfeld lapsed into a prolonged, exhausted silence. Gabriel could see that in her mind a door had closed. On one side was an old woman living alone in Amsterdam; on the other, a child who had mistakenly betrayed her family. Gabriel suggested they stop for the night. And a part of him wondered whether to continue at all. For what purpose? For a painting that was probably lost forever? But much to his surprise, it was Lena who insisted on pressing forward, Lena who demanded to tell the rest of the story. Not for the sake of the Rembrandt, she assured him, but for herself. She needed to explain how severely she had been punished for those few stolen moments in the garden. And she needed to atone. And so, for the first time in her life, she described how her family had been dragged from the attic under the shamed gaze of the de Graaf children. And how they were taken by truck to, of all places, the Hollandsche Schouwburg, once the most glamorous theater in Amsterdam.

"The Germans had turned it into a detention center for captured Jews. It was nothing like I remembered, of course. The seats had been removed from the orchestra, the chandeliers had been ripped from the ceiling, and there were ropes hanging like nooses above what was left of the stage."

Her memories were something from a nightmare. Memories of laughing Schalkhaarders swapping stories about the evening's hunt. Memories of a young boy who'd attempted to flee and was beaten senseless. Memories of a dozen elderly men and women who had been pulled from their beds at a home for the aged and were seated calmly in their frayed nightgowns as if waiting for the performance to begin. And memories, too, of a tall man dressed entirely in black striding godlike across the stage, a portrait by Rembrandt in one hand, a sack of diamonds in the other.

"The man was SS?"

"Yes."

"Were you ever told his name?"

She hesitated. "I learned it later, but I will not say it."

Gabriel gave a placatory nod. Lena closed her eyes and continued. What she remembered most about him, she said, was the smell of leather rising from his freshly polished boots. His eyes were deep brown, the hair dark and richly oiled, the skin sallow and bloodless. His manner was aristocratic and shockingly courteous.

"This was no village bumpkin in a nice uniform. This was a man from a good family. A man from the upper reaches of German society. Initially, he spoke to my father in excellent

Dutch. Then, after establishing that my father spoke German, he switched."

"Did you speak German?"

"A little."

"Were you able to understand what was happening?"

"Bits and pieces. The SS man scolded my father for having violated the decrees concerning Jewish financial assets and valuables such as jewelry and works of art. He then informed my father that both the diamonds and the Rembrandt would have to be confiscated before our deportation to the labor camps. But there was just one thing he required first. He wanted my father to sign a piece of paper."

"A forfeiture document?"

She shook her head. "A bill of sale, not for the diamonds, only for the Rembrandt. He wanted my father to *sell* him the painting. The price would be one hundred guilders—payable at a future date, of course. One hundred guilders . . . less than the Jew hunters earned on a good night of roundups."

"You saw the actual contract?"

She hesitated, then nodded slowly. "The Germans were precise in all things, and paperwork was very important to them. They recorded everything. The number of people murdered each day in the gas chambers. The number of shoes left behind. The weight of the gold wrenched from the dead before they were thrown into the crematoria."

Again Lena's voice trailed off, and for a moment Gabriel feared she was lost to them. But she quickly composed herself and continued. Tonight, Lena Herzfeld had chosen Gabriel and Chiara to hear her testimony. Tonight there was no turning back.

"Only later did I understand why the SS man required my

father's signature. Stealing a bag of diamonds was one thing. But stealing a painting, especially a Rembrandt, was quite another. Isn't it ironic? They killed six million people, but he wanted a bill of sale for my father's Rembrandt—a piece of paper so he could claim he had acquired it legally."

"What did your father do?"

"He refused. Even now, I cannot imagine where he found the courage. He told the SS man that he had no illusions about the fate that awaited us and that under no circumstances would he sign anything. The SS man seemed quite startled. I don't think a Jew had dared to speak to him like that in a very long time."

"Did he threaten your father?"

"Actually, quite the opposite. For a moment, he seemed stumped. Then he looked down at Rachel and me and smiled. He said the labor camps were no place for children. He said he had a solution. A trade. Two lives for one painting. If my father signed the bill of sale, Rachel and I would be allowed to go free. At first, my father resisted, but my mother convinced him there was no choice. At least they will have each other, she said. Eventually, my father capitulated, and signed the papers. There were two copies, one for him, one for the SS man."

Lena's eyes shone suddenly with tears, and her hands began to tremble, not with sadness but with anger.

"But once the monster had what he wanted, he changed his mind. He said he had misspoken. He said he could not take *two* children, only one. Then he pointed at me and said, 'That one. The one with the blond hair and blue eyes.' It was my sentence."

The SS man instructed the Herzfeld family to say its last good-byes. *And be quick about it,* he added, his voice full of false cordiality. Lena's mother and sister wept as they embraced a final time, but her father managed to maintain an outward composure. Holding Lena close, he whispered that he would love her forever and that someday soon they would all be together again. Then Lena felt her father place something in her coat pocket. A few seconds later, the monster was leading her out of the theater. *Just keep walking, Miss Herzfeld,* he was saying. *And whatever you do, don't look back. If you look back, even once, I'll put you on the train, too.*

"And what do you think I did?" she asked.

"You kept walking."

"That's correct. Miss Herzfeld kept walking. And she never looked back. Not once. And she never saw her family again. Within three weeks, they were dead. But not Miss Herzfeld. She was alive because she had blond hair. And her sister had been turned to ashes because hers was dark."

21

AMSTERDAM

Lena Herzfeld went into hiding a second time. Her odyssey began in the building directly across the street from the theater, at Plantage Middenlaan 31. A former day-care center for working-class families, it had been turned by the Nazis into a second detention center reserved for infants and toddlers. But during the period of the deportations, several hundred small children were smuggled out in crates and potato sacks and turned over to the Dutch Resistance.

"The SS man personally walked me into the nursery and handed me over to the staff. I'm amazed he kept his word at all, but he had his painting. The war was full of such inexplicable contradictions. One moment, a heartless monster. The next, a man capable of a modicum of human decency."

Lena was spirited to Friesland in northwestern Holland in

the trunk of a car and surrendered to a childless couple active in the Dutch Resistance. They gave her a new name and told neighbors she had been orphaned in the German bombing of Rotterdam in May 1940. Because they were devout Calvinists, they expected Lena to attend church services on Sunday for the sake of her cover. But inside the security of the home, she was encouraged to maintain her Jewish identity.

"You might find this difficult to understand, but I consider myself to be one of the lucky ones. Many of the children who were hidden with Christian families had dreadful experiences. But I was treated kindly and with a great deal of warmth and affection."

"And when the war ended?"

"There was no place for me to go. I stayed in Friesland until I was eighteen. Then I attended university and eventually became a teacher. I thought many times about emigrating to Israel or America. But in the end, I decided to stay. I felt it was my duty to remain in Amsterdam with the ghosts of the dead."

"Did you ever try to reclaim your family home?"

"It wasn't possible. After the war the Dutch government declared that the rights of current owners were *equal* to those of the prior Jewish owners. It meant that unless I could prove that the man who purchased our home had done so in bad faith, I couldn't dislodge him. Furthermore, I had no proof my father had ever owned the house or even proof of his death, both of which were required by law."

"And the Rembrandt?"

"I came to regard the woman in that painting as an accomplice in my family's murder. I never wanted to see her again."

"But you kept the receipt," Gabriel said.

The child of the attic fixed him with a suspicious stare.

"Isn't that what your father placed in your pocket as you were saying good-bye?"

Still she didn't answer.

"And you kept it with you in hiding, didn't you, Lena? You kept it because it was the only thing of your father's you had." Gabriel was silent for a moment. "Where's the receipt, Lena?"

"It's in the top drawer of my nightstand. I look at it every night before I go to sleep."

"Will you let me have it?"

"Why would you want such a thing?"

"Your Rembrandt is out there somewhere. And we're going to find it."

"That painting is covered in blood."

"I know, Lena. I know."

22

AMSTERDAM

It was approaching eleven o'clock when they left Lena Herzfeld's house and a hard rain was hammering on the pavement. Chiara wanted to find a taxi but Gabriel insisted on walking. They stood for a long time outside the Hollandsche Schouwburg theater, now a memorial to those who had been imprisoned there, before making their way to Rembrandt's old house at the top of Jodenbreestraat. Gabriel could only marvel at the shortness of the distance. A kilometer, no more. He was certain the next link in the chain would be longer.

They ate with little appetite at a quiet restaurant near their hotel, talking about anything but the horror they had just heard, and climbed into bed shortly after one. Chiara's sleep was disturbed by nightmares, though much to her surprise she found that Ivan Kharkov had been displaced from his starring role by a man in black attempting to rip a child from her arms. She forced herself awake to find Gabriel seated at the writing desk in their room, the lamp burning brightly, a pen scratching furiously across a sheet of paper.

"What are you doing?"

"Go back to sleep."

"I was dreaming about him."

"I know."

In the morning, while Gabriel was still sleeping, she discovered the product of his nocturnal labors. Attached to the receipt for the painting was a document many pages in length, written on hotel stationery in Gabriel's distinctive left-handed script. At the top of the first page was the date and the city followed by the words *The Testimony of Lena Herzfeld*. Chiara leafed rapidly through the pages, astonished by what she was reading. Blessed with a flawless memory, Gabriel had created a verbatim transcript of the entire conversation. And on the final page he had written a short note to himself.

Sometimes the best way to find a painting is to find where it's been.

Find Kurt Voss.

Find the painting.

PART TWO

ATTRIBUTION

23

SOUTHWARK, LONDON

There are few things in the newspaper business more excruciating than a staff meeting that convenes at five o'clock on a Friday afternoon. Half those present are already thinking about their plans for the weekend while the rest are on deadline and therefore anxious about work still to be done. At the moment, Zoe Reed fell into neither category, though admittedly her mind had begun to wander.

Like nearly everyone else gathered in the fifth-floor conference room of the *Financial Journal*, Zoe had heard it all many times before. The once-mighty tablet of global business was now a financial basket case. Circulation and advertising revenue were locked in a downward spiral with no bottom in sight. Not only was the *Journal* unprofitable, it was hemorrhaging cash at an alarming and unsustainable rate. If trends continued, the paper's corporate parent, Latham International Media, would have no choice but to immediately seek a buyer—or, more likely, shut the paper down. In the meantime, newsroom expenditures would once again have to be slashed to the bone. No more costly lunches with sources. No more unapproved travel. And no more paid subscriptions to other publications. From this moment forward, *Journal* reporters could consume their news just like everyone else in the world—on the Internet for free.

The bearer of this gloomy report was Jason Turnbury, the *Journal*'s editor in chief. He was prowling the conference room like a matador, his necktie artfully loosened, his face still tanned from a recent Caribbean holiday. Jason was a rocket, a corporate shooting star who possessed an unrivaled ability to sidestep oncoming trouble. If there was blood to be shed over the *Journal*'s declining fortunes, it wasn't going to be his. Zoe knew for a fact Jason was being groomed for a corner office at Latham headquarters. She knew this because, against all better judgment, they had once had a brief affair. Though they were no longer lovers, he still confided in her and regularly sought her advice and approval. Therefore it came as no surprise to Zoe when, five minutes after the meeting broke up, he phoned her at her desk.

"How was I?"

"A bit maudlin for my taste. Surely it's not as bad as all that."

"Worse. Think *Titanic*."

"You don't really expect me to do my job without a proper travel and entertainment budget."

"The new rules apply to all editorial personnel. Even you."

"Then I quit."

"Good. That makes one fewer person I'll have to sack. Actually, *two*. My God, but we pay you an outrageous amount of money."

"That's because I'm special. It even says so in my title, Special Investigative Correspondent. You gave it to me yourself."

"Biggest mistake of my career."

"For the record, it was your *second* biggest, Jason."

The line had been delivered with Zoe's trademark acid wit. Low and sultry, Zoe's voice was one of the most dreaded sounds within the London financial world. It regularly reduced arrogant CEOs to mush and transformed even the most combative lawyers into blabbering idiots. Among the most respected and feared investigative journalists in Britain, Zoe and her small team of reporters and researchers had left a trail of broken companies and careers in their wake. She had exposed crooked accounting schemes, insider-trading practices, crimes against the environment, and countless cases involving bribery and kickbacks. And though most of her work involved British firms, she routinely reported on corporate shenanigans in other European countries and in America. Indeed, during the chaotic autumn of 2008, Zoe had spent several weeks trying to prove that an American wealth-management firm run by a highly respected strategist was actually a giant Ponzi scheme. She had been within forty-eight hours of confirming the story when Bernard Madoff was arrested by FBI agents and charged with securities fraud. Zoe's previous reporting gave the *Journal* a distinct advantage over its competitors as the scandal unfolded, though privately she never forgave herself for not getting Madoff before the authorities. Fiercely competitive and disdainful of those who broke rules of any sort, Zoe Reed had vowed to never let another corrupt, thieving businessman slip through her grasp.

At the moment, she was plugging the final holes in an upcoming exposé about a rising Labor MP who had accepted at least one hundred thousand pounds in illicit payments from Empire Aerospace Systems, a leading British defense contractor. The *Journal*'s publicity department had tipped off the broadcast news networks that Zoe had an important piece in the works, and appearances had already been quietly scheduled on the BBC, CNBC, Sky News, and CNN International. Unlike most print reporters, Zoe was a fluid television performer who had the rare ability to forget she was sitting in front of a camera. What's more, she invariably was the most attractive person on the set. The BBC had been trying to lure Zoe away from the *Journal* for years, and she had recently flown to New York to meet with executives at CNBC. Zoe now possessed the power to quadruple her salary simply by picking up the telephone. Which meant she was in no mood to listen to a lecture from Jason Turnbury about budget cuts.

"May I explain why your new cost-cutting measures will make it impossible to do my job?"

"If you must."

"As you well know, Jason, my sources come from the inside, and they have to be seduced into giving me information. Do you really expect me to convince a senior executive to betray his company over an egg-and-dill sandwich at Pret A Manger?"

"Did you look at your expense form last month before you signed it? I could have employed two junior editors for the amount of money you spent in the Grill Room of the Dorchester alone."

"Some conversations can't be done over the telephone."

"I agree. So why don't you meet me at Café Rouge for a drink so we can continue this in person?"

"You know that's not a good idea, Jason."

"I'm suggesting a cordial drink between two professionals."

"That's bollocks, and you know it."

Jason made light of her rejection and quickly changed the subject.

"Are you watching television?"

"Are we still allowed to watch television or is that now considered a waste of expensive corporate electricity?"

"Turn to Sky News."

Zoe switched the channel and saw three men standing before a gathering of reporters at the United Nations complex in Geneva. One was the UN secretary-general, the second was an Irish rock star who had worked tirelessly to eradicate poverty in Africa, and the third was Martin Landesmann. A fabulously wealthy Geneva-based financier, Landesmann had just announced he was donating one hundred million dollars to improve Third World food production. It was not the first time Landesmann had made such a gesture. Referred to as "Saint Martin" by detractors and supporters alike, Landesmann reportedly had given away at least a billion dollars of his own money to various charitable enterprises. His enormous wealth and generosity were matched only by his reclusiveness and scorn for the press. Landesmann had granted just one interview in his entire life. And Zoe had been the reporter.

"When was this?"

"Earlier this afternoon. He refused to take questions."

"I'm surprised they were able to convince Martin to even come."

"I didn't realize you two were on a first-name basis."

"Actually, I haven't spoken to him in months."

"Maybe it's time you renewed your relationship."

"I've tried, Jason. He's not interested in talking."

"Why don't you give him a call now?"

"Because I'm going home to take a very long bath."

"And the rest of the weekend?"

"A trashy book. A couple of DVDs. Maybe a walk in Hampstead Heath if it's not raining."

"Sounds rather dull."

"I like dull, Jason. That's why I've always been so fond of you."

"I'll be at Café Rouge in an hour."

"And I'll see you Monday morning."

She hung up the phone and watched Martin Landesmann exit the news conference in Geneva, his silver hair aglow in the flashing of a hundred cameras, his stunning French-born wife, Monique, at his side. For a devoutly private man, Landesmann certainly knew how to cut a striking figure on those rare occasions when he stepped onto the public stage. It was one of Martin's special gifts, his matchless ability to control what the world knew and saw of him. Zoe was quite confident she knew more about Martin Landesmann than any reporter in the world. Yet even she acknowledged that there was much about Saint Martin and his financial empire that was beyond her grasp.

Landesmann's image was replaced by that of the new American president, who was launching an initiative to improve relations between the United States and one of its most implacable foes, the Islamic Republic of Iran. Zoe switched off the television, glanced at her watch, and swore softly. It was already a few minutes past six. Her plans for the weekend were not as lackluster as she had led Jason to believe. In fact, they were quite extensive. And she was now running late.

She checked her e-mail, then conducted a harsh purge of her voice mail. By 6:15, she was pulling on her overcoat and heading across the newsroom. From inside his large glass-enclosed office, Jason was admiring his magnificent view of the Thames. Sensing Zoe behind him, he pirouetted and engaged in a flagrant attempt to catch her eye. Zoe lowered her gaze toward the carpet and ducked into a waiting elevator.

As the carriage sunk toward the lobby, Zoe examined her reflection in the stainless steel doors. *You were left on our doorstep by Gypsies,* her mother used to say. It seemed the only possible explanation for how a child of Anglo-Saxon heritage had come into the world with black hair, dark brown eyes, and olive-complected skin. As a young girl, Zoe had been self-conscious about her appearance. But by the time she went up to Cambridge, she knew it was an asset. Zoe's looks made her stand out from the crowd, as did her obvious intelligence and biting sense of humor. Jason had been smitten the first time she walked into his office. He'd hired her on the spot and expedited her ascent up the ladder of success. In moments of honesty, Zoe admitted that her career had been helped by her looks. But she was also smarter than most of her colleagues. And no one in the newsroom worked harder.

As the elevator doors opened, she spotted a knot of reporters and editors gathered in the lobby, debating a proper setting for that evening's drinking session. Zoe slipped past with a polite smile—she had acquaintances on the staff but no true friends—and stepped into the street. As usual, she headed across the Thames to the Cannon Street Underground Station. Had home been her true destination, she would have taken a westbound Circle Line train to Embankment and transferred to a Northern Line train to Hampstead. Instead, she stepped onto an eastbound train and rode it as far as St. Pancras Station, the new London terminal for high-speed Eurostar trains.

Tucked into the outside flap of Zoe's briefcase was a ticket for the 7:09 train to Paris. She purchased several magazines before clearing passport control, then made her way to the departure platform, where the boarding process was already under way. She found her seat in the first-class cabin and in short order was presented with a rather good glass of champagne. *A trashy book. A couple of DVDs. Maybe a walk in Hampstead Heath if it's not raining . . .* Not quite. She peered out the window as the train eased from the station and saw an attractive dark-haired woman gazing back at her. *This is the last time, Gypsy girl,* she thought. *This is the very last time.*

24

AMSTERDAM

Few people noticed Eli Lavon's arrival in Amsterdam the following day, and those who did mistook him for someone else. It was his special talent. Regarded as the finest street surveillance artist the Office had ever produced, Lavon was a ghost of a man who possessed a chameleon-like ability to change his appearance. His greatest asset was his natural anonymity. On the surface, he appeared to be one of life's downtrodden. In reality, he was a natural predator who could follow a highly trained intelligence officer or hardened terrorist down any street in the world without attracting even a flicker of interest. Ari Shamron liked to say that Lavon could disappear while shaking your hand. It was not far from the truth.

It was Shamron himself, in September 1972, who introduced Lavon to a promising young artist named Gabriel Allon. Though they did not realize it then, both had been selected to take part in what would become one of the most celebrated and controversial missions ever undertaken by Israeli intelligence—Wrath of God, the secret operation to hunt down and assassinate the perpetrators of the Munich Olympics massacre. In the Hebrew-based lexicon of the team, Lavon was an *ayin*, a tracker and surveillance specialist. Gabriel was an *aleph*. Armed with a .22 caliber Beretta pistol, he personally assassinated six of the Black September terrorists responsible for Munich. Under Shamron's unrelenting pressure, they stalked their prey across Western Europe for three years, killing both at night and in broad daylight, living in fear that at any moment they would be arrested and charged as murderers. When they finally returned home, Gabriel's temples were the color of ash, his face that of a man twenty years his senior. Eli Lavon, who had been exposed to the terrorists for long periods of time with no backup, suffered innumerable stress disorders, including a notoriously fickle stomach that troubled him to this day.

When the Wrath of God unit was formally disbanded, neither Gabriel nor Lavon wanted anything more to do with intelligence work or killing. Gabriel took refuge in Venice to heal paintings while Lavon fled to Vienna, where he opened a small investigative bureau called Wartime Claims and Inquiries. Operating on a shoestring budget, he managed to track down millions of dollars' worth of looted Holocaust assets and played a significant role in prying a multibillion-dollar settlement from the banks of Switzerland. Lavon's activities earned him few friends, and in 2003 a bomb exploded inside his office, seriously wounding him and killing two of his employees. Lavon never attempted to rebuild in Vienna, choosing instead to return to Israel and pursue his first love, archaeology. He now served as an adjunct professor at

Hebrew University and regularly took part in digs around the country. And twice a year he returned to the Office academy to lecture the new recruits on the fine art of physical surveillance. Invariably, one would ask Lavon about his work with the legendary assassin Gabriel Allon. Lavon's response never varied: "Gabriel *who*?"

By training and temperament, Lavon was prone to handle delicate objects with care. That was especially true of the single sheet of paper he accepted in the sitting room of a suite at the Ambassade Hotel. He examined it for several moments in the half-light before placing it on the coffee table and peering curiously at Gabriel and Chiara over his gold half-moon reading glasses.

"I thought you two were hiding out from Shamron in the deepest corner of Cornwall. How in the world did you get this?"

"Is it real?" asked Gabriel.

"Absolutely. But where did it come from?"

Gabriel gave Lavon an account of the investigation thus far, beginning with Julian Isherwood's unannounced appearance on the cliffs of Lizard Point and ending with the story of Lena Herzfeld. Lavon listened intently, his brown eyes darting back and forth between Gabriel and Chiara. At the conclusion, he studied the document again and shook his head slowly.

"What's wrong, Eli?"

"I've spent years searching for something like this. Leave it to you to stumble on it by accident."

"Something like what, Eli?"

"Proof of his guilt. Oh, I found scraps of corroborating evidence scattered across the graveyards of Europe, but nothing as damning as this."

"You recognize the name?"

"Kurt Voss?" Lavon nodded his head slowly. "You might say that SS-Hauptsturmführer Kurt Voss and I are old friends."

"And the signature?"

"To me, it's as recognizable as Rembrandt's." Lavon glanced down at the document. "Whether you ever manage to find Julian's painting, you've already made a major discovery. And it needs to be preserved."

"I'd be more than happy to entrust it to your capable hands, Eli."

"I assume there's a price involved."

"A small one," said Gabriel.

"What's that?"

"Tell me about Voss."

"It would be my distinct displeasure. But order us some coffee, Gabriel. I'm a bit like Shamron. I can't tell a story without coffee."

25

AMSTERDAM

Eli Lavon began with the basic facts of Kurt Voss's appalling biography.

Born into an upper-class trading family in Köln on October 23, 1906, Voss was sent to the capital for schooling, graduating from the University of Berlin in 1932 with degrees in law and history. In February 1933, within weeks of Hitler's rise to power, he joined the Nazi Party and was assigned to the Sicherheitsdienst, or SD, the security and intelligence service of the SS. For the next several years, he worked at headquarters in Berlin compiling dossiers on enemies of the Party, both real and imagined. Ambitious in all things, Voss courted Frieda Schuler, the daughter of a prominent Gestapo officer, and the two were soon wed at a country estate outside Berlin. Reichsführer-SS Heinrich Himmler was in attendance, as was SD chief Reinhard Heydrich, who serenaded the happy couple on the violin. Eighteen months later, Frieda gave birth to a son. Hitler himself sent a note of congratulations.

Voss soon grew bored with his work at SD headquarters and made it clear to his powerful backers he was interested in a more challenging assignment. His opportunity came in March 1938, when German forces rolled unchallenged into Austria. By August, Voss was in Vienna, assigned to the Zentralstelle für jüdische Auswanderung, the Central Office for Jewish Emigration. The bureau was led by a ruthless young SS officer who would change the course of Voss's life.

"Adolf Eichmann," said Gabriel.

Lavon nodded his head slowly. *Eichmann . . .*

The Zentralstelle was headquartered in an ornate Viennese palace appropriated from the Rothschild family. Eichmann's orders were to cleanse Austria of its large and influential Jewish population through a mechanized program of rapid coerced flight. On any given day, the splendid old rooms and wide halls were overflowing with Jews clamoring to escape the wave of virulent anti-Semitic violence sweeping the country. Eichmann and his team were more than willing to show them the door, provided they first pay a steep toll.

"It was a giant fleecing operation. Jews entered at one end with money and possessions and came out the other with nothing but their lives. The Nazis would later refer to the process as the 'Vienna model,' and it was regarded as one of Eichmann's finest accomplishments. In truth, Voss deserved much of the credit, if you can call it that. He was never far from Eichmann's side. They used to prowl the corridors of the palace in their black SS uniforms like a pair of young gods. But there was one difference.

Eichmann was transparently cruel to his victims, but those who encountered Voss were often struck by his impeccable manners. He always carried himself as though he found the entire process distasteful. In reality, it was just a disguise. Voss was a shrewd businessman. He would search out the well-to-do and pull them into his office for a private chat. Invariably, their money would end up in his pocket. By the time he left Vienna, Kurt Voss was a wealthy man. And he was just getting started."

By the autumn of 1941, with the Continent engulfed in war, Hitler and his senior henchmen decided that the Jews were to be exterminated. Europe was to be scoured from west to east, with Eichmann and his "deportation experts" operating the levers of death. The able-bodied would be used as slave labor. The rest—the young, the old, the sick, the disabled—would immediately be subjected to "special treatment." For the nine and a half million Jews living under direct or indirect German rule, it was a catastrophe, a crime without a name.

"But not for Voss," said Lavon. "For Kurt Voss, it was the business opportunity of a lifetime."

As the lethal summer of 1942 commenced, Voss and the rest of Eichmann's team were headquartered in Berlin at 116 Kurfürstenstrasse, an imposing building which, much to Eichmann's delight, had once housed a Jewish mutual aid society. Known as Department IVB4, these were the men who kept the Continent-wide enterprise of mass murder humming along smoothly.

"Voss had an office just down the hall from Eichmann," Lavon said. "But he was rarely there. Voss had a roving commission. He approved the deportation lists, supervised the roundups, and secured the necessary trains. And, of course, he expanded his thriving side business, robbing his victims blind before dispatching them to their deaths."

But Voss's most lucrative transaction would occur late in the war and in the last country to be ravaged by the fires of the Holocaust: Hungary. When Eichmann arrived in Budapest, he had one goal—finding each and every one of Hungary's 825,000 Jews and sending them to their deaths at Auschwitz. His trusted aide, Kurt Voss, wanted something else.

"The Bauer-Rubin industrial works," said Lavon. "The owners were a consortium of highly assimilated Jews, most of whom had either converted to Catholicism or were married to Catholic women. Within days of his arrival in Budapest, Voss summoned them and explained that their days were numbered. But as usual, he had a proposition. If the Bauer-Rubin industrial works were transferred to his control, Voss would make certain that the owners and their families would be granted safe passage to Portugal. As you might expect, the owners quickly agreed to Voss's demands. The following day, the managing partner, a man named Samuel Rubin, accompanied Voss on a trip to Zurich."

"Why Zurich?"

"Because that's where the vast majority of the firm's assets were held for safekeeping. Voss pulled the company apart piece by piece and moved its holdings to accounts under his control. When his greed was finally satisfied, he allowed Rubin to leave for Portugal and promised that everyone else would follow in short order. It never happened. Rubin was the only one to survive. The rest ended up in Auschwitz along with more than four hundred thousand other Hungarian Jews."

"And Voss?"

He returned to Berlin on Christmas Eve 1944. But with the war all but lost, Voss and the rest of Eichmann's desk murderers were treated as outcasts and pariahs, even by some of their colleagues in the SS. As the city shook beneath the Allied air raids, Eichmann turned his lair into a heavily guarded fortress and began hastily destroying his most damning files. Voss the lawyer knew that concealment of such vast crimes was not possible, not with evidence scattered across a continent and thousands of survivors waiting to come forward to tell their stories. Instead, he used his remaining time to more productive ends—gathering his ill-gotten riches and preparing for his escape.

"Eichmann was woefully unprepared when the end finally came. He had no false papers, no money, and no safe house. But not Voss. Voss had a new name, places to hide, and, of course, a great deal of money. On April 30, 1945, the night Hitler committed suicide in his bunker beneath the Reich Chancellery, Kurt Voss shed his SS uniform and slipped out of his office at 116 Kurfürstenstrasse. By morning, he had vanished."

"And the money?"

"It was gone, too," said Lavon. "Just like the people it once belonged to."

26

AMSTERDAM

Gabriel Allon had confronted evil in many forms: terrorists, murderous Russian arms dealers, professional assassins who shed the blood of strangers for briefcases filled with cash. But none could compare to the genocidal evil of the men and women who had carried out the single greatest act of mass murder in history. They had been a constant if unacknowledged presence inside Gabriel's childhood home in the Jezreel Valley of Israel. And now that night had fallen over Amsterdam, they had crept into the suite at the Ambassade Hotel. Unable to bear their company any longer, he stood abruptly and informed Eli Lavon and Chiara that he needed to continue the conversation outside. They drifted along the banks of the Herengracht through yellow lamplight, Gabriel and Lavon shoulder to shoulder, Chiara trailing several paces behind.

"She's too close."

"She's not tailing us, Eli. She's just watching our back."

"It doesn't matter. She's still too close."

"Shall we stop so you can give her a bit of instruction?"

"She never listens to me. She's unbelievably stubborn. And far too pretty for street work." Lavon gave Gabriel a sideways glance. "I'll never understand what she saw in a fossil like you. It must have been your natural charm and cheerful disposition."

"You were about to tell me more about Kurt Voss."

Lavon paused to allow a bicycle to pass. It was ridden by a young woman who was steering with one hand and sending a text message with the other. Lavon gave a fleeting smile, then resumed his lecture.

"Keep one thing in mind, Gabriel. We know a great deal about Voss now, but in the aftermath of the war we barely knew the bastard's name. And by the time we fully understood the true nature of his crimes, he'd disappeared."

"Where did he go?"

"Argentina."

"How did he get there?"

"How do you think?"

"The Church?"

"But of course."

Gabriel shook his head slowly. To this day, historians bitterly debated whether Pope Pius XII, the controversial wartime pontiff, had helped the Jews or turned a blind eye to their suffering. But it was Pius's actions *after* the war that Gabriel found most damning. The Holy Father never uttered a single word of sorrow or regret over the murder of six million human beings and seemed far more concerned about the perpetrators of the crime than its victims. Not only was the pope an outspoken critic of the

Nuremburg trials, he allowed the good offices of the Vatican to be used for one of history's greatest mass flights from justice. Known as the Vatican ratline, it helped hundreds, if not thousands, of Nazi war criminals to escape to sanctuaries in South America and the Middle East.

"Voss got to Rome with the help of old friends from the SS. Occasionally, he would stay in small inns or safe houses, but for the most part he found shelter in Franciscan monasteries and convents."

"And after he arrived?"

"He stayed at a lovely old villa at Number 23 Via Piave. An Austrian priest, Monsignor Karl Bayer, took very good care of him while the Pontifical Commission of Assistance saw to his travel arrangements. Within a few days, he had a Red Cross passport in the name of Rudolf Seibel and a landing permit for Argentina. On May 25, 1949, he boarded the *North King* in Genoa and set sail for Buenos Aires."

"The ship sounds familiar."

"It should. There was another passenger on board who'd also received help from the Vatican. His Red Cross passport identified him as Helmut Gregor. His real name was—"

"Josef Mengele."

Lavon nodded. "We don't know whether the two men ever met during the crossing. But we *do* know that Voss's arrival went more smoothly than Mengele's. Apparently, the Angel of Death described himself to immigration officials as a technician, but his luggage was filled with medical files and blood samples from his time at Auschwitz."

"Did Voss have anything interesting in his luggage?"

"You mean something like a Rembrandt portrait?" Lavon shook his head. "As far as we know, Voss came to the New World empty-handed. He listed his occupation as bellman and was admitted to the country without delay. His mentor, Eichmann, arrived a year later."

"It must have been quite a reunion."

"Actually, they didn't get on terribly well in Argentina. They met for coffee a few times at the ABC Café in downtown Buenos Aires, but Voss apparently didn't care for Eichmann's company. Eichmann had spent several years in hiding, working as a lumberjack and a farmer. He was no longer a young god who held the fate of millions in the palm of his hand. He was a common laborer in need of work. And he was seething with bitterness."

"And Voss?"

"Unlike Eichmann, he had a formal education. Within a year, he was working as a lawyer in a firm that catered to the German community in Argentina. In 1955, his wife and son were smuggled out of Germany, and the family was reunited. By all accounts, Kurt Voss lived a rather ordinary but comfortable middle-class life in the Palermo district of Buenos Aires until his death in 1982."

"Why wasn't he ever arrested?"

"Because he had powerful friends. Friends in the secret police. Friends in the army. After we grabbed Eichmann in 1960, he went underground for a few months. But for the most part, the man who put Lena Herzfeld's family on a train to Auschwitz lived out his life without fear of arrest or extradition."

"Did he ever publicly talk about the war?"

Lavon gave a faint smile. "You might find this difficult to believe, but Voss actually granted an interview to *Der Spiegel* a few years before his death. As you might expect, he maintained his innocence to the end. He denied ever deporting anyone. He denied ever killing anyone. And he denied ever stealing a thing."

"So what happened to all that money Voss *didn't* steal?"

"There's general consensus among Holocaust restitution experts, myself included, that he was never able to get it out of Europe. In fact, the exact fate of Kurt Voss's fortune is regarded as one of the great unsolved mysteries of the Holocaust."

"Any ideas where it might be?"

"Come now, Gabriel. You don't need me to tell you that."

"Switzerland?"

Lavon nodded. "As far as the SS was concerned, the entire country was a giant safe-deposit box. We know from American OSS records that Voss was a frequent visitor to Zurich throughout the war. Unfortunately, we don't know who he was meeting with or where he did his private banking. While I was in Vienna, I worked with a family whose ancestors had been fleeced by Voss at the Zentralstelle in 1938. I spent years knocking on doors in Zurich searching for that money."

"And?"

"Not a trace, Gabriel. Not a single trace. As far as the Swiss banking industry is concerned, Kurt Voss never existed. And neither did his looted fortune."

27

AMSTERDAM

They had arrived, coincidentally, at the top of Jodenbreestraat. Gabriel lingered for a moment outside the house where Hendrickje Stoffels had posed for her lover, Rembrandt, and asked her a single question. How had her portrait, stolen from Jacob Herzfeld in Amsterdam in 1943, ended up in the Hoffmann Gallery of Lucerne twenty-one years later? She could not answer, of course, and so he put the question to Eli Lavon instead.

"Perhaps Voss disposed of it before his escape from Europe. Or perhaps he brought it with him to Argentina and sent it back to Switzerland later to be sold quietly." Lavon glanced at Gabriel and asked, "What are the chances the Hoffmann Gallery might show us the record of that sale in 1964?"

"Zero," replied Gabriel. "The only thing more secretive than a Swiss bank is a Swiss art gallery."

"Then I suppose that leaves us with only one option."

"What's that?"

"Peter Voss."

"The son?"

Lavon nodded. "Voss's wife died a few years after him. Peter is the only one left. And the only one who might know more about what happened to the painting."

"Where is he?"

"Still in Argentina."

"What are his politics like?"

"Are you asking whether he's a Nazi like his father?"

"I'm just asking."

"Few children of Nazis share the beliefs of their fathers, Gabriel. Most are deeply ashamed, including Peter Voss."

"Does he really use that name?"

"He dropped his alias when the old man died. He's established quite a reputation for himself in the Argentine wine business. He owns a very successful vineyard in Mendoza. Apparently, he produces some of the best Malbec in the country."

"I'm happy for him."

"Try not to be too judgmental, Gabriel. Peter Voss has tried to atone for his father's sins. When Hezbollah blew up the AMIA Jewish community center in Buenos Aires a few years back, someone sent a large anonymous donation to help rebuild. I happen to know it was Peter Voss."

"Will he talk?"

"He's very private, but he's granted interviews to a number of prominent historians. Whether he'll speak to an Israeli agent named Gabriel Allon is another question entirely."

"Haven't you heard, Eli? I'm retired."

"If you're retired, why are we walking down an Amsterdam street on a freezing night?" Greeted by silence, Lavon answered his own question. "Because it never ends, does it, Gabriel? If Shamron had tried to lure you out of retirement to hunt down a terrorist, you would have sent him packing. But this is different, isn't it? You can still see that tattoo on your mother's arm, the one she always tried to hide."

"Have you finished psychoanalyzing me, Professor Lavon?"

"I know you better than anyone in the world, Gabriel. Even better than that pretty girl walking behind us. I'm the closest thing to family you have—other than Shamron, of course." Lavon paused. "He sends his best, by the way."

"How is he?"

"Miserable. It seems the sun is finally setting on the era of Shamron. He's puttering around his villa in Tiberias with nothing to do. Apparently, he's driving Gilah to distraction. She's not at all sure how much longer she can put up with him."

"I thought Uzi's promotion meant Shamron would have carte blanche at King Saul Boulevard."

"So did Shamron. But much to everyone's surprise, Uzi's decided he wants to be his own man. I had lunch with him a few weeks ago. Bella's given the poor boy quite a makeover. He looks more like a corporate CEO than an Office chief."

"Did my name come up?"

"Only in passing. Something tells me Uzi likes the fact you're hiding at the end of the earth in Cornwall." Lavon gave him a sideways glance. "Any regrets about not taking the job?"

"I never wanted the job, Eli. And I'm genuinely pleased for Uzi."

"But he might not be so pleased to hear you're thinking of running off to Argentina to talk to the son of Adolf Eichmann's right-hand man."

"What Uzi doesn't know won't hurt him. Besides, it's an in-and-out job."

"Where have I heard that one before?" Lavon smiled. "If you want my opinion, Gabriel, I think the Rembrandt is probably long gone. But if you're convinced Peter Voss might be able to help, let me go to Argentina."

"You're right about one thing, Eli. I can still see that tattoo on my mother's arm."

Lavon exhaled heavily. "At least let me make a phone call and see if I can arrange the meeting. I wouldn't want you to go all the way to Mendoza to be turned away empty-handed."

"Quietly, Eli."

"I don't know any other way. Just promise me you'll watch your step down there. Argentina is filled with the sort of people who would love nothing better than to see your head on a stick."

They had reached Plantage Middenlaan. Gabriel led Lavon into a side street and stopped before the narrow little house with the narrow black door. Lena Herzfeld, the child of darkness, sat alone in a gleaming white room without memory.

"Do you remember what Shamron told us about coincidences when we were kids, Eli?"

"He told us that only idiots and dead men believed in them."

"What do you think Shamron would have to say about the disappearance of a Rembrandt that had once been in the hands of Kurt Voss?"

"He wouldn't like it."

"Can you keep an eye on her while I'm in Argentina? I'd never forgive myself if anything happened. She's suffered enough already."

"I was already planning to stay."

"Be careful around her, Eli. She's fragile."

"They're all fragile," Lavon said. "And she'll never even know I'm here."

28

AMSTERDAM

Zentrum Security of Zurich, Switzerland, operated by a simple creed. For the right amount of money, and under the proper circumstances, it would undertake almost any task. Its investigative division conducted inquiries and background checks into businesses and individuals. A counterterrorism unit provided advice on asset hardening and published an authoritative daily newsletter on current global threat levels. A personal protection unit provided uniformed security guards for businesses and plainclothes bodyguards for individuals. Zentrum's computer security division was regarded as among Europe's finest while its international consultants provided entrée to firms wishing to do business in dangerous corners of the world. It operated its own private bank and maintained a vault beneath the Talstrasse used for storage of sensitive client assets. At last estimate, the value of the items contained in the vault exceeded ten billion dollars.

Filling Zentrum's various divisions with qualified staff provided a unique challenge since the company did not accept applications for employment. The process of recruitment never varied. Zentrum talent spotters identified targets of interest; then, without the target's knowledge, Zentrum investigators conducted a quiet but invasive background check. If the target was deemed "Zentrum material," a team of recruiters would swoop in for the kill. Their task was made easier by the fact that Zentrum's salaries and perks far exceeded those of the overt business world. Indeed, Zentrum executives could count on one hand the number of targets who had turned them down. The firm's workforce was highly educated, multinational, and multiethnic. Most employees had spent time in the military, law enforcement, or the intelligence services of their respective countries. Zentrum recruiters demanded fluency in at least three languages, though German was the language of the workplace and was therefore a requirement for employment. Resignations were almost unheard of, and terminated employees rarely found work again.

Like the intelligence services it sought to emulate, Zentrum had two faces—one it reluctantly showed the world, another it kept carefully hidden. This covert branch of Zentrum handled what were euphemistically referred to as special tasks: blackmail, bribery, intimidation, industrial espionage, and "account termination." The name of the unit never appeared in Zentrum's files nor was it spoken in Zentrum's offices. The select few who knew of the unit's existence referred to it as the Cellar Group, or Kellergruppe, and its chief as the Kellermeister. For the past fifteen years, that position had been held by the same man, Ulrich Müller.

The two operatives Müller had sent to Amsterdam were

among his most experienced. One was a German who specialized in all things audio; the other was a Swiss with a flair for photography. Shortly after six p.m., the Swiss operative snapped a photo of the trim Israeli with gray temples gliding through the entrance of the Ambassade Hotel, accompanied by the tall, dark-haired woman. A moment later, the German raised his parabolic microphone and aimed it toward the third-floor window on the left side of the hotel's façade. The Israeli appeared there briefly and stared into the street. The Swiss snapped one final picture, then watched as the curtains closed with a snap.

29

MONTMARTRE, PARIS

The steps of the rue Chappe were damp with morning drizzle. Maurice Durand stood at the summit, kneading the patch of pain in his lower back, then made his way through the narrow streets of Montmartre to an apartment house on the rue Ravignan. He peered up at the large windows of the unit on the top floor for a moment before lowering his gaze to the intercom. Five of the names were neatly typed. The sixth was rendered in distinctive script: *Yves Morel . . .*

For a single night, twenty-two years earlier, the name had been on the lips of every important collector in Paris. Even Durand, who normally kept a discreet distance from the legitimate art world, felt compelled to attend Morel's auspicious debut. The collectors pronounced Morel a genius—a worthy successor to such greats as Picasso, Matisse, and Vuillard—and by evening's end every canvas in the gallery was spoken for. But that all changed the following morning when the all-powerful Paris art critics had their say. Yes, they acknowledged, young Morel was a remarkable technician. But his work lacked boldness, imagination, and, perhaps most important, originality. Within hours, every collector had withdrawn his offer, and a career that seemed destined for the stratosphere came crashing ignominiously to the ground.

At first, Yves Morel was angry. Angry at the critics who had savaged him. Angry at the gallery owners who then refused to show his work. But most of his rage was reserved for the craven, deep-pocketed collectors who had been so easily swayed. "They're sheep," Morel declared to anyone who would listen. "Moneyed phonies who probably couldn't tell a fake from the real thing." Eventually, the remarkable technician whose work supposedly lacked originality decided to prove his point by becoming an art forger. His paintings now hung on the walls of mansions around the world and even in a couple of small museums. They had made Morel rich—richer than some of the fools who bought them.

Though Morel no longer sold his forgeries on the open market, he occasionally did work for friends from the naughty end of the art trade. One such friend was Maurice Durand. In most cases, Durand utilized Morel's talents for replacement jobs—robberies in which a copy of the stolen painting was left behind to deceive the owner into believing his beloved masterpiece was safe and sound. Indeed, as Durand entered Morel's studio, the forger was putting the finishing touches on a Manet that would soon be hanging in a small Belgian museum. Durand inspected the canvas admiringly before coaxing the Rembrandt from a long cardboard tube and placing it gently on Morel's worktable. Morel whistled between his teeth and said, *"Merde."*

"I couldn't agree more."

"I assume that's a *real* Rembrandt?"

Durand nodded. "And unfortunately so is the bullet hole."

"What about the stain?"

"Use your imagination, Yves."

Morel leaned close to the canvas and rubbed gently at the surface. "The blood is no problem."

"And the bullet hole?"

"I'll have to adhere a new patch of canvas to the original, then retouch a portion of the forehead. When I'm finished, I'll cover it with a coat of tinted varnish to match the rest of the painting." Morel shrugged. "Dutch Old Masters aren't exactly my strong suit, but I think I can pull it off."

"How long will it take?"

"A couple of weeks. Maybe longer."

"A client is waiting."

"You wouldn't want your client to see this." Morel probed at the bullet hole with his fingertip. "I'm afraid I'm also going to have to reline it. Looks to me as if the last restorer used a technique called a blind canvas."

"What's the difference?"

"In a traditional relining, the glue is spread across the entire back of the painting. In a blind canvas, it's only placed along the edges."

"Why would he have done that?"

"Hard to say. It's a bit easier and much quicker." Morel looked up and shrugged. "Maybe he was in a hurry."

"Can you do that sort of thing?"

"Reline a picture?" Morel appeared mildly offended. "I reline all my forgeries to make them appear older than they really are. For the record, it's not without risk. I once ruined a fake Cézanne."

"What happened?"

"Too much glue. It bled through the canvas."

"Try not to put too much glue on this one, Yves. She has enough problems already."

"I'll say," Morel said with a frown. "If it would make you feel better, I'll remove the blind canvas right now. It won't take long. Make yourself comfortable."

"I haven't been comfortable in twelve years."

"The back?"

Durand nodded and eased himself into a paint-smudged wing chair while Morel laid the painting facedown on the worktable. Using the tip of a utility knife, he carefully detached the top left corner of the blind canvas from the original, then worked his way slowly around the entire perimeter. Ten minutes later, the separation was complete.

"Mon Dieu!"

"What have you done to my Rembrandt, Yves?"

"I didn't do anything, but someone else did. Come here, Maurice. You'd better have a look."

Durand walked over to the worktable. The two men stood side by side, staring silently down at the back of the painting.

"Do me a favor, Yves."

"What's that?"

"Put it back in the tube and forget it was ever here."

"Are you sure, Maurice?"

Durand nodded and said, "I'm sure."

30

MENDOZA, ARGENTINA

LAN Airlines flight 4286 sank slowly from the cloudless Argentine sky toward Mendoza city and the distant saw-toothed peaks of the Andes. Even from twenty thousand feet, Gabriel could see the vineyards stretching in an endless green sash along the far edge of the high desert valley. He looked at Chiara. She was reclined in her first-class seat, her beautiful face in repose. She had been in the same position, with only slight variations, throughout most of the thirty-hour journey from Amsterdam. Gabriel was envious. Like most Office agents, his career had been marked by near-constant travel, yet he had never mastered the ability to sleep on airplanes. He had passed the long transatlantic flight reading about Kurt Voss in a dossier hastily prepared by Eli Lavon. It included the only known photograph of Voss in his SS uniform—a snapshot taken not long after his arrival in Vienna—along with a posed portrait that appeared in

Der Spiegel not long before his death. If Voss had been troubled by a guilty conscience late in life, he had managed to conceal it from the camera lens. He appeared to be a man at peace with his past. A man who slept well at night.

A flight attendant woke Chiara and instructed her to raise her seat back. Within a few seconds, she was once again sleeping soundly and remained so even after the aircraft thudded onto the runway of Mendoza's airport. Ten minutes later, as they entered the terminal, she was brimming with energy. Gabriel walked next to her, legs heavy, ears ringing from lack of sleep.

They had cleared passport control earlier that morning upon their arrival in Buenos Aires, and there were no formalities to see to other than the acquisition of a rental car. In Europe, such indignities were usually handled by couriers and other Office field operatives. But here in distant Mendoza, Gabriel had no choice but to join the long queue at the counter. Despite his printed confirmation, his request for a car seemed to come as something of a surprise to the clerk, for try as she might she could find no record of Gabriel's reservation in the computer. Locating something suitable turned into a thirty-minute Sisyphean ordeal requiring multiple phone calls and much scowling at the computer screen. A car finally materialized, a Subaru Outback that had been involved in an unfortunate mishap during a recent trip into the mountains. Without apology, the clerk handed over the paperwork, then delivered a stern lecture about what the insurance did and did not cover. Gabriel signed the contract, all the while wondering what sort of unfortunate mishap he could inflict on the car before returning it.

Keys and luggage in hand, Gabriel and Chiara stepped into the tinder-dry air. It had been the depths of winter in Europe, but here in the Southern Hemisphere it was high summer. Gabriel located the car in the rental lot; then, after searching it for explosives, they climbed inside and headed into town. Their hotel was located in the Plaza Italia, named for the many Italian immigrants who had settled in the region in the late nineteenth and early twentieth centuries. Entering the room, Gabriel was tempted to climb into the freshly turned-down bed. Instead, he showered and changed into clean clothing, then headed back down to the lobby. Chiara was waiting at the front desk, searching for a map of the local wineries. The concierge produced one. Bodega de la Mariposa, the winery owned by Peter Voss, was not on it.

"I'm afraid the owner is very private," the concierge explained. "No tastings. No tours."

"We have an appointment with Senor Voss," Gabriel said.

"Ah! In that case . . ."

The concierge circled a spot on the map approximately five miles to the south and traced the quickest route. Outside, a trio of bellmen were trading barbed comments on the deplorable condition of the rental car. Seeing Chiara, they all rushed simultaneously to open her door, leaving Gabriel to climb behind the wheel unassisted. He turned into the street and for the next thirty minutes meandered the tranquil boulevards of central Mendoza, searching for evidence of surveillance. Seeing nothing out of the ordinary, he sped southward along an archipelago of vineyards and wineries until they came to an elegant stone-and-steel gate marked PRIVATE. On the opposite side, leaning against the door of a white Suburban, was a square-shouldered security man wearing a large cowboy hat and reflective sunglasses.

"Senor Allon?"

Gabriel nodded.

"Welcome." He smiled warmly. "Follow me, please."

Gabriel waited for the gate to open, then set off after the Suburban. It did not take long to see how Bodega de la Mariposa, which roughly translated means Wine Cellar of the Butterflies, had acquired its name. A great undulating cloud of swallowtails floated above the vineyards and in the wide gravel forecourt of Peter Voss's sprawling Italianate villa. Gabriel and Chiara parked in the shade of a cypress tree and followed the security man across a cavernous entry hall, then down a wide corridor to a terrace facing the snowcapped peaks of the Andes. A table had been laid with cheese, sausage, and figs, along with Andean mineral water and a bottle of 2005 Bodega de la Mariposa Reserva. Leaning against the balustrade, resplendent in his newly polished leather riding boots, was SS-Hauptsturmführer Kurt Voss. "Welcome to Argentina, Mr. Allon," he said. "I'm so glad you were able to come."

31

MENDOZA, ARGENTINA

It was not Kurt Voss, of course, but the resemblance between father and son was astonishing. Indeed, with only a few minor alterations, the figure coming toward them across the terrace might well have been the same man Lena Herzfeld had watched striding across the stage of the Hollandsche Schouwburg theater, a portrait by Rembrandt in one hand, a sack of diamonds in the other.

Peter Voss was somewhat trimmer than his father had been late in life, a bit more rugged in appearance, and had retained more of his hair, which was now completely white with age. On closer inspection, his boots were not as resplendent as Gabriel had first imagined. Deep brown in color, they were coated by a thin layer of powdery dust from his afternoon ride. He shook their hands warmly, bowing slightly at the waist, then guided them proprietarily to the sunlit table. As they settled into their places, it was clear Peter Voss was aware of the effect his appearance was having on his two guests. "There's no need to avert your eyes," he said, his tone conciliatory. "As you might expect, I'm used to people staring at me by now."

"I didn't mean to, Herr Voss. It's just—"

"Please don't apologize, Mr. Allon. He was my father, not yours. I don't talk about him often. But when I do, I've always found it's best to be direct and honest. It's the least I can do. You've come a very long way, surely not without good reason. What is it you would like to know?"

The straightforward nature of Voss's question took Gabriel by surprise. He had interrogated a Nazi war criminal once, but never had he spoken to the child of one. His instincts were to proceed with caution, as he had with Lena Herzfeld. And so he nibbled at the edge of a fig and, in an informal tone, asked Voss when he first became aware of his father's wartime activities.

"Activities?" Voss repeated, his voice incredulous. "Please, Mr. Allon, if we are going to have a candid discussion about my father, let's not mince words. My father didn't engage in *activities.* He committed atrocities. As for when I learned about them, it came to me in bits and pieces. In that respect, I suppose, I'm much like any other son who discovers his father is not the man he claimed to be."

Voss poured them each a glass of the garnet-colored wine and recounted a pair of incidents that had occurred just weeks apart when he was a teenager.

"I was walking home from school in Buenos Aires and stopped at a café to meet my father. He was seated at a corner table conversing quietly with another man. I'll never forget the look on that man's face when he saw me—shock, horror, pride, amazement, all at the same time. He was trembling slightly as he shook my hand. He said I looked just like my father when they had worked together in the old days. He introduced himself as Ricardo Klement. I'm sure you know his real name."

"Adolf Eichmann."

"In the flesh," Voss said. "Not long after, I went to a bakery frequented by Jewish refugees. There was an old woman standing in line. When she saw me, the blood drained from her face and she became hysterical. She thought I was my father. She accused me of killing her family."

Voss reached for his wineglass but stopped. "Eventually, I learned that my father was indeed a murderer. And not an ordinary murderer. A man with the blood of millions on his hands. What did it say about me that I could love someone guilty of such horror? What did it say about my mother? But the worst part, Mr. Allon, is that my father never atoned for his sins. He never felt ashamed. In fact, he was quite proud of his accomplishments until the very end. I am the one who shoulders his burden. And I feel his guilt to this day. I am entirely alone in the world now. My wife died several years ago. We never had children. Why? Because I was afraid of my father's evil. I wanted his bloodline to end with me."

Voss seemed temporarily exhausted by the admission. He retreated into a meditative silence, his gaze fixed on the distant mountains. Finally, he turned back to Gabriel and Chiara and said, "But surely you didn't come all the way to Mendoza to listen to me condemn my father."

"Actually, I came because of this."

Gabriel placed a photograph of *Portrait of a Young Woman* in front of Voss. It lay there for a moment untouched, like a fourth guest who had yet to find cause to join the conversation. Then Voss lifted it carefully and examined it in the razor-sharp sun.

"I've always wondered what it looked like," he said distantly. "Where is it now?"

"It was stolen a few nights ago in England. A man I knew a long time ago died trying to protect it."

"I'm truly sorry to hear that," Voss said. "But I'm afraid your friend wasn't the first to die because of this painting. And unfortunately he won't be the last."

32

MENDOZA, ARGENTINA

In Amsterdam, Gabriel listened to the testimony of Lena Herzfeld. Now, seated on a grand terrace in the shadow of the Andes, he did the same for the only child of Kurt Voss. For his starting point, Peter Voss chose the night in October 1982 when his mother had telephoned to say that his father was dead. She asked her son to come to the family home in Palermo. There were things she needed to tell him, she said. Things he needed to know about his father and the war.

"We sat at the foot of my father's deathbed and spoke for hours. Actually, my mother did most of the talking," Voss added. "I mostly listened. It was the first time that I fully understood the extent of my father's crimes. She told me how he had used his power to enrich himself. How he had robbed his victims blind before sending them to their deaths at Auschwitz, Treblinka, and Sobibor. And how, on a snowy night in Amsterdam, he had accepted a portrait by Rembrandt in exchange for the life of a single child. And to make matters worse, there was proof of my father's guilt."

"Proof he had acquired the Rembrandt through coercion?"

"Not just that, Mr. Allon. Proof he had profited wildly from history's greatest act of mass murder."

"What sort of proof?"

"The worst kind," said Voss. "Written proof."

Like most SS men, Peter Voss continued, his father had been a meticulous keeper of records. Just as the managers of the extermination centers had maintained voluminous files documenting their crimes, SS-Hauptsturmführer Kurt Voss had kept a kind of balance sheet where each of his illicit transactions was carefully recorded. The proceeds of those transactions were concealed in dozens of numbered accounts in Switzerland. "Dozens, Mr. Allon, because my father's fortune was so vast he thought it unwise to keep it in a single, conspicuously large account." During the final days of the war, as the Allies were closing in on Berlin from both east and west, Kurt Voss condensed his ledger into one document detailing the sources of his money and the corresponding accounts.

"Where was the money hidden?"

"In a small private bank in Zurich."

"And the list of account numbers?" asked Gabriel. "Where did he keep that?"

"The list was far too dangerous to keep. It was both a key to a fortune and a written indictment. And so my father hid it in a place where he thought no one would ever find it."

And then, in a flash of clarity, Gabriel understood. He had seen the proof in the photos on Christopher Liddell's computer in Glastonbury—the pair of thin surface lines, one perfectly vertical, the other perfectly horizontal, that converged a few centimeters from Hendrickje's left shoulder. Kurt Voss had used *Portrait of a Young Woman* as an envelope, quite possibly the most expensive envelope in history.

"He hid it inside the Rembrandt?"

"That's correct, Mr. Allon. It was concealed between Rembrandt's original canvas and a second canvas adhered to the back."

"How long was the list?"

"Three sheets of onionskin, written in my father's own hand."

"And how was it protected?"

"It was sealed inside a sheath of wax paper."

"Who did the work for him?"

"During my father's time in Paris and Amsterdam, he came in contact with a number of people involved in Special Operation Linz, Hitler's art looters. One of them was a restorer. He was the one who devised the method of concealment. And when he'd finished the job, my father repaid the favor by killing him."

"And the painting?"

"During his escape from Europe, my father made a brief stop in Zurich to meet with his banker. He left it in a safe-deposit box. Only one other person knew the account number and password."

"Your mother?"

Peter Voss nodded.

"Why didn't your father simply transfer the money to Argentina at that time?"

"Because it wasn't possible. The Allies were keeping a close watch on financial transactions carried out by Swiss banks. A large transfer of cash and other assets from Zurich to Buenos

Aires would have raised a red flag. As for the list, my father didn't dare attempt to carry it with him during his escape. If he'd been arrested on his way to Italy, the list would have guaranteed him a death sentence. He had no choice but to leave the money and the list behind and wait until the dust had settled."

"How long did he wait?"

"Six years."

"The year you and your mother left Europe?"

"That's correct," Voss said. "When my father was finally able to send for us, he instructed my mother to make a stop in Zurich. The plan was for her to collect the painting, the list, and the money. I didn't understand what was happening at the time, but I remember waiting in the street while my mother went into the bank. Ten minutes later, when she came out, I could see she'd been crying. When I asked what was wrong, she snapped at me to be quiet. After that, we climbed onto a streetcar and rode aimlessly in circles through the city center. My mother was staring out the window. She was saying the same words over and over again. 'What am I going to tell your father? What am I going to tell your father?'"

"The painting was gone?"

Voss nodded. "The painting was gone. The list was gone. The money was gone. The banker told my mother that the accounts never existed. 'You must be mistaken, Frau Voss,' he told her. 'Perhaps a different bank.'"

"How did your father react?"

"He was furious, of course." Voss paused. "Ironic, isn't it? My father was angry because the money he had stolen had been *stolen* from him. You could say the painting became his punishment. He avoided justice, but he became obsessed with the Rembrandt and with finding the key to a fortune hidden inside it."

"Did he try again?"

"One more time," Voss said. "In 1967, an Argentine diplomat agreed to go to Switzerland on my father's behalf. Under their arrangement, half of any money recovered would be turned over to the Argentine treasury, with the diplomat taking a cut for himself."

"What happened?"

"Shortly after the diplomat arrived in Switzerland, he sent word that he had met with my father's banker and was confident of a successful outcome. Two days later, his body was found floating in Lake Zurich. The Swiss inquest found he had slipped from the end of a jetty while sightseeing. My father didn't believe it. He was convinced the man had been murdered."

"Who was the diplomat?"

"His name was Carlos Weber."

"And you, Herr Voss?" Gabriel asked after a long pause. "Did you ever look for the money?"

"To be honest, I considered it. I thought it might be a way to return some money to my father's victims. To atone. But in the end, I knew it was a fool's errand. The gnomes of Zurich guard their secret treasures very carefully, Mr. Allon. Their banks might look clean and tidy, but the truth is, they're dirty. After the war, the bankers of Switzerland turned away deserving people who had the temerity to come looking for their deposits, not because the banks didn't have the money but because they didn't want to give it up. What chance did the son of a murderer have?"

"Do you know the name of your father's banker?"

"Yes," Voss said without hesitation. "It was Walter Landesmann."

"Landesmann? Why is that name familiar?"

Peter Voss smiled. "Because his son is one of the most powerful financiers in Europe. In fact, he was just in the news the other day. Something about a new program to combat hunger in Africa. His name is—"

"Martin Landesmann?"

Peter Voss nodded. "How's that for a coincidence?"

"I don't believe in coincidences, Herr Voss."

Voss lifted his wine toward the sun. "Neither do I, Mr. Allon. Neither do I."

33

MENDOZA, ARGENTINA

Gabriel and Chiara drove out of the vineyard, trailed by a cumulus cloud of butterflies, and returned to Mendoza. That evening they had dinner at a small outdoor restaurant opposite their hotel in the Plaza Italia.

"You liked him, didn't you?" asked Chiara.

"Voss?" Gabriel nodded slowly. "More than I wanted to."

"The question is, do you believe him?"

"It's a remarkable story," said Gabriel. "And I believe every word of it. Kurt Voss was an easy mark. He was a notorious war criminal, a wanted man. For more than twenty years, the fortune was sitting in Landesmann's bank growing by the day. At some point, Landesmann decided Voss was never coming back, and he convinced himself the money was his for the taking. So he closed out the accounts and destroyed the records."

"And a fortune of looted Holocaust assets vanished into thin air," Chiara said bitterly.

"Just like the people it once belonged to."

"And the painting?"

"If Landesmann had had any sense, he would have burned it. But he didn't. He was a greedy bastard. And even in 1964, before art prices skyrocketed, the painting was worth a great deal. I suspect he entrusted it to the Hoffmann Gallery of Lucerne and arranged for a quiet sale."

"Did he know about the list?"

"In order to find it, he would have had to pull apart the two canvases and look inside. But he had no reason to do that."

"So it was still inside the painting at the time of the 1964 sale?"

"Without question."

"There's one thing I don't understand," Chiara said after a silence. "Why kill Carlos Weber? After all, Landesmann had quietly turned away Voss's wife when she came looking for the money. Why didn't he do the same when Weber appeared in Zurich?"

"Perhaps it was because Weber's visit was quasi-official. Remember, he was representing not just Voss but the government of Argentina. That made him dangerous." Gabriel paused. "But I suspect there was something else that made Weber even more dangerous. He knew about the Rembrandt and the list of account numbers hidden inside it. And he made that clear to Landesmann during their meeting."

"And Landesmann realized that he had a serious problem," Chiara said. "Because whoever was in possession of the Rembrandt also had proof that Kurt Voss's fortune had been hidden in Landesmann's bank."

Gabriel nodded. "Obviously, Landesmann said something encouraging to Weber to keep him in Zurich long enough to arrange his death. Then, after Weber's unfortunate fall into Lake Zurich, he no doubt undertook a frantic search for the painting."

"Why didn't he just go back to the Hoffmann Gallery and ask for the name of the person who bought it in 1964?"

"Because in Switzerland, a private sale means a *private* sale, even for the likes of Walter Landesmann. Besides, given Landesmann's precarious situation, he would have been very reluctant to call attention to himself like that."

"And Martin?"

"I suspect that, at some point, the father confessed his sins to his son, and Martin took up the search. That Rembrandt has been floating around out there like a ticking time bomb for more than forty years. If it were ever to come to light . . ."

"Then Martin's world would be shattered in an instant."

Gabriel nodded. "At the very least, he would find himself swamped by a tidal wave of litigation. In the worst-case scenario, he might be forced to surrender hundreds of millions, even billions, of dollars in compensation and damages."

"Sounds to me like a rather strong motive to steal a painting," Chiara said. "But what do we do now? Walter Landesmann is long dead. And we can't exactly go knocking on his son's door."

"Maybe Carlos Weber can help us."

"Carlos Weber was murdered in Zurich in 1967."

"A fortunate occurrence from our point of view. You see, when diplomats die, their governments tend to get annoyed. They conduct investigations. And invariably they write reports."

"There's no way the Argentine government is going to give us a copy of the inquiry into Weber's death."

"That's true," said Gabriel. "But I know someone who might be able to get it for us."

"Does this someone have a name?"

Gabriel smiled and said, "Alfonso Ramirez."

AT THE conclusion of the meal, as the subjects were strolling hand in hand across the darkened plaza toward their hotel, a digitized audio file was dispatched to the headquarters of Zentrum Security in Zurich along with several surveillance photographs. One hour later, headquarters sent a reply. It contained a set of terse instructions, the address of an apartment house in the San Telmo district of Buenos Aires, and the name of a certain former colonel who had worked for the Argentine secret police during the darkest days of the Dirty War. The most intriguing aspect of the communication, however, was the date of the operatives' return home. They were scheduled to leave Buenos Aires the following night. One would take Air France to Paris; the other, British Air to London. No reason for their separate travel was given. None was needed. The two operatives were both veterans and knew how to read between the lines of the cryptic communiqués that flowed from corporate headquarters. An account termination order had been handed down. Cover stories were being written, exit strategies put in place. It was too bad about the woman, they thought as they glimpsed her briefly standing on the balcony of her hotel room. She really did look quite lovely in the Argentine moonlight.

34

BUENOS AIRES

On the night of August 13, 1979, Maria Espinoza Ramirez, poet, cellist, and Argentine dissident of note, was hurled from the cargo hold of a military transport plane flying several thousand feet above the South Atlantic. Seconds before she was pushed, the captain in charge of the operation slashed open her abdomen with a machete, a final act of barbarism that ensured her corpse would fill rapidly with water and thus remain forever on the bottom of the sea. Her husband, the prominent antigovernment journalist Alfonso Ramirez, would not learn of Maria's disappearance for many months, for at the time he, too, was in the hands of the junta's henchmen. Had it not been for Amnesty International, which waged a tireless campaign to bring attention to his case, Ramirez would almost certainly have suffered the same fate as his wife. Instead, after more than a year in captivity, he was freed on the condition he refrain from ever writing about politics again. "Silence is a proud tradition in Argentina," said the generals at the time of his release. "We think Senor Ramirez would be wise to discover its obvious benefits."

Another man might have heeded the generals' advice. But Alfonso Ramirez, fueled by rage and grief, waged a fearless campaign against the junta. His struggle did not end with the regime's collapse in 1983. Of the many torturers and murderers Ramirez helped to expose in the years afterward was the captain who had hurled his wife into the sea. Ramirez wept when the panel of judges found the captain guilty. And he wept again a few moments later when they sentenced the murderer to just five years in prison. On the steps of the courthouse, Ramirez declared that Argentine justice was now lying on the bottom of the sea with the rest of the disappeared. Arriving home that evening, he found his apartment in ruins and his bathtub filled with water. On the bottom were several photos of his wife, all of which had been slashed in half.

Having established himself as one of the most prominent human rights activists in Latin America and the world, Alfonso Ramirez turned his attention to exposing another tragic aspect of Argentina's history, its close ties to Nazi Germany. *Sanctuary of Evil,* his 2006 historical masterwork, detailed how a secret arrangement among the Perón government, the Vatican, the SS, and American intelligence allowed thousands of war criminals to find safe haven in Argentina after the war. It also contained an account of how Ramirez had assisted Israeli intelligence in the unmasking and capture of a Nazi war criminal named Erich Radek. Among the many details Ramirez left out was the name of the legendary Israeli agent with whom he had worked.

Though the book had made Ramirez a millionaire, he had resisted the pull of the smart northern suburbs and still resided in the southern barrio of San Telmo. His building was a large Parisian-style structure with a courtyard in the center and a winding staircase covered by a faded runner. The apartment itself served as both his residence and office, and its rooms were filled to capacity with tens of thousands of dog-eared files and dossiers. It was rumored that Ramirez's personal archives rivaled those of the government. Yet in all his years of rummaging through Argentina's dark past, he had never digitized or organized his vast holdings in any way. Ramirez believed that in clutter lay security, a theory supported by empirical evidence. On numerous occasions, he had returned home to find his files in disarray, but none of his important documents had ever been stolen by his adversaries.

One section of the living room was largely free of historical debris, and it was there Ramirez received Gabriel and Chiara. Propped in one corner, exactly where she had left it the night of her abduction, was Maria's dusty cello. On the wall above were two handwritten pages of poetry, framed and shielded by glass, along with a photograph of Ramirez at the time of his release from prison. He bore little resemblance to that emaciated figure now. Tall and broad-shouldered, he looked more like a man who wrestled with machinery and concrete than words and ideas. His only vanity was his lush gray beard, which in the opinion of right-wing critics made him look like a cross between Fidel Castro and Karl Marx. Ramirez did not take the characterization as an insult. An unrepentant communist, he revered both.

Despite the abundance of irreplaceable paper in the apartment, Ramirez was a reckless, absent-minded smoker who was forever leaving burning cigarettes in ashtrays or dangling off the end of tables. Somehow, he remembered Gabriel's aversion to tobacco and managed to refrain from smoking while holding forth on an array of topics ranging from the state of the Argentine economy to the new American president to Israel's treatment of the Palestinians, which, of course, he considered deplorable. Finally, as the first drops of afternoon rain made puddles on the dusty windowsill, he recalled the afternoon several years earlier when he had taken Gabriel to the archives of Argentina's Immigration Office. There, in a rat-chewed box of crumbling files, they discovered a document suggesting that Erich Radek, long assumed dead, was actually living under an assumed name in the first district of Vienna.

"I remember one thing in particular about that day," Ramirez said now. "There was a beautiful girl on a motor scooter who followed us wherever we went. She wore a helmet the entire time, so I never really saw her face. But I remember her legs quite clearly." He glanced at Chiara, then at Gabriel. "Obviously, your relationship was more than professional."

Gabriel nodded, though by his expression he made it clear he wished to discuss the matter no further.

"So what brings the two of you to Argentina this time?" Ramirez asked.

"We were doing a bit of wine tasting in Mendoza."

"Find anything to your liking?"

"The Bodega de la Mariposa Reserva."

"The '05 or the '06?"

"The '05, actually."

"I've had it myself. In fact, I've had the opportunity to speak with the owner of that vineyard on a number of occasions."

"Like him?"

"I do," Ramirez said.

"Trust him?"

"As much as I trust anyone. And before we go any further, perhaps we should establish the ground rules for this conversation."

"The same as last time. You help me now, I help you later."

"What exactly are you looking for?"

"Information about an Argentine diplomat who died in Zurich in 1967."

"I assume you're referring to Carlos Weber?" Ramirez smiled. "And given your recent trip to Mendoza, I also assume that you're searching for the missing fortune of one SS-Hauptsturmführer Kurt Voss."

"Does it exist, Alfonso?"

"Of course it exists. It was deposited in Bank Landesmann in Zurich between 1938 and 1945. Carlos Weber died trying to bring it to Argentina in 1967. And I have the documents to prove it."

35

BUENOS AIRES

There was just one problem. Alfonso Ramirez had no idea where he had hidden the documents. And so for the next half hour, as he shuffled from room to room, lifting dusty covers and frowning at stacks of faded paper, he recited the details of Carlos Weber's disgraceful curriculum vitae. Educated in Spain and Germany, Weber was an ultranationalist who served as a foreign policy adviser to the parade of military officers and feeble politicians who had ruled Argentina in the decade before the Second World War. Profoundly anti-Semitic and antidemocratic, he tilted naturally toward the Third Reich and forged close ties to many senior SS officers—ties that left Weber uniquely positioned to help Nazi war criminals find sanctuary.

"He was one of the linchpins of the entire shitty deal. He was close to Perón, close to the Vatican, and close to the SS. Weber didn't help the Nazi murderers come here merely out of the goodness of his heart. He actually believed they could help build the Argentina of his dreams."

Ramirez yanked open the top drawer of a battered metal file cabinet and fingered his way quickly through the tabs of several dozen manila folders.

"Is there any chance his death was an accident?" asked Gabriel.

"None," Ramirez replied emphatically. "Carlos Weber was known to be an excellent athlete and a strong swimmer. There's no way he slipped into the lake and drowned."

Ramirez rammed the file drawer closed and opened the next. A moment later, he smiled and triumphantly withdrew a folder. "Ah, here's the one I was looking for."

"What is it?"

"About five years ago the government announced it was going to release another batch of so-called Nazi files. Most of it was rubbish. But the archivists let a couple of gems slip through." Ramirez held up the folder. "Including these."

"What are they?"

"Copies of the cables Weber sent from Switzerland during his trip in 1967. Take a look."

Gabriel accepted the documents and read the first dispatch:

PLEASE INFORM THE MINISTER THAT MY MEETING WAS PRODUCTIVE AND I EXPECT A FAVORABLE OUTCOME IN SHORT ORDER. ALSO, PLEASE PASS ALONG A SIMILAR MESSAGE TO THE INTERESTED PARTY, AS HE IS QUITE ANXIOUS FOR NEWS OF ANY SORT

"Weber was clearly referring to his meetings with Walter Landesmann," Ramirez said. "And the interested party was obviously a reference to Kurt Voss."

Gabriel looked at the second dispatch:

PLEASE INFORM THE MINISTER BANK LANDESMANN HAS LOCATED THE ACCOUNTS IN QUESTION. ALERT THE TREASURY TO EXPECT A TRANSFER OF FUNDS IN SHORT ORDER.

"The next day, Carlos Weber was found dead." Ramirez picked up a stack of thick files, bound by metal clasps and heavy elastic bands. He held them silently for a moment, then said, "I need to warn you, Gabriel. Everyone who goes looking for that money ends up dead. These files were assembled by a friend of mine, an investigative reporter named Rafael Bloch."

"Jewish?"

Ramirez nodded gravely. "At university, he was a communist like me. He was arrested briefly during the Dirty War, but his father paid a very large bribe and managed to secure his release. Rafi was damn lucky. Most of the Jews who were arrested never stood a chance."

"Go on, Alfonso."

"Rafi Bloch specialized in financial stories. Unlike the rest of us, he studied something useful—namely, economics and business. Rafi knew how to read a ledger sheet. Rafi knew how to trace wire transfers. And Rafi never, ever took no for an answer."

"It's hereditary."

"Yes, I know," said Ramirez. "Rafi spent years trying to prove what happened to that money. But along the way he found something else. He discovered that the entire Landesmann empire was dirty."

"Dirty? How?"

"Rafi never went into specifics with me. But in 2008, he finally felt confident he had his story."

"What did he do?"

"He went to Geneva to have a word with a man named Landesmann. *Martin* Landesmann. And he never came back again."

In retrospect, said Ramirez, a journalist with Rafael Bloch's experience should have proceeded with a bit more caution. But given the impeccable public reputation of the man in question, Bloch foolishly allowed himself to believe he was in no danger.

The first contact was made on the morning of October the fifteenth—a telephone call, placed by Bloch from his hotel room to the headquarters of Global Vision Investments, requesting an interview with its chairman. The request was denied, and it was made clear to Bloch that further inquiries were not welcome. Bloch recklessly responded with an ultimatum. Unless he was granted an interview, he would take his material to Washington and show it to the relevant congressional committees and government agencies.

That seemed to get the attention of the person at the other end of the line, and an appointment was scheduled for two days later. Rafi Bloch would never keep that appointment—or any other, for that matter. A climber found his corpse the following spring in the French Alps, headless, handless, frozen solid. Martin Landesmann's name never even came up in the investigation.

36

BUENOS AIRES

The electricity failed with the first flash of lightning. They gathered in the semidarkness of the living room and leafed through the files of Rafael Bloch while the entire building shook with thunder.

"Behind every fortune lies a great crime," said Ramirez.

"Honoré de Balzac," said Chiara.

Ramirez gave her an admiring nod. "The old boy could have been referring to Walter and Martin Landesmann when he wrote those words. Upon his death, Walter Landesmann bequeathed to his son a small private bank in Zurich—a bank with a great deal of blood money on its balance sheets—and Martin turned it into an empire." Ramirez looked at Gabriel. "How much do you know about him?"

"Landesmann?" Gabriel shrugged. "He's one of the world's richest men but likes to play the role of reluctant billionaire."

Gabriel furrowed his brow in mock concentration. "Remind me of the name of that foundation of his."

"One World," said Ramirez.

"Ah, yes, how could I forget?" Gabriel asked sardonically. "Landesmann's devoted followers regard him as something of a prophet. He preaches debt relief, corporate responsibility, and renewable energy. He's also engaged in a number of development projects in Gaza that have caused him to form rather close ties to Hamas. But I doubt that would upset his friends in Hollywood, the media, or leftist political circles. As far as they're concerned, Martin Landesmann never puts a foot wrong. He's pure of heart and noble of intent. He's a saint." Gabriel paused. "Have I left anything out?"

"Just one thing. It's all a lie. Well, not all of it. Saint Martin does have many friends and admirers among the smart set. But I doubt even the sheep in Hollywood would stand by him if they ever discovered the true source of his enormous wealth and power. As for his charitable activities, they're funded by capitalism at its most base and ruthless. Saint Martin pollutes, drills, mines, and exploits with the best of them."

"Money makes the world go round, Alfonso."

"No, my friend. As the good book says, 'For the love of money is the root of all evil.' And the fount of Saint Martin's wealth is an unspeakable evil. That's why Martin disposed of his father's bank within a year of the old man's death. And why he moved from Zurich to the shores of Lake Geneva. He wanted to flee the scene of the crime and shed his Alemannic roots. Do you know he refuses to even speak German in public anymore? Only English and French."

"Why didn't you ever pursue the story?"

"I considered it."

"But?"

"There were things Rafi knew that he didn't put into his files—things I was never able to duplicate on my own. In short, I didn't have the goods. Saint Martin has very deep pockets, and he's a litigious son of a bitch. To properly investigate him would require the resources of a powerful law enforcement agency." Ramirez gave Gabriel a knowing smile. "Or perhaps an intelligence service."

"Any chance you can let me have those cables?"

"No problem," Ramirez said. "I might even allow you to borrow Rafi's files. But those are going to cost you."

"Name your price."

"I want to know the rest of the story."

"Get a pen."

"Mind if I record it, for accuracy's sake?"

"Surely you jest, Alfonso."

"Sorry," Ramirez said. "I almost forgot who I was talking to."

IT WAS APPROACHING three p.m. when they finished, leaving Gabriel and Chiara just enough time to make the evening KLM flight back to Amsterdam. Ramirez offered to drive them to the airport, but Gabriel insisted on taking a taxi. They bade farewell to Ramirez at the door of his apartment and headed quickly down the spiral staircase, the cables and Rafi Bloch's files tucked safely inside Gabriel's shoulder bag.

The events of the next few seconds would play incessantly in Gabriel's mind for months to come. Unfortunately, they were images he had seen too many times before—images of a world he thought he had finally left behind. Another man might have missed the warning signs—the large suitcase in the corner of the lobby that had not been there earlier, the muscular figure with blond hair and sunglasses stepping rather too quickly into the street, the car waiting curbside with its back door ajar—but Gabriel noticed them all. And without a word he wrapped his arm around Chiara's waist and swept her through the doorway.

Neither he nor Chiara would ever be able to recall the actual sound of the explosion, only the searing wave of air and the helpless sensation of being hurled into the street like toys thrown by a petulant child. They came to rest side by side, Gabriel facedown with his hands flung over his head, Chiara on her back with her eyes tightly closed in pain. Gabriel managed to shield her from the hailstorm of masonry and shattered glass that rained down upon them but not from the sight of Alfonso Ramirez. He was lying in the center of the street, his clothing blackened by fire. Fluttering all around them were thousands of pieces of paper, the priceless files of Ramirez's archives. Gabriel crawled to Ramirez's side and felt his neck for a pulse. Then he rose and returned to Chiara.

"Are you all right?"

"I think so."

"Can you stand up?"

"I'm not sure."

"You have to try."

"Help me."

Gabriel pulled Chiara gently to her feet, then picked up his bag and slung it over his shoulder. Chiara's first steps were unsteady, but by the time the sirens began to sound in the distance she was moving along the devastated street at a brisk pace. Gabriel led her around a corner, then pulled out his mobile phone and dialed a number from memory. A female voice answered calmly in Hebrew; in the same language, Gabriel recited a code phrase followed by a series of numbers. After a few seconds, the female voice asked, "What is the nature of your emergency?"

"I need an extraction."

"How soon?"

"Immediately."

"Are you alone?"

"No."

"How many in your party?"

"Two."

"What is your present location?"

"Avenida Caseros, San Telmo, Buenos Aires . . ."

37

BEN GURION AIRPORT, ISRAEL

There is a room at Ben Gurion Airport known to only a handful of people. It is located to the left of passport control, behind an unmarked door kept locked at all times. Its walls are faux Jerusalem limestone; its furnishings are typical airport fare: black vinyl couches and chairs, modular end tables, cheap modern lamps that cast an unforgiving light. There are two windows, one looking onto the tarmac, the other onto the arrivals hall. Both are fashioned of high-quality one-way glass. Reserved for Office personnel, it is the first stop for operatives returning from secret battlefields abroad, thus the permanent odor of stale cigarettes, burnt coffee, and male tension. The cleaning staff has tried every product imaginable to expel it, but the smell remains. Like Israel's enemies, it cannot be defeated by conventional means.

Gabriel had entered this room, or versions of it, many times before. He had entered it in triumph and staggered into it in failure.

He had been fêted in this room, consoled in it, and once he had been wheeled into it with a bullet wound in his chest. Usually it was Ari Shamron who was waiting to receive him. Now, as Gabriel slipped through the door with Chiara at his side, he was greeted by the sight of Uzi Navot. He had shed at least thirty pounds since Gabriel had seen him last and was wearing a new pair of stylish spectacles that made him look like the editor of a trendy magazine. The stainless steel chronometer he had always worn to emulate Shamron was gone, replaced by a tank-style watch that went well with his tailored navy blue suit and white open-collared dress shirt. The metamorphosis was complete, thought Gabriel. Any trace of the hard-bitten field operative had been carefully erased. Uzi Navot was now a headquarters man, a spy in the prime of life.

Navot stared at them wordlessly for a moment, a look of genuine relief on his face. Then, satisfied that Gabriel and Chiara had suffered no serious injuries, his expression darkened.

"This is a special occasion," he said finally. "My first personnel crisis as chief. I suppose it's only fitting that you're involved. Then again, it was rather mild by your exalted standards—just an apartment building in ruins and eight people dead, including one of Argentina's most prominent journalists and social critics."

"Chiara and I are fine, Uzi, but thank you for asking."

Navot made a placatory gesture, as if to say he wanted the tone of the conversation to remain civil.

"I realize your status is somewhat vague at the moment, Gabriel, but there is no ambiguity over the rules governing your movements. Because your passports and identities are still managed by the Office, you're supposed to tell me when you travel." Navot paused. "You *do* recall making that promise, don't you, Gabriel?"

With a nod, Gabriel conceded the point.

"When were you planning to tell me about your little adventure?"

"It was a private matter."

"Private? There's no such thing where you're concerned." Navot frowned. "And what the hell were you doing in Alfonso Ramirez's apartment?"

"We were looking for a portrait by Rembrandt," Gabriel said. "And a great deal of money."

"And I thought it was going to be something dull." Navot sighed heavily. "I assume that you were the target of that bomb, and not Alfonso Ramirez?"

"I'm afraid so."

"Any suspects?"

"Just one."

THEY CLIMBED into the back of Navot's armored limousine, with Chiara between them like a separation fence, and headed up Highway 1 toward Jerusalem. Navot appeared intrigued by Gabriel's account at first, but by the time the briefing was concluded his arms were folded defensively across his chest and his face was fixed in an expression of transparent disapproval. Navot was like that. A veteran field agent trained to conceal his emotions, he had never been good at hiding the fact he was annoyed.

"It's a fascinating story. But if the point of your little excursion was to find your friend Julian Isherwood's painting, you don't seem much closer. And it appears you've tread on some serious toes. You and Chiara are lucky to be alive right now. Take the hint. Drop the case down a very deep hole and forget about it. Julian will survive. Go back to your cottage by the sea in Cornwall. Live your life." Navot paused, then asked, "That's what you wanted, wasn't it?"

Gabriel left the question unanswered. "This may have started out as a search for a stolen painting, Uzi, but it's become much more. If everything we've learned is correct, Martin Landesmann is sitting on a mountain of stolen money. He and his father have killed several people to protect that secret, and someone just tried to kill us in Buenos Aires. But I can't prove it on my own. I need—"

"The resources of the Office?" Navot stared incredulously. "Perhaps it's escaped your notice, but at the moment the State of Israel is confronting more serious threats. Our friends in Iran are on the verge of becoming a nuclear power. In Lebanon, Hezbollah is arming for an all-out war. And, in case the news hasn't reached Cornwall, we're not exactly popular in the world right now. It's not that I don't take what you've discovered seriously, Gabriel. It's just we have other things to worry about."

Chiara interjected for the first time. "You might feel otherwise if you met Lena Herzfeld."

Navot raised a hand in his own defense. "Listen, Chiara, in a perfect world we would go after all the Martin Landesmanns out there. But it's not a perfect world. If it was, the Office could close its doors, and we could all spend the rest of our days thinking pure thoughts."

"So what should we do?" Gabriel asked. "Wash our hands of it?"

"Let Eli handle it. Or give it to the bloodhounds at the Holocaust restitution agencies."

"Landesmann and his lawyers will swat them away like flies."

"Better them than you. Given your history, you're not exactly the best candidate to take on a man like Landesmann. He has friends in high places."

"So do I."

"And they'll disown you if you try to bring down a man who's given away as much money as he has." Navot was silent for a moment. "I'm going to say something I'll probably regret later."

"Then maybe you shouldn't say it."

Navot didn't heed Gabriel's advice. "If you had taken the director's job the way Shamron wanted, then you would be the one making the decisions like this. But you—"

"Is that what this is about, Uzi? Putting me in my place?"

"Don't flatter yourself, Gabriel. My decision is based on my need to set priorities. And one of those priorities is maintaining good relations with the security and intelligence services of Western Europe. The last thing we need is some ill-conceived cowboy operation against Martin Landesmann. This discussion is now officially over."

Gabriel peered silently out the window as the car turned into Narkiss Street. Near the end was a small limestone apartment house largely concealed by a sprawling eucalyptus tree growing in the front garden. As the car came to a stop at the entrance, Navot was shifting uneasily in his seat. Personal confrontation had never been his strong suit.

"I'm sorry about the circumstances, but welcome home. Go upstairs and lie low for a few days until we've had a chance to sort through the wreckage in Buenos Aires. And try to get some rest. Don't take this the wrong way, Gabriel, but you look like hell."

"I can't sleep on airplanes, Uzi."

Navot smiled. "It's good to know some things never change."

38

RUE DE MIROMESNIL, PARIS

By the afternoon of Gabriel Allon's unheralded return to Jerusalem, Maurice Durand was thoroughly regretting that he had ever heard the name Rembrandt van Rijn or laid eyes on the portrait of his delectable young mistress. Durand's predicament was now twofold. He was in possession of a bloodstained painting too badly damaged to deliver to his client, along with a very old list of names and numbers that had been gnawing at the edges of his conscience from the moment he saw it. He decided to confront his problems sequentially. Methodical in all things, he knew no other way.

He dealt with the first problem by dispatching a brief e-mail to an address at yahoo.com. It stated that, much to the regret of Antiquités Scientifiques, the item requested by the client had not arrived as scheduled. Sadly, Durand added, it never would, for it had been involved in a tragic warehouse fire and now was little more than a worthless pile of ash. Given the fact that the item was a one-of-a-kind and therefore irreplaceable, Antiquités Scientifiques had no choice but to immediately refund the client's deposit—two million euros, a figure not included in the communiqué—and to offer its deepest apologies for any inconvenience caused by the unforeseen turn of events.

Having dealt with his first dilemma, Durand turned his attention to the troubling three pages of decaying onionskin paper he had found inside the painting. This time he chose a more archaic solution, a box of wooden matches from Fouquet's. Striking one, he lifted it toward the bottom right corner of the first page. For the next several seconds, he tried to close the three-inch gap between fuel and flame. The names, however, would not allow it.

Katz, Stern, Hirsch, Greenberg, Kaplan, Cohen, Klein, Abramowitz, Stein, Rosenbaum, Herzfeld . . .

The match extinguished itself in a puff of smoke. Durand tried a second time, but with the same result. He didn't bother to make a third attempt. Instead, he carefully returned the document to its wax paper sheath and placed it in his safe. Then he picked up his phone and dialed. A woman answered after the first ring.

"Is your husband there?"

"No."

"I need to see you."

"Hurry, Maurice."

ANGÉLIQUE BROSSARD was a good deal like the glass figurines lining the display cases of her shop—small, delicate, and pleasing to look at provided one's gaze did not linger too long or in too critical a manner. Durand had known her for nearly ten years. Their liaison fell under the heading of what Parisians politely refer to as a *cinq à sept,* a reference to the two hours in late afternoon traditionally reserved for the commission of adultery. Unlike Durand's other relationships, it was relatively uncomplicated. Pleasure was given, pleasure was demanded in return, and the word love was never spoken. That is not to say their attachment lacked affection or commitment. A thoughtless word or forgotten birthday could send Angélique into a fury. As for Durand, he had long ago given up on the idea of marriage. Angélique Brossard was the closest thing to a wife he would ever have.

Invariably, their encounters took place on the couch in Angélique's office. It was not large enough for proper lovemaking, but through many years of regular use they had trained themselves to utilize its limited geography to its full potential. On that afternoon, however, Durand was in no mood for romance. Clearly disappointed, Angélique lit a Gitane and looked at the cardboard tube in Durand's hand.

"You brought me a present, Maurice?"

"Actually, I was wondering whether you could do something for me."

She gave him a wicked smile. "I was hoping you'd say that."

"It's not that. I need you to keep this for me."

She glanced at the tube again. "What's inside?"

"It's better you don't know. Just keep it someplace where no one will find it. Someplace where the temperature and humidity are relatively stable."

"What is it, Maurice? A bomb?"

"Don't be silly, Angélique."

She picked a fleck of tobacco thoughtfully from the tip of her tongue. "Are you keeping secrets from me, Maurice?"

"Never."

"So what's inside the package?"

"You wouldn't believe me if I told you."

"Try me."

"It's a Rembrandt portrait worth forty-five million dollars."

"Really? Is there anything else I should know?"

"It has a bullet hole, and it's covered in blood."

She blew a stream of smoke dismissively toward the ceiling. "What's wrong, Maurice? You don't seem yourself today."

"I'm just a bit distracted."

"Problems with your business?"

"You might say that."

"My business is hurting, too. Everyone on the street is in trouble. I never thought I would say this, but the world was a much better place when the Americans were still rich."

"Yes," Durand said absently.

Angélique frowned. "Are you sure you're all right?"

"I'm fine," Durand assured her.

"Are you ever going to tell me what's really in the package?"

"Trust me, Angélique. It's nothing."

39

TIBERIAS, ISRAEL

To describe the influence of Ari Shamron on the defense and security of the State of Israel was tantamount to explaining the role played by water in the formation and maintenance of life on earth. In many respects, Ari Shamron *was* the State of Israel. After fighting in the war that led to Israel's reconstitution, he had spent the subsequent sixty years protecting the country from a host of enemies bent on its destruction. His star had burned brightest in times of crisis. He had penetrated the courts of kings, stolen the secrets of tyrants, and killed countless foes, sometimes with his own hands, sometimes with the hands of men such as Gabriel. Yet for all of Shamron's clandestine achievements, a single act had made him an icon. On a rainy night in May 1960, Shamron had leapt from the back of a car in Argentina and seized Adolf Eichmann, managing director of the Holocaust and immediate superior of SS-Hauptsturmführer Kurt Voss. In a way, all roads had been leading to Shamron from the moment Gabriel had entered Lena Herzfeld's sitting room. But then all roads usually did.

Shamron's role in the affairs of state had been drastically reduced in recent years, as had the size of his domain. He was now master of little more than his honey-colored villa overlooking the Sea of Galilee, yet even there he served mainly as a minister without portfolio to Gilah, his long-suffering wife. Shamron was now the worst thing a once-powerful man could be—unwanted and unneeded. He was regarded as a pest and a nuisance, someone to be tolerated but largely ignored. In short, he was underfoot.

Shamron's mood improved dramatically, however, when Gabriel and Chiara telephoned from Jerusalem to invite themselves to dinner. He was waiting in the entrance hall when they arrived, his pale blue eyes shimmering with an impish excitement. Despite his obvious curiosity over the reason for Gabriel's sudden return to Israel, he managed to restrain himself at dinner. They spoke of Shamron's children, of Gabriel's new life in Cornwall, and, like everyone else these days, the dire state of the global economy. Twice Shamron tried to broach the subjects of Uzi Navot and King Saul Boulevard, and twice Gilah deftly steered him into less turbulent waters. During a stolen moment in the kitchen, Gabriel quietly asked her about the state of Shamron's health. "Even I can't remember all the things that are wrong with him," she said. "But don't worry, Gabriel. He's not going anywhere. Shamron is eternal. Now go sit with him. You know how happy that makes him."

There is a familial quality to the intelligence services of Israel that few outsiders ever manage to grasp. More often then not, major operations are conceived and planned not in secure briefing rooms but in the homes of their participants. Few venues had played a more prominent role in the secret wars of Israel—or in Gabriel's own life—than Shamron's large terrace overlooking the Sea of Galilee. It was now noteworthy in Shamron's life as the only place where Gilah permitted him to smoke his wretched unfiltered Turkish cigarettes. He lit one over Gabriel's objections and lowered himself into his favorite chair facing the looming black mass of the Golan Heights. Gabriel ignited a pair of gas patio heaters and sat next to him.

"Chiara looks wonderful," Shamron said. "But that's hardly surprising. You've always had a knack for repairing beautiful objects."

Shamron gave a faint smile. He had been responsible for sending Gabriel to Venice to study the craft of restoration but had always been mystified by his prodigy's ability to paint in the manner of the Old Masters. As far as Shamron was concerned, Gabriel's remarkable talent with a brush was akin to a parlor trick or a magician's sleight of hand. It was something to be exploited, like Gabriel's unique gift for languages and his ability to get a Beretta off his hip and into firing position in the time it takes most men to clap their hands.

"All you have to do now," Shamron added, "is have a baby."

Gabriel shook his head in amazement. "Is there no aspect of my life that you regard as private or out-of-bounds?"

"No," Shamron replied without hesitation.

"At least you're honest."

"Only when it suits my purposes." Shamron drew heavily on his cigarette. "So I hear Uzi is giving you a hard time."

"How do you know?"

"I still have plenty of sources at King Saul Boulevard, despite the fact that Uzi has decided to cast me into the wilderness."

"What did you expect? Did you think he was going to give you a big office on the top floor and reserve a place for you at the operational-planning table?"

"What I expected, my son, was to be treated with a certain amount of respect and dignity. I've earned it."

"You have, Ari. But may I speak bluntly?"

"Tread carefully." Shamron clamped his large hand around Gabriel's wrist and squeezed. "I'm not as frail as I look."

"You suck the oxygen out of any room you enter. Every time you set foot in King Saul Boulevard, the troops want to bask in your glow and touch the hem of your garment."

"Are you taking Uzi's side?"

"I wouldn't dream of it."

"Wise boy."

"But you should at least consider the possibility that Uzi can run the Office without your constant input. After all, that's why you recommended him for the job in the first place."

"I recommended him because the man I really wanted wasn't available. But that's a topic for another conversation." Shamron tapped his cigarette against the side of his ashtray and gave Gabriel a sideways glance. "No regrets?"

"None whatsoever. Uzi Navot is the director of the Office, and he's going to be the director for a very long time. You'd better make peace with that fact. Otherwise, your final years on this earth are going to be filled with bitterness."

"You sound like Gilah."

"Gilah is a very wise woman."

"She is," Shamron agreed. "But if you're so pleased with the way Uzi is running things, then what are you doing here? Surely you didn't come all the way up to Tiberias for the pleasure of my company. You're here because you want something from Uzi and he won't give it to you. Try as I might, I haven't been able to figure out what it is. But I'm getting close."

"How much do you know?"

"I know that Julian Isherwood retained your services to track down a missing portrait by Rembrandt. I know that Eli Lavon is watching over an old woman in Amsterdam. And I know you've set your sights on one of the most successful businessmen in the world. What I don't quite yet understand is how these things are connected."

"It has something to do with an old acquaintance of yours."

"Who's that?"

"Eichmann."

Shamron slowly crushed out his cigarette. "You have my attention, Gabriel. Keep talking."

ARI SHAMRON, the only survivor of a large Jewish family from Poland, captor of Adolf Eichmann, knew much about the unfinished business of the Holocaust. But even Shamron appeared spellbound by the story Gabriel told him next. It was the story of a hidden child from Amsterdam, a murderer who had traded lives for property, and a painting stained with the blood of all those who had ever attempted to find it. Concealed inside the painting was a deadly secret—a list of names and numbers, proof that one of the most powerful business empires in the world had been built upon the looted assets of the dead.

"The boy king is right about one thing," Shamron said at the conclusion of Gabriel's briefing. "You should have told us about your travel plans. I could have arranged an escort for you in Argentina."

"I was looking for a missing painting, Ari. I didn't think I needed one."

"It's possible you were simply in the wrong place at the wrong time. After all, Alfonso Ramirez was one of the few people in the world with nearly as many enemies as you."

"It's possible," Gabriel conceded. "But I don't believe it." He paused, then said, "And neither do you, Ari."

"No, I don't." Shamron lit another cigarette. "You've managed to build an impressive case against Martin Landesmann in a short period of time. But there's just one problem. You'll never be able to prove it in a court of law."

"Who said anything about a court of law?"

"What exactly are you suggesting?"

"That we find a way to convince Martin to make amends for the sins of his father."

"What do you need?"

"Enough money, resources, and personnel to mount an operation on European soil against one of the world's richest men."

"It sounds expensive."

"It will be. But if I'm successful, the operation will fund itself."

The concept seemed to appeal to Shamron, who still acted as though operational expenditures came from his own pocket. "I suppose the next thing you're going to request is your old team."

"I was getting to that."

Shamron studied Gabriel in silence for a moment. "What happened to the tired warrior who sat on this terrace not long ago and told me he wanted to run away with his wife and leave the Office for good?"

"He met a woman in Amsterdam who's alive because her father gave Kurt Voss a Rembrandt." Gabriel paused, then asked, "The only question is, can you convince Uzi to change his mind?"

"Uzi?" Shamron waved his hand dismissively. "Don't worry about Uzi."

"How are you going to handle it?"

Shamron smiled. "Did I ever tell you that the prime minister's grandparents were from Hungary?"

40

JERUSALEM

Uzi Navot inherited many traditions from the eight men who had served as director before him, including a weekly private breakfast meeting with the prime minister at his Jerusalem office. Navot regarded the sessions as invaluable, for they provided an opportunity to brief his most important client on current operations without having to compete with the heads of Israel's other intelligence services. Usually, it was Navot who did most of the talking, but on the morning after Gabriel's pilgrimage to Tiberias the prime minister was curiously expansive. Just forty-eight hours earlier, he had been in Washington for his first summit with the new American president, a former academic and U.S. senator who hailed from the liberal wing of the Democratic Party. As predicted, the encounter had not gone well. Indeed, behind the frozen smiles and posed handshakes a palpable tension had crackled between the two men. It was now clear the close relationship the prime minister had enjoyed with the last occupant of the Oval Office would not be duplicated in the new administration. Change had definitely come to Washington.

"But none of this comes as a surprise to you, does it, Uzi?"

"I'm afraid we saw it coming even during the transition," Navot said. "It was obvious that the special operational bond we had forged with the CIA after 9/11 wasn't going to carry over."

"Special operational bond?" The prime minister treated Navot to a campaign-poster smile. "Spare me the Officespeak, Uzi. Gabriel Allon practically had an office at Langley during the last administration."

Navot made no response. He was used to toiling in Gabriel's long shadow. But now that he had reached the pinnacle of Israel's intelligence community, he didn't enjoy being reminded of his rival's many exploits.

"I hear Allon's in town." The prime minister paused, then added, "I also hear he got into a bit of trouble in Argentina."

Navot steepled his forefingers and pressed them tightly to his lips. A trained interrogator would have recognized the gesture as a transparent attempt to conceal discomfort. The prime minister recognized it, too. He also was clearly relishing the fact that he had managed to surprise the chief of his foreign intelligence service.

"Why didn't you tell me about Buenos Aires?" the prime minister asked.

"I didn't feel it was necessary to burden you with the details."

"I like details, Uzi, especially when they involve a national hero."

"I'll keep that in mind, Prime Minister."

Navot's tone displayed a transparent lack of enthusiasm, and his temper was now at a slow simmer. The prime minister had obviously been talking to Shamron. Navot had been expecting something like this from the old man for some time. But how to proceed? With care, he decided.

"Is there something you wish to say to me, Prime Minister?"

The prime minister refilled his coffee cup and contemplatively added a few drops of cream. Clearly, there was something he wished to say, but he seemed in no hurry to come to the point. Instead, he launched into a lengthy homily on the burdens of leadership in a complex and dangerous world. Sometimes, he said, decisions were influenced by national security, other times by political expediency. Occasionally, though, it boiled down to a simple question of right and wrong. He allowed this last statement to hang in the air for a moment before lifting his white linen napkin from his lap and folding it deliberately.

"My father's family came from Hungary. Did you know that, Uzi?"

"I suspect the entire country knows that."

The prime minister gave a fleeting smile. "They lived in a dreadful little village outside Budapest. My grandfather was a tailor. They had nothing to their name other than a pair of silver Shabbat candlesticks and a *kiddush* cup. And do you know what Kurt Voss and Adolf Eichmann did before putting them on a train to Auschwitz? They stole everything they had. And then they gave them a receipt. I have it to this day. I keep it as a reminder of the importance of the enterprise we call Israel." He paused. "Do you understand what I'm saying to you, Uzi?"

"I believe I do, Prime Minister."

"Keep me informed, Uzi. And remember, I like details."

Navot stepped into the anteroom and was immediately accosted by several members of the Knesset waiting to see the prime minister. Claiming an unspecified problem requiring his urgent attention, he shook a few of the more influential hands and patted a few of the more important backs before beating a hasty retreat to the elevators. His armored limousine was waiting outside, surrounded by his security detail. Fittingly, the heavy gray skies were pouring with rain. He slipped into the back and tossed his briefcase onto the floor. As the car lurched forward, the driver sought Navot's eyes in the rearview mirror.

"Where to, boss? King Saul Boulevard?"

"Not yet," Navot said. "We have to make one stop first."

The eucalyptus tree perfumed the entire western end of Narkiss Street. Navot lowered his window and peered up at the open French doors on the third floor of the limestone apartment house. From inside came the faint strains of an aria. *Tosca? La Traviata?* Navot didn't know. Nor did he much care. At this moment, he was loathing opera and anyone who listened to it with an unreasonable passion. For a mad instant, he considered returning to the prime minister's office and tendering his immediate resignation. Instead, he opened his secure cell phone and dialed. The aria went silent. Gabriel answered.

"You had no right going behind my back," Navot said.

"I didn't do a thing."

"You didn't have to. Shamron did it for you."

"You left me no choice."

Navot gave an exasperated sigh. "I'm down in the street."

"I know."

"How long do you need?"

"Five minutes."

"I'll wait."

The volume of the aria rose to a crescendo. Navot closed his window and luxuriated in the deep silence of his car. God, but he hated opera.

41

ST. JAMES'S, LONDON

The one name not spoken that morning in Jerusalem was the name of the man who had started it all: Julian Isherwood, owner and sole proprietor of Isherwood Fine Arts, 7-8 Mason's Yard, St. James's, London. Of Gabriel's many discoveries and travails, Isherwood knew nothing. Indeed, since securing a set of yellowed sales records in Amsterdam, his role in the affair had been reduced to that of a worried and helpless bystander. He filled the empty hours of his days by following the British end of the investigation. The police had managed to keep the theft out of the papers but had no leads on the painting's whereabouts or the identity of Christopher Liddell's killer. This was not an amateur looking for a quick score, the detectives muttered in their own defense. This was the real thing.

As with all condemned men, Isherwood's world shrank. He

attended the odd auction, showed the odd painting, and tried in vain to distract himself by flirting with his latest young receptionist. But most of his time was devoted to planning his own professional funeral. He rehearsed the speech he would give to the hated David Cavendish, art adviser to the vastly rich, and even produced a rough draft of a mea culpa he would eventually have to send to the National Gallery of Art in Washington. Images of flight and exile also filled his thoughts. Perhaps a little villa in the hills of Provence or a shack on the beach in Costa Rica. And the gallery? In his worst moments, Isherwood imagined having to drop it in Oliver Dimbleby's lap. Oliver had always coveted the gallery. Now, thanks to *Portrait of a Young Woman,* oil on canvas, 104 by 86 centimeters, Oliver could have it at no cost other than cleaning up Julian's mess.

It was complete twaddle, of course. Isherwood was not about to spend the rest of his life in exile. Nor would he ever allow his beloved gallery to fall into the grubby hands of Oliver Dimbleby. If Isherwood had to face a public firing squad, he would do it without a blindfold and with his chin held high. For once in his life, he would be courageous. Just like his old father. And just like Gabriel Allon.

Coincidentally, these were the very images occupying Isherwood's thoughts when he spotted a solitary figure coming across the damp paving stones of Mason's Yard, coat collar turned up against the late-autumn chill, eyes on the prowl. The man was in his early thirties, built like an armored fighting vehicle, and dressed in a dark suit. For an instant, Isherwood feared the man was some sort of heavy-fisted debt collector. But a few seconds later, he realized he had seen the man before. He worked in the security section of a certain embassy located in South Kensington—an embassy that, regrettably, was forced to employ many others like him.

A moment later, Isherwood heard the drowsy voice of his receptionist announcing there was a Mr. Radcliff to see him. It seemed Mr. Radcliff, a nom de plume if ever there was one, had a few minutes to kill between appointments and was wondering whether he might have a peek at the gallery's inventory. Isherwood normally turned away such drop-ins. But on that morning, for all the obvious reasons, he made an exception.

He greeted the man circumspectly and led him to the privacy of the upper exhibition room. Just as Isherwood suspected, Mr. Radcliff's tour was brief. He frowned at a Luini, clucked his tongue at a Bordone, and appeared puzzled by a luminous landscape by Claude. "I think I like it," he said, handing Isherwood an envelope. "I'll be in touch." Then he lowered his voice to a whisper and added, "Make sure you follow the instructions carefully."

Isherwood saw the young man to the door, then, in the privacy of his washroom, unsealed the envelope. Inside was a brief note. Isherwood read it once, then a second time, just to be sure. Leaning against the basin to steady himself, he was overcome by an immense wave of relief. Though Gabriel had not found the painting, his investigation had produced a critical piece of information. Isherwood's original search of the painting's provenance had failed to reveal it had been stolen during the Second World War. Therefore the rightful owner of the painting was not the mysterious unnamed client of David Cavendish but an elderly woman in Amsterdam. For Julian Isherwood, the discovery meant that the cloud of financial ruin had been lifted. Typically, matters involving looted art might be litigated for years. But Isherwood knew from experience that no decent court in the world would ever force him to compensate a man for a painting that was not rightly his. The Rembrandt was still missing and might never be found. But, simply put, Isherwood was now off the hook.

His relief, however, was soon followed by a pang of deep guilt. Guilt over the tragedy of the Herzfeld family, a story Isherwood understood all too well. Guilt over the fate of Christopher Liddell, who had sacrificed his life trying to protect the Rembrandt. And guilt, too, over the present circumstances of one Gabriel Allon. It seemed Gabriel's quest to recover the painting had earned him a powerful new enemy. And once more it seemed he had fallen under the spell of Ari Shamron. Or perhaps, thought Isherwood, it was the other way around.

Isherwood read the note a final time, then as instructed touched it to the open flame of a match. In an instant, the paper vanished in a burst of fire that left no trace of ash. Isherwood returned to his office, hands shaking, and gingerly sat at his desk. *You might have warned me about the flash paper, petal,* he thought. *Nearly stopped my bloody heart.*

PART THREE

AUTHENTICATION

42

KING SAUL BOULEVARD, TEL AVIV

The operation began in earnest when Gabriel and Chiara arrived at Room 456C. A subterranean chamber located three levels beneath the lobby of King Saul Boulevard, it had once been a dumping ground for obsolete computers and worn-out furniture, often used by the night staff for romantic trysts. Now it was known throughout the Office only as Gabriel's Lair.

A strip of bluish fluorescent light shone from beneath the closed door, and from the opposite side came the expectant murmur of voices. Gabriel smiled at Chiara, then punched the code into the pad and led her inside. For a few seconds, none of the nine people sprawled around the dilapidated worktables seemed to notice their presence. Then a single face turned, and there arose a loud cheer. When the cacophony finally subsided, Gabriel and Chiara made their way slowly around the room, greeting each member of the fabled team.

There was Yossi Gavish, a tweedy, Oxford-educated analyst from Research, and Yaakov Rossman, a pockmarked former officer from Shabak's Arab Affairs Department who was now running agents into Syria. There was Dina Sarid, a terrorism specialist from History who seemed to carry the grief of her work wherever she went, and Rimona Stern, a former military intelligence officer who happened to be Shamron's niece by marriage and was now assigned to the Office's special Iran task force. There were Mordecai and Oded, a pair of all-purpose fieldhands, and two computer sleuths from Technical of whom it was said no database or server in the world was safe. And there was Eli Lavon, who had flown in from Amsterdam the previous evening after turning over the Lena Herzfeld watch to a local security team.

Within the corridors and conference rooms of King Saul Boulevard, these men and women were known by the code name Barak—the Hebrew word for lightning—because of their ability to gather and strike quickly. They had operated together, often under conditions of immense stress, on secret battlefields from Moscow to the Caribbean. But one member of the team was not present. Gabriel looked at Yossi and asked, "Where's Mikhail?"

"He *was* on a leave of absence."

"Where is he now?"

"Standing right behind you," said a voice at Gabriel's back.

Gabriel turned around. Propped against the jamb was a lanky figure with eyes the color of glacial ice and a fine-boned, bloodless face. Born in Moscow to a pair of dissident scientists, Mikhail Abramov had come to Israel as a teenager within weeks of the Soviet Union's collapse. Once described by Shamron as "Gabriel without a conscience," Mikhail had joined the Office after serving in the Sayeret Matkal special forces, where he had assassinated several of the top terrorist masterminds of Hamas and Palestinian Islamic Jihad. But he would forever be linked to Gabriel and Chiara by the terrifying hours they had spent together in the hands of Ivan Kharkov in a birch forest outside Moscow.

"I thought you were supposed to be in Cornwall," Mikhail said.

"I got a little stir-crazy."

"So I hear."

"Are you up for this?"

Mikhail shrugged. "No problem."

Mikhail took his usual seat in the back left corner while Gabriel surveyed the four walls. They were papered over with surveillance photos, street maps, and watch reports—all corresponding to the eleven names Gabriel had written on the chalkboard the previous summer. Eleven names of eleven former KGB agents, all of whom had been killed by Gabriel and Mikhail. Now Gabriel wiped the names from the board with the same ease he had wiped the Russians from the face of the earth and in their place adhered an enlarged photograph of Martin Landesmann. Then he settled atop a metal stool and told his team a story.

It was a story of greed, dispossession, and death spanning more than half a century and stretching from Amsterdam to Zurich to Buenos Aires and back to the graceful shores of Lake Geneva. It featured a long-hidden portrait by Rembrandt, a twice-stolen fortune in looted Holocaust assets, and a man known to all the world as Saint Martin who was anything but. Like a painting, said Gabriel, Saint Martin was merely a clever illusion. Beneath the shimmering varnish and immaculate brushwork of his surface were base layers of shadows and lies. And perhaps there was an entire hidden work waiting to be brought to the surface. They were going to attack Saint Martin by focusing on his lies. Where there was one, Gabriel said, there would be others. They were like loose threads at the edge of an otherwise undamaged canvas. Pull on the right one, Gabriel promised, and Saint Martin's world would fall to pieces.

43

KING SAUL BOULEVARD, TEL AVIV

They divided his life in half, which Martin, had he known of their efforts, would surely have found appropriate. Dina, Rimona, Mordecai, and Chiara were given responsibility for his highly guarded personal life and his philanthropic work while the rest of the team took on the Herculean task of deconstructing his far-flung financial empire. Their goal was to find evidence that Saint Martin knew his astonishing wealth had been built upon a great crime. Eli Lavon, a battle-scarred veteran of many such investigations, privately despaired of their chances for success. The case against Landesmann, while compelling to a layman, was based largely on the fading memories of a few participants. Without original documentation from Bank Landesmann or an admission of guilt from Saint Martin himself, any allegations of wrongdoing might ultimately be impossible to prove. But as Gabriel reminded Lavon time and time again, he was not necessarily looking for legal proof, only a hammer that he might use to beat down the doors of Saint Martin's citadel.

Gabriel's first priority, however, was to break open the doors of Uzi Navot's executive suite. Within hours of the team's formation, Navot had issued a collegial directive to all department heads instructing them to cooperate fully with its work. But the written directive was soon followed by a verbal one that had the effect of sending all requests for intelligence or resources to Navot's sparkling desk, where invariably they languished before receiving his necessary signature. Navot's personal demeanor only reinforced the notion of indifference. Those who witnessed his encounters with Gabriel described them as tense and abbreviated. And during his daily planning meetings, Navot referred to the investigation of Martin Landesmann only as "Gabriel's project." He even refused to assign the venture a proper code name. The message, while carefully encrypted, was clear to all those who heard it. The Landesmann case was a tin can Navot intended to kick down the road. As for Gabriel, yes, he was a legend, but he was yesterday's man. And anyone foolish enough to hitch his wagon to him would at some point feel Uzi's wrath.

But as the work of the team quietly progressed, the siege slowly lifted. Gabriel's requests began clearing Navot's desk in a more timely fashion, and the two men were soon conferring in person on a regular basis. They were even spotted together in the executive dining room sharing a dietetic lunch of steamed chicken and wilted greens. Those fortunate few who were able to gain admittance to Gabriel's subterranean realm described the mood as one of palpable excitement. Those who labored there under Gabriel's unrelenting pressure might have described the atmosphere in another manner, but, as always, they kept their own counsel.

Gabriel made few demands of his team other than loyalty and hard work, and they rewarded him with absolute discretion. They regarded themselves as a family—a boisterous, quarrelsome, and sometimes dysfunctional family—and outsiders were never privy to family secrets.

The true nature of their project was known only to Navot and a handful of his most senior aides, though even a glance inside the team's cramped lair would have left very little to the imagination. Stretching the entire length of one wall was a complex diagram of Saint Martin's global business empire. At the top were the companies directly owned or controlled by Global Vision Investments of Geneva. Below that was a directory of firms owned by known subsidiaries of GVI, and farther down lay a substrata of enterprises held by corporate shells and offshore fronts.

The diagram proved Alfonso Ramirez's contention that, for all Saint Martin's corporate piety, he was remorseless in pursuit of profit. There was a textile mill in Thailand that had been cited repeatedly for using slave labor, a chemical complex in Vietnam that had destroyed a nearby river, and a cargo vessel recycling center in Bangladesh that was regarded as one of the most fouled parcels of land on the planet. GVI also controlled a Brazilian agribusiness that was destroying several hundred acres of the Amazon rain forest on a daily basis, an African mining company that was turning a corner of Chad into a dust bowl, and a Korean offshore-drilling firm that had caused the worst environmental disaster in the history of the Sea of Japan. Even Yaakov, who had seen mankind at its worst, was stunned by the vast chasm between Landesmann's words and his deeds. "The word that leaps to mind is *compartmentalized,*" said Yaakov. "Our Saint Martin makes Ari Shamron look one-dimensional."

If Landesmann were troubled by the contradictions in his business affairs, it was not visible on the face he showed in public. For on the opposite wall of Room 456C there emerged a portrait of a righteous, enlightened man who had achieved much in life and was eager to give much in return. There was Martin the philanthropist, and Martin the mystic of corporate responsibility. Martin who gave medicine to the sick, Martin who brought water to the thirsty, and Martin who built shelter for the homeless, sometimes with his own hands. Martin at the side of prime ministers and presidents, and Martin cavorting in the company of famous actors and musicians. Martin discussing sustainable agriculture with the Prince of Wales, and Martin fretting about the threat of global warming with a former senator from America. There was Martin with his photogenic family: Monique, his beautiful French-born wife, and Alexander and Charlotte, their teenage children. Finally, there was Martin making his annual pilgrimage to the World Economic Forum at Davos, the one time each year when the oracle spoke for attribution. Were it not for Davos, Saint Martin's legion of devoted followers might have been forgiven for assuming that its prophet had taken a vow of silence.

It would not have been possible to assemble so complete a picture of Martin in so short a period of time if not for the help of someone who had never even set foot in Room 456C. His name was Rafael Bloch, and his contribution was the treasure trove of files gathered during his long and ultimately fatal investigation into Martin Landesmann. Bloch had left behind many pieces of the puzzle. But it was Eli Lavon who unearthed the true prize, and Rimona Stern who helped decode it.

Buried in an unlabeled tan folder were several pages of handwritten notes concerning Keppler Werk GmbH, a small metallurgy firm based in the former East German city of Magdeburg. Apparently, Landesmann had secretly purchased the company in 2002, then poured millions into transforming the once-dilapidated facility into a modern technological showpiece. It seemed that Keppler's assembly lines now manufactured some of the finest industrial-grade valves in Europe—valves it shipped to customers around the world. It was a list of those customers that raised alarm bells, for Keppler's distribution chain corresponded rather nicely to a global smuggling route well known to Office analysts. The network began in the industrial belt of Western Europe, snaked its way across the lands of the former Soviet Union, then looped through the shipping lanes of the Pacific Rim before finally reaching its terminus at the Islamic Republic of Iran.

It was this discovery, made on the fourth day of the team's effort, that prompted Gabriel to announce that they had just discovered Martin's loose thread. Uzi Navot immediately christened the operation Masterpiece and headed to Kaplan Street in Jerusalem. The prime minister wanted details, and Navot finally had a critical one to share. Gabriel's project was no longer simply about a missing Rembrandt portrait and a pile of looted Holocaust assets. Martin Landesmann was in bed with the Iranians. And only God knew who else.

THE NEXT EVENING, Martin Landesmann became the target of active, if distant, Office surveillance. The setting for this milestone was Montreal; the occasion was a charity gala at a downtown hotel for a cause Saint Martin supposedly held dear. The watchers took several photos of Landesmann as he arrived for the party—accompanied by Jonas Brunner, his personal security chief—and snapped several more as he departed in the same manner. When next they saw him he was stepping off his private business jet at Geneva International Airport and into the back of an armored Mercedes Maybach 62S limousine, which delivered him directly to Villa Elma, his palatial estate on the shores of Lake Geneva. Martin, they would soon discover, spent almost no time at GVI's headquarters on the Quai de Mont-Blanc. Villa Elma was his base of operations, the true nerve center of his vast empire, and the repository of Martin's many secrets.

As the surveillance operation settled into place, it began to produce a steady stream of intelligence, most of it useless. The watchers took many pretty pictures of Martin and recorded the occasional snatch of long-range audio, but their efforts produced nothing resembling an actionable piece of information. Martin conducted conversations they could not hear with men they could not identify. It was, said Gabriel, like listening to a melody without words.

The problem lay in the fact that, despite repeated efforts, Technical had been unable to penetrate GVI's well-fortified computer systems or to crack into Martin's ever-present mobile phone. Given no advance warning of Martin's hectic schedule, Gabriel's watchers were little more than a pack of hounds chasing a crafty fox. Only the flight plans filed by Martin's pilots betrayed his movements, but even those proved to be of little value. Ten days into the Landesmann watch, Gabriel announced that he never wanted to see another photo of Martin getting on or off an airplane. Indeed, Gabriel declared, he would be happy if he never saw Martin's face again. What he needed was a way inside Martin's world. A way to get his phone. A way to get his computer. And for that he needed an accomplice. Given Martin's daunting security, it would not be possible to create one out of whole cloth. Gabriel needed the help of someone close to Martin. He needed an agent in place.

AFTER A WEEK of around-the-clock searching, the team found its first potential candidate while staking out Martin at his luxury penthouse apartment located at 21 Quai de Bourbon, on the northern edge of the Île Saint-Louis in Paris. She was delivered to his door by way of a chauffeured Mercedes at five minutes past nine in the evening. Her hair was dark and cut fashionably short; her eyes were large and liquid and brimming with an obvious intelligence. The surveillance team judged her to be a self-assured woman and, after hearing her bid good night to her driver, British. She punched the code into the entry keypad as though she had performed the task many times before, then disappeared through the doorway. They saw her again two hours later admiring the view of the Seine from Martin's window with Martin at her back. The intimacy of their pose, combined with the fact that her torso was bare, left no doubt about the nature of their relationship.

She departed at 8:15 the next morning. The watchers took several additional photos as she climbed into the back of a chauffeured Mercedes, then followed her to the Gare du Nord where she boarded the 9:13 Eurostar train to London. After three days of surveillance, Gabriel knew her name, her address, her telephone number, and the date of her birth. Most important, he knew where she worked.

It was the last piece of information—the place of her employment—that caused Uzi Navot to immediately declare her "flagrantly unsuitable" for recruitment. Indeed, during the heated argument that followed, an exasperated Navot would once again say things he would later regret. Not only did he call into question Gabriel's judgment but his sanity as well. "Obviously, the Cornish wind has affected your brain," he snapped at one point. "We don't recruit people like her. We avoid them at all costs. Cross her off your list. Find someone else."

In the face of Navot's tirade, Gabriel displayed a remarkable equanimity. He patiently refuted Navot's arguments, calmed Navot's fears, and reminded Navot of the formidable nature of Martin's many defenses. The woman they had first seen in Paris was the proverbial bird in the hand, he said. Release her to the wind, and it might be months before they found another candidate. Navot finally capitulated, as Gabriel had known he would. Given Martin's secret commercial ties to the Iranians, he was no longer a can that could be kicked down the road. Martin had to be dealt with and dealt with quickly.

The global nature of Martin's sins, combined with the passport carried by the potential recruit, meant it was not possible for the Office to proceed alone. A partner was required, perhaps two for good measure. Navot issued the invitations; the British quickly agreed to act as host. Gabriel had one final request, and this time Navot did not object. One didn't bring a knife to a gunfight, Navot conceded. And one never went to war against a man like Martin Landesmann without Ari Shamron in his back pocket.

44

THE MARAIS, PARIS

Many years earlier, Maurice Durand had stumbled across a newspaper article about the case of Christoph Meili, a private security guard who had the misfortune of being assigned to work at the Union Bank of Switzerland's headquarters on the Bahnhofstrasse in Zurich. While making his rounds on a January afternoon in 1997, the devoutly Christian father of two entered the bank's shredding room and discovered a pair of large rolling bins filled with old documents, including several ledgers detailing transactions conducted between UBS and Hitler's Germany. Meili found the presence of the material in the shredding room more than a little suspicious, since weeks earlier Swiss banks had been prohibited by federal law from destroying wartime documents. Sensing something was amiss, he stuffed two of the ledgers under his shirt and smuggled them to his modest home outside Zurich. The next morning, he handed the documents over to the Israeli Cultural Center, at which point his problems began.

The head of the center quickly called a press conference to denounce UBS for its wanton destruction of records. UBS dismissed the shredding as a regrettable mistake and promptly laid blame at the feet of the bank's archivist. As for Christoph Meili, he was summarily fired from his job and soon became the target of a criminal investigation into whether *he* had violated Swiss bank-secrecy laws by stealing the wartime records. Meili was hailed around the world as a "document hero," but in his native land he was hounded by public denunciations and death threats. Much to Switzerland's shame, the security guard who acted on his conscience had to be granted political asylum by the U.S. Senate and was quietly resettled with his family in New York.

At the time, Maurice Durand concluded that Meili's actions, while admirable and courageous, were ultimately foolhardy. Which made it all the more strange that Durand had now decided he had no choice but to embark on a similar path. Ironically, his motivations were identical to Meili's. Though Monsieur Durand was a career criminal who habitually violated two of God's most sacred commandments, he regarded himself as a deeply spiritual and honorable man who tried to operate by a certain code. That code would not allow him to ever accept payment for a painting stained in blood. Nor would it permit him to suppress the document he had discovered hidden inside. To do so would not only be a crime against history but make him an accessory after the fact to a mortal sin.

There were, however, two aspects of the Meili affair Maurice Durand was determined not to repeat—public exposure and the threat of prosecution. Meili's lapse, he concluded, had been to place his trust in a stranger. Which explained why, late that afternoon, Durand decided to close his shop early and personally deliver a pair of eighteenth-century lorgnette opera glasses to one of his most valued clients, Hannah Weinberg.

Fifty years of age and childless, Madame Weinberg had two passions: her impressive collection of antique French eyewear and her tireless campaign to rid the world of racial and religious hatred in all its forms. Hannah's first passion had caused her to form an attachment to Antiquités Scientifiques. Her second had compelled her to found the Isaac Weinberg Center for the Study of Anti-Semitism in France, named for her paternal grandfather who was arrested during *Jeudi noir,* Black Thursday, the roundup of Jews in Paris, on July 16, 1942, and subsequently murdered at Auschwitz. Hannah Weinberg was now regarded as the most prominent so-called memory militant in France. Her fight against anti-Semitism had earned her a legion of admirers—including the current French president—but many determined enemies as well. The Weinberg Center was the target of constant threats, as was Hannah Weinberg herself. As a result, Maurice Durand was one of the few people who knew that she lived in her grandfather's old apartment at 24 rue Pavée, in the fourth arrondissement.

She was waiting for him on the landing outside her apartment, dressed in a dark sweater, a pleated wool skirt, and heavy stockings. Her dark hair was streaked with gray; her nose was narrow and aquiline. She greeted Durand warmly with kisses on each cheek and invited him inside. It was a large apartment, with a formal entrance hall and a library adjoining the sitting room. Antique furniture covered in faded brocade stood sedately about, thick velvet curtains hung in the windows, and an ormolu clock ticked quietly on the mantel. The effect of the décor was to create the impression of a bygone era. Indeed, for a moment Durand felt as though he were standing in an annex of Antiquités Scientifiques.

Durand formally presented Hannah with her opera glasses and informed her about a number of interesting pieces that might soon be coming into his possession. Finally, he opened his attaché case and in an offhanded tone said, "I stumbled upon some interesting documents a few days ago, Madame Weinberg. I was wondering whether you might have a moment to take a look."

"What are they?"

"To be honest, I have no idea. I was hoping you might know."

He handed the sheath of old wax paper to Hannah Weinberg and watched as she removed the delicate sheets of paper.

"It was hidden inside a telescope I purchased a few weeks ago," he said. "I found it while I was doing some repair work."

"That's odd."

"I thought so, too."

"Where did the telescope come from?"

"If it's all right with you, Madame Weinberg, I'd rather not—"

She held up a hand. "Say no more, Monsieur Durand. You owe your clients absolute discretion."

"Thank you, madame. I knew you would understand. The question is, what is it?"

"The names are clearly Jewish. And it obviously has something to do with money. Each name is assigned a corresponding figure in Swiss francs, along with an eight-digit number of some sort."

"It looks like wartime paper to me."

She fingered the edge of one page carefully. "It is. You can tell by the shoddy quality. In fact, it's a miracle the pages are even intact."

"And the eight-digit numbers?"

"Hard to say."

Durand hesitated. "Is it possible they're account numbers of some sort, Madame Weinberg?"

Hannah Weinberg looked up. "*Swiss* bank accounts?"

Durand gave a deferential smile. "You're the expert, madame."

"I'm not, actually. But it's certainly plausible." She studied the pages again. "But who would assemble a list like this? And why?"

"Perhaps you know someone who might be able to answer that question. Someone at the center, for example."

"We really don't have anyone who focuses purely on financial matters. And if you're right about the meaning of the numbers, these documents need to be reviewed by someone who knows a thing or two about Swiss banking."

"Do you happen to know someone like that, madame?"

"I'm sure I can track down someone qualified." She looked at him for a moment, then asked, "Is that your wish, Monsieur Durand?"

He nodded. "But I have a small favor. I would appreciate it if you would keep my name out of it. My business, you understand. Some of my clients might—"

"Don't worry," Hannah Weinberg said, cutting him off. "Your secret is safe with me, Maurice. This will be strictly *entre nous.* I give you my word."

"But you'll call if you learn anything interesting?"

"Of course."

"Thank you, madame." Maurice Durand closed his attaché

case and gave her a conspiratorial smile. "I hate to admit it, but I've always loved a good mystery."

HANNAH WEINBERG stood in the window of her library and watched Maurice Durand recede into the gathering darkness along the rue Pavée. Then she gazed at the list.

Katz, Stern, Hirsch, Greenberg, Kaplan, Cohen, Klein, Abramowitz, Stein, Rosenbaum, Herzfeld . . .

She wasn't at all sure she believed Durand's story. Regardless, she had made a promise. But what to do with the list? She needed an expert. Someone who knew a thing or two about Swiss banks. Someone who knew where the bodies were buried. In some cases, literally.

She opened the top drawer of her writing desk—a desk that had once belonged to her grandfather—and removed a single key. It opened a door at the end of an unlit corridor. The room behind it was a child's room, Hannah's old room, frozen in time. A four-poster bed with a lace canopy. Shelves stacked with stuffed animals and toys. A faded pinup of an American heartthrob actor. And hanging above a French provincial dresser, shrouded in heavy shadow, was a painting, *Marguerite Gachet at Her Dressing Table,* by Vincent van Gogh. Several years earlier, she had lent it to a man who was trying to find a terrorist—a man from Israel with the name of an angel. He had given her a number where he could be reached in an emergency or if she needed a favor. Perhaps it was time to renew their relationship.

45

THAMES HOUSE, LONDON

The conference room was preposterously large, as was the gleaming rectangular table that ran nearly the entire length of it. Shamron sat at his assigned place, dwarfed by his executive swivel chair, and gazed across the river toward the Emerald City-like headquarters of MI6. Gabriel sat next to him, hands neatly folded, eyes flickering over the two men opposite. On the left, dressed in an ill-fitting blazer and crumpled gabardine trousers, was Adrian Carter, director of the CIA's National Clandestine Service. On the right was Graham Seymour, deputy director of MI5.

The four men seated around the table represented a secret brotherhood of sorts. Though each remained loyal to his own country, their close bond transcended time and the fickle whims of their political masters. They did the unpleasant chores no one else was willing to do and worried about the consequences later. They had fought for one another, killed for one another, and in some cases bled for one another. During multiple joint operations, all conducted under conditions of extreme stress, they had also developed an uncanny ability to sense one another's thoughts. As a result, it was painfully obvious to both Gabriel and Shamron that there was tension on the Anglo-American side of the table.

"Something wrong, gentlemen?" asked Shamron.

Graham Seymour looked at Carter and frowned. "As our American cousins like to say, I'm in the doghouse."

"With Adrian?"

"No," Carter interjected quickly. "We revere Graham. It's the White House that's angry with him."

"Really?" Gabriel looked at Seymour. "That's quite an accomplishment, Graham. How did you manage that?"

"The Americans had an intelligence failure last night. A significant failure," he added. "The White House has gone into full damage-control mode. Tempers are flaring. Fingers are pointing. And most of them seem to be pointing at me."

"What exactly was this failure?"

"A Pakistani citizen who sometimes resides in the United Kingdom attempted to blow himself up on a flight from Copenhagen to Boston. Luckily, he was as incompetent as the last fellow, and international passengers seem to have become quite adept at taking matters into their own hands."

"So why is anyone angry with you?"

"Good question. We alerted the Americans several months ago that he was associating with known radicals and was probably being groomed for an attack. But according to the White House, I wasn't forceful enough in my warnings." Seymour glanced at Carter. "I suppose I could have written an op-ed piece in the *New York Times,* but I thought that might be a bit excessive."

Gabriel looked at Carter. "What happened?"

"His name was misspelled by someone on our end when it was entered into the database of suspected militants."

"So he never made it onto the no-fly list?"

"That's correct."

Graham Seymour shook his head in amazement. "There's a ten-year-old American Boy Scout who can't get his name *off* the no-fly list, but I can't get a known jihadi *on* it. Quite the contrary, they gave him an open-ended visa and allowed him to get on an airplane with a one-way ticket and explosive powder in his carry-on."

"Is that true, Adrian?" asked Gabriel.

"In a nutshell," Carter conceded morosely.

"So why take it out on Graham?"

"Political convenience," Carter said without hesitation. "In case you haven't noticed, there are powerful people around our new president who like to pretend there's no such thing as a war on terror. In fact, I'm no longer allowed to utter those words. So when something does happen . . ."

"The powerful men around your president go looking for a scapegoat."

Carter nodded.

"And they picked Graham Seymour?" asked Gabriel incredulously. "A loyal friend and ally who's been at your side from the beginning of the war on terror?"

"I've pointed that out to the president's counterterrorism adviser, but he's in no mood to listen. Apparently, his job is less than secure at the moment. As for Graham, he'll survive. He's the only person in Western intelligence who's been in his job longer than I have."

Seymour's mobile telephone purred softly. He dispatched the call to his voice mail with the press of a button, then rose from his chair and walked over to the credenza for a cup of coffee. He was dressed, as usual, in a perfectly fitted charcoal gray suit and a regimental tie. His face was even featured, and his full head of hair had a rich silvery cast that made him look like a model one sees in ads for costly but needless trinkets. Though he had worked briefly as a field officer, he had spent the lion's share of his career toiling behind locked doors at MI5 headquarters. Graham Seymour waged war against Britain's enemies by attending briefings and reading dossiers. The only light that shone upon his patrician features emanated from his halogen desk lamp. And the only surface his handmade English shoes ever trod upon was the fine woolen carpet stretching between his office and the director-general's.

"How goes the search for the missing Rembrandt?" Seymour asked.

"It's evolved."

"So I'm told."

"How much do you know, Graham?"

"I know that after leaving Christopher Liddell's studio with a rubber glove filled with evidence, you headed to Amsterdam. From there, you traveled to Argentina, where, two days later, one of the country's most important voices of conscience was killed in a bombing." Seymour paused. "Was it an old enemy or have you already managed to make a new one?"

"We believe it was Martin Landesmann."

"Really?" Seymour brushed a bit of invisible lint from his trousers.

"You don't seem terribly surprised, Graham."

"I'm not."

Gabriel looked at Adrian Carter and saw he was doodling on his MI5 notepad.

"And you, Adrian?"

Carter looked up briefly from his labors. "Let's just say I've never been one to bow at the altar of Saint Martin. But do tell me the rest of it, Gabriel. I could use a good story after the day I've had."

ADRIAN CARTER was easily underestimated, an attribute that had served him well throughout his career at the CIA. Little about Carter's churchy appearance or clinical demeanor suggested he oversaw the most powerful covert intelligence apparatus in the world—or that before his ascension to the seventh floor at Langley he had operated on secret battlefields from Poland to Central America to Afghanistan. Strangers mistook him for a university professor or a therapist of some sort. When one thought of Adrian Carter, one pictured a man grading a senior thesis or listening to a patient confessing feelings of inadequacy.

But it was Carter's ability to listen that set him apart from lesser rivals at Langley. He sat transfixed throughout Gabriel's story, legs crossed, hands thoughtfully bunched beneath his chin. Only once did he move and that was to brandish his pipe. This gave Shamron license to draw his own weapon, despite Seymour's halfhearted attempt to enforce MI5's ban on smoking. Having heard Gabriel's story already, Shamron occupied his time by contemptuously inspecting his imposing surroundings. He had begun his career in a building with few amenities other than electricity and running water. The grandness of Britain's intelligence monuments always amused him. Money spent on pretty buildings and nice furniture, Shamron always said, was money that couldn't be spent on stealing secrets.

"For the record," Graham Seymour said at the conclusion of Gabriel's presentation, "you've already managed to violate several provisions of our agreement. We allowed you to take up residence in the United Kingdom on the proviso that you were retired and that your only work would be *art* related. This affair stopped being *art* related when you stumbled back into the arms of your old service after the bombing in Buenos Aires. And it certainly stopped being *art* related when your prime minister signed off on a full-scale investigation of Martin Landesmann. Which, by the way, is long overdue."

"What do you know about Martin that the rest of the world doesn't?"

"A few years ago, Her Majesty's Revenue and Customs began a major effort to crack down on British subjects who were concealing money in offshore tax havens. During the course of their investigation, they discovered an unusually large number of our citizens, many with questionable sources of income, had deposited money in something called Meissner Privatbank of Liechtenstein. After some digging, they concluded that Meissner wasn't much of a bank at all but a portal to a massive money-laundering operation. And guess who owned it?"

"Global Vision Investments of Geneva?"

"Through various fronts and subsidiaries, of course. When the boys at Revenue and Customs were preparing to go public with their findings, they expected a big pat on the back. But much to their surprise, word came from on high to shut down the investigation, and the case was dropped."

"Any reason given?"

"Not one that anyone dared to say aloud," Seymour said. "But it was clear Downing Street didn't want to jeopardize the flow of Swiss investment money into the United Kingdom by starting a public row with a man regarded as Switzerland's patron saint of corporate responsibility."

Carter tapped his pipe like a gavel against an ashtray and began slowly reloading the bowl.

"Is there something you wish to add, Adrian?" asked Gabriel.

"Zentrum Security."

"What is it?"

"A corporate security firm based in Zurich. A couple of years ago, a number of American firms doing business in Switzerland became convinced they were the targets of corporate espionage. They approached the administration and asked for help. The administration quietly dropped it in my lap."

"And?"

"We discovered that all the firms involved in the complaint had been targeted by Zentrum. It isn't merely a 'guns, guards, and gates' kind of firm. Along with the usual range of protective services, it does a lucrative trade in what it refers to as overseas consulting."

"Translation?"

"It arranges deals between clients and foreign entities, be they corporate or government."

"What kind of deals?"

"The kind that can't be handled in the traditional manner," Carter said. "And you can guess who owns Zentrum Security."

"Global Vision Investments."

Carter nodded.

"Have they ever arranged any deals for a company called Keppler Werk GmbH of Magdeburg, Germany?"

"Keppler has never popped up on our radar screens," Carter said. "But as you know, thousands of international companies are currently doing business in Iran. Our friends in China are among the worst offenders. They'll do business with anyone, but the Germans aren't much better. Everyone wants their market share, and in times like these, they're reluctant to give it up over something as trivial as Iran's nuclear ambitions. At least seventeen hundred German firms are doing business in Iran, many of them makers of sophisticated industrial equipment. We've been pleading with the Germans for years to scale back their business ties to the Iranians, but they refuse. Some of our closest allies are in bed with Tehran for one reason and one reason only. Greed."

"Isn't it ironic," said Shamron. "The country that brought us the last Holocaust is doing a brisk business with the country promising to bring us the next one."

All four men lapsed into an uncomfortable silence. It was Gabriel who broke it.

"The question is," he said, "is Martin Landesmann shipping sensitive material to the Iranians through the back door? If that's the case, we need to know two things. What exactly is he selling them? And how is it getting there?"

"And how do you propose we find out?" asked Seymour.

"By getting inside his operation."

"Good luck. Martin runs a very tight ship."

"Not as tight as you might think." Gabriel laid a surveillance photograph on the table. "I assume you recognize her?"

"Who wouldn't?" Seymour tapped the photo with his forefinger. "But where did you take this?"

"Outside Martin's apartment in Paris. She spent the night with him."

"You're sure?"

"Would you like to see more photos?"

"God, no!" Seymour said. "I've never cared for operations involving matters of the heart. They can be extremely messy."

"Life is messy, Graham. That's what keeps people like you and me in business."

"Perhaps. But if this recruitment of yours isn't handled carefully, I won't be in this business for long." Seymour looked down at the photo and shook his head slowly. "Why couldn't Martin fall for a waitress like every other cad?"

"He has excellent taste."

"I'd withhold judgment on that until you meet her. She has something of a reputation. It's quite possible she'll turn you down." Seymour paused, then added, "And, of course, there's another possibility."

"What's that?"

"She could be in love with him."

"She won't be when I'm finished."

"Don't be so sure. Women have a way of looking past the faults of the men they love."

"Yes," Gabriel said. "I've heard that somewhere before."

46

THAMES HOUSE, LONDON

Operation Masterpiece became a joint American-British-Israeli undertaking at 11:45 the following morning, when Graham Seymour emerged from No. 10 Downing Street with the last of the required ministerial authorizations tucked safely inside his secure briefcase. The speed with which the agreement was concluded was a testament to Seymour's current standing in Whitehall. It was also, Seymour would later admit, a rather astute display of good old-fashioned realpolitik. If Martin Landesmann were to go down, the mandarins reckoned, chances were good a great deal of British money would go down with him. In their calculation, it was better to be a party to Gabriel's operation than a spectator. Otherwise, there might be nothing left of Martin's financial carcass but bleached bones and a bit of loose change.

For the moment, the Americans were content to play the role of confidant and trusted adviser. Indeed, within hours of the interservice gathering at Thames House, Adrian Carter was Langley-bound aboard his Gulfstream V executive jet. Gabriel Allon had no airplane of his own, nor did he have any intention of leaving his operation solely in the hands of even a trusted friend like Graham Seymour. Gabriel had found the target and Gabriel intended to personally close the deal. This presented MI5's lawyers with a bit of a problem. Yes, they declared after much deliberation, it was permissible for an officer of a foreign intelligence service to take part in such a discussion. But only after said officer had been told, in no uncertain terms, the legal facts of life.

And so shortly after two that afternoon, Gabriel was once more seated at the preposterous table in the ninth-floor conference room, this time confronted by what appeared to be the entire legal department of MI5. After a brief review of Gabriel's past actions on British soil—their catalogue was remarkably complete—the lawyers laid down the rules of engagement for Masterpiece. Given the sensitive nature of the target's work, the recruitment would have to be handled with extreme care. There would be no coercion of any kind, nor a whiff of anything that smelled remotely of blackmail. Any Israeli surveillance of the subject on British soil was to cease forthwith. And any future surveillance of the subject on British soil, if approved, would be carried out only by MI5. "Now sign this," said one of the lawyers, thrusting an impressive-looking document into Gabriel's hand, along with an impressive-looking gold pen. "And God help you if you violate a word of it."

Gabriel had no such intentions—at least none at the time—so he scribbled something illegible on the line indicated and retreated to the anteroom. Waiting there was Nigel Whitcombe, a young

MI5 field officer who had cut his operational teeth working with Gabriel against Ivan Kharkov. Whitcombe's pious appearance concealed a mind as devious as any career criminal's.

"I'm surprised you're still in one piece," he said.

"They managed to do it without leaving any cuts or bruises."

"They're good at that." Whitcombe tossed aside a two-week-old copy of *The Economist* and stood. "Let's head downstairs. Wouldn't want to miss the opening act."

They rode a lift to the lowest level of the building and followed a harshly lit corridor to a secure door marked OPS CENTER. Whitcombe punched the code into the keypad and led Gabriel inside. At the front of the room was a wall of large video monitors, watched over by a select group of senior operations officers. The chair marked SEYMOUR was empty—hardly surprising, since the man who usually occupied it was at that moment preparing to make his much-anticipated return to the field. Whitcombe tapped Gabriel's arm and pointed to a CCTV image at the center of the video wall.

"Here comes your girl."

Gabriel glanced up in time to see a rain-spattered sedan passing through a security gate outside a grim-looking modern office building. At the bottom left of the image was the location of the camera that had captured it: Wood Lane, Hammersmith. Ten minutes later, Nigel Whitcombe pointed to a new image on the video wall, a direct feed of the British Broadcasting Corporation. One of the technicians turned up the audio in time to hear the news presenter read the introduction.

"There were new allegations today . . ."

Whitcombe looked at Gabriel and smiled. "Something tells me this is going to be an interesting evening."

IT WAS fitting commentary on the deplorable state of print journalism that Zoe Reed, regarded as one of the brightest stars of the British press, spent the final hours before her recruitment bathed in the flattering glow of television lights. Ironically, her appearances that evening would prove to be a major embarrassment to Downing Street, for they involved allegations that yet another Labor MP had been caught up in the Empire Aerospace bribery scandal. The BBC got first crack at her, followed by Sky News, CNBC, and finally CNN International.

It was upon Zoe's departure from CNN's studios, located at 16 Great Marlborough Street, that she had the first inkling her evening might not go as planned. It was brought about by the sudden disappearance of the car and driver retained by the *Financial Journal* to ferry her from appearance to appearance. As she was reaching for her mobile, a middle-aged man in a mackintosh coat approached and informed her that, due to a scheduling problem, she had been assigned a new car, a gleaming Jaguar limousine parked on the opposite side of the street. Anxious to return home after a long day, she hurried across through the rain and climbed into the back without hesitation. At which point she realized she was not alone. Seated next to her, a mobile phone pressed to his ear, was a well-dressed man with even features and a full head of pewter-colored hair. He lowered the phone and looked at Zoe as if he had been expecting her.

"Good evening, Ms. Reed. My name is Graham Seymour. I work for the Security Service, and through no fault of my own I've been promoted to a senior position, which you can verify by speaking to the person at the other end of this call." He handed her the mobile. "It's my director-general. I trust you'll remember her voice, since you interviewed her just last month. You were a bit hard on her in my opinion, but your article made for good reading."

"Is that why I'm here?"

"Of course not, Ms. Reed. You're here because we have a serious problem—a problem involving the security of the country and the entire civilized world—and we need your help."

Zoe lifted the phone cautiously to her ear. "Good evening, Zoe, my dear," she heard a familiar matronly voice say. "Rest assured you are in very good hands with Graham. And do accept my apology for disturbing your evening, but I'm afraid there was no other way."

IN THE operations room at Thames House, there was a communal sigh of relief as they watched the Jaguar slip away from the curb. "Now the fun begins," said Nigel Whitcombe. "We'd better get moving or we'll be late for the second act."

47

HIGHGATE, LONDON

The safe house stood at the end of a hushed cul-de-sac in Highgate, three stories of sturdy Victorian red brick with chimneys at each end of its roof. Gabriel and Nigel Whitcombe arrived first and were seated before a panel of video monitors in the upstairs study when Zoe Reed came through the front entrance. A pair of docile-looking female officers immediately took possession of her raincoat, briefcase, and mobile phone; then Graham Seymour ushered her into the drawing room. It had the comfortable, musty air of a private London club. There was even a dreadful print of a country hunt scene above the fireplace. Zoe examined it with a slightly bemused expression, then, at Seymour's invitation, sat in a leather wing chair.

Seymour walked over to the sideboard, which had been laid with an array of food and drinks, and drew two cups of coffee from the pump-action thermos. The care with which he performed this task was an accurate reflection of his mood. Zoe Reed was no run-of-the-mill target for recruitment. Yes, she had been left vulnerable by her relationship with Martin Landesmann, but Seymour knew he could not be seen to exploit the affair in any way. To do so, he reckoned, would not only place his own career at risk but spoil any chance of obtaining what they needed most. Like all veterans, Seymour knew that successful recruitments, much like successful interrogations, were usually the result of playing to the dominant aspects of the target's personality. And Graham Seymour knew two critical things about Zoe Reed. He knew she despised corruption in all its forms and he knew that she was not afraid of powerful men. He also suspected she was not the sort of woman who would react well when told she had been deceived. But then few women did.

It was into this minefield of human emotion that Graham Seymour waded now, a cup of hot coffee balanced in each hand. He gave one to Zoe, then, almost as an afterthought, instructed her to sign the document lying on the table in front of her.

"What is it?"

"The Official Secrets Act." Seymour's tone was repentant. "I'm afraid you'll need to sign it before this conversation can continue. You see, Ms. Reed, the information I'm about to share with you can't be written about in the pages of the *Journal*. In fact, once you sign—"

"I'll be forbidden from discussing it even with members of my own family." She fixed him with a mocking stare. "I know all about the Official Secrets Act, Mr. Seymour. Who do you think you're dealing with?"

"I'm dealing with one of Britain's most accomplished and respected journalists, which is why we've gone to such lengths to keep this conversation private. Now, if you would please sign, Ms. Reed."

"It's not worth the paper it's printed on." Greeted by silence, Zoe gave an exasperated sigh and signed the document. "There," she said, pushing the paper and pen toward Seymour. "Now, why don't you tell me exactly why I'm here."

"We need your help, Ms. Reed. Nothing more."

Seymour had composed the words carefully that afternoon. They were a call to colors—an appeal to patriotism without uttering so unfashionable a word—and they elicited the precise response he had been hoping for.

"Help? If you needed my help, why didn't you just call me on the telephone and ask? Why the spy games?"

"We couldn't contact you openly, Ms. Reed. You see, it's quite possible someone is watching you and listening to your phones."

"Who on earth would be watching me?"

"Martin Landesmann."

Seymour had tried to drop the name as casually as possible. Even so, its impact was instantly visible on Zoe's face. Her cheeks flushed slightly, then quickly regained their normal complexion. And though she did not realize it, Zoe Reed had just answered two of Gabriel's most pressing questions. She was embarrassed by her relationship with Martin Landesmann. And she had the ability to handle pressure.

"Is this some kind of a joke?" she asked, her tone even.

"I'm the deputy director of MI5, Ms. Reed. I don't have time for much of anything, let alone jokes. You should know from the outset that Martin Landesmann is the target of an investigation being conducted by the United Kingdom and two of our allies. You should also be assured that you are not a target in any way."

"What a relief," she said. "So why am I here?"

Seymour advanced cautiously and according to his script. "It's come to our attention that you and Mr. Landesmann have a close relationship. We would like to borrow your access to Mr. Landesmann to assist us in our investigation."

"I interviewed Martin Landesmann once. I hardly think that falls into the category of—"

Seymour raised his hand, interrupting her. He had been prepared for this. In fact, he had expected nothing less. But the last thing he wanted was to place Zoe in a position where she felt compelled to lie.

"Obviously, this is not a court of law, Ms. Reed. You are under no legal obligation to talk to us, and I'm certainly not here to pass judgment on anyone. Heaven knows, we've all made mistakes, myself included. But having said that, we need to be honest with each other. And I'm afraid we don't have much time."

Zoe appeared to give his words careful deliberation. "Why don't you go first, Mr. Seymour? Be honest with me."

She was testing him—Seymour could see that. He seized the opportunity without hesitation, though his tone remained one of clinical detachment.

"We know that approximately eighteen months ago you obtained an exclusive interview with Mr. Landesmann, the first and only such interview he has ever granted. We know that you are now romantically involved with him. We also know that you spend time together on a regular basis, most recently at his apartment on the Île Saint-Louis in Paris." Seymour paused. "But none of that is important."

This time Zoe made no attempt to deny the facts. Instead, she displayed a flash of her famous temper.

"Not important?" she snapped. "How long have you been following me?"

"We've never followed you."

"So much for honesty."

"I am being honest, Ms. Reed. We found out about you by accident. Martin Landesmann was under surveillance when you visited his apartment. Unfortunately, you were swept up in the wash."

"Is that a legal term?"

"It is what it is, Ms. Reed."

Zoe dispensed with denials and resorted to righteous indignation, the trusted friend of journalists the world over. "Even if this came into your possession in the manner you claim, you had no right to act upon it or even handle it."

"In point of fact, we did. I can show you the Home Secretary's signature if you like. But that said, we are not interested in your personal life. We asked you here because we have some sensitive information—information we will share with you if you help us."

Seymour's offer of classified intelligence did nothing to mollify Zoe's anger. "Actually," she said pointedly, "I think it's time I had a word with my barrister."

"That's not necessary, Ms. Reed."

"How about my publisher?"

"Latham? I doubt they would react well to being dragged into this."

"Really? And how do you think the British public would react to an exposé on how MI5 is spying on reporters?"

After years of being hounded by the press, Seymour was tempted to point out that the British public was more likely to enjoy reading about her affair with Martin Landesmann than yet another dreary scandal involving MI5. Instead, he lifted his gaze reflectively toward the ceiling and allowed the anger of the exchange to dissipate. In the quiet of the upstairs study, the two men seated before the video monitors had conflicting reactions to the verbal sparring. Nigel Whitcombe feared Zoe was a lost cause, but Gabriel saw her defiance as a positive sign. As Ari Shamron always said, a recruit who agreed too quickly was a recruit who couldn't be trusted.

"Unfortunately," Seymour resumed, "Martin Landesmann is not the man you think he is. That shiny image is nothing but a carefully constructed cover. And you're not the first to be fooled. He's involved in money laundering, tax evasion, corporate espionage, and much worse." Seymour gave Zoe a moment to absorb his words. "Martin Landesmann is dangerous, Ms. Reed. *Extremely* dangerous. And, present company excepted, he doesn't care for reporters—not because of some false modesty, but because he doesn't like people digging into his affairs. One of your fellow journalists discovered that not long ago when he made the mistake of asking Martin the wrong question. That man is now dead."

"Martin Landesmann? A murderer? Are you completely mad? Martin Landesmann is one of the most respected and admired businessmen in the world. My God, he's practically—"

"A saint?" Seymour shook his head. "I read all about Saint Martin's good works in your article. But if I were you, I'd hold off on Martin's canonization until you hear all the evidence. This may be hard to accept at the moment, but he's deceived you. I'm offering you a chance to hear the truth."

Zoe appeared to wrestle for a moment over the word truth. Gazing at her face in the video monitors, Gabriel thought he detected the first signs of doubt in her eyes.

"You're not offering me anything," she shot back. "You're trying to blackmail me. Do you not see anything remotely unethical about that?"

"I've spent my entire professional life working for the Security Service, Ms. Reed. I'm conditioned to deal not in black-and-white but shades of gray. I see the world not as I would like it to be but as it is. And, for the record, we are not blackmailing you or pressuring you in any way. Quite simply, you have a choice."

"What sort of choice?"

"Option one, you can agree to help us. Your work will be extremely limited in scope and short in duration. No one will ever know a thing—unless you choose to violate the Official Secrets Act, which, obviously, we strongly discourage."

"And the second option?"

"I'll take you home, and we'll pretend this never happened."

She appeared incredulous. "And what happens to all the dirt you and your *allies* have accumulated? I tell you what will happen to it. It will find its way into a nice little file that will remain within easy reach of powerful fingers. And if I ever step out of line, or do anything to irritate Her Majesty's Government, the contents of that file will be used against me."

"If that were the case, Ms. Reed, we would have used it to prevent you from going to print with the Empire Aerospace scandal. But that's not the way it works in the real world, only in bad television dramas. The Security Service exists to protect the British people, not oppress them. We aren't bloody Russians, for

God's sake. And you have my word that the material you refer to will bc destroyed the moment you leave here."

She hesitated. "And if I stay?"

"You will be told an extremely compelling story by a very interesting man." Seymour leaned forward in his chair, elbows resting on his knees, fingers intertwined. "You have a reputation as a consummate professional, Ms. Reed. I'm counting on that reputation to help us get past any uncomfortable feelings this conversation might have provoked. Everything you think you know about Martin Landesmann is a lie. This is a chance for you to bring down a corrupt and dangerous businessman from the inside. It's also an opportunity for you to help make us all a bit safer."

In the upstairs study, Nigel Whitcombe and Gabriel stared at the screens, awaiting her reply. Whitcombe would later say he felt they were doomed. But not Gabriel. He saw in Zoe a kindred spirit, a woman cursed with an exaggerated sense of right and wrong. Whatever she had once felt for Saint Martin was now dissolving under the weight of Seymour's words. Gabriel could see it in the expression on her telegenic face. And he could hear it in the decisive tone of her voice when she looked Graham Seymour directly in the eyes and asked, "And this very interesting man? Who is he?"

"He's connected to a foreign intelligence service. The fact that he is willing to meet with someone in your profession is evidence of how seriously we all take this matter. I should point out in advance that it is quite possible you may recognize him. But under no circumstances are you ever to write about him or the things that he's about to tell you. And I should add that there's no point to asking him any questions about himself. He won't answer them. Ever."

"You still haven't told me what it is you want me to do."

"I'll leave that to him. Shall I bring him in, Ms. Reed? Or shall I take you home?"

48

HIGHGATE, LONDON

Gabriel slipped silently into the room. At first, Zoe seemed unaware of his presence. Then her head turned slowly, and she studied him for a moment with an obvious curiosity, one half of her face illuminated by lamplight, the other concealed by shadow. Her pose was so motionless that for an instant Gabriel imagined he was gazing upon a portrait. Then she rose to her feet and extended a hand. "I'm Zoe," she said. "Who are you?"

Gabriel shot a glance at Graham Seymour before accepting the outstretched hand. "I'm a friend, Zoe. I'm also a great admirer of your work."

"And you're evading my question."

Seymour was about to intervene, but Gabriel stilled him with a small shake of his head. "I'm afraid that evading questions is an affliction common to men like Graham and me. We demand truthfulness in others while concealing ourselves behind a cloak of lies."

"Is it your intention to lie to me tonight?"

"No, Zoe. If you are prepared to listen to what I have to say, then you will be told only the truth."

"I'll listen. But no commitments beyond that."

"Do you have a problem with commitment, Zoe?"

"No," she said, holding his gaze. "Do you?"

"Actually, some people tell me I'm too committed."

"Committed to what?"

"I care about some of the same things you do, Zoe. I don't like powerful men who prey on the weak. I don't like men who take things that don't belong to them. And I certainly don't like men who do business with regimes that speak openly about wiping my country from the face of the earth."

She looked at Seymour, then at Gabriel again.

"You're obviously referring to Iran."

"I am."

"Which means you're Israeli."

"I'm afraid so."

"And the other country involved in this operation?"

"That would be the United States of America."

"Lovely." She sat down again and scrutinized him for a moment without speaking.

"Is there something you wish to ask me, Zoe?"

"Your name."

"I suspect you already know it."

She hesitated, her dark eyes flickering over his face, then said, "You're Gabriel Allon, the one who rescued the American ambassador's daughter outside Westminster Abbey."

"If memory serves, the two men who rescued Elizabeth Halton were officers of the SO19 division of the Metropolitan Police."

"That was the story put out to cover up your role in the operation. The kidnappers demanded that you deliver the ransom money. They'd planned to kill you and Elizabeth Halton together. It was never determined exactly how you were able to escape. There were rumors you tortured the cell leader to death in a field north of London."

"You really mustn't believe everything you read in the papers, Zoe."

"Isn't *that* the truth." Her eyes narrowed. "So are the rumors correct, Mr. Allon? Did you really torture that terrorist in order to save Elizabeth Halton's life?"

"And what if the answer was yes?"

"As an orthodox left-wing journalist, I would be predictably appalled."

"And if you were Elizabeth Halton?"

"Then I suppose I would hope the bastard suffered a great deal before you put him out of his misery." She scrutinized him carefully. "So are you going to tell me what happened in that field?"

"What field?"

Zoe frowned. "So you get to know all my darkest secrets and I get to know nothing about you."

"I don't know *all* your secrets."

"Really?" Her tone was sardonic. "What other terrible things would you like to know about me?"

"For the moment, I don't want to know anything at all. I just want you to listen to a story. It's a story about a missing masterpiece by Rembrandt, a fortune in looted Holocaust assets, an Argentine reporter named Rafael Bloch, and a company called Keppler Werk GmbH of Magdeburg, Germany." Gabriel paused, then added, "A company secretly owned by Martin Landesmann."

"Sounds like something that could sell a few newspapers." She glanced at Graham Seymour. "Am I to assume this is all covered by the Official Secrets Act as well?"

Seymour nodded.

"What a pity."

Zoe looked at Gabriel and asked him to tell her the rest of it.

ZOE WAS moved by the story of Lena Herzfeld, fascinated by the torment of Peter Voss, and heartbroken by the deaths of Rafael Bloch and Alfonso Ramirez. But it was the long list of Martin Landesmann's many sins that horrified her the most. Gabriel could see that the skepticism Zoe displayed earlier in the evening had now given way to anger—an anger that seemed to grow more intense with each new revelation he laid on the table.

"Are you saying Martin Landesmann is selling critical equipment to the Iranian nuclear program?"

"That's what we suspect, Zoe."

"Suspect?"

"As you know, there are few absolutes in intelligence work, but here's what we've discovered. We know Martin is selling high-grade industrial equipment to Iran through its state-sponsored nuclear-smuggling network. We know he's making a tremendous amount of money doing it. And we know he's going to a great deal of trouble to keep it a secret. At a time when the Iranians are moving rapidly toward developing a nuclear weapons capability, we can't afford to be in the dark about anything. It's essential that we uncover exactly what Martin is selling them." He paused. "And for that we need you."

"Me? Everything I know about Martin's business is contained in an article that Mr. Seymour now says was inaccurate. What can I possibly do to help you discover what he's shipping to the Iranians?"

"More than you realize," Gabriel said. "But before we get to that, there are a few things I need to know."

"Such as?"

"How did it happen, Zoe? How did you become involved with a man like Martin Landesmann?"

She gave him a wry smile. "Perhaps social customs are different in Israel, Mr. Allon, but here in Britain there are some things that are still regarded as private—unless you're a politician or a famous footballer, of course."

"I can assure you, Zoe, I have no desire to hear any intimate details about your relationship."

"What would you like to know?"

"Let's start with something simple," he said. "How did you meet?"

Zoe made a brief show of thought. "It was two years ago, in Davos. Martin had just given his yearly address, and he'd been electrifying. I filed my story from the pressroom, then headed over to the Belvedere Hotel. It was the usual scene—movie stars and politicians rubbing shoulders with the world's richest businessmen. That's where the real action takes place in Davos, at the cocktail parties and in the bars of the swankiest hotels."

"And Martin was there?"

She nodded. "He and his entourage were having drinks in the corner, protected by a wall of bodyguards. I ordered a glass of wine and immediately found myself in a horrendously boring conversation with a finance minister from Africa about debt relief. After ten minutes, I was ready to slit my wrists. Then I felt a tap on my shoulder. It was a blond chap, dark suit, buzz cut, German accent. Said his name was Jonas Brunner. Said he worked for Mr. Landesmann. Said Mr. Landesmann was wondering whether I might join him for a drink. I accepted, of course, and a few seconds later I was seated next to the man himself."

"And what did the man want?"

"I'd been badgering him for months for an interview. He told me he wanted to meet the world's most persistent woman, or so he said at the time."

"Why would any businessman in his right mind want to give you an interview?"

"It wasn't going to be that kind of piece. I wanted to do something different from my usual scorched-earth investigations. I wanted to write about a wealthy businessman who was actually doing something decent with his money. I told Martin I wanted my readers to meet the man behind the curtain."

"But your conversation that night was off the record?"

"Completely."

"What did you talk about?"

"Remarkably, *me*. Martin wanted to know about my work. My family. My hobbies. Anything but himself."

"And you were impressed?"

"Dazzled, actually. It's hard not to be. Martin Landesmann is incredibly handsome and wealthy beyond belief. And not many of the men I meet ever want to talk about anything but themselves."

"So you were attracted to him?"

"At the time, I was intrigued. And remember, I was after an interview."

"And Martin?"

She gave a faint smile. "As the evening wore on, he became quite flirtatious—in an understated, subliminal *Martin* sort of way," she added. "He finally asked whether I would have dinner with him in the privacy of his suite. He said it would give us a chance to get to know each other better. When I told him that I didn't think it was appropriate, he seemed quite shocked. Martin isn't used to people telling him no."

"And the interview?"

"I thought I'd lost any chance of getting it. But the opposite turned out to be true. Scott Fitzgerald was right about the rich, Mr. Allon. They are different from you and me. They want everything. And if they can't have something, they want it more."

"And Martin wanted you?"

"So it seemed."

"How did he pursue you?"

"Quietly and persistently. He would call every couple of days, just to chat and swap insights. British politics. Bank of England monetary policy. The budget deficit in America." She paused, then added, "Very sexy stuff."

"Nothing personal?"

"Not then," she said. "After about a month, he finally called me late one night and said a single word: Yes. I got on the next plane to Geneva and spent three days inside Martin's bubble. Even for a jaded reporter like me, it was an intoxicating experience.

When the piece ran, it was an earthquake. It was required reading for businessmen and politicians around the world. And it cemented my reputation as one of the top financial journalists in the world."

"Did Martin like it?"

"At the time, I didn't have a clue."

"No phone calls?"

"Radio silence." She paused. "I confess I was disappointed when I didn't hear from him. I was curious to know what he thought of the article. Finally, two weeks after publication, he called again."

"What did he want?"

"He said he wanted to celebrate the fact that he was the first businessman to survive the slashing pen of Zoe Reed. He invited me to dinner. He even suggested I bring a date."

"You accepted?"

"Instantly. But I didn't bring a date. Martin and I had dinner here in London at L'Autre Pied. Afterward, I let him take me back to his hotel. And then . . ." Her voice trailed off. "Then I let him take me to bed."

"No qualms about journalistic ethics? No guilt about sleeping with a married man?"

"Of course I had qualms. In fact, I swore to myself it would never happen again."

"But it did."

"The very next afternoon."

"You began seeing him regularly after that?"

She nodded.

"Where?"

"Anywhere but London. My face is far too recognizable here.

We always met somewhere on the Continent, usually in Paris, sometimes in Geneva, and occasionally at his chalet in Gstaad."

"How do you communicate?"

"The normal way, Mr. Allon. Martin's communications are very secure."

"For good reason," Gabriel said. "Any plans to see him in the future?"

"After what you've just told me?" Zoe laughed. "Actually, I'm supposed to see him in Paris four days from now. A week after that, I'm scheduled to go to Geneva. That's actually a work trip—Martin's annual Christmas gala at Villa Elma. Each year three hundred very rich, very lucky people are allowed to spend a few hours inside Martin's inner sanctum. The price of admission is a hundred-thousand-euro contribution to his One World foundation. Even then, he has to turn away hundreds of people each year. I go for free, of course. Martin enjoys bringing me to Villa Elma." She paused, then added, "I'm not sure Monique feels the same way."

"She knows about you?"

"I've always thought she must suspect something. Martin and Monique pretend to have the perfect relationship, but in reality their marriage is a sham. They reside under the same roof but for the most part lead completely separate lives."

"Has he ever discussed the possibility of leaving her for you?"

"Surely you're not as old-fashioned as that, Mr. Allon." She frowned. "Being around Martin Landesmann is very exciting. Martin makes me happy. And when it's over . . ."

"He'll go back to his life, and you'll go back to yours?"

"Isn't that the way it always works?"

"I suppose," said Gabriel. "But it might not be so easy for you."

"Why would you say that?"

"Because you're in love with him."

Zoe's cheeks turned vermilion. "Is it that obvious?" she asked quietly.

"I'm afraid so."

"And you still want to use me?"

"Use you? No, Zoe, I have no intention of using you. But I would be honored if you would agree to join our endeavor as a full partner. I promise it will be the experience of a lifetime. And you'll see things no other British reporter has seen before."

"Perhaps now might be a good time to tell me exactly what it is you want me to do, Mr. Allon."

"I need you to see Martin Landesmann at his apartment in Paris one more time. And I need you to do me a favor while you're there."

IT WAS a few minutes after midnight when the Jaguar limousine bearing Zoe Reed and Graham Seymour eased away from the curb outside the Highgate safe house. Gabriel departed five minutes later, accompanied by Nigel Whitcombe. They headed south through the quiet streets of London, Whitcombe chattering with edgy excitement, Gabriel emitting little more than the occasional murmur of agreement. He climbed out of the car at Marble Arch and made his way on foot to an Office safe flat overlooking Hyde Park on Bayswater Road. Ari Shamron was waiting anxiously at the dining-room table, wreathed in a fog of cigarette smoke.

"Well?" he asked.

"We havc our agent in place."

"How long do we have to get her ready?"

"Three days."

Shamron smiled. "Then I suggest you get busy."

49

HIGHGATE, LONDON

It was an alarmingly short period of time, even for an intelligence service used to working under the pressure of a ticking clock. They would have just three days to turn a British investigative reporter into a professional spy. Three days to prepare her. Three days to train her in the basics of tradecraft. And three days to teach her how to perform a pair of critical procedures—one involving Martin Landesmann's secure mobile phone, a Nokia N900, the other involving his Sony VAIO Z Series notebook computer.

Their task was made even more difficult by Gabriel's decision to leave Zoe's work schedule unchanged, a step he took to avoid any disruption in her daily routine. It meant the team would have her for only a few hours each evening, and only after she had already put in an exhausting day at the office. Graham Seymour quietly voiced doubts as to whether she would be ready, as did the

Americans, who were now following the affair closely. But Gabriel held firm. Zoe had a date with Martin in Paris in three days. Break that date, and Martin might become suspicious. Send her into Martin's bed too many times with her head filled with secrets, and she might end up like Rafael Bloch.

For his classroom, Gabriel chose the familiar surroundings of the Highgate safe house, though by the time Zoe arrived for her first session it no longer bore any resemblance to a private London club. Its walls were covered with maps, photographs, and diagrams, and its rooms were occupied by a large group of Israelis who seemed more like harried graduate students than accomplished intelligence operatives. They greeted the new arrival as though they had been expecting her for a long time, then crowded around the dining-room table for a quick takeaway curry. The warmth displayed by Gabriel's team was genuine, even if the names they hid behind were not. Zoe gravitated naturally toward the tweedy, Oxbridge-educated Yossi, though she was clearly intrigued by an attractive woman with long dark hair who referred to herself as Rachel.

The enormous operational constraints forced Gabriel to dispense with normal methods of training and design a true crash course in the basics of espionage. It began immediately after dinner when Zoe was placed on a conveyor belt of sorts that whisked her from room to room, briefing to briefing. They trained her in the basics of countersurveillance and impersonal communication. They taught her how to move in public and how to conceal emotion and fear. And they even gave her a few lessons in self-defense. "She's naturally aggressive," Rimona told Gabriel, a bag of frozen peas pressed to her swollen eye. "And she has a wicked left elbow."

She was a gifted pupil, but then they had expected nothing less. By the end of the first night, the team unanimously declared her an amazingly quick study—high praise, given the quality of past recruits. Blessed with the skills of an elite reporter, she was able to store, sort, and retrieve vast amounts of information with remarkable speed. Even Dina, who carried a database of terrorism in her brain, was impressed by Zoe's power of recall. "She's used to working under a deadline," Dina said. "The harder we push, the better she reacts."

Her final stop each night was the small upstairs study. There, alone with Gabriel, she would repeatedly rehearse the procedures that were the central purpose for her recruitment. If successful, Gabriel promised, Martin's world would be an open book. One mistake, he cautioned, and she would sink the entire operation and place herself in grave danger. She was to assume that the wolf was just outside the door waiting to catch her in the ultimate act of betrayal. To defeat him would require speed and near silence. Speed came easily; silence proved far more elusive. It was finally achieved late on the second night, when a recording of the session revealed nothing audible to the human ear.

Zoe's rapid training, however, was only one of Gabriel's concerns. There were vehicles to rent, additional personnel to move into place, and a safe flat to acquire on the Right Bank of the river Seine, not far from the Hôtel de Ville. And given the high-profile involvement of the British, there were many high-profile meetings to attend. The Iran team from MI6 found its way to the planning table, as did representatives of the Foreign Office and the Ministry of Defence. Indeed, each time Gabriel entered Thames House, the crowd seemed larger. There were obvious risks to working in such close proximity to sister intelligence services—

namely, that those same services were taking careful note of every operational tendency they were able to observe. Gabriel's exposure was increased by the fact that he was living and working inside an MI5 safe house. Though Graham Seymour denied he was listening in on the preparations, Gabriel was confident that every word uttered by his team was being recorded and analyzed by MI5. But such was the price to be paid for British cooperation against Martin Landesmann. And for Zoe.

Gabriel remained faithful to the original operational accord and grudgingly allowed Graham Seymour to handle Zoe's surveillance. Over the objections of the lawyers, Seymour extended the zone of coverage to include Zoe's telephone and computer inside the offices of the *Financial Journal.* The intercepts of her calls and electronic correspondence exposed no indiscretion or second thoughts of any kind. Nor did they reveal any undisclosed contact from one Martin Landesmann, chairman of Global Vision Investments of Geneva.

On Zoe's final night at the Highgate safe house, she seemed more focused than ever. And if she was at all frightened by what lay ahead, she gave no sign of it. She resolutely stepped onto Gabriel's conveyor belt and was whisked one last time from room to room, briefing to briefing. Her night ended, as usual, in the upstairs study. Gabriel switched off the lights and listened carefully while she rehearsed for a final time.

"Done," she said. "How long did it take?"

"Two minutes, fourteen seconds."

"That's good?"

"Very good."

"Did you hear anything?"

"Not a sound."

"Are we finished?"

"Not quite." Gabriel switched on the lights and looked at her thoughtfully. "It's not too late to change your mind, Zoe. We'll find some other way of getting to him. And I promise that none of us will think any less of you."

"Yes, but I might." She was silent for a moment. "You should know something about me, Mr. Allon. Once I've made a decision, I stick to it. I never break promises, and I hate to make mistakes."

"We share that affliction."

"I thought so."

Zoe picked up the rehearsal phone. "Any last-minute advice?"

"My team has prepared you well, Zoe."

"Yes, they have." She looked up at him. "But they're not you."

Gabriel took the phone from her grasp. "Once you start, move quietly but quickly. Don't creep around like a cat burglar. Visualize your actions before you take them. And don't think about the bodyguards. We'll worry about the bodyguards. All you have to worry about is Martin. Martin is your responsibility."

"I'm not sure I can pretend to be in love with him."

"Humans are natural liars. They mislead and dissemble hundreds of times each day without even realizing it. Martin Landesmann happens to be an extraordinary liar. But with your help, we can beat him at his own game. The mind is like a basin, Zoe. It can be filled and emptied at will. When you walk into his apartment tomorrow night, we don't exist. Only Martin. You just have to be in love with him one more night."

"And after that?"

"You go back to your life and pretend none of it ever happened."

"And what if that's not possible?"

"The mind is like a basin, Zoe. Pull the plug, and the memory drains away."

With that, Gabriel walked her downstairs and helped her into the back of an MI5 Rover. As usual, Zoe immediately switched on her mobile phone to conduct a bit of work during the short drive home to Hampstead. Because the device had spent a few minutes in the capable hands of Mordecai earlier that evening, the team now knew Zoe's altitude, latitude, longitude, and the speed at which she was traveling. They were also able to hear everything she was saying to her MI5 minder and were able to monitor both ends of a call she placed to her editor in chief, Jason Turnbury. Within five minutes of the call's termination, they had downloaded her e-mail, text messages, and several months' worth of Internet activity. They also downloaded several dozen photographs, including one she snapped six months earlier of a shirtless Martin Landesmann sunning himself on the deck of his chalet in Gstaad.

The presence of the photograph on Zoe's telephone provoked a fierce debate among Gabriel's team, which they conducted in a terse form of colloquial Hebrew no MI5 listener would ever be able to translate. Yaakov, a man with a complicated personal life of his own, moved for immediate termination of the entire operation. "There's just one reason why a woman would keep a picture like that. She's still in love with him. And if you send her into his apartment tomorrow night, she'll sink us all." But it was Dina—Dina of the much-broken heart—who talked Yaakov down from his ledge. "Sometimes a woman likes to stare at a man she hates just as much as one she loves. Zoe Reed hates Martin more than she's ever hated anyone in her life. And she wants to bring him down just as much as we do."

Oddly enough, it was Zoe herself who settled the dispute an hour later, when Martin phoned from Geneva to say how much he was looking forward to seeing her in Paris. The call was brief; Zoe's performance, exemplary. After severing the connection, she immediately dialed Highgate to report the call, then settled into bed for a few hours of sleep. As she switched off her bedside lamp, they overheard a single word that left little doubt about her true feelings for Martin Landesmann.

"Bastard . . ."

The following morning when Gabriel arrived at Thames House, it seemed the whole of Whitehall was waiting in the ninth-floor conference room. After enduring an hour of rigorous questioning, he was made to swear a blood oath that, if caught on French soil, he would say nothing of British or American involvement in the affair. Seeing no papers to sign, Gabriel raised his right hand, then slipped quickly out the door. Much to his surprise, Graham Seymour insisted on driving him to St. Pancras Station.

"To what do I owe the honor?" Gabriel asked as the car pulled into Horseferry Road.

"I wanted a word in private."

"About?"

"Zoe's mobile phone." Seymour looked at Gabriel and frowned. "You signed an agreement to let us handle her surveillance and you violated it the moment our backs were turned."

"Did you really think I was going to send her into Martin's apartment without audio coverage?"

"Just make sure you shut down the feed once she's safely back on British soil. So far, we've managed to avoid shooting ourselves in the foot. I'd prefer to keep it that way."

"The best way to shoot ourselves in the foot would be to lose Zoe in Paris tomorrow night."

"But that's not going to happen, is it, Gabriel?"

"Not if we run the operation my way."

Seymour gazed out the window at the Thames. "I don't have to remind you that a good many careers are in your hands, mine included. Do whatever you need to do to get Martin's phone and computer. But make sure you bring our girl home in one piece."

"That's the plan, Graham."

"Yes," Seymour said distantly. "But you know what they say about the best laid schemes of mice and men. They sometimes go astray with disastrous results. And if there's one thing Whitehall doesn't like, it's a disaster. Especially one that occurs in France."

"Would you like to come and personally supervise?"

"As you well know, Gabriel, I'm forbidden by law from operating on foreign soil."

"How do you manage to gather any intelligence with all these rules?"

"We're not like you, Gabriel. We're British. Rules make us happy."

50

MAYFAIR, LONDON

As with nearly every other aspect of Masterpiece, choosing the location of an operational command post was the source of tense negotiation. For reasons of both design and statute, the ops center at MI5 was deemed unsuitable for a foreign venture, even one as close as Paris. MI6 made a predictable play to stage the event at Vauxhall Cross—an offer summarily rejected by Graham Seymour, who was already fighting a losing battle to keep his glamorous rival out of what he regarded as his operation. Since the Israelis had no London operations center—at least not a declared one—that left only the Americans. Running the show from the CIA's shop made sense for both political and technical reasons since American capabilities on British soil far exceeded those of the British themselves. Indeed, after Seymour's last visit to the Agency's colossal underground facility he had concluded that the Americans could run a world war from beneath

Grosvenor Square with Whitehall none the wiser. "Who allowed them to build it?" the prime minister had asked. "You did, sir," Seymour had replied.

Having settled on the venue, there was the small matter of the invitees. As Seymour feared, the list of those wishing to attend quickly grew atrociously long—so long, in fact, he felt compelled to remind his brethren it was an intelligence operation they were staging, not a West End premiere. Moreover, since the operation was likely to produce material inappropriate for broad dissemination, it had to be conducted with more than the usual sensitivity. Other agencies would eventually be briefed on the haul, Seymour declared, but under no circumstances could they be present when it was obtained. The guest list would be limited to the three principals—the three members of a secret brotherhood who did the unpleasant chores no one else was willing to do and worried about the consequences later.

Though the precise location of the CIA's London ops center was a carefully guarded secret, Graham Seymour knew with considerable certainty that it was located some forty feet beneath the southwest corner of Grosvenor Square. He had always been somewhat amused by this, since on any given day several hundred anxious visa applicants were queued overhead, including the occasional jihadi bent on attacking the American homeland. Because the facility did not officially exist, it had no official name. Those in the know, however, referred to it as the annex and nothing else. Its centerpiece was an amphitheater-like control room dominated by several large video screens capable of projecting images securely from almost anywhere on the planet. Directly adjacent was a glass-enclosed soundproof meeting room known affectionately as the fishbowl, along with a dozen gray cubicles reserved for the alphabet soup of American agencies involved in counterterrorism and intelligence collection. Even Graham Seymour, whose primary task remained counterespionage, could scarcely remember them all. The American security establishment, he thought, was much like American automobiles—large and flashy but ultimately inefficient.

It was a few minutes after six p.m. by the time Seymour finally gained admittance to the annex. Adrian Carter was seated in his usual chair on the back deck of the control room with Ari Shamron perched at his right, looking as though he were already in the throes of a full-blown nicotine fit. Seymour settled into his usual spot at Carter's left and fixed his gaze on the video screens. In the center of the display was a static CCTV image of the exterior of the *Financial Journal*, workplace of their soon-to-be agent in place, Zoe Reed.

Unlike her colleagues at the *Journal*, Zoe's day had been the subject of close scrutiny by the intelligence services of three nations. They knew that it had begun badly with a twenty-minute delay on the dreaded Northern Line tube. They knew she arrived for work at 9:45 looking deeply annoyed, that she lunched with a source at a quaint bistro near St. Paul's, and that she ducked into a Boots pharmacy on the way back to work to pick up a few personal items, which they were never able to identify. They also knew she had been forced to endure several unpleasant hours with a *Journal* lawyer because of a threatened libel suit stemming from her Empire Aerospace exposé. And that she was then dragooned into Jason Turnbury's office for yet another lecture about her expenses, which were even higher than the previous month.

Zoe finally emerged from *Journal* headquarters at 6:15, a few minutes later than Gabriel had hoped, and hailed a taxi. By no accident, one pulled to the curb immediately and ferried her at inordinate speed to St. Pancras. She navigated passport control in record time and headed to the boarding platform, where she was recognized by a lecherous City banker who proclaimed himself her biggest fan.

Zoe feared the man would be seated near her on the train but was relieved when her traveling companion turned out to be the quiet, dark-haired girl from Highgate who called herself Sally. Four other members of the team were also aboard Zoe's carriage, including an elfin figure with wispy hair she knew as Max and the tweedy Englishman who called himself David. Neither bothered to inform the ops center at Grosvenor Square that Zoe had made her train. CCTV did it for them.

"So far, so good," said Shamron, his gaze fastened on the video screens. "All we need now is our leading man."

BUT EVEN as Shamron uttered those words, the three spymasters already knew that Martin Landesmann was running alarmingly behind schedule. After starting his day with an hour-long scull across the flat waters of Lake Geneva, he boarded his private jet along with several top aides for the short hop to Vienna. There he visited the offices of a large Austrian chemical concern, emerging at three in the afternoon into a light snow. At which point, the intelligence gods decided to throw a spanner in the works. Because in the time it took Landesmann and his entourage to reach Schwechat Airport, the light snowfall had turned into a full-fledged Austrian blizzard.

For the next two hours, Saint Martin sat with monastic serenity in the VIP lounge of Vienna Aircraft Services while his entourage worked feverishly to obtain a departure slot. All available weather data pointed to a long delay or perhaps even airport closure. But by some miracle, Martin's jet received the only clearance that night and by half past five was Paris bound. In accordance with Gabriel's standing order, no photographs were snapped as Martin and his entourage deplaned at Le Bourget and filed into a waiting convoy of black S-Class Mercedes sedans. Three of the cars headed to the Hôtel de Crillon, one to the graceful cream-colored apartment house on the Île Saint-Louis.

For Gabriel Allon, standing in the window of the safe flat directly across the river Seine, the arrival of Martin Landesmann was a momentous occasion since it represented the first time he saw his quarry in the flesh. Martin emerged from the back of his car, a smart leather computer bag in one hand, and slipped unaccompanied through the entrance of the building. Martin the man of the people, thought Gabriel. Martin who was a few hours away from being an open book. Like nearly all his public appearances, it had been brief, though the impression it left was indelible. Even Gabriel could not help but feel a certain professional admiration for the completeness of Martin's cover.

Gabriel raised his night-vision binoculars to his eyes and surveyed the battlefield. Yaakov was in a Peugeot sedan parked along the river, Oded was in a Renault hatchback wedged into the narrow street at the side of Martin's building, and Mordecai was in a Ford van parked near the foot of the Pont Marie. All three would maintain a sleepless vigil for the duration of the evening, as would the three men in the black S-Class Mercedes parked outside 21 Quai de Bourbon. One was Henri Cassin, Martin's usual driver in Paris. The other two were officially licensed bodyguards employed by Zentrum Security. Just then, Gabriel heard a sharp crackle of static. Lowering his binoculars, he turned to Chiara, who was hunched over a laptop computer monitoring the live audio stream from Zoe's mobile phone.

"Is there a problem?"

Chiara shook her head. "It just sounds like the train is passing through a tunnel."

"Where is she?"

"Less than a kilometer north of the station."

Gabriel turned toward the window again and raised his binoculars. Martin was now standing at the edge of his rooftop terrace, his gaze fixed on the river, his Nokia phone pressed to his ear. A few seconds later, Gabriel heard a two-note ring emanating from Chiara's computer, followed by Zoe's voice.

"Hello, darling."

"Where are you?"

"The train's pulling into the station."

"How was the trip?"

"Not bad."

"And your day?"

"Indescribably dreadful."

"What's wrong?"

"Lawyers, darling. The bloody lawyers are what's wrong."

"Anything I can do to help?"

"I certainly hope so."

"See you in a few."

The connection went dead. Chiara looked up from the computer screen and said, "She's good."

"Yes, she is. But it's easy to lie on the telephone. Much harder when you're face-to-face."

Gabriel returned to his post at the window. Martin was talking on his mobile phone again, but this time Gabriel could not hear the conversation.

"Is Zoe off the train yet?"

"She's stepping onto the platform right now."

"Is she heading in the right direction?"

"At considerable speed."

"Wise girl. Now let's hope she makes it to her car before anyone can steal her bag."

IT HAD always been a mystery to Zoe why the London-to-Paris Eurostar, arguably the most glamorous rail link in the world, terminated in a dump like the Gare du Nord. It was an inhospitable place in the light of day, but at 10:17 on a cold winter's night it was positively appalling. Paper cups and food wrappers spilled from overflowing rubbish bins, dazed drug addicts wandered aimlessly about, and weary migrant workers dozed on their battered luggage waiting for trains to nowhere. Stepping outside into the darkness of the Place Napoléon III, Zoe was immediately set upon by no fewer than three panhandlers. Lowering her head, she slipped past without a word and climbed into a black sedan with the name REED in the window.

As the car lurched forward, Zoe felt her heart banging against the side of her rib cage. For an instant, she considered ordering the driver to take her back to the station. Then she peered out the window and saw the comforting sight of a motorcycle ridden by a single helmeted figure. Zoe recognized the shoes. They belonged to the lanky operative with blond hair and gray eyes who spoke with a Russian accent.

Zoe looked straight ahead and politely fended off the driver's attempt to engage in conversation. She didn't want to make small talk with a stranger. Not now. She had more important things on her mind. The two tasks that were the reason for her recruitment. The two tasks that would turn Martin's life into an open book. She rehearsed one final time, then closed her eyes and tried her best to forget. Gabriel had given her a series of simple exercises to perform. Tricks of memory. Tricks of the trade. Her assignment was made easier by the fact she didn't have to become someone else. She only had to turn back the hands of time a few days to the moment before she was summoned into Graham Seymour's car. She had to become Zoe before revelation. Zoe before truth. Zoe who was keeping a secret from her colleagues at the *Journal*. Zoe who was risking her reputation for a man known to all the world as Saint Martin.

The mind is like a basin, Zoe. It can be filled and emptied at will . . .

And so it was this version of Zoe Reed who alighted from her car and bade good night to her driver. And this Zoe Reed who punched the code into the entry keypad from memory and stepped into the elegant lift. *There is no safe house in Highgate,* she told herself. No tweedy Englishman called David. No green-eyed assassin named Gabriel Allon. At that moment, there was only Martin Landesmann. Martin who was now standing in the doorway of his apartment with a bottle of her favorite Montrachet in his hand. Martin whose lips were pressing against hers. And Martin who was telling her how much he adored her.

You just have to be in love with him one more night.

And after that?

You go back to your life and pretend none of it ever happened.

News of Zoe's arrival flashed on the screens of the ops center at 9:45 p.m. London time. In contravention of long-standing regulations, Ari Shamron immediately ignited one of his foul-smelling Turkish cigarettes. Nothing to do now but wait. God, but he hated the waiting.

51

ÎLE SAINT-LOUIS, PARIS

He was dressed like the lower half of a gray scale: slate gray cashmere pullover, charcoal gray trousers, black suede loafers. Combined with his glossy silver hair and silver spectacles, the outfit gave him an air of Jesuitical seriousness. It was Martin as he wished to see himself, thought Zoe. Martin as freethinking Euro-intellectual. Martin unbound by notions of conventionality. Martin who was anyone but the son of a Zurich banker named Walter Landesmann. Zoe realized her thoughts were straying into unguarded territory. *You know nothing about Walter Landesmann,* she reminded herself. Nothing about a woman named Lena Herzfeld, or a Nazi war criminal named Kurt Voss, or a Rembrandt portrait with a dangerous secret. At this moment, there was only Martin. Martin whom she loved. Martin who had removed the cork from the Montrachet and was now pouring the honey-colored wine carefully into two glasses.

"You seem distracted, Zoe." He handed her a glass and raised his own a fraction of an inch. "Cheers."

Zoe touched her glass to Martin's and tried to compose herself. "I'm sorry, Martin. Do forgive me. It's been a perfectly ghastly day."

Since ghastly days were not a part of Martin's repertoire, his attempt to adopt an expression of sympathy fell somewhat short. He drank more wine, then placed the glass on the edge of the long granite-topped island in the center of his glorious kitchen. It was artfully lit by a line of recessed halogen lamps, one of which shone upon Martin like a spotlight. He turned his back to Zoe and opened the refrigerator. It had been well stocked by his housekeeper that afternoon. He removed several white cardboard containers of prepared food and laid them out in a neat row along the counter. Martin, she realized, did everything neatly.

"I always thought we could talk about anything, Zoe."

"We can."

"So why won't you tell me about your day?"

"Because I have very little time with you, Martin. And the last thing I want to do is burden you with the dreary details of my work."

Martin gave her a thoughtful look—the one he always wore when taking a few prescreened questions at Davos—and began opening the lids of the containers. His hands were as pale as marble. Even now, it seemed surreal to watch him engage in so domestic a chore. Zoe realized it was all part of the illusion, like his foundation, his good deeds, and his trendy politics.

"I'm waiting," he said.

"To be bored?"

"You never bore me, Zoe." He looked up and smiled. "In fact, you never fail to surprise me."

His Nokia emitted a soft chime. He removed it from the pocket of his trousers, frowned at the caller ID, and returned it to his pocket unanswered.

"You were saying?"

"I might be sued."

"By Empire Aerospace?"

Zoe was genuinely surprised. "You read the articles?"

"I read everything you write, Zoe."

Of course you do. And then she remembered the first awkward moments of her encounter with Graham Seymour. *We couldn't contact you openly, Ms. Reed. You see, it's quite possible someone is watching you and listening to your phones . . .*

"What did you think of the articles?"

"They made for compelling reading. And if the Empire executives and British politicians are truly guilty, then they should be punished accordingly."

"You don't seem convinced."

"About their guilt?" He raised an eyebrow thoughtfully and placed a portion of haricots verts at one end of the rectangular serving platter. "Of course they're guilty, Zoe. I just don't know why everyone in London is pretending to be surprised. When one is in the business of selling arms to foreign countries, paying bribes to politicians is de rigueur."

"Perhaps," Zoe agreed, "but that doesn't make it right."

"Of course not."

"Have you ever been tempted?"

Martin placed two slices of quiche next to the green beans. "To do what?"

"To pay a bribe to secure a government contract?"

He smiled dismissively and added a few slices of stuffed chicken breast to the platter. "I think you know me well enough to answer that question yourself. We're very choosy about the companies we acquire. And we never go anywhere near defense contractors or arms makers."

No, thought Zoe. Only a textile mill in Thailand worked by slaves, a chemical complex in Vietnam that fouled every river within a hundred miles, and a Brazilian agribusiness firm that was destroying the very same rain forests Martin had sworn to defend to his dying breath. And then there was a small industrial plant in Magdeburg, Germany, that was doing a brisk but secret trade with the Iranians, champions of all the principles Martin held dear. But once again her thoughts were straying onto dangerous ground. *Avoid,* she reminded herself.

Martin placed a few slices of French ham on the platter and carried the food into the dining room, where a table had already been set. Zoe paused in the window overlooking the Seine before taking her usual seat. Martin filled her plate decorously with food and added wine to her glass. After serving himself, he asked about the basis of the threatened lawsuit.

"Malicious disregard for the truth," Zoe said. "The usual drivel."

"It's a public relations stunt?"

"Of the worst kind. I have the story nailed."

"I know the CEO of Empire quite well. If you'd like me to have a word with him, I'm sure I could make the matter—"

"Go away?"

Martin was silent.

"That might be a little awkward, Martin, but I do appreciate the thought."

"Do you have the support of management?"

"For the moment. But Jason Turnbury is already looking for the nearest foxhole."

"Jason isn't long for his job."

Zoe looked up sharply from her plate. "How on earth do you know that?"

"I know everything, Zoe. Haven't you learned that by now?"

Zoe felt her cheeks begin to burn. She gave an overly bright smile and said, "You always say that, darling. But I'm actually beginning to believe it."

"You should. You should also know your newspaper is in worse shape than you think. Jason has a lifeboat waiting for him at Latham headquarters. But I'm afraid the rest of the *Journal*'s management will have to fend for itself, along with the editorial staff."

"How much longer can we stay afloat?"

"Without a buyer or a massive infusion of cash . . . not long."

"How do you know all this?"

"Because Latham approached me last week and asked whether I'd be willing to take the *Journal* off its hands."

"You're joking." His expression made clear he wasn't. "That would make our relationship more complicated than it already is, Martin."

"Don't worry, Zoe. I said I wasn't interested. Media is a rather small portion of our overall investment picture at the moment, and I have no interest in taking on a newspaper that's bleeding to death." He held up his mobile phone. "How do you expect people to pay for something when you're giving it away for free?"

"And the *Journal*?"

"I suspect you'll get a lifeline."

"From whom?"

"Viktor Orlov."

Zoe recognized the name. Viktor Orlov was one of the original Russian oligarchs who had made billions gobbling up the valuable assets of the old Soviet state while ordinary Russians were struggling for survival. Like most of the first-generation oligarchs, Viktor had worn out his welcome in Russia. He now lived in London in one of the city's most valuable homes.

"Viktor got his British passport a few months ago," Martin said. "Now he wants a British newspaper to go with it. He thinks owning the *Journal* will grant him the social standing in London he craves most. He also wants to use it as a club to beat his old adversaries in the Kremlin. If he succeeds in getting his hands on it, your publication will never be the same."

"And if he doesn't buy us?"

"The paper could fold in short order. But remember, Zoe, you didn't hear that from me."

"I *never* hear anything from you, darling."

"I certainly hope not."

Zoe laughed in spite of herself. She was surprised at how easily she had fallen into the familiar, comfortable pattern of their relationship. She tried not to resist these feelings, just as she tried not to think about the mobile phone at Martin's elbow or the notebook computer resting on the island in the kitchen.

"How well do you know Viktor?"

"Well enough." Martin jabbed at his food. "He forced me to invite him to the fund-raiser at Villa Elma next week."

"How did he manage that?"

"By writing a million-euro check to One World. I don't care for Viktor or the way he does business, but at least you'll have a chance to rub shoulders with your new owner." He looked at her seriously. "You are still planning to come, aren't you, Zoe?"

"I suppose that depends on whether I'll be safe there."

"What are you talking about?"

"Your wife, Martin. I'm talking about Monique."

"Monique lives her life, and I live mine."

"But she might not enjoy seeing your life paraded in front of her wearing a Dior evening gown with the most scandalous neckline I've ever seen."

"You got my gift?"

"Yes, Martin, I did. And you absolutely shouldn't have."

"Of course I should have. And I expect you to be wearing it next week."

"I'm sure my date will enjoy it very much."

He looked down at his plate and casually asked who Zoe was planning to bring to the party.

"Jason was hoping to come again, but I haven't decided yet."

"Maybe you could bring someone other than one of your old lovers."

"Jason and I weren't lovers, Martin. We were a mistake."

"But he obviously still cares for you a great deal."

She gave him a playful look. "Martin Landesmann, I do believe you're jealous."

"No, Zoe, I'm not. But I don't want to be deceived, either."

Her expression turned serious. "If you're wondering whether there's another man in my life, there isn't, Martin. For better or worse, there's only you."

"You're sure about that?"

"Very sure. And if you're interested, I'd be more than willing to prove it."

"Finish your dinner, Zoe."

Zoe smiled. "I am finished."

Thirty minutes later, in the safe flat on the other side of the Seine, Gabriel sat hunched over his computer, fists to his temples, eyes closed, listening. Somewhere inside him, buried beneath a thousand lies and the scar tissue of countless wounds, there was an ordinary man who wanted desperately to lower the volume. Professionalism would not allow it. It was for her own good, he told himself. For her own protection. Sorry, Zoe. Had to be done.

To distract himself, Gabriel walked to the window, night-vision binoculars pressed to his eyes, and checked the disposition of his troops. Yaakov was in his Peugeot. Oded was in his Renault. Mordecai was in his Ford van. Mikhail and Yossi were drinking beer with a group of young toughs along the quay. Rimona and Dina were sitting astride a pair of motor scooters near the Hôtel de Ville. He gave them each a tap on the shoulder by way of encrypted radio. They replied one by one, crisp and alert, Gabriel's soldicrs of the night.

The last stop of Gabriel's battlefield tour was the entrance of the cream-colored apartment house at 21 Quai de Bourbon, where one of Martin's Zentrum bodyguards was pacing slowly in the lamplight. *I know how you feel*, thought Gabriel. The waiting can be hell.

52

ÎLE SAINT-LOUIS, PARIS

Moonlight shone through the uncurtained window and cast a rhombus of pale blue light across the tangled satin sheets of Martin Landesmann's enormous bed. Zoe lay very still, listening to the wet hiss of the early-morning traffic moving along the Seine. Somewhere two drunken lovers were having a noisy quarrel. Martin's breathing ceased momentarily, then resumed its normal rhythm. Zoe looked at the clock on the bedside table. It had not changed since the last time she checked it: *3:28* . . .

She looked carefully at Martin. After completing the act of love for a second time, he had retreated with marital discretion to his usual side of the bed and fallen into a satisfied slumber. His pose had not changed in nearly an hour. Bare to the hips, he was lying prone, with his legs in something akin to a running position and one hand stretched longingly toward Zoe. In sleep, his face had assumed a peculiar childlike innocence. Zoe felt compelled to look away. In the street the lovers' quarrel had ended, replaced now by male voices murmuring in German. It was nothing, she assured herself. Just the 3:30 a.m. shift change at Zentrum Security.

Don't think about the bodyguards, Gabriel had reminded her on the final night in Highgate. *We'll worry about the bodyguards. All you have to worry about is Martin. Martin is your responsibility . . .*

Martin still hadn't moved. Neither had Zoe. Only the clock.

3:32 . . .

Once you start, move quietly but quickly. Don't creep around like a cat burglar . . .

She closed her eyes and pictured the location of the four items she would need to complete her assignment. Two of the items—her mobile phone and the USB flash drive—were tucked into her handbag, which lay on the floor next to the bed. Martin's Nokia was still on the dining-room table; the Sony computer was still on the kitchen counter.

Visualize your actions before you take them. Once you get his phone and computer in a secure location, follow my instructions to the letter, and Martin will have no more secrets . . .

She reached into her bag, took hold of her phone and the flash drive, and slipped quietly from the bed. Her clothing lay scattered across the floor. Ignoring it, she padded quickly toward the door, her heart banging against her breastbone, and stepped into the hallway. Though Gabriel had advised against it, she couldn't help but take one final look at Martin. He appeared to still be sleeping soundly. She closed the door halfway and made her way silently through the apartment to the dining room. Their dishes were still on the table, as was Martin's telephone. She snatched it up and headed to the kitchen, dialing her own mobile as she moved. Gabriel answered after a single ring.

"Hang up. Count to sixty. Then go to work."

The connection went dead as Zoe entered the kitchen. In the darkness, she could just make out the faint outline of the black Sony VAIO computer at the end of the island. Martin had left the computer on standby mode. Zoe immediately shut it down and inserted the flash drive into one of the USB ports. Then she picked up the Nokia again and stared at the screen, counting silently to herself.

Twenty-five . . . twenty-six . . . twenty-seven . . . twenty-eight . . .

AFTER SEVERING his connection to Zoe, Gabriel quickly informed the rest of the team via secure radio that the operation was now hot. Only Mordecai had a task to perform at that point, and it required merely throwing the power switch on the device resting on the passenger seat of the Ford van. Essentially, the apparatus was a cell tower in a suitcase, designed to deceive Martin's phone into thinking it was on his usual network when in reality it was on the Office's. Its signal, while tightly focused on the building at 21 Quai de Bourbon, would temporarily obliterate most cellular service on the Île Saint-Louis. At that moment, any inconvenience to French telecom customers was the least of Gabriel's worries. He was standing in the window of the safe flat, gaze focused on the darkened windows of Martin Landesmann's bedroom, counting silently in his head.

Fifty-seven . . . fifty-eight . . . fifty-nine . . . sixty . . .

Now, Zoe. Now . . .

As if on cue, Zoe began punching a number into Martin's phone. It was a number she had dialed hundreds of times in the Highgate safe house. A number she knew as well as her own. After entering the last digit, she pressed the call button and lifted the phone to her ear. A single ringtone sounded, followed by several sharp beeps. Zoe looked at the display screen. A dialogue box appeared, asking whether she wished to accept an over-the-air software update. She immediately pressed YES on the touch screen. A few seconds later, another message appeared: DOWNLOAD IN PROGRESS.

Zoe placed the phone gently on the counter, then powered on the Sony notebook while holding down the F8 key. Rather than starting normally, the computer automatically took Zoe to the boot menu. She clicked on the option to enable boot logging, then instructed the computer to start up using the software contained on the flash drive. It did so without objection, and within a few seconds a box appeared on the screen, informing her that an upload was in progress. Because of its large size—every bit of data stored on Martin's hard drive—the upload would take one hour and fifteen minutes. Unfortunately, it was necessary to leave the flash drive in the USB port throughout the process, which meant Zoe would have to make a second trip to the kitchen to remove it when the task was complete.

She dimmed the brightness on the computer screen and picked up Martin's mobile phone again. The "software update" was complete. All that was required now was rebooting, a simple matter of switching the phone off and on once. She did so, then quickly checked the list of recent calls. There was no evidence of the one call Zoe had placed. In fact, according to the directory, the last call made from the phone was at 10:18, when Martin had phoned Monique in Geneva. As for the last call received, it was the one that had come through while Martin was preparing dinner. Zoe looked at the number.

Monique . . .

Zoe returned the phone to standby mode and opened the refrigerator. On the top shelf was a one-liter bottle of Volvic. She removed it, closed the door gently, and headed into the dining room, staying just long enough to deposit Martin's phone. Returning to the bedroom, she found the door slightly ajar, just as she had left it. Martin was lying motionless on the bed, the pale skin of his torso aglow in the moonlight. She padded to her side of the bed and dropped her mobile phone into her handbag. Then she slipped beneath the satin sheets and looked at Martin. His eyes opened suddenly, and his expression appeared childlike no more.

"I was beginning to get worried about you, Zoe. Where have you been?"

THERE ARE MOMENTS in even the simplest of operations when time stops. Gabriel had experienced more such moments than most professional intelligence officers. And he certainly experienced one at 3:36 a.m. in Paris while waiting for Zoe Reed, special investigative correspondent of the venerable *Financial Journal* of London, to respond to her lover, Martin Landesmann. He did not tell London about the potential problem. He did not tell his team. Instead, he stood in the window of the safe flat, binoculars to his eyes, Chiara at his side, and did what every experienced fieldhand does at a time like that. He held his breath.

The silence seemed to last an eternity. Later, when reviewing the recording, he would discover it was only three seconds. She began by complaining of a ferocious thirst, then playfully chastised Martin for hurling her clothing across the floor in his frenzy to undress her. And finally she suggested several things they might do now that they both happened to be awake at 3:36 in the morning.

Somewhere inside Gabriel was an ordinary man who wanted desperately not to eavesdrop. Professionalism would not allow it. And so he stood in the window of the safe flat with his wife at his side and listened while Zoe Reed made love one final time to a man whom Gabriel had convinced her to hate. And he listened, too, one hour and fifteen minutes later, as Zoe rose from Martin's bed to retrieve the flash drive from Martin's computer—a flash drive that had beamed the contents of Martin's hard drive to a sturdy redbrick Victorian house in Highgate.

Gabriel's partners in London would never hear the recordings from that night in Paris. They had no right. They would only know that Zoe Reed emerged from the apartment building on Île Saint-Louis at 8:15 a.m. and that she climbed in the back of a chauffeured Mercedes-Benz with the name REED in the window. The car ferried her directly to the Gare du Nord, where she was once again waylaid by several panhandlers and drug addicts as she hurried across the ticket hall toward her waiting train. A dread-locked Ukrainian with a mud-caked leather jacket proved to be the most persistent of her suitors. He finally backed down when confronted by a man with short dark hair and pockmarks on his face.

Not by coincidence, that same man was seated next to Zoe on the train. His forged New Zealand passport identified him as Leighton Smith, though his real name was Yaakov Rossman, one of four members of Gabriel's team who accompanied Zoe on her return to London. She passed most of the train ride reading the morning papers, and upon her arrival at St. Pancras was covertly returned to the custody of MI5. They drove her to work in an ersatz taxi and snapped several pictures as she disappeared through the entrance. As promised, Gabriel ordered the digital tap on Zoe's phone disconnected, and within minutes she vanished from the Office's global surveillance grid. Few members of the Masterpiece team seemed to notice. Because by then they were all listening to the voice of Martin Landesmann.

53

HIGHGATE, LONDON

To some extent, computer networks and communications devices can be shielded from outside penetration. But if the attack occurs from the inside—or by gaining access to the devices themselves—there is little the target can do to defend himself. With but a few lines of well-crafted code, a mobile phone or laptop computer can be convinced to betray its owner's most closely guarded secrets—and continue betraying them for months or even years. The machines are perfect spies. They do not require money or validation or love. Their motives are beyond question, for they have none of their own. They are reliable, dependable, and willing to work extraordinarily long hours. They do not become depressed or drink too much. They do not have spouses who berate them or children who disappoint them. They do not become lonely or frightened. They do not burn out. Obsolescence is their only weakness. More often than not, they are discarded merely because something better comes along.

The nature of the intelligence assault on Martin Landesmann, while breathtaking in scale, was routine in the world of twenty-first-century espionage. Gone were the days when the only option for eavesdropping on a target involved planting a battery-powered radio transmitter in his home or office. Now the targets willingly carried transmitters with them in the form of their own cellular phones and other mobile devices. Intelligence operatives didn't have to recharge weakening batteries because the targets did that themselves. Nor was it necessary for operatives to spend endless hours sitting in dreary listening posts since material acquired from a wi-fi device could be fed via the Internet to computers anywhere in the world.

In the case of Operation Masterpiece, those computers were tucked away in a redbrick Victorian house located at the end of a hushed cul-de-sac in the Highgate section of London. After working around the clock preparing for the operation in Paris, Gabriel and his team now worked around the clock sorting and analyzing the immense haul. In the blink of an eye, the life of one of the world's most reclusive businessmen was now an open book. Indeed, as Uzi Navot would describe it to the prime minister during their weekly breakfast meeting, "Anywhere Martin goes, we go with him."

They listened to his phone calls, they read his e-mail, they peered quietly over his shoulder while he surfed the Web. They negotiated deals with him, ate lunch with him, and went to cocktail receptions tucked in his breast pocket. They slept with him, bathed with him, exercised with him, and overheard a quarrel with Monique over his frequent trips to Paris. They accompanied him on a flying visit to Stockholm and were forced to endure an excruciating evening of Wagner with him. They knew his exact position on the planet at all times, and if he happened to be in motion, they knew the speed he was traveling. They also discovered that Saint Martin liked to spend a great deal of time alone sequestered in his office at Villa Elma, an expansive room located on the southeast corner of the mansion overlooking Lake Geneva, at precisely 1,238 feet above sea level.

There can be an obvious drawback to receiving such a vast amount of intelligence—the possibility that a vital piece of the puzzle might be swamped by a tsunami of useless information. Gabriel sought to avoid this pitfall by making certain that at least half the team remained focused on the true prize of the Paris operation, Martin's laptop. The haul was not limited to the material contained on the computer the night of the operation in Paris. Indeed, through a clever feat of engineering, the computer automatically sent an update each time data was added or subtracted. It meant that whenever Martin opened a document, Gabriel's team opened it, too. They even instructed the computer to transmit video from its built-in camera in thirty-minute loops. Most of the video was silent and black. But for an hour or so each day, whenever Martin was at task, he seemed to be peering directly into the Highgate safe house, watching Gabriel's team as it rummaged through the secrets of his life.

The contents of Martin's computer were encrypted, but the barriers quickly crumbled under the assault led by the two MIT-educated geniuses from Technical. Once they had penetrated the outer walls, the computer quickly belched forth thousands of documents that laid bare the inner workings of the Landesmann empire. Though the information was potentially worth millions to Martin's many competitors, it had little value to Gabriel, for it provided no additional intelligence on GVI's links to Keppler Werk GmbH or precisely what Keppler was secretly selling to the Iranians. Gabriel had learned from experience not to focus on what was visible in a computer's memory but on what was no longer there—the temporary files that floated like ghosts across the hard drive, the discarded documents that had lived there briefly before being tossed into the trash. Files are never truly deleted from a computer. Like radioactive waste, they can live on forever. Gabriel directed the technicians to focus their efforts on Martin's recycle bin, especially on a ghost folder lurking there that had been impervious to all attempts at retrieval.

Gabriel's team did not toil in isolation. Indeed, because Masterpiece was an international endeavor, dissemination of its hard-earned product was international as well. The Americans received a feed over a secure link from Highgate to Grosvenor Square, while the British, after much internal bickering, decided that MI6 was the logical first recipient since Iran was its responsibility. Graham Seymour managed to retain overall operational ascendancy, however, and Thames House remained the nightly meeting point for the principals. The atmosphere remained largely collegial, despite the fact each side brought to the table different assumptions about Iranian intentions, different styles of analysis, and different national priorities. For the Americans and the British, a nuclear Iran represented a regional challenge; for Israel, an existential threat. Gabriel didn't dwell on such issues at the conference table. But then he didn't need to.

His final stop at Thames House each night was the windowless cell of Nigel Whitcombe, who been handed control of the Zoe Reed watch. Despite the potential hazards involved in surveilling a British journalist, Whitcombe accepted the assignment without reservation. Like nearly everyone involved in Masterpiece, he had developed a bit of a schoolboy crush on Zoe and relished the opportunity to admire her for a few more days, even if from afar. The daily watch reports revealed no transgressions on her part and no evidence that she had broken discipline in any way. Each time Martin made contact with her, she duly reported it. She even forwarded to MI5 a brief message he had left on her home machine.

"What did it say?" asked Gabriel.

"The usual. I so enjoyed our time together, *darling.* Can't wait to see you in Geneva next week, *darling.* Something about a dress. I didn't understand that part." Whitcombe straightened the papers on his little headmasterly desk. "At some point, we're going to decide whether she has to attend Martin's little soirée or whether she should come down with a sudden case of swine flu instead."

"I'm aware of that, Nigel."

"May I offer an opinion?"

"If you must."

"Swine flu."

"And what if her absence makes Martin suspicious?"

"Better a suspicious Martin Landesmann than a dead British investigative reporter. That might not be good for my career."

It was nearly midnight by the time Gabriel returned to the Highgate safe house. He found his team hard at work and an intriguing message from King Saul Boulevard waiting in his encrypted in-box. It seemed an old acquaintance from Paris wanted a word. Reading the message a second time, Gabriel ordered himself to be calm. Yes, it was *possible* this was what they were looking for, but it was probably nothing. A mistake, he thought. A waste of time when he had none to spare. But it was also possible he had just been granted the first piece of good fortune since Julian Isherwood had appeared on the cliffs of Cornwall to ask him to find a missing portrait by Rembrandt. Someone would have to check it out. But given the demands of Operation Masterpiece, it would have to be someone other than Gabriel. All of which explains why Eli Lavon, surveillance artist, archaeologist, and tracker of missing Holocaust assets, returned to Paris early the next morning. And why, shortly after one that afternoon, he was walking along the rue des Rosiers, twenty paces behind a memory militant named Hannah Weinberg.

54

THE MARAIS, PARIS

She rounded the corner into rue Pavée and disappeared into the apartment house at No. 24. Lavon walked the length of the street twice, searching for evidence of surveillance, before presenting himself at the doorway. The directory identified the resident of apartment 4B as MME. BERTRAND. Lavon pressed the call button and peered benignly into the security camera.

"Oui?"

"I'm here to see Madame Weinberg, please."

A silence, then, "Who are you, monsieur?"

"My name is Eli Lavon. I'm—"

"I know who you are, Monsieur Lavon. Just a moment."

The entry buzzer moaned. Lavon crossed the damp interior courtyard, entered the foyer, and headed up the stairs. Waiting on the fourth-floor landing, arms folded, was Hannah Weinberg.

She admitted Lavon into her apartment and quietly closed the door. Then she smiled and formally extended her hand.

"It is an honor to meet you, Monsieur Lavon. As you might expect, you have many admirers at the Weinberg Center."

"The honor is mine," Lavon said humbly. "I've been watching you from a distance. Your center is doing marvelous work here in Paris. Under increasingly difficult conditions, I might add."

"We do what we can, but I'm afraid it's probably not enough." A sadness crept into her gaze. "I'm so sorry about what happened in Vienna, Monsieur Lavon. The bombing affected all of us very deeply."

"These are emotional issues," Lavon said.

"On both sides." She managed a smile. "I was just making some coffee."

"I'd love some."

She led Lavon into the sitting room and disappeared into the kitchen. Lavon looked around at the stately old furnishings. He had worked on the operation that had drawn Hannah Weinberg into the gravitational pull of the Office and knew her family history well. He also knew that in a room located at the end of the hall hung a painting by Vincent van Gogh called *Marguerite Gachet at Her Dressing Table.* The blood-soaked operation involving the little-known work was one of many Gabriel Allon productions Lavon had tried hard to forget. He tamped down the memory now as Hannah Weinberg returned carrying two cups of *café au lait.* She handed one to Lavon and sat.

"I assume this isn't a courtesy call, Monsieur Lavon."

"No, Madame Weinberg."

"You're here because of the documents?"

Lavon nodded and sipped his coffee.

"I didn't realize you were connected to . . ." Her voice trailed off.

"To what?" Lavon asked.

"Israeli intelligence," she said sotto voce.

"Me? Do I really look cut out for that sort of work?"

She examined him carefully. "I suppose not."

"After the bombing in Vienna, I returned to my first love, which is archaeology. I'm on the faculty of Hebrew University in Jerusalem, but I still have many contacts in the Holocaust restitution field."

"So how did you hear about the documents?"

"When you called the embassy here in Paris, they immediately contacted a friend of mine who works at Yad Vashem. He knew I was coming to Paris on other business and asked whether I would be willing to look into it for him."

"And what sort of business brought you to Paris?"

"An academic conference."

"I see." She drank some of her coffee.

"Are the documents here, Madame Weinberg?"

She nodded.

"May I see them, please?"

She peered at him over the rim of her coffee cup as if judging the veracity of his words, then rose and entered the library. When she returned, she was holding a discolored sheath in her hand. Lavon felt his heart begin to beat a little faster.

"Is that wax paper?" he asked as casually as possible.

She nodded. "That's how it came to me."

"And the documents?"

"They're inside." She handed the sheath to Lavon and said, "Be careful. The paper is quite fragile."

Lavon lifted the covering and carefully removed three pages of brittle onionskin paper. Then he slipped on a pair of half-moon glasses, fingers trembling slightly, and read the names.

Katz, Stern, Hirsch, Greenberg, Kaplan, Cohen, Klein, Abramowitz, Stein, Rosenbaum, Herzfeld . . .

Herzfeld . . .

He stared at the name a moment longer, then lifted his eyes slowly to Hannah Weinberg.

"Where did you get this?"

"I'm afraid I'm not in a position to say."

"Why not?"

"Because I promised the person complete confidentiality."

"I'm afraid that's not a promise you should have made."

She noticed the change in Lavon's tone. "You obviously seem to know something about this document."

"I do. And I also know that many people have died because of it. Whoever gave you this is in very serious danger, Madame Weinberg. And so are you."

"I'm used to that." She regarded him silently. "Were you telling me the truth when you said a friend from Yad Vashem asked you to come here?"

Lavon hesitated. "No, Madame Weinberg, I wasn't."

"Who sent you?"

"A mutual friend." Lavon held up the list. "And he needs to know the name of the person who gave you this."

"Maurice Durand."

"And what does Monsieur Durand do for a living?"

"He owns a small shop that sells antique scientific instruments. He says he found the documents while doing some repair work on a telescope."

"Did he?" Lavon asked skeptically. "How well do you know him?"

"I've done a great deal of business with him over the years." She nodded toward a circular wooden table arrayed with several dozen antique lorgnettes. "They're something of a passion of mine."

"Where's his shop?"

"In the eighth."

"I need to see him right away."

Hannah Weinberg rose. "I'll take you."

55

RUE DE MIROMESNIL, PARIS

The Weinberg Center was located just around the corner on rue des Rosiers. Hannah and Lavon stopped there long enough to make several copies of the list and lock them away. Then, with the original tucked safely inside Lavon's leather satchel, they rode the Métro to the rue de Miromesnil and made the two-minute walk to Antiquités Scientifiques. The sign in the door read OUVERT. Lavon spent a moment admiring the window display before trying the latch. It was locked. Hannah rang the bell, and they were admitted without delay.

The man waiting to receive them was equal to Lavon in height and weight, though in every other respect was his precise opposite. Where Lavon was shoddily attired in several layers of crumpled clothing, Maurice Durand wore an elegant blue suit and a wide necktie the color of Beaujolais nouveau. And where Lavon's hair was wispy and unkempt, Durand's monkish tonsure was cropped short and combed close to the scalp. He kissed Hannah Weinberg formally on both cheeks and offered Lavon a surprisingly strong hand. As Lavon accepted it, he had the uncomfortable feeling he was being eyed by a professional. And unless Lavon was mistaken, Maurice Durand felt exactly the same way.

"You have a beautiful shop, Monsieur Durand."

"Thank you," the Frenchman replied. "I consider it my shelter against the storm."

"What storm is that, monsieur?"

"Modernity," Durand replied instantly.

Lavon gave an empathetic smile. "I'm afraid I feel the same way."

"Really? And what is your field, monsieur?"

"Archaeology."

"How fascinating," Durand said. "When I was young, I was very interested in archaeology. In fact, I considered studying it."

"Why didn't you?"

"Dirt."

Lavon raised an eyebrow.

"I'm afraid I don't like to get my hands dirty," Durand explained.

"That would be a liability."

"A rather large one, I think," Durand said. "And what is your area of expertise, monsieur?"

"Biblical archaeology. I do most of my work in Israel."

Durand's eyes widened. "The Holy Land?"

Lavon hesitated, then nodded.

"I've always wanted to see it for myself. Where are you working now?"

"The Galilee."

Durand seemed genuinely moved.

"You are a believer, Monsieur Durand?"

"Devout." He looked at Lavon carefully. "And you, monsieur?"

"At times," said Lavon.

Durand looked at Hannah Weinberg. "That shipment of lorgnettes has finally arrived. I set aside the best pieces for you. Would you like to see them now?"

"Actually, my friend has something he needs to discuss with you."

Durand's gaze returned to Lavon. It betrayed nothing but a mild curiosity, though Lavon once again had the feeling Durand was taking his measure.

"How can I help you?"

"Would it be possible to speak in private?"

"But of course."

Durand gestured toward the doorway at the back of the shop. Lavon entered the office first and heard the door close behind him. When he turned around, the expression on Maurice Durand's face was far less amiable than it had been a moment earlier.

"Now what is this all about?"

Lavon removed the wax paper sheath from the satchel. "This."

Durand's eyes didn't move from Lavon's face. "I gave that document to Madame Weinberg on the condition she keep my name out of it."

"She tried. But I convinced her to change her mind."

"You must be very persuasive."

"Actually, it wasn't hard. All I had to do was explain how many people have been killed because of these three pieces of paper."

Durand's expression remained unchanged.

"Most people would be a bit uncomfortable after hearing something like that," Lavon said.

"Perhaps I'm not easily frightened, monsieur."

Lavon returned the sheath to his satchel. "I understand you found the document inside a telescope."

"It was a piece from the late eighteenth century. Brass and wood. Dollond of London."

"That's odd," Lavon said. "Because I know for a fact that very recently it was hidden inside a painting by Rembrandt called *Portrait of a Young Woman*. I also know that the painting was stolen and that a man was killed during the robbery. But that's not why I'm here. I don't know how you got these documents, but you should know there are people looking for them who are very dangerous. And they assume these papers are still inside the painting." Lavon paused. "Do you understand what I'm trying to say, Monsieur Durand?"

"I believe I do," Durand said carefully. "But I know nothing at all about a painting by Rembrandt—or anyone else, for that matter."

"You're sure, monsieur?"

"I'm afraid so."

"But perhaps you hear things from time to time. Or perhaps you have friends in the business who hear things. Friends who might know the whereabouts of this painting."

"I don't make a habit of associating with people from the art business. They tend to look down their noses at people like me."

Lavon handed Durand a business card. "But if you do happen to hear anything about the Rembrandt—anything at all, monsieur—please call this number. I can guarantee you complete confidentiality. Rest assured recovery of the painting is our *only* concern. And do be careful. I wouldn't want anything unpleasant to happen to you."

Durand slipped the card into his pocket, obviously anxious to end the conversation. "I wish I could be of help, monsieur, but I'm afraid I can't. Unless there's something else you require, I really should be getting back to the shop."

"No, nothing. Thank you for your time."

"Not at all."

Durand opened the door. Lavon started to leave, then stopped and turned.

"Actually, Monsieur Durand, there is one more thing."

"What's that?"

"Just remember that God is watching you. Please don't disappoint Him."

"I'll keep that in mind, Monsieur Lavon."

ELI LAVON and Hannah Weinberg parted at dusk in the Place de la Concorde. Hannah took the Métro back to the Marais, while Lavon made the short walk to 3 rue Rabelais, location of the Israeli Embassy. There, by the power vested in him by Operation Masterpiece, he instructed the Office station chief to put a security detail on Hannah Weinberg and a team of watchers on Maurice Durand. Then he requisitioned a car and driver to run him out to Charles de Gaulle Airport. "And make sure the driver has a gun in his pocket," Lavon said. "Maybe someday I'll be able to explain why."

Lavon was able to secure an economy-class seat on the 8:50

Air France flight to Heathrow and by eleven that night was making his way wearily up the walkway of the Highgate safe house. Stepping inside, he was greeted by the sight of the entire team engaged in a tumultuous celebration. He looked at Gabriel and asked, "Would someone like to tell me what's going on?"

"Valves, pipes, vacuum pumps, bellows, autoclaves, feed and withdrawal systems, frequency converters, motor housings, molecular pumps, rotors, magnets."

"He's selling them centrifuges?"

"Not just centrifuges," Gabriel said. "Saint Martin Landesmann is selling the Iranians everything they need to build their uranium enrichment plants."

"And I thought I had a good day."

"What have you got?"

"Nothing much." Lavon held up the wax paper sheath. "Just Kurt Voss's list of Zurich bank accounts."

PART FOUR

UNVEILING

56

THE PLAINS, VIRGINIA

The farm lay some fifty miles to the west of Washington, at the point where the first foothills of the Blue Ridge begin to sprout from the edge of the Shenandoah Valley. Residents of The Plains, a quaint hamlet located along the John Marshall Highway, believed the owner to be a powerful Washington lawyer with a great deal of money and many important friends in government, thus the black limousines and SUVs that were frequently seen roaring through town, sometimes at the oddest hours.

On a bitterly cold morning in mid-December, a dozen such vehicles were spotted in The Plains, far more than usual. All followed the same route—a left at the BP gas station and mini-mart, a right after the railroad tracks, then straight for a mile or so on County Road 601. Because it was a Friday and close to the Christmas holidays, it was assumed in The Plains that the farm was playing host to a weekend Washington retreat—the sort of gathering where lobbyists and politicians gather to swap money and favors, along with tips on how to improve one's golf swing and love life. As it turned out, the rumors were no accident. They had been planted by a division of the Central Intelligence Agency, which owned and operated the farm through a front company.

The security gate bore a handsome brass sign that read HEWITT, a name chosen at random by one of Langley's computers. Beyond it stretched a gravel road, bordered on the right by a narrow streambed and on the left by a broad pasture. Both were buried beneath more than two feet of snow, the remnants of a cataclysmic blizzard that had pummeled the region and paralyzed the federal government. Like most things these days, the storm had prompted a furious debate in Washington. Those who dismissed global warming as a hoax seized on the weather as validation of their point while prophets of climate change said it was yet more evidence of a planet in peril. The professional spies at Langley were not surprised by the discord. They knew all too well that two people could look at the same set of facts and come to radically different conclusions. Such was the nature of intelligence work. Indeed, such was the nature of life itself.

At the end of the gravel road, atop a low wooded hill, stood a two-story Virginia farmhouse with a double-decker porch and a copper roof. The circular drive had been plowed the previous night; even so, there was not enough room to accommodate the armada of sedans and SUVs. Indeed, the drive was so crammed with vehicles that the last to arrive could find no pathway to the house—a problem, since it contained the most important participants of the conference. As a result, they had no choice but to abandon their SUV and trudge the final fifty yards through the snow. Gabriel led the way, with Uzi Navot following a step behind and Shamron in the trail position, holding the arm of Rimona.

The entrance of the Israeli delegation prompted a round of cautious applause from the large group already gathered inside. The British had sent just two representatives—Graham Seymour of MI5 and Edmund Radcliff of MI6—but the Americans had shown no such restraint. Adrian Carter was there, along with Shepard Cantwell, the CIA's deputy director for intelligence, and Tom Walker, its top Iran analyst. There was also someone named Blanchard from the Office of National Intelligence and Redmond from the Defense Intelligence Agency. Representing the National Security Council was Cynthia Scarborough, and from the FBI was Steven Clark, though how the Bureau secured an invitation to the conference would forever remain one of Masterpiece's many mysteries.

They gathered around the formal dining room table, behind nameplates, towers of black briefing books, and cups of weak coffee. Adrian Carter made a few introductory remarks before switching on the PowerPoint. A map of Iran appeared on the screen with four locations clearly labeled. Carter shone the red light of a laser pointer at each in succession and read the names.

"Bushehr, Arak, Isfahan, Natanz. The key sites in the Iranian nuclear program. We all know the facilities well, but allow me to review them briefly. Bushehr is the nuclear power station built with German and Russian help. Isfahan is a conversion facility where uranium ore is turned into hexafluoride gas and uranium oxide. Arak is a heavy-water plant. And Natanz, of course, is Iran's primary uranium-enrichment facility." Carter paused, then added, "Or so it claims."

Carter lowered the laser pointer and turned to face his audience. "Our governments have long suspected those four sites are just the tip of the iceberg and that Iran is also building a chain of secret underground enrichment facilities. Now, thanks to our friends from Tel Aviv, we appear to have proof of our suspicions. And we believe Martin Landesmann, chairman of Global Vision Investments, is helping the Iranians do it."

Carter looked toward the Israeli delegation. "While it's true we've all been seeing the same intelligence on Landesmann for the past seventy-two hours, it was Rimona Stern who managed to connect the dots first. For those of you meeting her for the first time, Rimona is a former major in the Israel Defense Forces, an excellent field operative, and one of the country's most experienced intelligence analysts. You should also know that her uncle is none other than Ari Shamron. So I would advise you all to watch your step."

Shamron smiled and watched his niece intently as she rose and took Carter's place at the front of the room. Without a word, she advanced the PowerPoint presentation to the next image. Once again, it was a map of Iran. But this time, only one location was labeled.

The holy city of Qom . . .

IT WAS QOM that proved the mullahs were lying, Rimona began. Qom that shattered any last misplaced hopes the Iranian nuclear program was intended for anything other than producing weapons. Why else would they conceal a secret uranium-enrichment facility deep in a desert mountain? And why else would they refuse to disclose the facility to the International Atomic Energy Agency, nuclear watchdog of the United Nations? But there was a nagging problem with Qom, she reminded them. It was designed to house just three thousand centrifuges. And if those centrifuges were Iranian-made IR-1s, Qom could only manufacture enough highly enriched uranium to produce one bomb every two years, not enough for Iran to become a full-fledged nuclear power.

"Which should mean Qom is worthless," Rimona said. "Unless, of course, there are other Qoms, other secret enrichment facilities just like it scattered around the country. *Two* facilities with six thousand IR-1s spinning in tandem could produce enough highly enriched uranium to make a bomb each year. But what if there were *four* facilities with twelve thousand centrifuges? Or *eight* facilities with twenty-four thousand centrifuges?"

It was Tom Walker, Rimona's counterpart from the Agency, who answered. "Then Iran could produce enough enriched uranium to build an effective nuclear arsenal in a matter of months. They could throw the nuclear inspectors out of the country and go for nuclear breakout. And if the chain of secret facilities is well hidden and fortified, there would be almost nothing we could do to stop them."

"Correct," said Rimona. "But what if those centrifuges aren't wobbly, unreliable pieces of junk like the IR-1? What if they're similar to the P-2 models used by Pakistan? Or even better than the P-2? What if they're European designed and calibrated to the highest standards? What if they're manufactured under conditions where they don't end up with bothersome impurities like dust and fingerprints?"

This time it was Adrian Carter who answered. "Then we would be staring down the barrel of a nuclear Iran in a very short period of time."

"That's also correct. And I'm afraid that's exactly what's happened. While the civilized world has been talking, dithering, delaying, and wringing its hands, the Iranians have been quietly working to achieve their long-held nuclear ambitions. They've engaged in the time-honored deceptive practices of *khod'eh* and *taqiyya*. They've bluffed, deceived, and stalled their way to the doorstep of a nuclear arsenal. And Martin Landesmann has been helping them every step of the way. He's not just selling the Iranians the centrifuges. He's selling them the critical pumps, valves, and vacuums that link the centrifuges into a cascade. In short, Martin Landesmann is supplying the Islamic Republic of Iran with everything it needs to build uranium-enrichment plants."

"How?" asked Adrian Carter.

"Like this," said Rimona.

THE NEXT MAP that appeared on the screen depicted the Eurasian landmass stretching from Western Europe to the Sea of Japan. Scattered across Germany, Austria, Switzerland, and Belgium was a constellation of companies, more than a dozen industrial and technological firms, including Keppler Werk GmbH of Magdeburg. All the firms were connected by dotted lines leading to the southern Chinese city of Shenzhen, headquarters of XTE Hardware and Equipment.

"And guess who owns XTE Hardware and Equipment?" asked Rimona of no one in particular.

"Global Vision Investments," replied Adrian Carter.

"Through many fronts and subsidiaries, of course," Rimona added with a sardonic smile. "Mr. Landesmann also has a powerful partner, a Chinese private equity firm based in Shanghai that we believe is nothing more than a front company for the Ministry of State Security."

"The Chinese intelligence service," murmured Steven Clark of the FBI.

"Exactly." Rimona walked over to the map. "Landesmann's operation is much like the Iranian nuclear program it serves. It's dispersed, well concealed, and it contains redundancies and backups. Best of all, Saint Martin is completely untouchable because the entire supply chain is based on dual-use technology that's sold through cutouts. Martin is far too smart to sell the centrifuge cascades directly to the Iranians. Instead, he sells bits and pieces to XTE Hardware and Equipment. The Chinese then sell the finished product to trading companies in Dubai and Malaysia, which in turn deliver it to Iran."

"Can you tell how long it has been going on?" asked Cynthia Scarborough of the NSC.

"Not precisely, but we can make an educated guess. We know that Landesmann purchased Keppler Werk in 2002 and started adding other European industrial technology firms to his secret portfolio soon after."

"So we're talking about years then," Scarborough said.

"Several years," replied Rimona.

"Which means it's possible the secret chain of enrichment facilities could be at least partially completed?"

"That's our assumption. And recent Iranian behavior would seem to support that position."

"What sort of behavior?"

"For one thing, they're tunneling like moles. Your own satellite photographs show the Iranians are moving more and more of their nuclear program underground. And not just at Qom. They've added tunnel complexes at Isfahan and Natanz, and they're working on new ones at several other sites, including Metfaz, Khojir, and Parchin. Drilling tunnels into mountainsides isn't easy. And it certainly isn't cheap. We believe they're doing it for an obvious reason—to hide plants and to protect them from attack."

"What else?" asked Shepard Cantwell of the CIA.

"Natanz," replied Rimona.

"What about Natanz?"

"The Iranians have moved forty-three hundred pounds of low-enriched uranium, virtually their entire stockpile, to an aboveground storage facility. It's almost as if they're taunting us to attack them. Why would they take such a risk?"

"I suspect you have a theory."

"Iran's economy is on life support. Its young people are so restless they're willing to die protesting in the streets. We believe the mullahs might actually welcome an attack in order to reestablish their legitimacy with the Iranian people."

"But are they really willing to give up two tons of low-enriched uranium in the process?"

"They might be if other secret facilities are spinning away. In that case, an attack on Natanz gives them an excuse to throw out the UN inspectors and renounce their participation in the Nuclear Non-Proliferation Treaty."

"Which would then allow them to pursue a nuclear arsenal openly," Cynthia Scarborough pointed out. "Just like the North Koreans."

"That's correct, Ms. Scarborough."

"So what are you recommending?"

Rimona switched off the PowerPoint. "Stopping them, of course."

57

THE PLAINS, VIRGINIA

There is a point in any such gathering when those who collect intelligence part company with those who analyze it. That moment came at the conclusion of Rimona's briefing when Adrian Carter rose suddenly to his feet and began absently beating the pockets of his blazer for his pipe. Four other men rose in unison and followed him across the central hallway into the living room. A log fire was burning in the open hearth; Shamron warmed his liver-spotted hands against the flames before lowering himself into the nearest chair. Navot sat next to him while Gabriel remained on his feet, pacing slowly at the edges of the room. Graham Seymour and Carter sat at opposite ends of the couch, Seymour as if posed for a clothing advertisement, Carter like a doctor preparing to break bad news to a terminal patient.

"How long?" he asked finally. "How long before they're able to close the deal and build their first nuclear weapon?"

Gabriel and Shamron both deferred to their chief in name only, Uzi Navot.

"Even the IAEA has finally concluded that the Iranians already possess the capability to produce a bomb. And if Martin Landesmann is going to sell them the top-of-the-line centrifuges they need to produce a steady supply of fuel . . ."

"How long, Uzi?" Carter repeated.

"A year at the outside. Perhaps even sooner."

Carter inserted his pipe into his tobacco pouch. "For the record, gentlemen, my masters at 1600 Pennsylvania Avenue would be most grateful if you would refrain from attacking Iran's nuclear facilities now or at any time in the future."

"The feelings of the White House have been made clear to us."

"I'm just restating them now lest there be any confusion."

"There isn't. And as long as we're speaking for the record, no one wants to attack Iran any less than we do. This isn't some faction of the PLO we're dealing with. This is the Persian Empire. If we hit them, they'll hit us back. They're already arming Hezbollah and Hamas for a proxy war and priming their terror networks around the globe for attacks against Israeli and Jewish targets."

"They'll also turn Iraq into a flaming cauldron and the Persian Gulf into a war zone," Carter added. "The price of oil will skyrocket, which will plunge the global economy back into recession. And the world will blame you, of course."

"They always do," Shamron said. "We're used to that."

Carter struck a match and ignited his pipe. His next question was posed through a fog of smoke.

"Are you sure about the China connection?"

"We've been watching XTE for some time. The memos we dug out of Martin's laptop merely confirmed all our suspicions." Navot paused. "But surely you're not surprised by China's involvement in this?"

"I'm not surprised by anything China does these days, especially when it comes to Iran. The Islamic Republic is China's second-largest supplier of oil, and the state-run Chinese energy giants have invested tens of billions in Iranian oil-and-gas development. It's clear to us the Chinese view Tehran not as a threat but as an ally. And they're not at all concerned about the Iranians going nuclear. In fact, they might even welcome it."

"Because they think it will reduce American power in the Persian Gulf?"

"Precisely," said Carter. "And since the Chinese hold several hundred billion dollars' worth of American debt, we're in no position to call them on it. We've gone to them on numerous occasions to complain about restricted goods and weapons flowing from their ports to Iran, and the response is always the same. They promise to look into it. But nothing changes."

"We're not suggesting going to the Chinese," Navot said. "Or the Swiss, or the Germans, or the Austrians, or any other country linked to the supply chain. We already know it's a waste of time and effort. National interest and pure greed are powerful trump cards. Besides, the last thing we want is to confess to the Swiss that we're spying on their most prominent businessman."

"How many centrifuges do you think Martin has sold them?"

"We don't know."

"When was the first shipment?"

"We don't know."

"How about the last?"

"We don't know."

Carter waved a clear patch in the cloud of smoke in front of him. "All right, then. Why don't you tell us what you *do* know."

"We know the relationship has been lucrative and that it is ongoing. But more important we also know that in the near future a large shipment is scheduled to go from China to Dubai to Iran."

"How do you know that?"

"The information was contained in a temporary file we exhumed from Martin's hard drive. It was an encrypted e-mail sent to him by someone named Ulrich Müller."

Carter chewed silently on the tip of his pipe. "Müller?" he asked finally. "Are you sure?"

"Positive," Navot said. "Why?"

"Because we first came across Herr Müller during our investigation into Zentrum Security. Müller is former DAP, the Swiss security service, and a first-class shit. Martin and Müller go way back. Müller does Martin's dirty work."

"Like managing a nuclear-smuggling network that stretches from Western Europe to southern China and back to Iran?"

"It would make sense for someone like Müller to act as Martin's front man in all this. Martin wouldn't want the Iran portfolio anywhere near GVI. Better to let someone like Müller handle the details."

Carter lapsed into silence, his gaze moving between Navot and Shamron. Gabriel was still prowling the perimeter of the room.

"Rimona's final remarks indicate that you gentlemen have an

idea of how to proceed next," Carter said. "As your partners in this endeavor, Graham and I would like to know what you're thinking."

Navot glanced at Gabriel, who finally ceased pacing. "The material we gathered from Martin's laptop was helpful but limited. There's still a great deal we don't know. The number of units involved. The delivery dates. The method of payment. The shipping companies."

"I assume you have an idea where you might be able to find this information."

"On a computer located on the western shore of Lake Geneva," said Gabriel. "Twelve hundred thirty-eight feet above sea level."

"Villa Elma?"

Gabriel nodded.

"A break-in?" Carter asked incredulously. "Is that what you're suggesting? A second-story job at one of the most highly guarded private residences in Switzerland, a country notorious for the unusual vigilance of its citizenry?"

Greeted by silence, Carter's gaze moved from Gabriel to Shamron.

"I don't have to remind you of the pitfalls of operating in Switzerland, do I, Ari? In fact, I seem to recall an incident about ten years ago when an entire Office team was arrested while trying to tap the phone line of a suspected terrorist."

"No one is talking about breaking into Villa Elma, Adrian."

"So what do you have in mind?"

It was Gabriel who answered. "In four days, Martin Landesmann is throwing a lavish fund-raiser for three hundred of his closest and richest friends. We plan to attend."

"Really? And how do you plan on getting in? Are you going to pose as waiters and sneak in with canapés and caviar or just go for a good old-fashioned gate crash?"

"We're going as guests, Adrian."

"And how do you plan to get an invitation?"

Gabriel smiled. "We already have one."

"Zoe?" asked Graham Seymour.

Gabriel nodded.

"Do you happen to recall the words *limited* in scope and *short* in duration?"

"I was there, Graham."

"Good," said Seymour. "Then you might also recall we made a promise. We asked Zoe to perform one simple task. And that upon completion of that task she would go on her merry way with the expectation we would never darken her door again."

"The situation has changed."

"So you want her to break into a well-guarded office in the middle of a lavish party? An assignment like that would be extremely difficult and dangerous for a seasoned agent. For a novice recruit with no experience . . . impossible."

"I'm not asking Zoe to break into Martin's office, Graham. All she has to do is show up at the party." Gabriel paused, then added, "With a date on her arm, of course."

"A date you intend to provide for her?"

Gabriel nodded.

"Any candidates?" asked Adrian Carter.

"Just one."

"Since I assume you're not planning to fix her up with Ari or Eli Lavon, that leaves Mikhail."

"He looks excellent in a tux."

"I'm sure he does. But he also went through hell in Russia. Is he ready for something like this?"

Gabriel nodded. "He's ready."

Carter's pipe had gone dead. He immediately reloaded it and struck a match. "May I point out that right now we are seeing everything Martin does on his phone and laptop computer? If your proposed operation in Geneva goes bad, we stand to lose everything."

"And what if Martin decides to switch phones, or his security does a sweep of his laptop and discovers software that's not supposed to be there?"

"Your point?"

"Our window into Martin's world could close in the blink of an eye," Gabriel said, snapping his fingers to illustrate the point. "We have a chance to get into Villa Elma cleanly. Given what we know about how close the Iranians might be to a weapon, it seems to me we have no choice but to take it."

"You make a compelling case. But this discussion is moot unless Zoe agrees to go back in." Carter glanced at Seymour. "Will she do it?"

"I suspect she might be talked into it. But the prime minister will have to personally approve the operation. And no doubt my rivals from across the river will demand a role for themselves."

"They can't have one," Gabriel said. "This is our operation, Graham, not theirs."

"I'll be sure to give them the message," Seymour said, gesturing with his eyes toward the MI6 man in the dining room. "But there's just one thing we haven't covered."

"What's that?"

"What do you propose to do if we actually manage to find the shipment of centrifuges?"

"If we can find those centrifuges . . ." Gabriel's voice trailed off. "Let's just say the possibilities are endless."

58

SOUTHWARK, LONDON

Gerald Malone, chairman and CEO of Latham International Media, brought down the ax at three p.m. the following afternoon. It came in the form of an e-mail to all *Journal* employees, written in Malone's usual arid prose. It seemed that recent efforts to control costs had proven insufficient to keep the paper viable in its present form. Therefore, Latham management had no choice but to impose drastic and immediate staff reductions. The cuts would be both deep and wide, with the editorial division suffering the highest casualty rate by far. One newsroom unit, the special investigative team led by Zoe Reed, conspicuously managed to avoid any redundancies. As it turned out, the reprieve was a parting gift from Jason Turnbury, who would soon be joining the same management group that had just turned the *Journal* into a smoking ruin.

And so it was with a heavy sense of survivor's guilt that Zoe sat at her desk that evening, watching the ritual packing of personal effects that follows any mass firing. As she listened to the tear-stained speeches of farewell, she thought it might be time to leave newspapering and accept the television job that awaited her in New York. And not for the first time, she found herself daydreaming about the remarkable group of men and woman whom she had encountered at the safe house in Highgate. Much to her surprise, she missed the company of Gabriel and his team in ways she never imagined possible. She missed their determination to succeed and their unflinching belief that their cause was just, things she used to feel when she walked into the newsroom of the *Journal*. But more than anything, she missed the collegial atmosphere of the safe house itself. For a few hours each night, she had been part of a family—a noisy, quarrelsome, petulant, and at times dysfunctional family but a family nonetheless.

For reasons not clear to Zoe, it seemed the family had forsaken her. During the train ride home from Paris, the operative with short dark hair and pockmarks on his cheeks had clandestinely congratulated her on a job well done. But after that there had been only silence. No phone calls, no e-mails, no staged encounters on the street or tube, no quiet summons to MI5 headquarters to thank her for her service. From time to time, she had the sense she was being watched, but it might have only been wishful thinking. For Zoe, who was used to the instant gratification of daily journalism, the hardest part was not knowing whether her work had made a difference. Yes, she had a vague sense the Paris operation had gone well, but she had no idea whether it was producing the kind of intelligence Gabriel and Graham Seymour needed. She supposed it was quite possible she never would.

As for her feelings about Martin Landesmann, she had read once that the recovery time from a romantic relationship is equal to the life span of the relationship itself. But Zoe had discovered the time could be drastically reduced when one's former lover was secretly selling restricted goods to the Islamic Republic of Iran. Her hatred of Martin was now intense, as was her desire to sever contact with him. Unfortunately, that wasn't possible since her private life was now a matter of national security. MI5 had asked her to keep open the lines of communication to prevent Martin from becoming suspicious. Still unclear, though, was whether they wished her to attend Martin's gala fund-raiser in Geneva. Zoe had no desire to set foot in Martin's home. In fact, Zoe never wanted to see Martin's face again.

Her thoughts were interrupted by Jason Turnbury, who appeared in the newsroom to deliver the obligatory post-massacre eulogy about what an honor it had been to work with so talented and dedicated a group of journalists. At the conclusion of his remarks, the newsroom staff began slowly filing to the elevators like confused survivors of a natural disaster. Most headed straight for the Anchor, the historic pub located adjacent to the *Journal,* and began drinking heavily. Zoe felt compelled to put in an appearance but soon found herself desperate to escape. So she dried a few eyes and patted a few shoulders, then slipped quietly out the door into a drenching rain.

There were no taxis to be had, so she struck out across Southwark Bridge. A frigid wind was howling up the Thames; Zoe put up her compact umbrella, but it was useless against the horizontal deluge. At the far end of the bridge she spotted a familiar figure standing on the pavement as if oblivious to the weather. It was the middle-aged man in a mackintosh coat who had made the initial approach to Zoe outside CNN the night of her recruitment. As Zoe drew closer, he raised his hand to his mouth as if suppressing a cough. At which point a Jaguar limousine materialized and stopped next to her. The rear door opened. Graham Seymour beckoned her inside.

"I hear there was a fair amount of bloodletting at the *Journal* just now," Seymour said as the car drew away from the curb.

"Is there anything you *don't* know?"

"It was on the BBC."

The car turned left into Upper Thames Street.

"My tube stop is in the opposite direction."

"I need to have a word with you."

"I gathered."

"We were wondering what your plans were for the weekend."

"A trashy book. A couple of DVDs. Maybe a walk in Hampstead Heath if it's not raining."

"Sounds rather dull."

"I like dull, Mr. Seymour. Especially after Paris."

"We have something a bit more exciting if you're interested."

"What do you want me to do this time? Break into a bank? Take down an al-Qaeda cell?"

"All you have to do is attend a party and look ravishing."

"I think I can mange that. Any planning involved?"

"I'm afraid so."

"So it's back to Highgate?"

"Not right away. You have a dinner date at Mirabelle first."

"With whom?"

"Your new lover."

"Really? What's he like?"

"Young, handsome, rich, and Russian."

"Does he have a name?"

"Mikhail Danilov."

"How noble."

"Actually, he doesn't have a noble bone in his body. Which is exactly why he's going to be on your arm when you walk into Martin Landesmann's house Saturday night."

59

HIGHGATE, LONDON

In keeping with the spirit of Masterpiece, their romance was a whirlwind. They lunched together, window-shopped in New Bond Street together, strolled the markets of Covent Garden together, and were even spotted ducking hand-in-hand into an early-afternoon film in Leicester Square. Notoriously circumspect at work about her personal affairs, Zoe made no mention of anyone new in her life, though all agreed that her mood around the office seemed markedly improved. This prompted wild if uninformed speculation among her colleagues as to the identity of her new love interest and the source of his obvious wealth. Someone said he had made a fortune in Moscow real estate before the crash. Someone else said it was Russian oil that had made him rich. And from somewhere within the bowels of the copy desk came the completely unfounded rumor he was an arms dealer—just like the recently departed Ivan Kharkov, may God have mercy on his miserable soul.

The staff of the *Journal* would never learn the true identity of the tall, strikingly handsome Russian squiring Zoe about town. Nor would Zoe's colleagues ever discover that the new couple spent most of their time sequestered inside a redbrick Victorian house located at the end of a quiet cul-de-sac in Highgate. Any questions Zoe had regarding the success of the Paris operation were put to rest within seconds of her return, for the first voice she heard upon entering the drawing room was Martin Landesmann's. It was emanating from the speakers of a computer in the corner of the room, and would continue to do so, virtually uninterrupted, for the next three days of preparation. While Zoe was pleased that her work had paid dividends, she found the constant presence of Martin's voice deeply unsettling. Yes, she thought, Martin more than deserved the intrusion into his most private affairs. But she could not help but feel uneasy over the enormous powers of surveillance now possessed by the world's intelligence services. Mobile technology had given governments the capability to monitor their citizens' words, e-mails, and to some extent even their thoughts in ways that were once the stuff of science fiction. The brave new world had definitely arrived.

The team of operatives working at the safe house was largely the same with two notable additions. One was a rheumy-eyed octogenarian; the other, a strawberry-haired man with the physique of a wrestler. Zoe understood immediately that they were figures of authority. She would never be told, however, they were the former and present chiefs of the Israeli secret intelligence service.

Though her role in Geneva was to be largely one of entrée,

Zoe had to be prepared for the worst possible outcome. As a result, her rapid training focused largely on learning a tragic story. It was the story of a handsome Russian named Mikhail Danilov who had swept her off her feet. A man who had preyed on her vulnerability and deceived her into inviting him to Martin Landesmann's gala. This story, Gabriel reminded her at every turn, would be Zoe's only protection in the event the operation went badly. Thus the stroll along New Bond Street, the outing to Covent Garden, and the time-consuming afternoon film in Leicester Square. "Store every sordid detail in that formidable memory of yours," Gabriel said. "Learn it as though you reported it and wrote it yourself."

Unlike most crash preparations, the information did not flow just one way during those final sessions in Highgate. In fact, in a curious reversal of roles, Zoe was able to contribute significantly to the planning since she was the only one among those present to have ever set foot in Martin's enchanted lakeside residence. It was Zoe who described the entry protocol at Martin's front gate on the rue de Lausanne and Zoe who briefed the team on the probable disposition of Martin's security guards inside the mansion. Shamron was so impressed by her presentation that he told Navot to consider putting her on the Office payroll permanently.

"Something tells me our British partners might not appreciate that," Navot replied.

"Partnerships between intelligence services are like marriages based on physical attraction, Uzi. They burn brightly for a time and almost always end badly."

"I didn't realize you were a relationship counselor, boss."

"I'm a spy, Uzi. The mysteries of the human heart are my business."

The presence of so many powerful personalities in so confined a space might well have been a recipe for disaster. But for the most part, the atmosphere during those three intense days of preparation remained civil, at least when Zoe was present. Gabriel retained control over operational planning, but Navot took the Office's seat at the interagency meetings in Thames House. In many respects, it was a coming-out party for Navot, and those who witnessed his conduct during the gatherings came away impressed by his seriousness of purpose and his command of the issues. All agreed that the Office looked to be in good hands for years to come—unless, of course, Navot's promising career were to be derailed by a disaster on the shores of Lake Geneva.

It was the memories of disasters past that seemed to haunt Gabriel during those long days in Highgate. Time and time again, he warned his team to guard against any complacency arising from the success of the operation in Paris. They would be playing on Martin's turf now. Therefore, all the advantages would be his. Like his father before him, Martin had shown himself willing to resort to violence when faced with the threat of exposure. He had killed one reporter over his secret dealings with Iran and would surely kill another, even a reporter who happened to be sharing his bed.

But occasionally even Gabriel would pause and shake his head in wonder at the unlikely road he had traveled to reach this point—a road that had begun in Amsterdam in the luminous white sitting room of Lena Herzfeld. Lena was rarely far from Gabriel's thoughts, just as the list of names and account numbers was never far from his side. *Katz, Stern, Hirsch, Greenberg, Kaplan, Cohen, Klein, Abramowitz, Stein, Rosenbaum, Herzfeld . . .* Shamron referred to them as the invisible members of Gabriel's team.

Shamron displayed an admirable restraint within the walls of the safe house, but for an hour each day, on the wooden bench atop Parliament Hill, he would privately share with Gabriel his fears about the operation that lay ahead. He began their final meeting by expressing his concerns about Gabriel's leading man.

"Your entire operation hinges on Mikhail making one key decision. Can he get into Martin's office cleanly and stay there for an hour and fifteen minutes without anyone noticing his absence? If he makes the wrong decision, it's going to be a party to remember."

"You're concerned he might be too aggressive?"

"Not necessarily. Mikhail was a mess when he came home from Russia. Almost as bad as you and Chiara. After what he went through in that birch forest, he might not take the risks necessary to pull off his assignment."

"He's been trained by the Sayeret and the Office, Ari. When he walks through the door of Villa Elma tomorrow night, he won't be Mikhail Abramov. He'll be Mikhail Danilov, Russian millionaire and consort of Zoe Reed."

"Was it really necessary to give a hundred thousand euros of my money to Martin's foundation?"

"Mr. Danilov insisted."

"Did he?"

"Mr. Danilov wanted to make a good first impression. He's also not the sort of man who likes to come across as a freeloader. Mr. Danilov is quite well off. And he always pays his own way."

"Let's just hope Mr. Danilov makes the right choice about whether to go after the computer. Not only for his sake but for Zoe's, not to mention your friend Uzi Navot." Shamron ignited a cigarette. "I hear he's already won many friends and admirers at Thames House and Vauxhall Cross."

"And you?"

"I will admit to being impressed by Uzi's debut on the international stage. If this operation proves to be a success, it will go down as one of the greatest triumphs in the history of the Office. And to think Uzi actually tried to kill it before it could even take flight." Shamron glanced at Gabriel. "Maybe next time he won't let his ego get in the way when you try to tell him something."

Gabriel made no reply.

"I see you didn't include your wife on the team for Geneva," Shamron said. "I assume it wasn't an oversight."

"She's not happy about it, but I want her to stay here with you and Uzi."

"Maybe you should consider doing the same." Shamron smoked in silence for a moment. "I suppose I don't have to remind you that you operated in Switzerland quite recently or that there was a great deal of bloodshed involved. It's possible the Swiss are aware of your recent visits to the country. Which means that if anything goes wrong tomorrow evening, it might be a long time before I can get you out again."

"I'm not going to let anyone else run the show in Geneva, Ari."

"I assumed that would be your answer. Just make sure you abide by the Eleventh Commandment. Don't get caught."

"Do you have any other helpful advice?"

"Bring Zoe Reed home alive." Shamron dropped his cigarette to the ground. "I wouldn't want Uzi's London debut to close after its opening night."

IF THERE WAS a chink in the armor of the Office, it was the problem of passports. In most cases, undercover Israeli agents could not carry Israeli passports since Israeli citizens were not allowed to enter target countries or, as in the case of Switzerland, were regarded with suspicion by local authorities. Therefore, after a round of intense negotiations, it was decided that all eight members of the Geneva team would travel on false American or Commonwealth passports. It was a magnanimous but necessary gesture that guaranteed the operation would not crumble at the gates of passport control. Even so, Gabriel took the routine Office precaution of sending his team into Geneva on three different flights and by three different routes. There were some traditions that died hard, even in a multilateral world.

His own flight was KLM 1022, departing London Heathrow at 5:05 p.m., arriving Geneva International at ten after a brief stopover in Amsterdam, which Gabriel found fitting. He had an American passport that identified him as Jonathan Albright and a stack of business cards that said he worked for a hedge fund based in Greenwich, Connecticut. He carried clothing that didn't belong to him and performance charts he didn't understand. In fact, as Gabriel slipped out of the Highgate safe house that afternoon for the final time, everything about him was a lie. Everything but the beautiful woman with riotous dark hair watching from the window on the second floor. And the list of names and account numbers tucked safely into the zippered compartment of his briefcase.

60

GENEVA

The first trucks appeared at the gates of Villa Elma at the stroke of nine the following morning. Thereafter, they arrived in an unbroken stream, disgorging their contents into Martin Landesmann's graceful forecourt like the spoils of a distant war. There were crates of wine and spirits and ice chests filled with fresh crab flown in specially from Alaska. There were trolleys stacked with tables and chairs and polished wooden boxes filled with china, crystal, and silver. There were music stands for a full orchestra, a fifty-foot fir tree to adorn the front entrance hall, and enough lights to illuminate a midsize city. There was a team of audiovisual technicians bearing a theater-quality projection system, and, curiously, a pair of women dressed in khaki who arrived in late afternoon accompanied by a dozen wild animals. The animals turned out to be highly endangered species that Saint Martin was allegedly spending a small fortune attempting to save.

As for the projection system, Martin planned to bore his guests with an hour-long documentary he had produced on the perils of global warming. The timing was somewhat ironic since Europe was shivering through the coldest winter in living memory.

The intensity of the preparations at Villa Elma stood in stark contrast to the tranquil mood at the Grand Hotel Kempinski, located approximately a mile down the lakeshore, on the Quai de Mont-Blanc. In the ornate lobby, the atmosphere was one of permanent evening. Beneath a low ceiling studded with a galaxy of tiny lights, bellmen and valets spoke in hushed tones as if concerned about waking sleeping children. A decorative gas fire burned listlessly in the empty lounge; gold watches and pearl necklaces glowed seductively from the display cases of empty boutiques. Even at three p.m., a time when the lobby normally bustled with activity, the silence was oppressive. Privately, management was blaming the recent slump in business on the weather and on the collapse of the real estate market in a certain Gulf emirate known for its excess. To make matters worse, Swiss voters had recently offended many of the Kempinski's most reliably free-spending patrons by approving a nationwide ban on the construction of minarets. Like nearly everyone else in Geneva, management was beginning to wonder whether the usually sure-footed business enterprise sometimes referred to as Switzerland had finally lost a step.

As a result, management was overjoyed when Zoe Reed, the British journalist who was a fixture on hotel television screens around the world, entered the Kempinski's lobby at 3:15, accompanied by a gold-plated Russian named Mikhail Danilov. After checking into separate rooms, Mr. Danilov sent a shirt and tuxedo down to the laundry for pressing, then proceeded to the fitness room for what witnesses would later describe as a terrifying workout. For her part, Ms. Reed spent a few minutes browsing the shops in the lobby, then headed to the salon to have her hair and makeup professionally done for the affair at Villa Elma. Two other female attendees were also in the salon, along with a woman who had been present in the Highgate safe house. Seated in the waiting area was the tweedy Englishman whom Zoe knew as David. He was leafing through a copy of *Vogue* magazine with an expression of spousal boredom and grumbling to himself about the quality of the maid service.

It was approaching five when Zoe left the salon and headed upstairs to her room to begin dressing for the party. Her escort, Mikhail Danilov, was staying in the adjacent room, while three doors down was a man who had checked into the hotel under the name Jonathan Albright, executive vice president of something called Markham Capital Advisers of Greenwich, Connecticut. His real name was Gabriel Allon, of course, and he was not alone. Seated on the opposite side of the small desk was Eli Lavon. Like Gabriel, he was wearing a pair of headphones and staring intently into a laptop computer. Lavon's was receiving a stream from the compromised phone of Zoe Reed while Gabriel's was taking in the feed from Martin Landesmann's. Zoe was watching the hourly news bulletin on the BBC. Martin was discussing security arrangements for the party with Jonas Brunner, his personal bodyguard.

The meeting concluded at 5:03. Martin conferred briefly with his chief party planner, then headed upstairs to the room located in the southeast corner of Villa Elma, 1,238 feet above sea level. Gabriel heard the now-familiar eight atonal beeps as Martin entered the security code into the keyless lock—eight digits that would soon be standing between Mikhail and Martin's most closely guarded secrets. A few seconds later came the sound of the office door opening and closing, followed by the clatter of Martin's fingers over the keyboard of his computer. It seemed Martin had a bit of work to do before the party. So did Gabriel. He handed his headphones to Eli Lavon and stepped into the corridor.

A DO NOT DISTURB sign hung from the latch. Gabriel knocked twice, paused, then knocked twice again. Zoe opened the door a few seconds later and peered at him over the security bar.

"What can I do for you?" she asked, feigning irritation.

"You can let me in, Zoe. We swept your room while you were gone. You're clean."

Zoe unlocked the door and stepped aside. She was barefoot and wearing only a white hotel bathrobe.

"Is that what you're planning to wear tonight?" asked Gabriel.

"I prefer it to that dress Martin bought me."

"He might be disappointed if you don't wear it."

"So will every other man in the room."

Gabriel walked over to the desk. Zoe's phone was lying on the blotter. He picked it up, pressed the power button, and held it until the screen turned to black.

"Is there something you need to tell me about my phone?" Zoe asked.

"It's just a precaution."

"Yes," she said, her tone sardonic. "And I came all the way to Geneva to bask in the glow of Martin Landesmann for a few hours."

Gabriel placed the phone on the desk again but said nothing.

"Just make sure you switch it off when this is over." She sat on the edge of the bed. "You never told me what you call it."

"What's that?"

"The procedure we carried out on Martin's phone and computer."

"I was born in the late seventeenth century, Zoe. Even I don't know the proper name for it."

"And the slang?"

"Some techs refer to it as backdooring, rooting, or popping. We like to call it owning."

"Meaning?"

"If we can get our hands on the target's phone, we *own* it. If we can get inside his bank accounts, we *own* them. If we can get to his home security system, we can *own* that, too. And if Mikhail can get inside Martin's office tonight . . ."

"Then we can find the centrifuges?"

Gabriel was struck by Zoe's use of the pronoun we. "Yes," he said with a nod of his head. "If we're lucky, we might be able to find the centrifuges."

"What are the odds?"

"Hard to say."

"I assume this isn't the first time your service has done something like this."

Gabriel hesitated, then answered. "There's been a not-so-secret war going on here in Europe for some time, Zoe. It involves the Iranians and European high-tech firms. And the computers of the bad guys are one of our greatest weapons."

"For example?"

"I'm not going to give you an example."

"How about a hypothetical?"

"All right. Let's say a hypothetical Iranian nuclear scientist goes to a hypothetical conference in Berlin. And let's say our hypothetical scientist has notes on his hypothetical computer on how to build a nuclear warhead."

"Then it might be difficult to keep a straight face when the Iranian president declares his program is strictly peaceful."

"That's correct."

"And are they building a warhead?"

"Without question," Gabriel said. "And they're getting closer every day. But to be an effective nuclear power, they need a steady supply of highly enriched uranium. And for that, they need centrifuges. Good ones. Centrifuges that don't break down. Centrifuges that spin at a reliable speed. Centrifuges that aren't contaminated."

"*Martin*'s centrifuges," Zoe said softly.

Gabriel was silent. Zoe glanced at the clock on the nightstand.

"Unless you intend to help me get dressed, I think I'll have to ask you to leave now."

"In a minute." Gabriel sat. "Remember, Zoe, when Mikhail makes his move, it's important you not appear to be alone or in any way unattached. Latch onto someone. Strike up a conversation. The worst thing you can do is be quiet or look nervous. Be the opposite of nervous. Be the life of the party. Do you understand?"

"I think I can manage that."

Gabriel smiled briefly, then his expression turned serious. "Now tell me again what happens if Mikhail gets caught."

"I'm to disown him. I'm to say he deceived me into bringing him. And then I'm to leave the party as quickly as possible."

"Even if it means leaving Mikhail behind."

She was silent for a moment. "Please don't make me say it."

"Say it, Zoe."

"Even if it means leaving Mikhail behind."

"Don't hesitate, Zoe. And don't look back. If one of Martin's guards tries to grab you, make a scene so everyone in the party knows there's a problem. Martin will have no choice but to let you leave." Gabriel paused, then asked, "Do you understand, Zoe?"

She nodded.

"Say it."

"I'll make a bloody scene. And I'll leave Mikhail behind."

"Very good. Any questions?"

Zoe shook her head. Gabriel rose and gave her the phone.

"Turn it on when I leave. And keep it close tonight."

Gabriel started toward the door.

"Actually, I do have one question, Mr. Allon."

He stopped and turned.

"What happened in that field outside London?"

"There is no field outside London. And there is no safe house in Highgate, either. The mind is like a basin, Zoe. Pull the plug, and the memory drains away."

Gabriel slipped out the door without another word. Zoe switched on her mobile and began to dress.

AMONG THE MANY logistical challenges faced by the team had been the acquisition of a suitable car to ferry Zoe and Mikhail to the party. An attempt was made to rent a vehicle in Geneva, but that proved impossible because Martin's other guests had already snatched up every luxury sedan in the canton. That left a hasty purchase as the only option. Gabriel handled the chore himself, choosing a black fully loaded S-Class Mercedes, which he paid for in full with a certified check from one of Navot's operational accounts in Zurich. When news of the procurement reached Highgate, Shamron flew into a seething rage. Not only had the Office just spent one hundred and twenty-five thousand dollars for a car but a German car at that.

It eased gracefully into the Kempinski's circular drive at 6:15 that evening with Yaakov behind the wheel, looking as though he were guiding an oil tanker through treacherous seas. After successful completion of the maneuver, he informed the doorman that he was there to collect Mr. Danilov. The doorman called Mr. Danilov, who in turn called Ms. Reed and Mr. Albright of Markham Capital Advisers. Mr. Albright immediately dispatched a secure message to his superiors in London that read DEPARTURE IMMINENT. Then he looked at his computer screen. A red light was blinking in the southeast corner of Villa Elma, 1,238 feet above sea level.

61

MAYFAIR, LONDON

The message from Geneva flashed on the screens of the CIA ops center beneath Grosvenor Square. Seated in their usual places in the back row were Graham Seymour, Adrian Carter, and Ari Shamron. In a significant break with tradition, they were joined that evening by two additional members of the Masterpiece team. One was Uzi Navot, the other was Chiara Allon. All five were staring at the message screens like stranded airline passengers waiting for a long-delayed flight. Shamron was already nervously turning over his old Zippo lighter in his fingertips. Two turns to the right, two turns to the left . . .

"Does anyone know the definition of the word *imminent*?"

"Ready to take place," offered Graham Seymour.

"Hanging threateningly over one's head," added Adrian Carter.

Shamron frowned heavily and looked at Chiara, who responded by typing a few characters into her laptop computer. A moment later, a new message appeared on the display screens at the front of the room.

DEPARTURE IN PROGRESS . . .

"What was the problem?" Shamron asked.

"Zoe's zipper was stuck."

"Who fixed it?"

"Mr. Albright of Markham Capital Advisers."

Shamron smiled. *Two turns to the right, two turns to the left . . .*

MIKHAIL STOOD outside the elevators on the sixth floor of the Grand Hotel Kempinski and examined his appearance in the decorative smoked-glass mirror. His clothing was simple but elegant: a Brioni tuxedo, a plain-fronted formal shirt, a traditional bow tie. The jacket had been specially fitted to accommodate the two pieces of technical equipment he was carrying at the small of his back. The crisp knot of his bow tie had been a collaborative effort involving three agents of Israeli intelligence and no small amount of preoperational hysteria.

He leaned closer to the mirror, made an adjustment to his blond forelock, and examined his face. Hard to believe he was the same boy from the derelict apartment blocks of Moscow. A boy who had been beaten and spat upon by Russian brethren every day merely for having been cursed with the name of the patriarch. The boy had moved to Israel with his dissident parents and had learned to fight. But tonight he would fight in a different way, against a man who was supplying the mullahs of Iran with the power to fulfill their wildest fantasies. Tonight he was no longer Mikhail Abramov. Tonight he was a real Russian with a proper Russian name and a great deal of money in his Russian pockets.

He heard the sound of a door closing just down the corridor. Zoe appeared a few seconds later, looking radiant in her Dior dress. Mikhail kissed her formally on both cheeks for the benefit of the hotel cameras, then stepped back to admire her.

"Something tells me you're going to be the center of attention tonight."

"Better me than you."

Mikhail laughed as he led Zoe into the elevator. In the lobby, Yossi and Rimona were drinking coffee near the gas fire while Dina and Mordecai were talking to the concierge about restaurants. Mikhail offered Zoe his arm and led her toward the entrance. A doorman intercepted them, a concerned look on his face.

"I'm afraid we have a slight problem, Mr. Danilov."

"What's that?"

"An overabundance of cars."

"Can you be a bit more clear?" Mikhail asked, adopting the impatient tone that comes naturally to the rich, Russian or otherwise. "I'm afraid we're running late for an important engagement."

The doorman turned and pointed through the revolving door toward the S-Class Mercedes. Yaakov was standing at the rear driver's-side door, hand on the latch, face a blank mask.

"That's *your* car, Mr. Danilov."

"So what's the problem?"

The doorman pointed to a second Mercedes, a Maybach 62S. Two well-dressed men in dark overcoats were standing near the trunk, hands in their pockets. Mikhail recognized the older of the two from surveillance photographs. It was Jonas Brunner.

"And *that* car," said the doorman, "is for Ms. Reed."

"Who sent it?"

"Mr. Martin Landesmann."

"Do me a favor then. Tell those gentlemen that Ms. Reed and I will be traveling to the party together in *my* car."

"They were quite insistent Ms. Reed ride with them."

Mikhail instructed Zoe to wait in the lobby, then stepped outside. Jonas Brunner immediately walked over and introduced himself.

"Do you mind telling me what this is all about?" Mikhail asked.

"Mr. Landesmann has made arrangements for your travel to Villa Elma. Forgive us for not telling you sooner. It was an oversight on our part."

"Us?"

"I work for Mr. Landesmann."

"In what capacity?" Mikhail asked needlessly.

"I'm a personal aide, of sorts," Brunner said evasively.

"I see. Well, please convey to Mr. Landesmann our thanks for his very generous offer, but we'll be taking our own car."

"I'm afraid Mr. Landesmann would be deeply offended to hear that." Brunner held out his hand toward the Maybach. "Please, Mr. Danilov, I'm sure you and Ms. Reed will find this one very comfortable."

Mikhail turned and looked at Zoe, who was watching him through the glass as though she found the entire spectacle faintly amusing. It was not, of course. In fact, it presented Mikhail with his first decision of the evening, far sooner than he had anticipated. To refuse the offer would look suspicious. But to accept meant they would be under Martin's control from the outset. Mikhail Abramov wanted to insist on taking his own car. But Mikhail Danilov knew he had no choice but to accept. Otherwise, the evening was going to get off to a very tense start. He looked at Brunner and managed a slight smile.

"We'll be delighted to ride in your car. Shall I dismiss my driver or will we need him to get back to the hotel?"

"We'll bring you back at the end of the party, Mr. Danilov."

Mikhail turned and gestured for Zoe to come outside. Brunner opened the rear door of the Maybach and smiled.

"Good evening, Ms. Reed."

"Good evening, Jonas."

"You look lovely this evening."

"Thank you, Jonas."

YAAKOV WATCHED the Maybach turn into the darkened Quai de Mont-Blanc, then lifted his wrist mic to his lips.

"Did you hear that?"

"I heard it," replied Gabriel."

"What do you want me to do?"

"Follow them. Carefully."

THIRTY SECONDS LATER, a new message flashed on the screens at Grosvenor Square. Shamron glared at Navot.

"How much did that car cost me, Uzi?"

"One hundred and twenty-five thousand, boss."

"And how much did Mikhail donate to Martin's foundation?"

"A hundred thousand."

"I once stole a Russian MiG for less than that, Uzi."

"What would you like me to do, boss?"

"Make sure that car survives the night. I want my money back."

62

GENEVA

They headed north along the shoreline through the drowsy elegance of Geneva's diplomatic quarter. Zoe sat behind the driver, hands folded in her lap, knees leaning to one side. Mikhail sat behind Jonas Brunner and stared silently at the lake.

"Your first time in Geneva, Mr. Danilov?"

"No. Why do you ask?"

"You seem very interested in the lake."

"I've always been very fond of the lake."

"So you come often then?"

"A couple of times a year."

"For business?"

"Is there any other reason to come to Geneva?"

"Some people come for holiday."

"Really?"

And do you interrogate all Mr. Landesmann's guests, Herr Brunner? Or only the friends of his mistress?

If Zoe was thinking the same thing, her expression did not show it. She turned her large brown eyes fondly toward Mikhail, then stared straight ahead. They were approaching the Botanical Gardens. The Palace of Nations floated past like a giant luxury liner and was swallowed by the mist. Mikhail looked out the window again and saw Brunner's eyes watching him in the side mirror.

"Mr. Landesmann asked me to thank you for the generous donation you made to One World. He intends to speak with you personally, if he has a chance."

"That's really not necessary."

"Try telling that to Mr. Landesmann."

"I will," Mikhail said jovially.

Brunner didn't seem to understand the irony. He turned robotically, his cross-examination apparently at an end, and murmured a few words in German into his wrist mic. They had left the diplomatic quarter and were speeding now along the rue de Lausanne. Towering hedgerows and stone walls lined both sides of the road, concealing some of the world's costliest and most exclusive real estate. The gates seemed to grow grander the farther they moved from central Geneva, though none matched the imposing elegance of the entrance of Villa Elma. A two-story stucco guardhouse stood just to the right, its turret poking vigilantly above the groomed hedge. Limousines lined the shoulder of the road, waiting to be admitted by the clipboard-wielding foot soldiers of Zentrum Security. Brunner motioned for the driver to go around.

Seeing the approaching Maybach, the guards stepped aside

and allowed it to pass unchecked through the gate. Directly ahead, at the apex of a long, tree-lined drive, Villa Elma glowed like a wedding cake. Another line of limousines stretched from the entrance, tailpipes gently smoking. This time, Brunner ordered the driver to join the queue. Then he looked over his shoulder at Zoe.

"When you're ready to leave, Ms. Reed, just tell one of the security guards and we'll have the car brought around." He glanced at Mikhail. "Enjoy your evening, Mr. Danilov."

"I intend to."

The car came to a stop at the entrance of the mansion. Mikhail climbed out and offered Zoe his hand.

"What just happened there?" Zoe whispered as they headed toward the entrance.

"I believe your friend Martin Landesmann just marked his territory."

"Is that all it was?"

"We're here, aren't we?"

She gave his arm a brief squeeze. "You handled that very well, Mr. Danilov."

"Not nearly as well as you, Ms. Reed."

They stepped into the soaring entrance hall and were immediately set upon by a phalanx of attendants in formal attire. One relieved Mikhail of his overcoat while a second saw to Zoe's wrap. Then, after being presented with an embossed reception card, they were instructed to join a short receiving line of jeweled women and envious men.

Standing at the foot of the spectacular light-strewn fir tree was Saint Martin Landesmann in all his glory. Martin of the careful handshake. Martin of the whispered confidence. Martin of the solicitous nod. Monique and the children seemed like mere accessories, like Martin's understated Patek Philippe wristwatch and the two Zentrum bodyguards standing with feigned detachment at his back. Monique was taller than Martin by an inch. Her long dark hair was swept directly back from her forehead, and she wore a sleeveless gown that flattered her slender arms. Martin seemed oblivious to her beauty. He had eyes only for his invited guests. And, briefly, for the famous British reporter who was now standing five feet away at the side of a Russian millionaire named Mikhail Danilov. Mr. Danilov handed the reception card to the attendant at the front of the line. Then he lowered his eyes to the marble floor and waited for their names to be called.

THERE EXISTS a snapshot of the encounter that followed. Unposed, it was captured by one of the commercial photographers hired for the event and was later stolen from his computer as part of the multinational inquiry conducted at the conclusion of the affair. In retrospect, it was a remarkably accurate predictor of the events that followed. Martin's expression was curiously dour for such a joyous occasion, and by a trick of the camera angle his gaze appeared fixed on both Mikhail and Zoe at the same time. Monique was looking at neither. In fact, Monique's elegant head was adroitly turned in the opposite direction.

The photograph did not reflect the brevity of the encounter, though the audio feed did. Just fifteen seconds in length, it was obtained by not one but two sources—the mobile phone in Zoe Reed's clutch and the Nokia N900 that, in violation of Monique's expressed wishes, was tucked into the breast pocket of Martin's formal jacket. Gabriel listened to the recording three times, then dashed off a message to London as Zoe and Mikhail waded into the party. The orchestra was playing "See, the Conqu'ring Hero Come" by Handel. Even Zoe had to laugh.

NOT FAR FROM Villa Elma, on the rue de Lausanne, is a small Agip gas station and mini-mart. Like most Swiss service stations, it is exceedingly neat. It also has a small bakery, which, surprisingly, sells some of Geneva's better bread and pastries. By the time Yaakov arrived, the bread was well past its prime, though the coffee was freshly made. He bought a large cup with milk and sugar, a box of Swiss chocolates, and a pack of American chewing gum, then returned to the Mercedes and settled behind the wheel for the long wait. He was supposed to be sitting inside the walls of Villa Elma with the rest of the limousine drivers. But Martin had necessitated a change in plan. Was his gesture innocent, or had he just sunk the entire operation with one simple maneuver? Whatever the case, Yaakov was certain of one thing. Mikhail and Zoe were now locked inside Martin's citadel, surrounded by Martin's bodyguards, and completely at Martin's mercy. Not exactly the way they'd drawn it up in Highgate. Funny how it always seemed to work out that way.

63

GENEVA

It was Martin's party, but it was Zoe's night. Zoe sparkled. Zoe dazzled. Zoe shone. Zoe was incomparable. Zoe was a star. She did not choose this role for herself. It was chosen for her. Zoe stood out that night because she was different. Zoe didn't own things or buy things. Zoe didn't lend money or drill for North Sea oil. Zoe wasn't even rich. But she was beautiful. And she was intelligent. And she was on television. And with a few strokes of her famous pen, she could turn anyone in the room into the next Martin Landesmann, no matter how grievous his private sins.

She listened a great deal and spoke only when necessary. And if she had opinions, she did not share them since she regarded herself as the last journalist in the world who actually tried to keep her personal politics out of her work. She flirted with the youthful owner of an American software giant, was pawed by a Saudi prince of untold wealth, and dispensed some sage advice to none other than Viktor Orlov, future owner of the *Financial Journal.* A reclusive Milanese billionaire offered to throw open the gates of his business empire to Zoe in exchange for a favorable story; a famous British actor associated with the "slow food" movement pleaded with her to do more to promote sustainable agriculture. And much to Monique Landesmann's displeasure, Zoe was even asked by the girls in khaki to hold a Eurasian lynx cub during the presentation on Martin's efforts to save the world's most endangered animals. When the cat nuzzled Zoe's cheek, one hundred fifty men sighed aloud, wishing they could do the same thing.

Throughout the evening, the handsome Mikhail Danilov was never far from Zoe's side. He seemed content merely to bask in Zoe's reflected glow, though he shook many hands, handed out many glossy business cards, and made many vague commitments to future London lunches. He was the perfect escort for a woman like Zoe, confident enough to not feel slighted by the attention paid to her and more than willing to float unseen in the background. Indeed, despite his striking good looks, no one seemed to notice Mr. Danilov's absence when the three hundred invited guests filed into the grand ballroom for the screening of Martin's movie.

The room had been converted into a theater with rows of colored folding chairs arrayed in a rainbow and the ubiquitous logo of the One World foundation projected onto the large screen. An empty lectern stood before it, waiting for Martin to grace it. Zoe took a seat at the back of the room and was immediately joined by the Saudi prince. He touched her thigh while lobbying her to write a piece about some of the exciting developments taking place in the Saudi oil industry. Zoe promised to consider it, then removed the Saudi's hand as Martin ascended to the lectern to rapt applause.

It was a performance Zoe had seen several times before in Davos, yet it was utterly compelling nonetheless. Martin was professorial one moment, revolutionary the next. He exhorted his fellow magnates to pursue social justice over pure profit. He spoke of sacrifice and service. He called for open borders and open hearts. And he demanded a world organized by new societal principles, ones based not on material acquisition but on sustainability and dignity. Had Zoe not known the truth about Martin, she might have been spellbound like the other three hundred people in the room. And she might have roared with approval at the conclusion of Martin's remarks. Instead, she managed only the politest applause and quickly surveyed the room as the lights went out. The One World logo dissolved and was replaced by a fierce orange sun beating down upon a parched desert landscape. A single cello played a haunting melody.

"Is something wrong, Ms. Reed?" the Saudi prince asked.

"I seem to have misplaced my date," Zoe said, recovering quickly.

"How fortunate for me."

Zoe smiled and said, "Don't you just adore films about the dangers of burning fossil fuel?"

"Doesn't everyone?" said the Saudi.

The parched desert gave way to a submerged coastal village in Bangladesh. Zoe casually glanced at her watch and marked the time. *Ninety minutes*, Gabriel had said. *If Mikhail's not back in ninety minutes, get into your car and leave*. But there was just one problem with that plan. Zoe had no car other than Martin's limousine. And Zentrum Security was doing the driving.

IRONICALLY, IT was Martin Landesmann himself, thanks to the compromised mobile phone in his pocket, who had taught the Masterpiece team about the back staircase that led from the service kitchen directly to his private office. He came that way each morning after his hour-long scull on the lake, rising from 1,226 feet above sea level to 1,238. Some mornings, he would pop into his bedroom suite to have a word with Monique, but usually he would proceed directly to his office and enter the eight digits into his keyless lock. Eight digits that would soon be standing between Mikhail and Martin's most closely guarded secrets.

Mikhail's first challenge was getting from the reception rooms into the service kitchen cleanly. His task was made easier by the fact that Martin's dark-suited security men were standing watch over the doors and corridors leading to sections of the mansion where the guests were not welcome. The entrance to the kitchen was completely unguarded, and the hallway leading to it was heavily trafficked by waiters rushing in both directions. None seemed to give a second look to the lanky blond-haired man who entered the kitchen carrying an empty silver tray. Nor did any of them seem to notice when the lanky blond-haired man deposited the same tray on a counter and mounted the back staircase as if it were an everyday occurrence.

Through the magic of global positioning technology, Mikhail

knew the route down to the inch. At the top of the stairs, he turned to the right and proceeded thirty-two feet along a dimly lit corridor. Then it was a left, to a pair of double doors leading to the small alcove outside Martin's office. As expected, the doors to the alcove were closed but unlocked.

Mikhail opened one of the doors, slipped through it, and closed it again quickly. The alcove was in pitch-darkness, precisely what he needed to perform the first step of the break-in. He removed a small ultraviolet light from the pouch at the small of his back and switched it on. The ghostly blue beam illuminated the pad for the keyless entry system. More important, the UV light revealed Martin's latent fingerprints on the pad. Five of the numerical keys bore fingerprints—2, 4, 6, 8, 9—along with the unlock button.

Mikhail quickly removed the cover of the keypad, exposing the electronic circuitry, and took a second item from his pouch. The size of an iPod, it had a numbered keypad of its own and a pair of wires with small alligator clips at the ends. Mikhail powered on the device and attached the clips to the exposed wiring of Martin's keyless lock. Then he pressed the same five numbers—2, 4, 6, 8, 9—followed by the enter key. In less than a second, the device fed every possible combination of numbers into the memory chip, and the lock instantly snapped open. Mikhail unclipped the device and replaced the cover on the keypad, then stepped into Martin's office and quietly closed the door. Mounted on the wall was an identical keypad. Mikhail illuminated it briefly with his UV light and pressed the lock button. The dead bolts slammed home with a solid thump.

Like the alcove, the office was in complete darkness. Mikhail had no need of light. He knew that Martin's computer was located precisely thirteen feet away, at roughly two o'clock. Martin had shut it down before leaving the office earlier that evening. All Mikhail had to do was insert his Sony flash drive into one of the USB ports and hold down the F8 key while pressing the power button. With a few keystrokes, the contents of Martin's hard drive were soon flowing through cyberspace at the speed of light. A dialogue box appeared on the screen: *TIME REMAINING FOR UPLOAD: 1:14:32 . . .* Nothing to do now but wait. He inserted the earpiece of his miniature secure radio and stared at the screen.

"Are they getting it?" Mikhail asked.

"They're getting it," Gabriel replied.

"Don't forget about me here."

"We won't."

Gabriel clipped out. Mikhail sat alone in the darkness, watching the countdown clock on the screen of Martin's computer.

TIME REMAINING FOR UPLOAD: 1:13:47 . . .

THE COMPUTER receiving the feed from Villa Elma was located in the glass-enclosed conference room of the London ops center known as the fishbowl. On its screen was a message identical to the one on Martin's. Shamron was the only one in the room who did not think it was cause for celebration. Experience would not permit it. Nor would the status boards. He had one operative locked in Martin's office, seven operatives sitting in a luxury Geneva hotel, and a Mercedes sedan parked at a gas station in one of the world's most secure neighborhoods. And then, of course, there was the small matter of a famous British reporter who was watching a movie about global warming at the side of a Saudi prince. *What could go wrong?* Shamron thought, his lighter rotating nervously in his fingertips. *What could possibly go wrong?*

64

ZURICH

It had been a humbling few months for the tiny Swiss Confederation, as evidenced by the ghostlike silence hanging over Zurich's Bahnhofstrasse that same damp December evening. Having been brought to the brink of insolvency, Switzerland's largest banks had been forced to suffer the indignity of a government bailout. Sensing weakness, foreign tax collectors were now clamoring for Swiss financial institutions to lift the veil of secrecy that had shielded their clients for centuries. The gnomes of Zurich, among the wiliest of God's creatures, had instinctively taken shelter and were waiting patiently for the inclement weather to pass. They did so secure in the knowledge that America's bankers could no longer hold steadfast to their claims of moral superiority. Say what you like about Swiss greed, they assured themselves, but never once had it plunged the entire planet into recession. That would forever be a singularly American achievement.

But economies, like ecosystems, are dynamic, and a threat to one species does not necessarily mean a threat to all. In fact, it can often mean opportunity, as was the case for the enterprise housed in the leaden office building located at the Kasernenstrasse, on the banks of the Sihl Canal. But that was the beauty of corporate security. Trouble tended to be oblivious to the business cycle.

Strangely enough, Ulrich Müller's Kellergruppe did not actually operate from the cellar of Zentrum headquarters. Quite the opposite, it occupied a suite of spacious offices on the top floor, a testament to the significant contribution made by the unit to Zentrum's healthy bottom line. Several senior staff members were on duty that evening, keeping careful watch over a pair of sensitive operations. One was a blackmail job in Berlin; the other, an "account termination" in Mexico City. The Mexico case was particularly critical since it involved a crusading government prosecutor who was poking his nose into matters that didn't concern him. The wet work itself was being handled by a local subcontractor, a professional hit man often used by Mexican drug lords. That was the Kellergruppe's preferred method of operation. Whenever possible, it utilized the services of skilled professionals and career criminals who had no idea whom they were working for. This reduced exposure for the firm and limited potential damage in those rare cases when an operation did not go as planned.

Despite the extreme sensitivity of the Berlin and Mexico City operations, Ulrich Müller was not present at Zentrum headquarters that evening. Instead, for reasons not yet known to him, he was parked in a deserted lot several miles south of the city center along the western shore of the Zürichsee. The location had been chosen by a man named Karl Huber, a former underling of Müller's at the Dienst für Analyse und Prävention, the Swiss domestic intelligence service. Huber said he had something important he needed to tell Müller. Something that couldn't be discussed over the phone or in an enclosed room. Huber had sounded worried, but Huber usually did.

Müller glanced at his wristwatch, then looked up again to watch a car approaching from the south. Huber, he thought, right on schedule. The car turned into the lot, headlamps doused, and parked a few inches behind Müller's bumper. Müller frowned. As always, Huber's tradecraft was impeccable. A moment later, the DAP man was slumped in Müller's passenger seat, a laptop computer on his lap, looking as though someone had just died.

"What's the problem, Karl?"

"This."

Huber powered on the laptop and clicked on an icon. A few seconds later, Müller heard the voice of Zentrum's owner having an extremely private conversation with his wife. It was obvious from the quality of the audio that the conversation was being conducted face-to-face and was being picked up by a microphone several feet away. Müller listened only for a moment, then, with a sharp wave of his hand, instructed his former underling to shut it down.

"Where did you get this?"

Huber glanced at the ceiling but said nothing.

"Onyx?"

Huber nodded.

"What's the source?"

"Landesmann's mobile phone."

"Why is the internal security service of Switzerland eavesdropping on the private conversations of Martin Landesmann?"

"We're not. But obviously someone else is. And they've managed to get to more than just his mobile."

"What else?"

"His laptop."

Müller went pale. "What are you seeing?"

"Everything, Ulrich. And I mean *everything*."

"Onyx?"

Huber nodded. "Onyx."

THE TWO MEN were not referring to the translucent form of quartz, but the signals intelligence service of the Swiss government. A scaled-down version of the National Security Agency's Echelon program, Onyx had the capability to intercept global communications and cellular traffic, as well as activity on the World Wide Web. Shortly after its completion in 2005, Onyx discovered one of the world's most explosive secrets when a ground station high in the Swiss Alps intercepted a fax between the Egyptian foreign minister and his ambassador in London. The fax would eventually help lead to the revelation of the CIA's secret black site prisons for suspected al-Qaeda terrorists. Despite the circumstances, Ulrich Müller couldn't help but marvel at the irony of the situation. Onyx had been conceived and built in order to steal the secrets of Switzerland's adversaries. Now it appeared the system had inadvertently stumbled upon the secrets of the country's most prominent businessman.

"How did Onyx find it?" Müller asked.

"The computers found it. The computers find everything."

"When?"

"Shortly after Martin's hard drive went up on the satellites, the Onyx filtering system hit on several keywords. The material was automatically flagged and delivered to an analyst at Zimmerwald for further investigation. After a few hours of poking around, the analyst discovered that Martin's phone was hot as well. My office was just notified, but Onyx has been monitoring the feed for several days. And the material is being shipped to the DAP for further investigation."

Müller closed his eyes. It was a disaster in the making.

"How long has the phone been compromised?"

"Hard to say." Huber shrugged. "At least a week. Maybe longer."

"And the computer?"

"The staff at Onyx thinks they were hit at the same time."

"What were the keywords that triggered the auto flagging?"

"Keywords having to do with certain goods being shipped to a certain country on the eastern side of the Persian Gulf. Keywords having to do with a certain Chinese company based in Shenzhen called XTE Hardware and Equipment." Huber paused, then asked, "Ever heard of it?"

"No," Müller said.

"Does Landesmann have any connection to it?"

Müller raised an eyebrow. "I didn't realize this was an official visit, Karl."

"It isn't."

Müller cleared his throat. "As far as I know, Mr. Landesmann has no interest whatsoever in XTE Hardware and Equipment of Shenzhen, China."

"That's good to hear. But I'm afraid the DAP suspects otherwise."

"What are you talking about?"

"Let's just say there's pressure on the chief to order a full investigation."

"Can you stop it?"

"I'm trying."

"Try harder, Karl. This firm pays you exceedingly well to make sure things like this don't happen to our clients, let alone the boss."

Huber frowned. "Why don't you say that a little louder? I'm not sure the Onyx ground station in the Valais was able to hear you."

Müller made no reply.

"You do have one thing working in your favor," Huber said. "The DAP and the Federal Police are going to be extremely reluctant to open a potentially embarrassing probe at a time like this, especially one involving a man as beloved as your owner. Martin is the patron saint of Switzerland. And you can be sure that his friends in the government will think twice about doing anything that tarnishes his reputation. Martin is good for the country."

"But?"

"There's always the potential it will leak to the press the way the Egyptian fax did. If that happens . . ." Huber paused. "As you know, these things have a way of taking on a life of their own."

"Zentrum will be most grateful if you can keep this matter out of the press, Karl."

"How grateful?"

"The money will be transferred first thing Monday morning."

Huber closed the laptop. "There's one other thing to keep in mind. Whoever did this is extremely good. And they had help."

"What kind of help?"

"Someone on the inside. Someone with access to Martin's phone and computer. If I were you, I'd start putting together a list of possible suspects. And then I'd handcuff each one to a radiator and find out who's responsible."

"Thank you for the advice, Karl, but we prefer subtler methods."

Huber gave a sardonic smile. "Try telling that to Rafael Bloch."

ULRICH MÜLLER headed back to the center of Zurich at considerable speed, turning over the implications of what he had just been told. *Someone on the inside . . . Someone with access to Martin's phone and computer . . .* While it was possible Martin had been betrayed by an employee, Müller considered it highly unlikely since all GVI staff were subjected to rigorous background checks and regular security reviews. Müller suspected the traitor was someone much closer to Martin. Someone who was sharing Martin's bed on a regular basis.

He parked in the Kasernenstrasse and headed upstairs. A Kellergruppe operative tried to give Müller an update on the Berlin and Mexico City operations; Müller brushed past without a word and entered his office. His computer was powered on. He hesitated for a few seconds, then called up the guest list for that evening's One World fund-raiser at Villa Elma. The overt side of Zentrum had done a cursory security check on all three hundred of the invitees. Near the bottom of the list, Müller found the name he was looking for. He snatched up his phone and started to dial the number for Martin's mobile. Realizing his mistake, he hung up and dialed Jonas Brunner instead. Brunner answered after three rings, his voice a whisper.

"Where are you?" Müller asked.

"In the ballroom."

"What's that noise?"

"Mr. Landesmann's movie."

Müller swore softly. "Can you see the British reporter?"

Brunner was silent for a few seconds. "She's at the back of the room."

"Is her date with her?"

Another silence, then, "Actually, I can't see him."

"Shit!"

"What's the problem?"

Müller didn't answer directly. Instead, he gave the bodyguard a set of precise instructions, then asked, "How many men do you have there tonight?"

"Forty."

Müller hung up the phone and quickly dialed Zentrum's travel desk.

"I need a helicopter."

"What's your destination?"

"I'll know when I'm airborne."

"How soon do you need it?"

"Now."

65

GENEVA

For a big man, Jonas Brunner was surprisingly quiet on his feet. Not a single head turned as he made his way to Martin's shoulder. Not a single eyebrow rose as he murmured a few words into Martin's ear. Martin appeared momentarily startled by the news, then quickly regained his usual composure and slipped a pale hand into his breast pocket. The Nokia telephone appeared; its screen flared briefly and went dark as the power was extinguished. Martin immediately surrendered it to Brunner, then rose to his feet and followed the security man from the ballroom. By now several of the guests were watching him intently, including the famous British reporter seated next to a Saudi prince of untold wealth. When Martin disappeared from view, she turned back to the film and tried desperately not to show the fear rising inside her. *He's probably just bored silly*, she told herself, but not with much conviction. Zoe could always tell when Martin was bored. Martin wasn't bored. Martin was furious.

GABRIEL REMOVED his headphones, checked the connection, checked the transmission status, jabbed at his keyboard. Then he looked at Lavon in frustration.

"Are you still hearing audio from Zoe's phone?"

"Loud and clear. Why?"

"Because Martin's just went down."

"Any GPS data?"

"Nothing."

"He probably just switched off his phone."

"Why would he do that?"

"Good question."

"What do we do?"

Gabriel typed four words into his computer and hit SEND. Then he keyed into Mikhail's earpiece.

"It's possible we have a problem."

"What's that?"

Gabriel explained.

"Any advice?"

"Sit tight."

"And if several men come through the door?"

"Pull the USB immediately."

"And do what with it?"

Gabriel clipped out.

GABRIEL'S MESSAGE appeared instantly on the status screens of the London ops center: *MARTIN'S PHONE DOWN . . . ADVISE . . .* Adrian Carter swore softly. Uzi Navot closed his eyes and exhaled deeply.

"People shut off their phones all the time," Graham Seymour suggested.

"That's true," Navot said. "But not Martin. Martin never shuts his phone down."

"It's your man in there, Uzi. That means it's your call."

"How much time left on the feed from Martin's computer?"

"Twenty-one and change."

"What are the chances we have what we need?"

"I'm not an expert, but I'd say they're fifty-fifty."

Navot looked at Shamron. Shamron looked stoically back, as if to say that these are the moments careers are made.

"I want better odds than fifty-fifty," Navot said.

"So we wait?"

Navot nodded. "We wait."

MIKHAIL MOVED quietly to the window, parted the curtain a fraction of an inch, and peered into Martin's garden. It was twenty feet down with a guard patrolling the perimeter. But that didn't matter. The office windows were bulletproof and didn't open. Mikhail returned to the desk and checked the status box on Martin's computer screen: *18:26 . . . 18:25 . . . 18:24 . . .*

Sitting tight, he thought. *But what about Zoe?*

JONAS BRUNNER and his security staff worked from an office on the ground floor of the mansion not far from the service kitchen. He led Martin Landesmann inside and dialed Ulrich Müller's number in Zurich.

"Why did you tell me to turn off my phone?"

"Because it's compromised."

"Compromised?"

"Your mobile is broadcasting your life to the world, Martin. So is your computer."

Landesmann's already pale face drained of color. "Who did this?"

"I'm not sure yet. But I think they may have come to your party tonight for a second helping."

"What are you talking about?"

Müller relayed his suspicions. Landesmann listened in silence, then slammed down the phone.

"What do you want me to do, Mr. Landesmann?"

"Find that Russian."

"And Zoe?"

"Give me a few of your men. I'll take care of Zoe."

IT DID NOT take Brunner more than a few minutes to confirm that Mikhail Danilov, companion of Zoe Reed, was not present in the ballroom for the screening of One World's newest production. The length of Mr. Danilov's absence was unclear, as was his present location, though it didn't take long for Brunner to decide where to begin his search.

Wisely, he chose not to go alone, bringing with him four of his most impressively built men. They climbed the back staircase as nonchalantly as possible; once out of sight, each man drew a SIG Sauer P226. At the top of the stairs, they proceeded wordlessly down the hallway, footfalls muted by lush carpeting. Thirty-two feet later, they stopped and turned to the left. The doors leading to the alcove were closed. They yielded without a sound. Brunner slipped inside and paused before the keyless lock, his right hand hovering over the pad. This was the point where the silent approach ended. But there was no choice. Brunner punched in the eight digits and pressed ENTER. Then he placed his hand on the latch and waited for the dead bolts to snap open.

MARTIN RETURNED to the ballroom as the film was nearing its conclusion and sat next to Monique.

"There's something I need to tell you," he said softly, his gaze focused on the screen.

"Perhaps this might not be the best time or place, Martin."

"Actually, I'm afraid it is."

Monique looked at him. "What have you done?"

"I need your help, Monique."

"And if I refuse?"

"We can lose everything."

THE MAN who sprang at Jonas Brunner and his men like a predatory cat had two advantages. One was the advantage of sight—after nearly an hour in the office, his eyes were accustomed to the gloom—while the other was training. Yes, Brunner and his men were all Swiss Army veterans, but the lanky Russian with eyes the color of glacial ice was ex-Sayeret Matkal and therefore expert in the ways of Krav Maga, the official martial art of the Israeli military and intelligence services. What it lacks in beauty it more than makes up for in efficiency and sheer brutality. Its doctrines are simple: continuous motion and constant attack. And once the battle is joined, it does not end until the opponent is on the ground and in need of serious medical attention.

The Russian fought bravely and in near silence. He broke two noses with palm strikes, fractured a cheekbone with an adroit elbow, and left a larynx so damaged its owner would speak with a rasp for the rest of his life. Eventually, though, he was overwhelmed by the greater numbers and combined weight of his opponents. After rendering him defenseless, Brunner and his men pummeled their opponent viciously until he lapsed into unconsciousness, at which point there arose a great swell of applause from one floor below. Brunner briefly imagined it was for him. It wasn't, though. The One World documentary had just ended, and Saint Martin was basking in the adulation of his guests.

GABRIEL DID NOT hear the applause, only the violent struggle that preceded it. Next came the voice of Jonas Brunner ordering his men to take Mr. Danilov quietly down to the cellar. When the signal from the radio vanished from the airwaves, Gabriel didn't bother trying to reestablish contact. Instead, he dialed Zoe's number and closed his eyes. *Answer your phone, Zoe. Answer your damn phone.*

Zoe was filing slowly out of the ballroom when she felt a tap on her shoulder. Turning around, she was greeted by the unexpected sight of Monique Landesmann, a pleasant smile on her face. Zoe felt her cheeks begin to burn but managed a smile of her own.

"I don't believe we've been properly introduced, Zoe." Monique extended her hand. "Martin's told me so much about you. He admires your work a great deal."

"If there were more businessmen like your husband, Mrs. Landesmann, I'm afraid I wouldn't have much to write about."

Zoe was not sure from where she summoned these words, but they seemed to please Monique.

"I hope you enjoyed the film. Martin's very proud of it."

"He should be."

Monique placed a jeweled hand lightly on Zoe's arm. "There's something I need to discuss with you, Zoe. Might we have a brief word in private?"

Zoe hesitated, unsure of what to do, then agreed.

"Wonderful," said Monique. "Come this way."

She led Zoe across the ballroom through a pair of towering doors, then down a marble hallway lit by chandeliers. At the end of the hallway was a small, ornate parlor that looked like something Zoe had seen on a tour of Versailles. Monique paused at the doorway and, with a smile, gestured for Zoe to enter. Zoe never saw the hand that immediately clamped over her mouth or the one that ripped the clutch from her grasp. She tried to struggle, but it was useless. She tried to scream but could barely breathe. As the bodyguards carried Zoe from the room, she managed to twist her head around and cast a pleading glance toward Monique. But Monique never saw it. She had already turned and was making her way back to the party.

MARTIN WAS standing at the center of the main reception room, surrounded as usual. Monique went to his side and slipped an arm proprietarily around his waist.

"Is everything all right?" he asked.

"Everything's fine, darling," she whispered, kissing his cheek. "But if you ever betray me again, I'll destroy you myself."

66

MAYFAIR, LONDON

A chapel silence had fallen over the London ops center by the time Gabriel's last message arrived. Adrian Carter and Graham Seymour, Anglicans both, sat with heads bowed and eyes closed as if in prayer. Shamron and Navot stood shoulder to shoulder, Navot with his wrestler's arms folded across his chest, Shamron with his cigarette lighter twirling anxiously between his fingertips. Chiara was in the fishbowl, scrolling through the contents of Martin Landesmann's hard drive.

"Martin wouldn't dare kill them in the house," said Carter.

"No," Shamron agreed. "First he'll have them driven into the Alps. *Then* he'll kill them."

"Perhaps your team can intercept them on the way out of Villa Elma," Seymour said.

"May I remind you that there are almost two hundred black luxury automobiles lined up in Martin's drive, all of which will be departing at roughly the same time? And then, of course, Martin has access to the lake and several very fast boats." Shamron paused. "Anyone know where we can get a boat on a freezing December night in Geneva?"

"I have friends in the DAP," Carter said without much conviction. "Friends who've occasionally been helpful in our efforts against al-Qaeda."

"They're your friends," Navot said, "not ours. And I can assure you that the DAP would love nothing more than to rub our noses in a very big pile of shit."

"Consider the alternative, Uzi. It might be better for you and your service to lose a little face than one of your best agents and one of Britain's most famous journalists."

"This isn't about pride, Adrian. This is about keeping several of my best people out of a Swiss jail."

"If I handle it, they might not have to go to jail."

"Have you forgotten the name of the man who's sitting in a room in the Grand Hotel Kempinski right now?" Greeted by silence, Navot continued, "I'm not willing to place the fate of Gabriel and the rest of the team in the hands of your friends from the DAP. If there's a deal that has to be made, we'll do it ourselves."

"It's your show, Uzi. What do you suggest?"

Navot turned to Shamron.

"How much of Martin's hard drive did we get before the feed was intercepted?" Shamron asked.

"Roughly ninety percent."

"Then I'd say the odds of finding something interesting just increased dramatically. If I were you, I'd get our computer technicians down here from Highgate and tell them to start looking through that data as if their lives depended on it."

Navot glanced at Seymour and asked, "How long will it take to get them here?"

"With a police escort . . . twenty minutes."

"Ten would be better."

Seymour reached for a phone. Shamron went quietly to Navot's side.

"May I make one other suggestion, Uzi?"

"Please."

"Get Gabriel, Eli, and the rest of the team out of the Kempinski before the Swiss police come knocking."

THE STEPS were built of stone and spiraled downward into the bowels of the old mansion. Zoe's feet never touched them. Five of Zentrum's finest bore her into the gloom, one man for each extremity, one to smother her cries for help. They carried her in the supine position with her head leading the way, so that she was able to see the faces of her tormentors. She recognized all of them from her previous life. Her life before revelation. Her life before truth. Her life before Keppler Werk GmbH of Magdeburg, Germany, and XTE Hardware and Equipment of Shenzhen, China. *Her life before Gabriel . . .*

The stairs emptied into a passageway with damp walls and an arched ceiling. Zoe had the sensation of floating through an Alpine tunnel. There was no light at the end of it, only the wet stench of the lake. Zoe began to thrash violently. One of the guards responded by squeezing her neck in a way that seemed to paralyze her entire body.

At the end of the passageway, they hurled her to the ground and restrained her with silver duct tape, ankles first, wrists next, finally her mouth. Then a single immense bodyguard hoisted her over his shoulder and carried her down another passage and into a small, darkened room that smelled heavily of mold and dust. There he placed Zoe on her feet and asked whether she was able to breathe. When she responded in the affirmative, he drove a huge fist into her abdomen. She folded like a pocketknife and collapsed to the stone floor, struggling for breath.

"How about now? Can you breathe now, Ms. Reed?"

She couldn't. Zoe couldn't breathe. Zoe couldn't see. Zoe couldn't even seem to hear. All she could do was writhe in agony and watch helplessly as lights exploded in her oxygen-starved brain. She did not know how long her contortions lasted. She only knew that at some point she became aware of the fact she was not alone. Lying facedown on the ground next to her—unconscious, tightly bound, wet with blood—was Mikhail. Zoe laid her head on his shoulder and tried to rouse him, but Mikhail made no movement. Then her body began to convulse with an uncontrollable fear, and tears flowed onto her cheeks.

AT THAT same moment, Jonas Brunner was standing alone in his office, staring down at the items on his desk. One Bally wallet with credit cards and identification in the name Mikhail Danilov. One room key from the Grand Hotel Kempinksi. One ultraviolet flashlight. One Sony USB flash drive. One small electronic device with a numeric keypad and wires with alligator clips. One miniature radio and earpiece of indeterminate manufacture. Taken together, the items added up to only one possible conclusion. The man now lying bleeding and unconscious in the cellar of Villa Elma was a professional. Brunner picked up his phone and shared that opinion with Ulrich Müller, who was now airborne over Canton Zurich.

"How long was he alone in the office?"

"We're not sure. Perhaps an hour, maybe more."

"What was the state of the computer?"

"It was on and connected to the Internet."

"Where are they now?"

Brunner answered.

"Can you get them out of the house with no one noticing?"

"No problem."

"Be careful, Jonas. He didn't do this alone."

"What do we do after we get them off the property?"

"I have a few questions I'd like to ask them. In private."

"Where should we take them?"

"East," Müller said. "You know the place."

Brunner did. "What about Monique and Martin?" he asked.

"As soon as the last guest leaves, I want them in the helicopter."

"Monique isn't going to be happy."

"Monique doesn't have a choice."

The line went dead. Brunner sighed and hung up the phone.

GIVEN THE jet-setting nature of the Kempinski's clientele, changes in itinerary were the norm rather than the exception. Regardless, the wave of early departures swamping the reception desk that evening was unusual. First there was an American couple who claimed to have a child in distress. Then there was a pair of Brits who argued bitterly from the time they stepped off the elevator until the moment they finally climbed into their rented Volvo. Five minutes later came a meek figure with disastrous hair who requested a taxi to the Gare de Cornavin, followed soon after by a trim man with gray temples and green eyes who said nothing while the receptionist prepared his bill. He endured a five-minute wait for his rented Audi A6 with admirable patience, though he was obviously annoyed by the delay. When the car finally came, he tossed his bags into the backseat and gave the valet a generous tip before driving away.

It was not the first time the staff of the Kempinski had been misled by guests, but the scale of the deception foisted upon them that night was unprecedented. There was no child in distress and no source of genuine anger between the bickering couple with British passports. In fact, only one of them was actually British, and that had been a long time ago. Within ten minutes of departing the hotel, both couples had taken up positions along the rue de Lausanne, along with the driver of the very expensive S-Class Mercedes sedan. As for the man with green eyes and gray temples, his destination was the Hôtel Métropole—though by the time he arrived at the check-in counter he was no longer Jonathan Albright of Greenwich, Connecticut, but Heinrich Kiever of Berlin, Germany. Upon entering his room, he hung the DO NOT DISTURB sign on his door and immediately established secure communications with his newly redeployed team. Eli Lavon arrived ten minutes later.

"Any change?" he asked.

"Just one," said Gabriel. "The first guests are starting to leave."

67

GENEVA

Zoe thought she heard the sound of approaching footsteps. Whether it was five men or five hundred, she could not tell. She lay motionless on the damp floor, her head still propped against Mikhail's shoulder. The duct tape around her wrists had cut off her circulation, and her hands felt as though a thousand needles were pricking them. She was shaking with cold and fear. And not just for herself. Zoe reckoned she had been locked in the cellar for at least an hour, and Mikhail had yet to regain consciousness. He was still breathing, though, deeply, steadily. Zoe imagined she was breathing for him.

The footfalls drew closer. Zoe heard the heavy door of the room swing open and saw the beam of a flashlight playing over the walls. Eventually, it found her eyes. Behind it, she recognized the familiar silhouette of Jonas Brunner. He examined Mikhail with little concern, then tore the duct tape from Zoe's mouth.

She immediately began to scream for help. Brunner silenced her with two hard slaps across the face.

"What in God's name are you doing, Jonas? This is—"

"Exactly what you and your friend deserve," he said, cutting her off. "You've been lying to us, Zoe. And if you continue to lie, you're only going to make your situation worse."

"My situation? Are you mad, Jonas?"

Brunner only smiled.

"Where's Martin?"

"Mr. *Landesmann,*" Brunner said pointedly, "is busy saying good night to his guests. He asked me to see you out. *Both* of you."

"See us out? Look at my friend, Jonas. He's unconscious. He needs a doctor."

"So do several of my best men. And he'll get a doctor when he tells us who he's working for."

"He works for himself, you idiot! He's a millionaire."

Brunner gave another smile. "You like men with money, don't you, Zoe?"

"If it wasn't for men with money, Jonas, you'd be writing parking tickets in some shitty little village in the Alps."

Zoe never saw the blow coming. A sweeping backhand, it drove her head sideways into Mikhail's blood-soaked neck. Mikhail seemed to stir, then went motionless again. Zoe's cheek radiated with pain, and she could taste blood in her mouth. She closed her eyes, and for an instant it seemed Gabriel was speaking quietly into her ear. *You're Zoe Reed,* he was saying. *You make mincemeat of people like Martin Landesmann. No one tells you what to do. And no one ever lays a hand on you.* She opened her eyes and saw Brunner's face floating behind the glow of the flashlight.

"Who do you work for?" he asked.

"The *Financial Journal* of London. Which means you just slapped the wrong fucking girl, Jonas."

"Tonight?" Brunner asked as if addressing a dull pupil. "Who are you working for tonight, Zoe?"

"I'm not working tonight, Jonas. I came here at Martin's invitation. And I was having a wonderful time until you and your thugs grabbed me and locked me in this godforsaken room. What the hell is going on?"

Brunner studied her for a moment, then looked at Mikhail. "You're here because this man is a spy. We found him in Mr. Landesmann's office during the film. He was stealing material from Mr. Landesmann's computer."

"A spy? He's a businessman. An oil trader of some sort."

Brunner held a small silver object before her eyes. "Have you ever seen this before?"

"It's a flash drive, Jonas. Most people have one."

"That's true. But most people don't have these." Brunner held up an ultraviolet flashlight, a device with wires and alligator clips, and a miniature radio with an earpiece. "Your friend is a professional intelligence officer, Zoe. And we believe you are, too."

"You've got to be kidding, Jonas. I'm a reporter."

"So why did you bring a spy into Mr. Landesmann's home tonight?"

Zoe stared directly into Brunner's face. The words she spoke were not hers. They had been written for her by a man who did not exist.

"I don't know much about him, Jonas. I bumped into him at a reception. He came on very strong. He bought me expensive gifts. He took me to nice restaurants. He treated me very well. In hindsight . . ."

"What, Zoe?"

"Maybe none of it was real. Maybe I was deceived by him."

Brunner stroked the inflamed skin of her cheek. Zoe recoiled.

"I'd like to believe you, Zoe, but I can't let you go without corroborating your story. As a good reporter, you surely understand why I need a second source."

"In a few minutes, my editor is going to be calling to ask about the party. If he doesn't hear from me—"

"He'll assume you're having a wonderful time and leave a message on your voice mail."

"More than three hundred people saw me here tonight, Jonas. And unless you let me out of here very soon, not one of them is going to see me leave."

"But that's not true, Zoe. We all saw you leave, including Mrs. Landesmann. The two of you had a very pleasant conversation shortly before you and Mr. Danilov got into your car and returned to your hotel."

"Are you forgetting that we don't have a car, Jonas? You brought us here."

"That's true, but Mr. Danilov insisted on having his own driver pick him up. I assume his driver is also an intelligence officer." Brunner gave her a humorless smile. "Allow me to present you with the facts of life, Zoe. Your friend committed a serious crime on Swiss soil tonight, and spies don't go running to the police when things go wrong. Which means you could vanish from the face of the earth and no one will ever know what happened."

"I told you, Jonas, I hardly—"

"Yes, yes, Zoe," Brunner said mockingly, "I heard you the first time. But I still need that second source."

Brunner motioned with the flashlight, prompting several of

his men to enter. They covered Zoe's mouth with duct tape again, then wrapped her in thick woolen blankets and bound her so tightly that even the slightest movement was impossible. Enveloped now in a suffocating blackness, Zoe could see but one thing—the terrible vision of Mikhail lying on the floor of the cellar, bound, unconscious, his shirt soaked in blood.

One of the guards asked Zoe if she could breathe. This time, she made no response. The foot soldiers of Zentrum Security seemed to find that amusing, and Zoe heard only laughter as she was lifted from the ground and borne slowly from the cellar as if to her own grave. It was not a grave where they placed her but the trunk of a car. As it moved forward, Zoe began to shake uncontrollably. *There is no safe house in Highgate,* she told herself. No girl named Sally. No tweedy Englishman named David. No green-eyed assassin named Gabriel Allon. There was only Martin. Martin whom she had once loved. Martin who now was sending her into the mountains of Switzerland to be killed.

68

GENEVA

The exodus of guests from Villa Elma began as a trickle at midnight, but by quarter past it had become a torrent of steel and tinted glass. As Shamron had predicted, Martin and his men held a distinct advantage since nearly all the cars leaving the party were black and of German manufacture. Roughly two-thirds headed left toward central Geneva while the remaining third turned right toward Lausanne and Montreux. Positioned in three separate vehicles along the road, Gabriel's team watched the passing vehicles for anything out of the ordinary. A car with two men in the front seat. A car traveling at an unusually high rate of speed. A car riding a bit low on its rear axle.

Twice pursuits were undertaken. Twice pursuits were quickly called off. Dina and Mordecai gave needless chase to a BMW sedan for several miles along the lakeshore while Yossi and Rimona briefly shadowed a Mercedes SL coupe as its occupants wandered Geneva apparently searching for the next party. From his holding point at the gas station, Yaakov saw nothing worth chasing. He just sat with his hands wrapped tightly around the wheel, berating himself for ever letting Zoe and Mikhail out of his sight. Yaakov had spent years running informants and spies in the worst hellholes of the West Bank and Gaza without getting a single one killed. And to think he was about to suffer the first loss of his career here, along the tranquil shores of Lake Geneva. Not possible, he thought. *Madness* . . .

But it was possible, and the likelihood of such an outcome seemed to increase with each whispered transmission flowing from Gabriel's desperate team to the new command center at the Hôtel Métropole. It was Eli Lavon who communicated directly with the team and Lavon who filed the updates to London. Gabriel monitored the radio traffic from his outpost in the window. His gaze was fixed on the lights of Villa Elma burning like bonfires on the far shore of the lake.

Shortly after one a.m., the lights were extinguished, signaling the official conclusion of Martin's annual gala. Within minutes, Gabriel heard the beating of rotors and saw the running lights of a helicopter descending slowly toward Martin's lawn. It remained there scarcely more than a minute, then rose once again and turned eastward over the lake. Lavon joined Gabriel at the window and watched the helicopter disappear into the darkness.

"Do you suppose Mikhail and Zoe are on that bird?"

"They could be," Gabriel conceded. "But if I had to guess, I'd say that's Martin and Monique."

"Where do you think they're going?"

"At this hour . . . I can think of only one place."

As IT turned out, it took just fifteen minutes for Graham Seymour to get the two Office computer technicians from the safe house in Highgate to Grosvenor Square. They were quickly joined by four cybersleuths from MI5, along with a team of Iran analysts from the CIA and MI6. Indeed, by midnight London time, more than a dozen officers from four intelligence services were huddled around the computer in the fishbowl, watched over intently by Chiara. As for the four most senior members of Operation Masterpiece, they remained at their posts, staring glumly at the messages streaming across the status boards.

"Looks as if our boy has decided to flee the scene of the crime," Seymour said, face buried in his hands. "Do you think there's any way Mikhail and Zoe are still inside that mansion?"

"I suppose there's always a chance," said Adrian Carter, "but Martin doesn't strike me as the sort to leave a mess lying around. Which means the clock is now definitely ticking."

"That's true," said Shamron. "But we have several things working in our favor."

"Really?" asked Seymour incredulously, gesturing toward the status boards. "Because from where I sit, it looks as though Zoe and Mikhail are about to disappear without a trace."

"No one's going to disappear." Shamron paused, then added gloomily, "At least, not right away." He laboriously lit a cigarette. "Martin isn't stupid, Graham. He'll want to know exactly who Mikhail and Zoe are working for. And he'll want to know how much damage has been done. Getting information like that takes time, especially when a man like Mikhail Abramov is involved. Mikhail will make them work for it. That's what he's trained to do."

"And what if they decide to take a shortcut?" asked Seymour. "How long do you expect Zoe to be able to hold up?"

"I'm afraid I have to side with Graham," said Carter. "The only way we're going to get them back is to make a deal."

"With whom?" asked Navot.

"At this point, our options are rather limited. Either we call Swiss security or we deal directly with Martin."

"Have you ever stopped to consider they might be the same thing? After all, this is Switzerland we're talking about. The DAP exists not only to protect the interests of the Swiss Confederation but of its financial oligarchy as well. And not necessarily in that order."

"And don't forget," Shamron said, "Landesmann owns Zentrum Security, which is filled with former officers of the DAP. That means we can't go to Martin on bended knee. If we do, he'll be able to rally the Swiss government to his defense. And we could lose everything we've worked for."

"The centrifuges?" Seymour drew a heavy breath and stared at the row of digital clocks at the front of the ops center. "Let me make something very clear, gentlemen. Her Majesty's Government has no intention of allowing harm to come to a prominent British subject tonight. Therefore, Her Majesty's Government will go to the Swiss authorities independently, if necessary, to secure a deal for Zoe's release."

"A separate peace? Is that what you're suggesting?"

"I'm not *suggesting* anything. I'm *telling* you my patience has limits."

"May I remind you, Graham, that you're not the only one with a citizen at risk? And may I also remind you that by going to the DAP you will be exposing our entire operation against Martin?"

"I'm aware of that, Ari. But I'm afraid my girl trumps your agent. And your operation."

"I didn't realize we were the only ones involved in this," Navot said acidly.

Seymour made no response.

"How long will you give us, Graham?"

"Six a.m. London time, seven a.m. Geneva."

"That's not long."

"I understand," Seymour said. "But it's all the time you have."

Shamron turned to Navot.

"I'm afraid the Geneva team has outlived its usefulness. In fact, at this point they're our biggest liability."

"Withdrawal?"

"Immediate."

"They're not going to like it."

"They don't have a choice." Shamron pointed at the technicians and analysts crowded around the computers in the fishbowl. "For the moment, our fate is in their hands."

"And if they can't find anything by six o'clock?"

"We'll make a deal." Shamron crushed out his cigarette. "That's what we do. That's what we always do."

IN THE finest tradition of Office field commands, the message that arrived on Gabriel's computer twenty seconds later was brief and entirely lacking in ambiguity. It came as no surprise—in fact, Gabriel had already instructed the team to prepare for such an eventuality—but none of that made the decision any easier.

"They want us out."

"How far out?" asked Eli Lavon.

"France."

"What are we supposed to do in France? Light candles? Keep our fingers crossed?"

"We're supposed to *not* get arrested by the Swiss police."

"Well, I'm not leaving here without Zoe and Mikhail," Lavon said. "And I don't think any of the others will agree to leave, either."

"They don't have a choice. London has spoken."

"Since when have you ever listened to Uzi?"

"The order didn't come from Uzi."

"Shamron?"

Gabriel nodded.

"I assume the order applies to you as well."

"Of course."

"And is it your intention to disregard it?"

"Absolutely."

"I thought that would be your answer."

"I recruited her, Eli. I trained her and I sent her in there. And there's no way I'm going to let her end up like Rafael Bloch."

Lavon could see there was no use arguing the point. "You know, Gabriel, none of this would have happened if I'd stopped you from going to Argentina. You'd be watching the sunset in Cornwall tonight with your pretty young wife instead of presiding over another deathwatch in yet another godforsaken hotel room."

"If I hadn't gone to Argentina, we would have never discovered that Saint Martin Landesmann built his empire upon the looted wealth of the Holocaust. And we would have never discovered that Martin was compounding his sins by doing business with a regime that talks openly about carrying out a second Holocaust."

"All the more reason you should have an old friend watching your back tonight."

"My old friend has been ordered to evacuate. Besides, I've given him enough gray hairs for two lifetimes."

Lavon managed a fleeting smile. "Just do me a favor, Gabriel. Martin may have managed to beat us tonight. But whatever you do, don't give him an opportunity to run up the score. I'd hate to lose my only brother over a shipload of centrifuges."

Gabriel said nothing. Lavon placed his hands on either side of Gabriel's head and closed his eyes. Then he kissed Gabriel's cheek and slipped silently out the door.

THE MERCEDES-BENZ S-Class sedan with a sticker price far in excess of a hundred thousand dollars slid gracefully to the curb outside the Hôtel Métropole. It had been purchased in order to ferry a striking young couple to a glamorous party. Now it was being used as a lifeboat, certainly one of the most expensive in the long and storied history of the Israeli intelligence services. It paused long enough to collect Lavon, then swung an illegal U-turn and headed across the Pont du Mont-Blanc, the first leg of its journey toward the French border.

Gabriel watched the taillights melt into the darkness, then sat down at his computer and reread the last encrypted dispatch from the ops center. *Six a.m. London time, seven a.m. Geneva time . . .* After that, Graham Seymour was planning to press the panic button and bring the Swiss into the picture. That left Gabriel, Navot, and Shamron just two and a half hours to strike a deal on better terms. Terms that didn't include exposing the operation. Terms that wouldn't allow Martin and his centrifuges to wriggle off Gabriel's hook.

In London, the computer technicians and analysts were searching the contents of Martin's hard drive for a bargaining chip. Gabriel already had one of his own—a list of names and account numbers hidden for sixty years inside *Portrait of a Young Woman,* 104 by 86 centimeters, by Rembrandt van Rijn. Gabriel laid the three pages of fragile onionskin carefully on the desk and photographed each with the camera of his secure mobile phone. Then he typed a message to London. Like the one he had received just a few minutes earlier, it was brief and entirely lacking in ambiguity. He wanted Ulrich Müller's telephone number. And he wanted it now.

69

GSTAAD, SWITZERLAND

The Swiss ski resort of Gstaad lies nestled in the Alps sixty miles northeast of Geneva in the German-speaking canton of Bern. Regarded as one of the most exclusive destinations in the world, Gstaad has long been a refuge for the wealthy, the celebrated, and those with something to hide. Martin Landesmann, chairman of Global Vision Investments and executive director of the One World charitable foundation, fell into all three categories. Therefore, it was only natural Martin would be drawn to it. Gstaad, he said in the one and only interview he had ever granted, was the place he went when he needed to clear his head. Gstaad was the one place where he could be at peace. Where he could dream of a better world. And where he could unburden his complex soul. Since he assiduously avoided traveling to Zurich, Gstaad was also a place where he could hear a bit of his native Schwyzerdütsch—though only occasionally, for even the Swiss could scarcely afford to live there anymore.

The comfortably well-off are forced to make the ascent to Gstaad by car, up a narrow two-lane road that rises from the eastern end of Lake Geneva and winds its way past the glaciers of Les Diablerets, into the Bernese Oberland. The immensely rich, however, avoid the drive at all costs, preferring instead to land their private jets at the business airport near Saanen or to plop directly onto one of Gstaad's many private helipads. Martin preferred the one near the fabled Gstaad Palace Hotel since it was only a mile from his chalet. Ulrich Müller stood at the edge of the tarmac, coat collar up against the cold, watching as the twin-turbine AW139 sank slowly from the black sky.

It was a large aircraft for private use, capable of seating a dozen comfortably in its luxurious custom-fitted cabin. But on that morning only eight people emerged—four members of the Landesmann family surrounded by four bodyguards from Zentrum Security. Well-attuned to the moods of the Landesmann clan, Müller could see they were a family in crisis. Monique walked several paces ahead, arms draped protectively around the shoulders of Alexander and Charlotte, and disappeared into a waiting Mercedes SUV. Martin walked over to Müller and without a word handed him a stainless steel attaché case. Müller popped the latches and looked inside. One Bally wallet with credit cards and identification in the name of Mikhail Danilov. One room key from the Grand Hotel Kempinksi. One ultraviolet flashlight. One Sony USB flash drive. One electronic device with a numeric keypad and wires with alligator clips. One miniature radio and earpiece of indeterminate manufacture.

There are many myths about Switzerland. Chief among them

is the long-held but misplaced belief that the tiny Alpine country is a miracle of multiculturalism and tolerance. While it is true four distinct cultures have coexisted peacefully within Switzerland's borders for seven centuries, their marriage is much more a defensive alliance than a union of true love. Evidence of that fact was the conversation that followed. When there was serious business to be done, Martin Landesmann would never dream of speaking French. Only Swiss German.

"Where is he?"

Müller tilted his head to the left but said nothing.

"Is he conscious yet?" asked Landesmann.

Müller nodded

"Talking?"

"Says he's ex-FSB. Says he works as an independent contractor for Russian private security companies and was hired by a consortium of Russian oligarchs to steal your most closely held business secrets."

"How did he get to my mobile phone and laptop?"

"He claims to have done it from the outside."

"How does he explain Zoe?"

"He says he learned of your relationship through surveillance and decided to exploit it in order to gain access to the party tonight. He says he deceived her. He claims she knows nothing."

"It's plausible," Landesmann said.

"Plausible," Müller conceded. "But there's something else."

"What's that?"

"The way he fought my men. He's been trained by an elite unit or intelligence service. He's no FSB thug. He's the real thing, Martin."

"Israeli?"

"I think so."

"If that's true, what does it say about Zoe?"

"She may be telling the truth. She may know nothing. But it's also possible they recruited her. Using an agent in place, especially a woman, is consistent with their operating doctrine. It's possible she's been spying on you from the beginning."

Landesmann glanced over toward the cars, where his family was waiting with visible impatience. "How much material has Onyx managed to intercept?"

"Enough to raise eyebrows."

"Can it be contained?"

"I'm working on it. But if a friendly service like the DAP is suspicious about what they're seeing, imagine how the material must look to an intelligence agency that doesn't have your best interests at heart."

"You're my chief security adviser, Ulrich. Advise me."

"The first thing we need to do is find out who we're dealing with and how much they know."

"And then?"

"One thing at a time, Martin. But do me one favor. Stay off the phone for the rest of the night." Müller glanced at the black sky. "Onyx is listening. And you can be sure everyone else is as well."

70

CANTON BERN, SWITZERLAND

Zoe did not know where they were taking her, of course. She only knew that the road they were now traveling was winding and that they were gaining altitude. The first fact was readily apparent by the violent lurching of the car, the second by the fact her ears were popping at regular intervals. To make matters worse, her abdomen ached where she had been struck, and she was intensely nauseated. Zoe was only grateful that she had been far too nervous to eat at Martin's party. Otherwise, it was quite possible she would have vomited into her duct-tape gag long ago and choked to death without Martin's bodyguards knowing a thing.

Her discomfort was made worse by the cold. The temperature seemed to be dropping by degrees with each passing minute. During the first part of the drive, the cold had been manageable. Now, in spite of the heavy blankets binding her body, it was eating away at her bones. She was so cold that she was no longer shivering. She was in agony.

In an attempt to ease her suffering, she played mind games. She wrote an article for the *Journal,* reread her favorite passages from *Pride and Prejudice,* and relived the moment in the bar of the Belvedere Hotel in Davos when Jonas Brunner had asked whether she would like to have a drink with Mr. Landesmann. But in this adaptation, she politely told Brunner to sod off and resumed her conversation with the African finance minister, now the most profoundly interesting exchange she had ever had in her life. This incarnation of Zoe Reed never met Martin Landesmann, never interviewed him, never slept with him, never fell in love with him. Nor was she ever scooped up by MI5 outside the London studios of CNN or taken to a safe house in Highgate. *There is no safe house in Highgate,* she reminded herself. No girl named Sally. No tweedy Englishman named David. No green-eyed assassin named Gabriel Allon.

Her thoughts were interrupted by the sudden slowing of the car. The road was much rougher now. In fact, Zoe doubted whether it was a road at all. The car lost traction, regained it, then fishtailed wildly for several seconds before finally staggering to a stop. The engine went dead, and Zoe heard four doors open and close in rapid succession. Then the trunk popped open, and she felt herself rise into the frigid air. Again they carried her on their shoulders like pallbearers carrying a coffin. Her journey was shorter this time, a few seconds, no more. Zoe could hear them sawing away at the duct tape. Then they rolled her twice to free her from the blankets.

Though not blindfolded, Zoe could see nothing. The place where they had taken her was black as pitch. They lifted her again, carried her a short distance, and placed her in a chair with no arms. Again they bound her with duct tape, this time to the back of the chair. Then lights came on, and Zoe screamed.

71

CANTON BERN, SWITZERLAND

Mikhail's position was a mirror image of Zoe's—hands and feet bound, torso secured to a straight-backed chair, duct tape over his mouth. He was fully conscious now and, judging from the blood flowing from his mouth, he had recently been struck. His tuxedo jacket had been removed; his shirt was torn in several places and soaked with blood. The contents of his wallet lay scattered on the cement floor at his feet, along with the USB flash drive and the ultraviolet light. Zoe tried not to look at the items. Instead, she kept her eyes focused on the tall, middle-aged man standing halfway between her and Mikhail. He was wearing a dark blue banker's suit and a woolen overcoat. The hair was Germanic blond going to gray, the expression on his face one of mild distaste. In one hand was a gun, in the other Mikhail's miniature radio. The gun had blood on it. Mikhail's blood, she thought. But that made sense. The man in the dark blue suit didn't look like the sort who liked to use his fists. He also looked vaguely familiar. Zoe was certain she had seen him somewhere before in close proximity to Martin. But in her current state she couldn't recall where it had been.

She glanced quickly around. They were in a commercial storage facility of some sort. It was cheaply made of corrugated metal and stank of dirty motor oil and rust. The overhead lights buzzed. For a moment, Zoe allowed herself to wonder whether Rafael Bloch had spent time in this same place before his body was taken across the border and dumped in the French Alps. Then she forced the thought from her mind. *Rafael Bloch? Sorry, doesn't ring a bell.* She looked at Mikhail. He was staring directly at her as if trying to communicate something. Zoe held his gaze for as long as she could bear it, then looked down at her hands. This movement seemed to prompt the well-dressed man into action. He came over and ripped the duct tape from her mouth. Zoe gave an involuntary scream of pain and immediately regretted it.

"Who are you?" she snapped. "And why in God's name am I here?"

"You know why you're here, Zoe. In fact, thanks to your associate, Mr. Danilov, we all know why you're here."

He spoke English with only the faintest accent and with the precision of a timepiece.

"Are you crazy? I'm here because Martin—"

"No, Zoe. You're here because you're a spy. And you came to Geneva to steal private documents and correspondence from Mr. Landesmann's computer, a very serious crime here in Switzerland."

"I presume kidnapping and assault are as well."

The man in the suit smiled. "Ah, the famous Zoe Reed wit. It's good to know that at least something about you isn't a lie."

"I'm a reporter, you idiot. And when I get out of here, I'm going to find out who you are and destroy you."

"But you're not really a reporter at all, are you, Zoe? Your job at the *Financial Journal* is nothing but a cover. Two years ago, you were ordered by your superiors at British intelligence to form a sexual relationship with Mr. Landesmann in order to spy on his business operations. You made contact with Mr. Landesmann by expressing interest in interviewing him. Then, twenty-two months ago, you made contact with him in Davos."

"That's madness. Martin tried to seduce *me* in Davos. He invited me to his suite for dinner."

"That's not the way Jonas Brunner and the rest of Mr. Landesmann's security detail remember the evening, Zoe. They recall that you were very flirtatious and aggressive. And that's what they'll tell the Swiss police." He paused, then added, "But it doesn't have to come to that, Zoe. The sooner you confess, the sooner we can resolve this unpleasant affair."

"I have nothing to confess other than foolishness. Obviously, I was a fool ever to believe Martin's lies."

"What lies are those, Zoe?"

"*Saint* Martin," she said, her voice dripping with contempt.

The man was silent for a moment. When he finally spoke again, he did so not to Zoe but to the gun in his hand.

"Say the words, Zoe. Confess your sins. Tell me the truth. Tell me that you're not a real reporter. Tell me that you were ordered by your superiors in London to seduce Mr. Landesmann and steal his private documents."

"I won't say it because it's not true. I loved Martin."

"Did you?" He looked up from the gun as if genuinely surprised, then at Mikhail. "And what about your friend, Mr. Danilov? Are you in love with him, too?"

"I hardly know him."

"That's not what he says. According to Mr. Danilov, you two are working together on the Landesmann case."

"I'm not working with anyone. And I don't know anything about a *Landesmann* case. I don't know why there would even be a *Landesmann* case."

"That's not what Mr. Danilov says."

Zoe looked directly at Mikhail for the first time since the interrogation had begun. He held her gaze for a few seconds, then almost imperceptibly shook his head. Zoe's inquisitor noticed. He walked slowly over to Mikhail and struck him hard across the face with the butt of the gun, opening another gash high on his cheek. Then the man took a fistful of Mikhail's hair and pressed the barrel of the gun against his temple. A guard standing on the opposite side took a hasty step backward. The man holding the gun screwed the barrel into Mikhail's skin, then turned his head and looked at Zoe.

"You have one chance to tell the truth, Zoe. Otherwise, Mr. Danilov is going to die. And if he dies, you die. Because we can't have witnesses lying around, can we? Confess your sins, Zoe. Tell me the truth."

Mikhail was wincing with pain. But this time he didn't try to hide his message to Zoe. He was shaking his head violently from side to side, shouting something into the duct tape covering his mouth. This earned him two more blows with the butt of the gun. Zoe closed her eyes.

"Last chance, Zoe."

"Put the gun down."

"Only if you tell me the truth."

"Put the gun down." She opened her eyes. "Put it down, and I'll tell you everything you want to know."

"Tell me now."

"Stop, damn it. You're hurting him."

"I'm going to do much worse if you don't start talking. Tell me the truth, Zoe. Tell me you're a spy."

"I'm not a spy."

"So why did you help them?"

"Because they asked me to."

"Who did?"

"British intelligence."

"Who else?"

"Israeli intelligence."

"Who's in charge of the operation?"

"I don't know."

"Who's in charge, Zoe?"

"I don't know his real name."

"You're lying, Zoe. Tell me his name."

"His name is Gabriel."

"Gabriel Allon?"

"Yes, Gabriel Allon."

"Was he in Geneva tonight?"

"I don't know."

"Answer me, Zoe. Was he in Geneva tonight?"

"Yes."

"Were there others?"

"Yes."

"Tell me their names, Zoe. All of them."

72

MAYFAIR, LONDON

The digital clock at the front of the London ops center read *05:53:17*. Less than seven minutes remaining until Graham Seymour's deadline. Shamron stared at the numbers despondently as if trying to mentally blunt their advance. It was odd, he thought, but in his youth time had always seemed to slow to a crawl at moments like these. Now the clock was roaring along at a gallop. He wondered whether it was yet another consequence of growing old. Time was his most implacable foe.

Regrettably, Shamron had lived through many such Office catastrophes and knew how the next few hours were likely to unfold. Once upon a time, the Europeans might have been expected to turn a blind eye. But no more. These days, they no longer had much use for the enterprise known as the State of Israel, and Shamron knew full well that the operation against Martin Landesmann was not going to go over well in the halls of

European power. Yes, the British and Americans had been along for the ride, but none of that would matter when the arrest warrants were issued. Not one would bear an American or British name. Only Israeli names. *Yossi Gavish, Dina Sarid, Yaakov Rossman, Rimona Stern, Gabriel Allon* . . . They had carried out some of the greatest operations in the history of the Office. But not tonight. Tonight, Saint Martin had beaten them.

Shamron turned his gaze toward Uzi Navot. He was seated in a cubicle reserved for the FBI, a secure telephone pressed to his ear. At the other end of the call was the prime minister. It was never pleasant to wake a prime minister—especially when the news involved a looming diplomatic and political disaster—and Shamron could only imagine the tirade Navot was now enduring. He could not help but feel an ache of guilt. Navot had wanted no part of Landesmann and would now be forced to pay the price for Shamron's folly. Shamron would do his best to shield Navot from harm, but he knew how these things went. A head would have to roll. And it was likely to be Navot's.

He looked at the clock again: *05:56:38* . . . Three and a half minutes until Graham Seymour telephoned the Swiss police. Three and a half minutes for the team of computer technicians and specialists to find the bargaining chip Shamron needed to achieve peace with honor. With Chiara peering anxiously over their shoulders, their labors were growing more frantic. Shamron wished he could help in some way. But he barely knew how to turn on a computer, let alone find a document buried in a pile of cybermush. Only the young knew how to do such things, Shamron thought gloomily. Yet more proof he had finally outlived his usefulness.

Another glance at the clock: *05:58:41* . . . Graham Seymour was now watching the time with an intensity matching Shamron's. At his right elbow was a telephone. An hour earlier, Seymour had taken the liberty of storing the DAP's emergency number in the phone's memory. One press of a button was all it would take.

The clock advanced: *05:59:57* . . . *05:59:58* . . . *05:59:59* . . . *06:00:00* . . .

Seymour lifted the receiver and looked at Shamron. "Sorry, Ari, but I'm afraid we've run out of time. I know it's not my call, but you might want to tell Gabriel to start heading for the border."

Seymour jabbed at the speed dial button and lifted the receiver to his ear. Shamron closed his eyes and waited for the words he would no doubt hear for the rest of his life. Instead, he heard the heavy glass door of the fishbowl open with a bang, followed by the triumphant voice of Chiara.

"We've got him, Graham! He's ours now! Hang up the phone! We've got him!"

SEYMOUR KILLED the connection. The receiver, however, was still in his hand.

"What exactly do you have?"

"The next shipment of centrifuges is due to leave Shenzhen in six weeks, arriving in Dubai sometime in mid-March, final payment due upon delivery to Meissner Privatbank of Liechtenstein."

"What's the source?"

"An encrypted temporary file that had once been attached to an e-mail."

"Who were the parties to the e-mail?"

"Ulrich Müller and Martin Landesmann."

"Let me see it."

Chiara handed Seymour a printout of the documents. Seymour examined them, then replaced the receiver.

"You just bought yourself one more hour, Ari."

Shamron turned to Chiara. "Can you get those documents to Gabriel securely?"

"No problem."

THE E-MAIL and supporting documentation were five pages in length. The computer technicians converted them to an encrypted PDF file and fired it to Gabriel over the secure link. It arrived on his computer at the Métropole at 7:05 local time, accompanied by the number for Ulrich Müller's mobile phone and his private e-mail address. Locating them had not been difficult. Both appeared hundreds of times in the memory of Martin's Nokia N900. Gabriel quickly prepared an e-mail to Müller with two PDF attachments and dialed his number. There was no answer. Gabriel killed the connection and dialed again.

ULRICH MÜLLER was driving past the floodlit Gstaad Palace Hotel when his mobile rang for the first time. Because he did not recognize the number, he did not answer. When the phone immediately rang a second time, he felt he had no choice. He tapped the CALL button and lifted the phone to his ear.

"*Ja?*"

"Good morning, Ulrich."

"Who is this?"

"Don't you recognize my voice?"

Müller did. He'd heard it on the surveillance tapes from Amsterdam and Mendoza.

"How did you get this number?" he asked.

"Are you driving, Ulrich? It sounds to me as if you're behind the wheel of a car."

"What do you want, Allon?"

"I want you to pull over, Ulrich. There's something you need to see."

"What are you talking about?"

"I'm going to send you an e-mail, Ulrich. I want you to look at it carefully. Then I want you to call me back at this number." A pause. "Did your phone capture this number?"

"I have it."

"Good. After you look at the e-mail, call me back. Right away. Otherwise, the next calls I make are to the Swiss Federal Police and the DAP."

"Don't you need my e-mail address, Allon?"

"No, Ulrich, I already have it."

The connection went dead. Müller pulled to the side of the road. Thirty seconds later, the e-mail came through.

Shit . . .

MÜLLER DIALED. Gabriel answered right away.

"Interesting stuff, don't you think, Ulrich?"

"I don't know what any of this means."

"Nice try. But before we go any further, I want to know whether my people are alive."

"Your people are fine."

"Where are they?"

"That's none of your concern."

"Everything is my concern, Ulrich."

"They're in my custody."

"Have they been mistreated?"

"They committed a serious crime in Martin Landesmann's home last night. They've been treated accordingly."

"If they've been harmed in any way, I'm going to hold you personally responsible. *And* your boss."

"Mr. Landesmann knows nothing about this."

"That's very admirable of you to try to take the blame for your employer, but it's not going to work, Ulrich. Not today."

"What do you want?"

"I want to talk to Martin."

"That's impossible."

"It's nonnegotiable."

"I'll see what I can do."

"You'd better, Ulrich. Or the next call I make is to the Swiss Federal Police."

"I need thirty minutes."

"You have five."

ZOE AND MIKHAIL sat face-to-face in the storage facility, each bound to a chair, mouths covered with duct tape. The guards had fled for the warmth of their cars. Before leaving, they had switched off the lights. The darkness was absolute, as was the cold. Zoe wanted to apologize to Mikhail for betraying the operation. Zoe wanted to tend to Mikhail's wounds. And more than anything, Zoe wanted reassurance that someone was looking for them. But none of that was possible. Not with the tape over their mouths. And so they sat in the cold, mute and motionless, and they waited.

Martin Landesmann's immense timbered chalet was ablaze with light as Ulrich Müller drove through the security gate and sped quickly up the long drive. A pair of guards stood watch outside the front entrance, shifting from foot to foot in the sharp early-morning cold. Müller walked past them without a word and entered the residence. Landesmann was seated alone before a fire in the great room. He was dressed in faded blue jeans and a heavy zippered sweater and holding a crystal snifter filled with cognac. Müller placed a finger to his lips and handed Landesmann the phone. Landesmann scrolled through the two PDF files, his face a blank mask. When he was finished, Müller took back the phone and switched it off before slipping it into the pocket of his overcoat.

"What does he want?" Landesmann asked.

"His people back. He'd also like to have a word with you."

"Tell him to go fuck himself."

"I tried."

"Is he in the country?"

"We'll know soon enough."

Landesmann carried his drink over to the fire. "Get him up here, Ulrich. And make sure he's in a less demanding mood by the time he arrives."

Müller powered on his phone and headed outside. The last

sound he heard as he was leaving was a crystal snifter exploding into a thousand pieces.

GABRIEL'S PHONE rang ten seconds later.

"You cut it very close, Ulrich."

"Mr. Landesmann has agreed to see you."

"A wise move on his part."

"Now, listen carefully—"

"No, Ulrich. *You* listen. I'll be in the parking lot above the Promenade in Gstaad in ninety minutes. Have your men meet me. And no bullshit. If my people don't hear from me by ten a.m. at the latest, that e-mail you just read goes to every intelligence service, law enforcement agency, justice ministry, and newspaper in the Western world. Are we clear, Ulrich?"

"The Promenade in Gstaad, ninety minutes."

"Well done, Ulrich. Now make sure my people are comfortable. If they're not, you'll make an enemy of me. And that's the last thing you want."

Gabriel killed the connection and quickly typed out a final message to London. Then he packed away the computer and headed for the elevator.

73

CANTON BERN, SWITZERLAND

A gust of freezing air scraped at the back of Zoe's neck as the door of the storage facility swung open. She closed her eyes and prayed for the first time in many years. *What now?* she wondered. Another round of interrogation? Another ride in the trunk of a car? Or had Martin finally decided the time had come to rid the world of another meddlesome reporter? Zoe feared there was no other possible outcome, especially now that she had betrayed the entire operation. Indeed, for the past several minutes she had found herself composing her own obituary. Only the lead eluded her. Martin and his thugs had yet to supply one crucial fact: the cause of her death.

She opened her eyes and looked at Mikhail. His face was illuminated by a shaft of gray light from the open door, and he was staring at the guards intently as they approached Zoe from behind. One of them removed the duct tape from her mouth, carefully this time, while another gently freed her hands and feet. Two other guards did the same for Mikhail while a third applied ointment and bandages to cuts on his face and scalp. The guards gave no explanation for their sudden hospitality, all of which was performed with typical Swiss efficiency. After handing each prisoner a blanket, they departed as suddenly as they had come. Zoe waited until the door was closed before speaking.

"What just happened?"

"Gabriel just happened."

"What are you talking about?"

Mikhail placed a finger to his lips. "Don't say another word."

A WAVE of jubilation and relief washed over the ops center when Gabriel's update flashed across the status screens. Even Graham Seymour, who had been in a state of near catatonia for the past several minutes, managed a brief smile. There were two people in the ops center, however, who seemed incapable of sharing in the joy of the moment. One was Ari Shamron; the other, Chiara Allon. Once again, an operation was in the hands of a man they loved. And once again they had no choice but to wait. And to swear to themselves that this was the last time. *The very last time . . .*

THE E63 MOTORWAY stretched eastward, immaculately groomed, empty of traffic. Gabriel kept both hands on the wheel of the Audi and his speed respectable. On the left side of the highway, neatly pruned vineyards advanced like columns of soldiers into the hills of Vaud. On his right lay Lake Geneva, with the Savoy Alps rising in the background. The base of the range was still shrouded in mist, but the highest peaks glowed with the first light of dawn.

He continued past Montreux to Aigle, then turned onto Route 11 and headed into the Vallée des Ormonts. It was a narrow, two-lane road, twisting and full of unexpected switchbacks. A few miles beyond Les Diablerets was the border separating Canton Vaud from Canton Bern. The signs immediately changed to German, as did the architecture of the houses. The first rays of sunlight were beginning to creep over the Bernese Alps, and by the time Gabriel reached the outskirts of Gstaad it was beginning to get light. He drove to the main lot in the center of the village and backed into a space in the far corner. In an hour, the lot would be jammed with cars. But for now it was empty except for a trio of snowboarders drinking beer around a battered VW van.

Gabriel left the engine running and watched the dashboard clock as the ninety-minute deadline he had imposed on Ulrich Müller came and went. He granted Müller a ten-minute grace period before finally reaching for the phone. He was in the process of dialing when a silver Mercedes GL450 sport-utility turned into the lot. It eased past the snowboarders and stopped a few yards from Gabriel's Audi. Inside were four men, all wearing matching dark blue ski jackets emblazoned with the insignia of Zentrum Security. The one in the rear passenger seat climbed out and motioned Gabriel over. Gabriel recognized him. It was Jonas Brunner.

Gabriel shut down the engine, locked his phone in the glove box, and climbed out. Brunner watched with a slightly bemused expression as though taken aback by Gabriel's modest stature.

"I'm told you speak German," Brunner said.

"Better than you," replied Gabriel.

"Are you armed?"

"No."

"Do you have a phone?"

"In the car."

"Radio?"

"In the car."

"What about a beacon?"

Gabriel shook his head.

"I'm going to have to search you."

"I can't wait."

Gabriel climbed into the back of the Mercedes and slid across to the center. Brunner got in after him and closed the door.

"Turn around and get on your knees."

"Here?"

"Here."

Gabriel did as he was told and was subjected to a more-than-thorough search, beginning with his shoes and ending with his scalp. When it was over, he turned around again and sat normally. Brunner signaled the driver, and the SUV eased forward.

"I hope you enjoyed that as much as I did, Jonas."

"Shut your mouth, Allon."

"Where are my people?"

Brunner didn't answer.

"How far are we going?"

"Not far. But we have to make a brief stop along the way."

"Coffee?"

"Yes, Allon. Coffee."

"I hope you didn't hurt my girl, Jonas. Because if you hurt her, I'm going to hurt you."

THEY HEADED due east along the edge of a narrow glacial valley. The road ducked in and out of the trees, leaving them in darkness one minute, blinding light the next. The blue-coated guards of Zentrum Security did not speak. Brunner's shoulder was pressing against Gabriel's. It was like leaning against a granite massif. The guard on Gabriel's left was flexing and unflexing his thick hands as if preparing for his solo. Gabriel had no illusions about the stop they were making on their way to see Martin. He wasn't surprised; it was a customary proceeding before a meeting like this, an aperitif before dinner.

At the head of the valley the road turned to a single-lane track before rising sharply up the slope of the mountain. A snowplow had passed through recently, but the Mercedes was barely able to maintain traction as it headed toward the summit. A thousand feet above the valley floor, it came to a stop next to a secluded grove of fir trees. The two men in front immediately climbed out, as did the one on Gabriel's left. Jonas Brunner made no movement.

"I don't think you'll enjoy this as much as you enjoyed the search."

"Is this the part where your men soften me up a bit before I get taken to see Saint Martin?"

"Just get out of the car, Allon. The sooner we get this over with, the sooner we can be on our way."

Gabriel sighed heavily and climbed out.

JONAS BRUNNER watched as his three best men marched Gabriel Allon into the trees, then marked the time. Five minutes, he'd told them. Not too much damage, just enough bruising to make him compliant and easy to handle. A part of Brunner was tempted to join in the festivities. He couldn't. Müller wanted an update.

He was dialing Müller's number when a movement in the trees caught his attention. Looking up, he saw a single figure walking purposefully out of the shadows. He glanced at his watch and frowned. He'd ordered his men to be judicious, but two minutes was hardly enough time to do the job right, especially when it involved a man like Gabriel Allon. Then Brunner looked at the figure closely and realized his mistake. It was not one of his own men coming out of the trees. *It was Allon . . .* In his hand was a gun, a SIG Sauer P226, the standard-issue sidearm of Zentrum Security. The Israeli ripped open Brunner's door and pointed the barrel of the gun directly into his face. Brunner didn't even think about reaching for his weapon.

"I'm told you speak German, Jonas, so listen carefully. I want you to give me your gun. Slowly, Jonas. Otherwise, I might be tempted to shoot you several times."

Brunner reached into his jacket, removed his weapon and handed it to the Israeli butt first.

"Give me your phone."

Brunner complied.

"Do you have a radio?"

"No."

"A beacon?"

Brunner shook his head.

"Too bad. You might need one later. Now get behind the wheel."

Brunner did as he was told and started the engine. The Israeli sat behind him, gun to the back of Brunner's head.

"How far are we going, Jonas?"

"Not far."

"No more stops?"

"No."

Brunner slipped the Mercedes into gear and continued up the slope of the mountain.

"Congratulations, Jonas. You just provided me with a weapon and turned yourself into a hostage. All in all, very well played."

"Are my men alive?"

"Two of them are. I'm not so sure about the third."

"I'd like to call for a doctor."

"Just drive, Jonas."

74

CANTON BERN, SWITZERLAND

They climbed another thousand feet into the mountains and stopped at the edge of a sunlit ledge of glistening snow and ice high above the valley floor. In the center of the glade was an AW139 helicopter, engines silent, rotors still. Martin Landesmann waited near the tail, eyes concealed by wraparound sunglasses, his expression that of a man who had dropped by on his way to somewhere else. Ulrich Müller hovered anxiously next to him. Gabriel glanced at Jonas Brunner's eyes in the rearview mirror and told him to shut off the engine. Brunner did as he was told.

"Give me the key."

Brunner removed it and handed it to Gabriel.

"Put both hands on the wheel, Jonas. And don't move."

Gabriel climbed out and tapped on Brunner's window with the barrel of the gun. Brunner emerged, hands in the air.

"Now we walk, Jonas, nice and slow. Don't do anything to make Martin nervous."

"He prefers to be called Mr. Landesmann."

"I'll try to remember that." Gabriel jabbed Brunner in the kidney with the barrel of the gun. "Move."

Brunner advanced slowly toward the helicopter, Gabriel two paces behind, the gun at his side. Ulrich Müller managed to maintain a placid expression, but Martin was clearly displeased by the ignominious arrival of his personal security chief. At Gabriel's command, Brunner stopped ten yards short of his masters. Gabriel raised the gun and pointed it at Müller.

"Are you armed?" Gabriel asked in German.

"No."

"Open your overcoat."

Müller unbuttoned his coat, then opened the sides simultaneously.

"Now the suit jacket," said Gabriel.

Müller did the same thing. No gun. Gabriel glanced at the pilot.

"What about him?"

"This isn't Israel," Müller said. "This is Switzerland. Helicopter pilots aren't armed."

"What a relief." Gabriel looked at Martin Landesmann. "And you, Martin? Do you have a gun?"

Landesmann made no response. Gabriel repeated the question in rapid French. This time, Landesmann gave a superior smile and in the same language said, "Don't be ridiculous, Allon."

Gabriel reverted to German. "I'd ask you to open your coat, Martin, but I know you're telling the truth. Men like you don't soil their hands with weapons. That's what people like Ulrich and Jonas are for."

"Are you finished, Allon?"

"I'm just getting started, Martin. Or is it *Saint* Martin? I can never remember which you prefer."

"Actually, I prefer to be called Mr. Landesmann."

"So I've been told. I assume you've had a chance to review the material I sent earlier this morning?"

"Those documents mean nothing."

"If that were true, Martin, you wouldn't be here."

Landesmann gave Gabriel a withering stare, then asked, "Where did you get it?"

"The information on your pending sale of centrifuges to the Islamic Republic of Iran?"

"No, Allon, the *other* document."

"You mean the list? The names? The accounts? The money deposited in your father's bank?"

"Where did you get it?" Landesmann repeated, his tone even.

"I got it from Lena Herzfeld, Peter Voss, Alfonso Ramirez, Rafael Bloch, and a young woman who kept it hidden and safe for many, many years."

Landesmann's face registered no change.

"Don't you recognize the names, Martin?" Gabriel glanced at Müller. "What about you, Ulrich?"

Neither man responded.

"Let me help," Gabriel said. "Lena Herzfeld was a young Dutch Jewish girl whose life was traded for a Rembrandt. Peter Voss was a decent man who tried to atone for the sins of his father. Alfonso Ramirez had proof that a small private bank in

Zurich was filled with looted Holocaust assets. And Rafael Bloch was the Argentine journalist who uncovered your ties to a German firm called Keppler Werk GmbH."

"And the young woman?" asked Landesmann.

"Oil on canvas, 104 by 86 centimeters." Gabriel paused. "But you already knew that, didn't you? You've been looking for her for a long time. She was the most dangerous one of all."

Landesmann ignored the last remark and asked, "What is it you want, Allon?"

"Answers," Gabriel said. "When did you learn the truth? When did you find out that your father had stolen the money that Kurt Voss hid in his bank?"

Landesmann hesitated.

"I have the list, Martin. It's not a secret anymore."

"He told me about it a few days before his death," Landesmann said after another pause. "The money, the painting, the visit from Voss's wife, Carlos Weber . . ."

"Your father admitted to killing Weber?"

"My father didn't kill Weber," Landesmann said. "It was handled for him."

"Who did it?"

Landesmann glanced at Müller. "An earlier version of Ulrich."

"They come in handy, don't they? Especially in a country like Switzerland. Concealing the more repugnant aspects of your past is a national tradition, rather like your chocolates and your clean streets."

"They're not as clean as they used to be," Landesmann said. "Especially in certain neighborhoods. Too many damn foreigners in the country all the time."

"It's good to know you haven't forsaken your Swiss German roots entirely, Martin. Your father would be proud."

"Actually, it was Father who suggested I leave Zurich. He knew the banks would eventually pay a price for their activities during the war. He thought it might hurt my image."

"Your father was a clever man." Gabriel was silent for a moment. "You built your empire on a great crime, Martin. Did your conscience ever bother you? Did you ever feel guilty? Did you ever lose a night's sleep?"

"It wasn't my crime, Allon. It was my father's. And as your own Scripture makes clear, the son will not bear the punishment for the father's iniquity."

"Unless the son compounds his father's sins by using the stolen fortune as the basis for a lucrative worldwide holding company called Global Vision Investments."

"I didn't realize Ezekiel contained such a passage."

Gabriel ignored Landesmann's sarcasm. "Why didn't you come forward, Martin? The original value of the accounts was a drop in the bucket compared to the wealth you created."

"A drop in the bucket?" Landesmann shook his head. "Do you remember the Swiss banking scandal, Allon? The autumn of 1996? Every day brought a new headline about our collaboration with Nazi Germany. We were being called Hitler's Swiss fences. Hitler's bankers. The jackals were circling. If anyone had ever discovered the truth, GVI would have been torn limb from limb. The litigation would have gone on for years. *Decades*. The descendants of *any* Jew in *any* country where Kurt Voss had operated could have come forward and made a claim against me. The class-action lawyers would have been falling over themselves to sign up clients and file suits. I would have lost everything. And for what? For something my father did a half century earlier? Forgive me, Allon, but I didn't feel it was necessary for me to endure such a fate because of him."

Landesmann made an impassioned case for his innocence, thought Gabriel. But like most things about him, it was a lie. His father had been driven by greed. And so was Martin.

"So you did exactly what your father did," Gabriel said. "You kept quiet. You profited wildly from the fortune of a mass murderer. And you continued to look for a lost masterpiece by Rembrandt that had the power to destroy you. But there was one difference. At some point, you decided to become a saint. Even your father wouldn't have had the nerve for that."

"I don't like to be referred to as Saint Martin."

"Really?" Gabriel smiled. "That might be the most encouraging thing I've ever heard about you."

"And why is that?"

"Because it suggests you might actually have a conscience after all."

"What are you going to do with that list, Allon?"

"I suppose that depends entirely on you, Martin."

75

CANTON BERN, SWITZERLAND

"What do you want, Allon? Money? Is that what this is about? A shakedown? How much will it cost me to make this matter go away? A half billion? A billion? Name your figure. I'll write you a check, and we'll call it a morning."

"I don't want your money," Gabriel said. "I want your centrifuges."

"Centrifuges?" Landesmann's tone was incredulous. "Where did you get the idea I was selling centrifuges?"

"From your computers. It's all there in black-and-white."

"I'm afraid you're mistaken. I own companies that sell dual-use components to trading companies that in turn sell them to other companies that may or may not be selling them to a certain manufacturer in Shenzhen, China."

"A manufacturer that you own through a Chinese partnership."

"Enjoy trying to prove that in court. I've done nothing illegal, Allon. You can't lay a finger on me."

"That might be true when it comes to Iran, but there's one thing that hasn't changed. You can still be torn to shreds by the class-action lawyers in America. And I have the evidence to bring you down."

"You have nothing."

"Are you really willing to take that chance?"

Landesmann made no reply.

"I have a hidden child in Amsterdam, a remorseful son in Argentina, contemporaneous diplomatic cables from Carlos Weber, and a list of names and numbers of accounts from your father's bank. And if you don't agree to cooperate, I'm going to take everything I have to New York City and give it to the most prominent law firm in town. They'll file suit against you in federal court for unjust enrichment and spend years picking through every aspect of your business. I doubt your saintly reputation will hold up under scrutiny like that. I also suspect your friends and protectors in Bern might resent you for reopening the most scandalous chapter in Swiss history."

"Allow me to impart a sad truth to you, Allon. If I wasn't doing business with the Iranians, one of my competitors would be. Yes, we make all the appropriate noises. But do you think we Europeans truly care whether Iran has a nuclear weapon? Of course not. We need Iranian oil. And we need access to the Iranian market. Even your so-called friends in America are doing a brisk business with the Iranians through their foreign subsidiaries. Face facts, Allon. You are alone. Again."

"We're not alone anymore, Martin. We have *you*."

Though Martin's eyes were concealed by sunglasses, he was

now having difficulty maintaining his veneer of confidence. Martin was wrestling, thought Gabriel. Wrestling with his father's sins. Wrestling with the illusion of his own life. Wrestling with the fact that, for all his money and power, Saint Martin had been bested on this morning by the child of a survivor. For a moment, Gabriel considered appealing to Martin's sense of decency. But Martin had none. Martin had only an instinct for self-preservation. And Martin had his greed. Greed had compelled Martin to conceal the truth about the source of his wealth. And greed would make Martin realize he had no choice but to reach for the lifeline Gabriel was offering him.

"What exactly are you proposing?" Landesmann said at last.

"A partnership," said Gabriel.

"What sort of partnership?"

"A *business* partnership, Martin. You and me. Together, we're going to do business with Iran. You will get to keep your money and your reputation. Your life will go on as though nothing has changed. But with one important difference. You work for me now, Martin. I *own* you. You've just been recruited by Israeli intelligence. Welcome to our family."

"And how long will this partnership last?"

"As long as we deem necessary. And if you step out of line, I'll throw you to the wolves."

"And the profits?"

"Couldn't resist, could you?"

"This *is* a business deal, Allon."

Gabriel looked toward the sky. "I think fifty-fifty sounds fair."

Landesmann frowned. "Do you see no ethical issue in the intelligence service of the State of Israel profiting from the sale of gas centrifuges to the Islamic Republic of Iran?"

"Actually, I think I rather like it."

"How long do I have to consider your offer?"

"About ten seconds."

Landesmann raised his sunglasses and looked at Gabriel for a moment in silence. "Your two agents will be dropped off at the base of Les Diablerets in one hour. Call me when you wish to finalize the details of our relationship." He paused. "I assume you have my numbers?"

"*All* of them, Martin."

Landesmann headed toward the door of the helicopter, then stopped.

"One last question."

"What's that?"

"How long was Zoe working for you?"

Gabriel smiled. "We'll be in touch, Martin."

Landesmann turned without another word and boarded the helicopter, followed by Müller and Brunner. The cabin door closed, the twin turbines whined, and within seconds Gabriel was awash in a cloud of blowing snow. Martin Landesmann stared at him through the window as if enjoying this one small measure of revenge. Then he ascended into the pale blue sky and vanished into the sun.

76

LES DIABLERETS, SWITZERLAND

Gabriel left Martin's Mercedes SUV in a tow-away zone in central Gstaad and drove to Les Diablerets in the Audi. He parked near the base of the gondola and entered a café to wait. It was filled with excited neon-clad skiers oblivious to the bargain that had just been struck on a sunlit glade a few miles away. As Gabriel ordered coffee and bread, he couldn't help but marvel at the incongruity of the scene. He was struck, too, by the fact that, despite his advancing age, he had never once been on skis. Chiara had been begging him for years to take her on a ski vacation. Perhaps he would finally succumb. But not here. Maybe Italy or America, he thought, but not Switzerland.

Gabriel carried his coffee and bread to the front of the café and sat at a table with a good view of the road and parking lot. A dark-haired woman with a young boy asked to join him; together, they watched as the gondola rose like a dirigible and disappeared into the mountains. Gabriel checked the time on his secure mobile phone. The deadline was still ten minutes away. He wanted to call Chiara and tell her he was safe. He wanted to tell Uzi and Shamron he had just closed the deal of a lifetime. But he didn't dare. Not over the air. It was a coup, perhaps the greatest of Gabriel's career, but it was his alone. He'd had accomplices, some willing, some not so willing. Lena Herzfeld, Peter Voss, Alfonso Ramirez, Rafael Bloch, Zoe Reed . . .

He glanced at the time again. Five minutes until the deadline. Five minutes until the first test of the Allon-Landesmann joint venture. Nothing to do now but wait. It was a fitting end, he thought. Like most Office veterans, he had made a career of waiting. Waiting for a plane or a train. Waiting for a source. Waiting for the sun to rise after a night of killing. And waiting now for Saint Martin Landesmann to surrender two agents who had very nearly disappeared from the face of the earth. The waiting, he thought. Always the waiting. Why should this morning be any different?

He turned over the phone, concealing the digital clock, and stared out the window. To help pass the time, he made small talk with the woman, who looked far too much like his mother for Gabriel's comfort, and with the boy, who was not much older than Dani had been on the night of his death in Vienna. And all the while he kept his eyes fastened on the road. And on the morning traffic streaming out of the Oberland. And, finally, on the silver Mercedes GL450 sport-utility vehicle now turning into the parking lot. It was driven by a man wearing a dark blue ski jacket emblazoned with the insignia of Zentrum Security. Two figures, a man and a woman, sat in back. They, too, wore Zentrum jackets. The man's eyes were concealed by large sunglasses. Gabriel turned over his phone and looked at the time. One hour exactly. There were certain advantages to doing business with the Swiss.

He bade the woman and child a pleasant morning and stepped outside into the sunlight. The Mercedes sport-utility had come to a stop. A striking woman and a lanky man with blond hair were in the process of climbing out. It was the woman who first noticed Gabriel. But in a stroke of professionalism belying her inexperience, she did not call out to him or even acknowledge his presence. Instead, she simply took her companion gently by the arm and led him over to the Audi. Gabriel had the engine running by the time they arrived. A moment later, they were heading down the Vallée des Ormonts, Zoe at Gabriel's side, Mikhail stretched out in the backseat.

"Lift your glasses," said Gabriel.

Mikhail complied.

"Who did that to you?"

"I never caught their names." Mikhail lowered the glasses and propped his head against the window. "Did you beat him, Gabriel? Did you beat Martin?"

"No, Mikhail. You and Zoe beat him. You beat him badly."

"How much of his computer did I get?"

"We own him, Mikhail. He's ours."

"Where to now?"

"Out of Switzerland."

"I'm in no condition to fly."

"So we'll drive instead."

"No more airplanes, Gabriel?"

"No, Mikhail. Not for a while."

PART FIVE

RECOVERY

77

NEW SCOTLAND YARD, LONDON

Detective Inspector Kenneth Ramsay, chief of Scotland Yard's Art and Antiques Squad, scheduled the news conference for two p.m. Within minutes of the announcement, rumors of a major recovery swept the pressroom. The speculation was fed mainly by the few surviving veterans of the Metropolitan Police beat, who read a great deal of significance into the timing of the news conference itself. An early-afternoon summons nearly always meant the news was flattering since it would leave reporters several hours to research and write their stories. If the news were bad, the veterans postulated, Ramsay would have summoned the press corps hard against their evening deadlines. Or, in all likelihood, he would have released a bland paper statement, the refuge of cowardly civil servants the world over, and slipped out a back door.

Naturally, the speculation centered around the Van Gogh self-portrait pinched from London's Courtauld Gallery several months earlier, although by that afternoon few reporters could even recall the painting's title. Sadly, not one of the masterpieces stolen during the "summer of theft" had been recovered, and more paintings seemed to be disappearing from homes and galleries by the day. With the global economy mired in a recession without end, it appeared art theft was Europe's last growth industry. In contrast, the police forces battling the thieves had seen their resources cut to the bone. Ramsay's own annual budget had been slashed to a paltry three hundred thousand pounds, barely enough to keep the office functioning. His fiscal straits were so dire he had recently been forced to solicit private donations in order to keep his shop running. Even *The Guardian* suggested it might be time to close the fabled Art Squad and shift its resources to something more productive, such as a youth crime-prevention program.

It did not take long for the rumors about the Van Gogh to breach the walls of Scotland Yard's pressroom and begin circulating on the Internet. And so it came as something of a shock when Ramsay strode to the podium to announce the recovery of a painting few people knew had ever been missing in the first place: *Portrait of a Young Woman,* oil on canvas, 104 by 86 centimeters, by Rembrandt van Rijn. Ramsay refused to go into detail as to precisely how the painting had been found, though he went to great pains to say no ransom or reward money was paid. As for its current location, he claimed ignorance and cut off the questioning.

There was much the press would never learn about the recovery of the Rembrandt. Even Ramsay himself was kept in the dark about most aspects of the case. He did not know, for example, that the painting had been quietly left in an alley behind a synagogue one week earlier in the Marais section of Paris. Or that it had been couriered to London by a sweating employee of the Israeli Embassy and turned over to Julian Isherwood, owner and sole proprietor of the sometimes solvent but never boring Isherwood Fine Arts, 7-8 Mason's Yard, St. James's. Nor would DI Ramsey ever learn that by the time of his news conference, the painting had already been quietly moved to a cottage atop the cliffs in Cornwall that bore a striking resemblance to the *Customs Officer's Cabin at Pourville* by Claude Monet. Only MI5 knew that, and even within the halls of Thames House it was strictly need to know.

IN KEEPING with the spirit of Operation Masterpiece, her restoration would be a whirlwind. Gabriel would have three months to turn the most heavily damaged canvas he had ever seen into the star attraction of the National Gallery of Art's long-awaited Rembrandt: A Retrospective. Three months to reline her and attach her to a new stretcher. Three months to remove the bloodstains and dirty varnish from her surface. Three months to repair a bullet hole in her forehead and smooth the creases caused by Kurt Voss's decision to use her as the costliest envelope in history. It was an alarmingly short period of time, even for a restorer used to working under the pressure of a ticking clock.

In his youth, Gabriel had preferred to work in strict isolation, but now that he was older he no longer liked to be alone. So with Chiara's blessing, he removed the furnishings from the living room and converted it into a makeshift studio. He rose before dawn each morning and worked until early evening, granting himself just one short break each day to walk the cliffs in the bitterly cold January wind. Chiara rarely strayed far from his side. She assisted with the relining and composed a small note to Rachel Herzfeld that Gabriel concealed against the inside of the new stretcher before tapping the last brad into place. She was even present the morning Gabriel undertook the unpleasant task of removing Christopher Liddell's blood. Rather than drop the soiled swabs onto the floor, Gabriel sealed them in an aluminum canister. And when it came time to remove the dirty varnish, he began on the curve of Hendrickje's breast, the spot where Liddell had been working the night of his murder.

As usual, Chiara was bothered by the dizzying stench of Gabriel's solvents. To help cover the smell, she prepared lavish meals, which they ate by candlelight at their table overlooking Mount's Bay. Though they tried not to relive the operation over dinner, the constant presence of the Rembrandt made it a difficult subject to avoid. Invariably, Chiara would remind Gabriel that he would never have undertaken the investigation if she had not insisted.

"So you enjoyed being back at the Office?" Gabriel asked, taunting her a bit.

"Parts of it," Chiara conceded. "But I would be just as happy if the Landesmann operation turned out to be your last masterpiece."

"It's not a masterpiece," Gabriel said. "Not until those centrifuges are in place."

"Does it bother you to leave it in Uzi's hands?"

"Actually, I prefer it." Gabriel looked at the battered painting propped on the easel in the living room. "Besides, I have other problems at the moment."

"Will she be ready in time?"

"She'd better be."

"Are we going to attend the unveiling?"

"I haven't decided yet."

Chiara gazed at the painting. "I understand all the reasons why Lena decided to let the National Gallery have it, but . . ."

"But what?"

"I think I would find it hard to give her up."

"Not if your sister had been turned to ash because her hair was dark."

"I know, Gabriel." Chiara looked at the painting again. "I think she's happy here."

"You wouldn't feel that way if you spent as much time with her as I do."

"She's misbehaving?"

"Let's just say she has her moods."

For the most part, Gabriel and Chiara managed to keep the outside world at bay after their return to Cornwall. But in late February, as Gabriel was laboring through the teeth of the restoration, Martin Landesmann managed to intrude on their seclusion. It seemed Saint Martin, after an unusually long absence from public view, had decided to raise the stakes on his annual appearance at Davos. After opening the forum by pledging an additional hundred million dollars to his African food initiative, he delivered an electrifying speech that was unanimously declared the highlight of the week. Not only did the oracle declare an end to the Great Recession, he described himself as "more hopeful than ever" about the future of the planet.

Saint Martin seemed particularly upbeat about the potential for progress in the Middle East, though events on the ground the very day of his remarks seemed to conflict with his optimism.

Along with the usual litany of terrorist horrors, there was an alarming report from the IAEA concerning the state of the Iranian nuclear program. The agency's director dispensed with his usual caution and predicted the Iranians were perhaps only months from a nuclear capability. "The time for talk is over," he said. "The time for action is finally upon us."

In a somewhat shocking break with past tradition, Martin ended his week at Davos by agreeing to make a brief appearance in the media center to take a few questions from the press. Not present was Zoe Reed, who had requested a leave of absence from the *Financial Journal* for reasons never made clear to her colleagues. Still more intriguing was the fact no one had seen her for some time. Like the Rembrandt, Zoe's whereabouts were strictly need to know. Indeed, even Gabriel was never told her exact location. Not that he could have been much help in her recovery. Hendrickje would never have allowed it.

In mid-April, on the first remotely pleasant day in Cornwall in months, Gerald Malone, CEO of Latham International Media, announced he was selling the venerable *Financial Journal* to the former Russian oligarch Viktor Orlov. Two days later, Zoe surfaced briefly to say she would be leaving the *Journal* to take a television job with CNBC in America. By coincidence, her announcement came on the very day Gabriel finished the retouching of Hendrickje's face. The next morning, when the painting was thoroughly dry, he covered it with a fresh coat of varnish. Chiara caught him standing in front of the canvas, one hand to his chin, head tilted slightly to one side.

"Is she ready for her coming-out party?" asked Chiara.

"I think so," said Gabriel.

"Does she approve of your work?"

"She's not speaking to me at the moment."

"Another quarrel?"

"I'm afraid so."

"Have you made a decision about Washington?"

"I think she needs us to be there."

"So do I, Gabriel. So do I."

78

WASHINGTON, D.C.

By the time Gabriel and Chiara arrived in America, their silent but demanding houseguest of three months was an international sensation. Her celebrity was not instant; it was rooted in an affair she'd had four hundred years earlier with a painter named Rembrandt and by the long and tragic road she had traveled ever since. Once upon a time, she would have been forced to live out her days in shame. Now they were lining up for tickets just to have a glimpse of her.

In an era when museums had been scorched repeatedly by provenance scandals, the director of the National Gallery of Art had felt compelled to reveal much of her sordid past. She had been sold in Amsterdam in 1936 to a man named Abraham Herzfeld, acquired by coercion in 1943 by an SS officer named Kurt Voss, and sold twenty-one years later in a private transaction conducted by the Hoffmann Gallery of Lucerne. At the request of the White House, the National Gallery never revealed the name of the Zurich bank where she had been hidden for several years, nor was there any mention of the document once hidden inside her. Her links to a looted Holocaust fortune had been carefully erased, just like the bullet hole in her forehead and the blood that had stained her garment. No one named Landesmann had ever laid hands on her. No one named Landesmann had ever killed to protect her terrible secret.

Her scandalous past did nothing to tarnish her reception. In fact, it only added to her allure. There was no escaping her face in Washington. She stared from billboards and buses, from souvenir shirts and coffee mugs, and even from a hot-air balloon that floated over the city the day before her unveiling. Gabriel and Chiara saw her for the first time minutes after stepping off their plane at Dulles Airport, gazing at them disapprovingly from an advertisement as they glided through customs on false passports. They saw her again peering from a giant banner as they hurried up the steps of the museum through an evening thunderstorm, this time as if urging them to quicken their pace. Uncharacteristically, they were running late. The fault was entirely Gabriel's. After years of toiling in the shadows of the art world, he'd had serious misgivings about stepping onto so public a stage, even clandestinely.

The exhibition opening was a formal, invitation-only affair. Even so, all guests had to have their possessions searched, a policy instituted at the gallery immediately after the attacks of 9/11. Julian Isherwood was waiting just beyond the checkpoint beneath the soaring main rotunda, gazing nervously at his wristwatch.

Seeing Gabriel and Chiara, he made a theatrical gesture of relief. Then, looking at Gabriel's clothing, he tried unsuccessfully to conceal a smile.

"I never thought I would live to see the day you put on a tuxedo."

"Neither did I, Julian. And if you make any more cracks—"

Chiara silenced Gabriel with a discreet elbow to the ribs. "If it would be at all possible, I'd like to get through the evening without you threatening to kill anyone."

Gabriel frowned. "If it wasn't for me, Julian would be trying to scrounge up forty-five million dollars right now. The least he can do is show me a modicum of respect."

"There'll be plenty of time for that later," Isherwood said. "But right now there are two people who are very anxious to see you."

"Where are they?"

"Upstairs."

"In separate rooms, I hope?"

Isherwood nodded gravely. "Just as you requested."

"Let's go."

Isherwood led them across the rotunda through a sea of tuxedos and gowns, then up several flights of wide marble steps. A security guard admitted them into the administrative area of the museum and directed them to a waiting room at the end of a long carpeted hallway. The door was closed; Gabriel started to turn the latch but hesitated.

She's fragile. They're all a bit fragile . . .

He knocked lightly. Lena Herzfeld, child of the attic, child of darkness, said, "Come in."

SHE WAS SEATED ramrod straight at the center of a leather couch, knees together, hands in her lap. They were clutching the official program of the exhibition, which was wrinkled and wet with her tears. Gabriel and Chiara sat on either side of her and held her tightly while she wept. After several minutes, she looked at Gabriel and touched his cheek.

"What shall I call you tonight? Are you Mr. Argov or Mr. Allon?"

"Please call me Gabriel."

She smiled briefly, then looked down at the program.

"I'm still amazed you were actually able to find her after all these years."

"We would never have been able to do it without the help of Kurt Voss's son."

"I'm glad he came tonight. Where is he?"

"Just down the hall. If you wouldn't mind, he'd like to have a word with you in private before the unveiling. He wants to apologize for what his father did."

"It wasn't his crime, Gabriel. And his apology won't bring my sister back."

"But it might help to hear it." Gabriel held her hand. "You've punished yourself long enough, Lena. It's time for you to let someone else bear the guilt for your family's murder."

Tears spilled onto her cheeks, though she emitted not a sound. Finally, she composed herself and nodded. "I'll listen to his apology. But I will not cry in front of him."

"There's something I need to warn you about, Lena."

"He looks like this father?"

"An older version," Gabriel said. "But the resemblance is striking."

"Then I suppose God decided to punish him, too." She shook her head slowly. "To live with the face of a murderer? I cannot imagine."

For Peter Voss's sake, Lena managed to conceal her shock when seeing him for the first time, though controlling her tears proved impossible. Gabriel remained in the room with them only a moment, then slipped into the corridor to wait with Chiara and Isherwood. Lena emerged ten minutes later, eyes raw, but looking remarkably composed. Gabriel took her hand and said there was one more person who wanted to see her.

Portrait of a Young Woman, oil on canvas, 104 by 86 centimeters, by Rembrandt van Rijn, was propped on an easel in a small holding room, covered by baize cloth, surrounded by several security guards and a nervous-looking curator. Chiara held Lena by the arm while Gabriel and Isherwood carefully removed the cover.

"She looks more beautiful than I remember."

"It's not too late to change your mind, Lena. If you don't want to give her up permanently, Julian can alter the terms of the contract so it's only a temporary loan."

"No," she said after a pause. "I can't care for her, not at my age. She'll be happier here."

"You're sure?" Gabriel pressed.

"I'm sure." Lena looked at the painting. "You put a prayer to my sister inside it?"

"Here," said Chiara, pointing to the center of the bottom portion of the frame.

"It will stay with her always?"

"The museum has promised to keep it there forever," said Gabriel.

Lena took a hesitant step forward. "I was never able to say good-bye to her that night in Amsterdam. There wasn't time." She looked at Gabriel. "May I touch her? One final time?"

"Carefully," said Gabriel.

Lena reached out and traced her finger slowly over the dark hair. Then she touched the bottom of the frame and walked silently from the room.

THE UNVEILING had been scheduled for eight, but due to circumstances never explained to the guests it was closer to half past before *Portrait of a Young Woman* was carried into the rotunda, cloaked in her shroud of baize. Unexpectedly, Gabriel felt as nervous as a playwright on opening night. He found a hiding place with Isherwood and Chiara at the edge of the crowd and stared at his shoes during several long and deeply boring speeches. Finally, the lights dimmed and the covering came off to tumultuous applause. Chiara kissed his cheek and said, "They adore it, Gabriel. Look around you, darling. They don't realize it, but they're cheering for you."

Gabriel looked up but immediately managed to find the one

person in the crowd who was not clapping. She was a woman in her mid-thirties with dark hair, olive-complected skin, and intoxicating green eyes that were focused directly on him. She raised a glass of champagne in his direction and mouthed the words, "Well done, Gabriel." Then she handed the glass to a passing waiter and headed toward the exit.

79

WASHINGTON, D.C.

"You never told me how much I look like her," said Zoe.

"Like Hendrickje?" Gabriel shrugged. "You're much prettier than she is."

"I'm sure you say that to all the girls."

"Only the ones I place in great danger."

Zoe laughed. They were walking along the edge of the Mall, the vast dome of the Capitol floating before them, the Washington Monument rising at their backs. Paris, Greece, and Egypt, thought Gabriel, all in the space of a few hundred yards. He looked at Zoe carefully. She was wearing an elegant evening gown, similar to the one she had worn to Martin's party, and a slender strand of pearls at her throat. Despite everything she had been through, she appeared relaxed and happy. It seemed to Gabriel that the burden of deception had been lifted from her shoulders. She was Zoe before the lies. Zoe before Martin.

"I didn't realize you were planning to come."

"I wasn't," she said. "But I decided I couldn't miss it."

"How did you manage to get a ticket?"

"Membership has its privileges, darling."

"You should have let me know."

"And how might I have done that? Call you? Drop you an e-mail or a text message?" She smiled. "Do you even *have* an e-mail address?"

"Actually, I do. But it doesn't work like a normal account."

"What a surprise," said Zoe. "How about a mobile phone? Do you carry one?"

"Only under duress."

"Mine's been acting up on me. You're not doing anything funny to it, are you?"

"You're off the grid, Zoe."

"I'm not sure I'll ever think of my phone quite the same way."

"You shouldn't."

They crossed the stone esplanade separating the main building of the National Gallery from its east wing.

"Do you always bring members of your team to openings or is that gorgeous creature on your arm tonight your wife?" Zoe gave him a sideways glance and smiled. "I do believe you're blushing, Mr. Allon. If you'd like, I can teach you a few tricks of the trade to help you better conceal your emotions."

Gabriel was silent.

"Is this the part where you're going to remind me that you demand truthfulness in others while concealing yourself behind a cloak of lies?"

"I'm not at liberty to discuss my personal life, Zoe."

"So we're not all going to be friends?"

"I'm afraid it doesn't work that way."

"Too bad," she said. "I always liked her. And, for the record, when we were all in Highgate together you two did a damn lousy job of hiding the fact you're madly in love."

"There is no safe house in Highgate, Zoe."

"Ah, yes, I forgot."

Gabriel changed the subject. "You look lovely, Zoe. New York obviously agrees with you."

"I still haven't managed to find a decent cup of tea."

"No second thoughts about leaving the newspaper business?"

"There *is* no newspaper business," Zoe said acidly. "What did you think of Martin's performance at Davos?"

"I sleep easier at night knowing that Martin is optimistic about our future."

"Has he been behaving himself?"

"I hear he's been a model prisoner."

"What's going on with the centrifuges?"

"There are no centrifuges, Zoe, at least none where Martin is concerned. Martin never puts a foot wrong. He's pure of heart and noble of intent. He's a saint."

"And to think I actually fell for that bilge."

"From our point of view, we're very glad you did." Gabriel smiled and guided her toward the main building. "Have you heard from him?"

"Martin? Not a peep. But it galls me to no end that he's actually going to get away with it. After what he and Müller did to Mikhail, I wish I could bring them down myself."

"You're still covered by the Official Secrets Act, Zoe. Even here in America."

"The MI6 station in Washington reminds me of that on a regular basis." Zoe smiled and asked about Mikhail.

"From what I hear, he's like new."

"Just like the Rembrandt?"

"I doubt Mikhail needed as much work as the Rembrandt."

"Do send him my best. I'm afraid I still see his face in my dreams every night."

"It won't last forever."

"Yes," she said distantly, "that's what the MI5 psychiatrists told me."

They had reached the gallery's front entrance. Chiara and Isherwood were waiting outside with Lena Herzfeld.

"Who's the woman with your wife?"

"She's the reason we recruited you," Gabriel said.

"Lena?"

Gabriel nodded. "Would you like to meet her?"

"If it's all right with you, I'll just admire her from afar." Zoe hailed a passing taxi. "If you ever need someone to do another dangerous job, you know where to find me."

"Go back to your life."

"I'm trying to," she said, smiling. "But it's just not as bloody interesting as yours."

Zoe kissed his cheek and climbed into the taxi. As it pulled away from the curb, Gabriel felt his phone vibrating in the breast pocket of his jacket. It was an e-mail from King Saul Boulevard, just one word in length.

Boom . . .

80

THE LIZARD PENINSULA, CORNWALL

As with nearly every other aspect of Operation Masterpiece, deciding precisely what to do with Martin Landesmann's centrifuges was the source of a contentious internal debate. Roughly speaking, there were three options—only fitting, since the political leadership and intelligence services of three nations were involved. Options one and two involved tampering and bugging while option three imagined a far more decisive course of action. Also known as the Hammer of Shamron, it called for concealing monitoring devices in the centrifuges along with enough high explosives to blow Iran's entire secret enrichment chain to kingdom come if the opportunity presented itself. The benefits, said Shamron, were twofold. Not only would a major act of sabotage deal a severe setback to the program but it would forever make the Iranians think twice about doing their nuclear shopping in Europe.

With the White House still hoping for a negotiated settlement to the Iran issue, the Americans entered the talks in the option two camp and remained there until the end. The British also liked the "wait and watch" approach, although in their mischievous hearts they wanted to do a bit of "messing about" as well. Option three was the most controversial of the plans—hardly surprising given its source—and in the end it was supported by only one country. Because that country also happened to be the one that would forever have to live under direct threat of a nuclear-armed Iran, its vote carried more weight. "Besides," argued Shamron emphatically, "Martin is ours. We found him. We fought for him. And we bled for him. We *own* those centrifuges. And we can do with them what we please."

A centrifuge cascade is a complex facility. It is also quite fragile, as the Iranians themselves have learned the hard way. One faulty gas centrifuge, spinning at several thousand rotations a minute, can break into deadly shrapnel and blow through a facility like a tornado, destroying adjacent centrifuges along with connective piping and assemblies. Years of painstaking work can be wiped out in an instant by a single fingerprint, smudge, or some other impurity.

In fact, that is precisely what the Iranians first suspected when a calamitous explosion swept through an undisclosed enrichment facility in Yazd at 4:42 a.m. Their suspicions quickly focused on sabotage, however, when a near-simultaneous blast shredded a second undisclosed facility at Gorgan near the Caspian Sea. When reports surfaced of explosions at two other secret enrichment plants, the Iranian president ordered an emergency shutdown of all nuclear facilities, along with an evacuation of nonessential personnel. By dawn Tehran time, the Hammer of Shamron had achieved its first goal. Four previously undisclosed plants lay in ruins. And the mullahs were in a panic.

BUT HOW TO explain the blasts publicly without revealing the great lie that was the Iranian nuclear program? For the first seventy-two hours, it seemed the mullahs and their allies in the Revolutionary Guards had chosen silence. It cracked, however, when rumors of the mysterious explosions reached the ears of a certain *Washington Post* reporter known for the infallibility of his sources inside the White House. He confirmed the reports with a few well-placed phone calls and published his findings the next morning in a front-page exclusive. The story ignited a firestorm, which is precisely what the men behind it had in mind.

Now under international pressure to explain the events, the Iranians shifted from silence to deception. Yes, they said, there had indeed been a string of unfortunate accidents at a number of civilian and military installations. Precisely how many facilities had been damaged the regime refused to say, only that all were nonnuclear in nature. "But this should come as a surprise to no one," the Iranian president said in an interview with a friendly journalist from China. "The Islamic Republic has no desire to produce nuclear weapons. Our program is entirely peaceful."

But still the leaks kept coming. And still the questions continued to be asked. If the four facilities involved were truly nonnuclear, why were they concealed in tunnels? And if they were for entirely peaceful purposes, why did the regime attempt to keep the explosions a secret? Since the mullahs refused to answer, the International Atomic Energy Agency did so for them. In a dramatic special report, the IAEA stated conclusively that each of the four facilities housed a cascade of centrifuges. There was only one possible conclusion to be drawn from the evidence. The Iranians were enriching uranium in secret. And they were planning to go for nuclear breakout.

The report was an earthquake. Within hours there were calls at the United Nations for crippling sanctions while the president of France suggested it might be time for allied military action—with the Americans taking the lead, of course. Painted into a rhetorical corner by years of deception, the Iranian regime had no option but to lash out, claiming it had been forced into a program of widespread concealment by constant Western threats. Furthermore, said the regime, its own investigation of the explosions had revealed they were caused by sabotage. High on the list of suspects were the Great Satan and its Zionist ally. "Tampering with our plants was an act of war," said the Iranian president. "And the Islamic Republic will respond in the very near future in a manner of our choosing."

The level of bombast rose quickly, as did the specificity of Iranian accusations of American and Israeli involvement. Sensing an opportunity to strengthen its position internally, the regime called on the Iranian people to protest this wanton violation of sovereignty. What they got instead was the largest rally in the history of the Iranian opposition movement. The mullahs responded by unleashing the dreaded Basij paramilitary forces. By the end of the day, more than a hundred protesters were dead and thousands more were in custody.

If the mullahs thought a display of naked brutality would end the protests, they were mistaken, for in the days to come, the streets of Tehran would become a virtual war zone of Green Movement rage and dissent. In the West, commentators speculated that the days of the regime might be numbered while security experts predicted a coming wave of Iranian-backed terrorism. Two questions, however, remained unanswered. Who had actually carried off the act of sabotage? And how had they managed to do it?

There were many theories, all wildly inaccurate. Not one referred to a long-lost Rembrandt now hanging in the National Gallery in Washington, or a former British newspaper reporter who was now a star on American cable news, or a Swiss financier known to all the world as Saint Martin who was anything but. Nor did they mention a man of medium build with gray temples who was often seen hiking alone along the sea cliffs of Cornwall—sometimes alone, sometimes accompanied by a broad-shouldered youth with matinee-idol good looks.

On a warmish afternoon in early June, while nearing the southern end of Kynance Cove, he spotted an elderly, bespectacled figure standing on the terrace of the Polpeor Café at Lizard Point. For an instant, he considered turning in the opposite direction. Instead, he lowered his head and kept walking. The old man had traveled a long way to see him. The least he could do was say a proper good-bye.

81

LIZARD POINT, CORNWALL

The terrace was in bright sunlight. They sat alone in the corner beneath the shade of a parasol, Shamron with his back to the sea, Gabriel directly opposite. He was dressed in hiking shorts and waterproof boots with thick socks pulled down to the ankle. Shamron stirred two packets of sugar into his coffee and in Hebrew asked whether Gabriel was armed. Gabriel glanced at the nylon rucksack resting on the empty chair next to him. Shamron pulled a frown.

"It's a violation of Office doctrine to carry weapons in separate containers. That gun is supposed to be at the small of your back where you can get to it quickly."

"It bothers my back on long walks."

Shamron, sufferer of chronic pain, gave a sympathetic nod. "I'm just relieved the British have finally given you formal permission to carry a gun at all times." He gave a faint smile. "I suppose we have the Iranians to thank for that."

"Are you hearing anything?"

Shamron nodded gravely. "They're convinced we were behind it and they're anxious to return the favor. We know that Hezbollah's top terror planner made a trip to Tehran last week. We also know that a number of operatives have been unusually chatty the last few days. It's only a matter of time before they hit us."

"Has my name come up?"

"Not yet."

Gabriel sipped his mineral water and asked Shamron what he was doing in the country.

"A bit of post-Masterpiece housekeeping."

"Of what sort?"

"The final interservice operational review," Shamron said disdainfully. "My personal nightmare. For the past few days, I've been locked in a room at Thames House with two dozen British and American spies who think it is their God-given right to ask me any question they please."

"It's a new world, Ari."

"I like the old ways better. They were less complicated. Besides, I've never played well with others."

"Why didn't Uzi handle the review himself?"

"Uzi is far too busy to deal with something so trivial," Shamron said sardonically. "He asked me to take care of it. I suppose it wasn't a complete waste of time. There were some fences that needed mending. Things got a little tense in the ops center on the final night."

"How did I manage to stay off the invitation list for this little gathering?"

"Graham Seymour felt you deserved a break."

"How thoughtful."

"I'm afraid he does have a couple of questions before the case file can be officially closed."

"What sort of questions?"

"About the *art* end of the affair."

"Such as?"

"How did Landesmann know the Rembrandt had resurfaced?"

"Gustaaf van Berkel of the Rembrandt Committee."

"What was the connection?"

"Who do you think was the committee's main source of funding?"

"Martin Landesmann?"

Gabriel nodded. "What better way to find a long-lost Rembrandt than to create the most august body of Rembrandt scholars in the world? Van Berkel and his staff knew the location of every known Rembrandt. And when new paintings were discovered, they were automatically brought to Van Berkel and his committee for attribution."

"How *Martin,*" said Shamron. "So when the painting was moved to Glastonbury for cleaning, Martin hired a professional to steal it for him?"

"Correct," said Gabriel. "But his thief turned out to have a conscience, something Martin was never burdened with."

"The Frenchman?"

"I assume so," said Gabriel. "But under no circumstances are you to say anything about Maurice Durand to the British."

"Because you made a deal with him?"

"Actually, it was Eli."

Shamron gave a dismissive wave of his hand. "As someone who's devoted your life to preservation of paintings, have you no misgivings about protecting the identity of a man who has stolen *billions* of dollars' worth of art?"

"If Durand hadn't given that list of names and account numbers to Hannah Weinberg, we would never have been able to break Martin. The list was Martin's undoing."

"So the end justifies the means?"

"You've made deals with people who are far worse than a professional art thief, Ari. Besides, Maurice Durand might come in handy the next time the Office needs to steal something. If I were Uzi, I'd stick him in my back pocket along with Martin Landesmann."

"He sends his regards, by the way."

"Uzi?"

"Landesmann," said Shamron, clearly enjoying the look of surprise on Gabriel's face. "He was wondering whether the two of you might meet on neutral territory for a quiet dinner."

"I'd rather take your place at the interservice operational review. But tell him thanks for the offer."

"I'm sure he's going to be disappointed. He says he has a great deal of respect for you. Apparently, Martin's become quite philosophical about the entire affair."

"How long before he tries to dissolve our partnership?"

"Actually, his efforts commenced not long after the explosions at the Iranian plants. Martin believes he's lived up to his end of the deal and would like to be released from any further obligations. What he doesn't quite understand is that our relationship is just beginning. Eventually, the Iranians will try to rebuild those enrichment plants. And we plan to make sure Martin is there to offer them a helping hand."

"Will the Iranians trust him?"

"We've given them no reason not to. As far as the mullahs are concerned, *we* tampered with the centrifuges while they were in transit. Which means Martin is going to pay dividends for years, and Uzi will be the primary beneficiary. No matter what happens for the rest of his term, Uzi will go down as one of the greatest directors in Office history. And all because of you."

Shamron scrutinized Gabriel. "It doesn't bother you that Uzi is getting all the credit for your work?"

"It wasn't my work, Ari. It was a team effort. Besides, after everything I've done to make Uzi's life miserable, he deserves to have a little glory thrown his way."

"The glory is yours, Gabriel. It's quite possible you've derailed the Iranian program for years. And in the process you've also managed to restore three remarkable women."

"Three?"

"Lena, Zoe, and Hendrickje. All in all, not bad for a few months' work." Shamron paused, then added, "Which leaves only you."

Gabriel made no response.

"I suppose this is the part where you tell me you're going to retire again?" Shamron shook his head slowly. "Maybe for a while. But then another Martin will come along. Or a new terrorist will carry out another massacre of innocents. And you'll be back on the field of battle."

"You're sure about that, Ari?

"Your mother named you Gabriel for a reason. You're eternal. Just like me."

Gabriel gazed silently at the purple thrift glowing atop the cliffs in the late-afternoon sun. Shamron seemed to sense that this time it was different. He looked around the terrace of the café and smiled reflectively.

"Do you remember the afternoon we came here a long time ago? It was after Tariq killed our ambassador and his wife in Paris."

"I remember, Ari."

"There was a girl," Shamron said after a long pause. "The one with all the earrings and bracelets. She was like a human wind chime. Do you remember her, Gabriel? She reminded me of—"

Shamron stopped himself. Gabriel seemed not to be listening anymore. He was staring at the cliffs, lost in memory.

"I'm sorry, Gabriel. I didn't mean to—"

"Don't apologize, Ari. I'll carry Leah and Dani with me for the rest of my life."

"You've given enough, Gabriel. Too much. I suppose it's fitting it should all end here."

"Yes," said Gabriel distantly, "I suppose it is."

"Can I at least give you a ride back to your cottage?"

"No," said Gabriel. "I'll walk."

He shouldered his rucksack and stood. Shamron remained seated, one final act of defiance.

"Learn from my mistakes, Gabriel. Take good care of your wife. And if you're fortunate enough to have children, take good care of them, too."

"I will, Ari."

Gabriel bent down and kissed Shamron's forehead, then started across the terrace.

"There's one more thing," Shamron called out in Hebrew.

Gabriel stopped and turned around.

"Put that gun at the small of your back where it belongs."

Gabriel smiled. "It's already there."

"I never saw a thing."

"You never did, Abba."

Gabriel left without another word. Shamron saw him one last time, as he made his way swiftly along the cliffs of Kynance Cove. Then Gabriel vanished into the fire of the setting sun and was gone.

AUTHOR'S NOTE

The Rembrandt Affair is a work of fiction. The names, characters, places, and incidents portrayed in the story are the product of the author's imagination or have been used fictitiously. Any resemblance to actual persons, living or dead, businesses, companies, events, or locales is entirely coincidental.

The statistics regarding art theft cited in the novel are accurate, as are the accounts of the theft of Leonardo's *Mona Lisa* in 1911 and Corot's *Le Chemin de Sèvres* in 1998. The *Portrait of a Young Woman* that appears in the pages of *The Rembrandt Affair* could never have been stolen, for it does not exist. If there was such a painting, it would look markedly like *Portrait of Hendrickje Stoffels*, oil on canvas, 101.9 by 83.7 centimeters, which hangs in Room 23 of the National Gallery in London.

There is no art gallery on the Herengracht called De Vries Fine Arts, though many dealers in Amsterdam and The Hague were all too happy to do a brisk trade with their German occupiers during the Second World War. The story of Lena Herzfeld and her family is fictitious, but, sadly, the details of the Holocaust in Holland cited during her "testimony" are not. Of the 140,000 Jews who resided in the Netherlands at the time the roundups began, only 25,000 managed to find a place to hide. Of those, one-third were either betrayed or arrested, oftentimes by their own countrymen. The famous Hollandsche Schouwburg theater did in fact serve as a detention center, and there was indeed a crèche across the street for young children. Several hundred young lives were saved due to the courage of the staff and the Dutch Resistance, one of the few bright spots on the otherwise bleak landscape of the Holocaust in the Netherlands.

The assistance given to fugitive Nazi war criminals by the Roman Catholic Church has been well documented. So, too, has the shameful wartime behavior of Switzerland's banks. Less well known, however, is the role played by Swiss high-technology firms in secretly supplying aspiring nuclear powers with the sophisticated equipment required to produce highly enriched uranium. In his authoritative book, *Peddling Peril,* proliferation expert David Albright describes how, in the 1990s, CIA operatives "witnessed Swiss government officials helping suppliers send sensitive goods to Pakistan, making a mockery of the official Swiss policy to maintain strict export control laws." Furthermore, Albright writes, "the Swiss government demonstrated an unwillingness to take action to disrupt these activities or to work with the CIA." Quite the opposite, in the summer of 2006, Swiss prosecutors threatened to bring criminal charges against several CIA officers involved in bringing down the global nuclear-smuggling network of A. Q. Khan. Only the intervention by officials at the highest levels of the American government convinced Bern to rethink its position.

While many Swiss firms have been willing proliferators—and no doubt remain so today—there is little disagreement among intelligence officials as to which Western European country has the most firms involved in the lucrative clandestine trade in nuclear materials. That dubious distinction belongs to Germany. Indeed, according to a very senior American intelligence official I spoke with while researching *The Rembrandt Affair,* much of the material required for Iran's secret nuclear program has been happily supplied by German high-tech firms. When I asked this official why German industrialists would be willing to sell such dangerous material to so unstable a regime, he gave me a somewhat puzzled look and responded with a single word: "Greed."

One would think that businessmen from Germany, the country that carried out the Holocaust, would have at least some qualms about doing business with a regime that has spoken openly about wiping the State of Israel from the face of the map. One would think, too, that Switzerland, the country that profited most from the Holocaust, would have similar reservations. But apparently not. If Iran succeeds in developing nuclear weapons, other countries in the region will surely want a nuclear capability of their own. Which means there is the potential for enormous future profits for firms willing to sell sensitive, export-restricted material to the highest bidder.

The intelligence services of three countries—the United States, Israel, and Great Britain—have worked the hardest to prevent such critical material from reaching Iran. The extent to which they have been successful is an open question. A senior American intelligence official with whom I spoke in the autumn of 2009 told me in no uncertain terms that Iran had other secret enrichment plants in addition to Qom—sites that could not have been constructed without at least some Western technology. And in March 2010, as I was completing this manuscript, the *New York Times* reported that Iran appears to be building at least two "Qom look-alikes" in defiance of the United Nations. The story was based on interviews with intelligence officials who insisted on anonymity because the information they were disclosing was based in part on "highly classified operations." No mention was made of a long-lost portrait by Rembrandt, a corrupt Swiss financier known to all the world as a saint, or a man of medium build with gray temples often seen hiking alone along the sea cliffs of Cornwall.

ACKNOWLEDGMENTS

This novel, like the previous books in the Gabriel Allon series, could not have been written without the assistance of David Bull, who truly is among the finest art restorers in the world. Usually, David advises me on how to clean paintings. This time, however, he assisted me in devising a plausible method for hiding a secret inside one. The technique known as a blind canvas is rarely used by modern restorers, though it turned out to be perfect for the task at hand. Also, I will forever be indebted to the brilliant Patrick Matthiesen, who instructed me in the sometimes wicked ways of the art world and helped to inspire one of my favorite characters in the series. Rest assured Patrick has few things in common with Julian Isherwood other than his passion for art, his sense of humor, and his boundless generosity.

Several Israeli and American officials spoke to me on background, and I thank them now in anonymity, which is how they would prefer it. Roger and Laura Cressey tutored me on American anti-proliferation efforts and helped me to better understand the ways of Washington's sprawling national security structure. A very special thanks to M, who taught me how to "own" a mobile phone or laptop computer. I don't think I will ever think of my smart phone in quite the same way, and neither should anyone else for that matter.

Anna Rubin, director of the New York State Banking Department's Holocaust Claims Processing Office, spoke with me about restitution issues and provenance searches. Peter Buijs taught me how to use the databases of the Jewish Historical Museum in Amsterdam while Sarah Feirabend of the Hollandsche Schouwburg memorial answered some final questions on the theater's terrible history. Sarah Bloomfield and Fred Zeidman, my colleagues at the United States Holocaust Memorial Museum in Washington, D.C., were a source of constant inspiration and encouragement. As always, I stand in awe of those who dedicate their lives to preserving the memory of the six million lost to the fires of the Shoah.

Yoav Oren gave me a terrifying tutorial in Krav Maga, though somehow he managed to make it look less like a lethal form of martial arts and more like ballet. Gerald Malone advised me on the wiretapping authority of the British government and provided much-needed laughter. Aline and Hank Day graciously allowed me to stage yet another high-level intelligence conference at their beautiful home. Marguerita and Andrew Pate made the twelve-hour flight to Argentina so Gabriel wouldn't have to.

I consulted hundreds of books, newspaper and magazine articles, and websites while preparing this manuscript, far too many to name here. I would be remiss, however, if I did not mention the extraordinary scholarship and reporting of Jacob Presser,

Debórah Dwork, Diane L. Wolf, Jean Ziegler, Isabel Vincent, Tom Bower, Martin Dean, Lynn H. Nicholas, David Cesarani, Uki Goñi, Steve Coll, and David Albright. David E. Sanger and William J. Broad of the *New York Times* have done an exemplary job of covering Iran's seemingly unstoppable march toward a nuclear weapon, and their learned, well-reported articles were an invaluable resource. So, too, were the authoritative reports issued by the Institute for Science and International Security and the Wisconsin Project on Nuclear Arms Control.

A special thanks to the National Gallery in London. Also, to the staffs of the Hotel de l'Europe in Amsterdam, the Hôtel de Crillon in Paris, and the Grand Hotel Kempinski in Geneva for taking good care of my family and me while I was conducting my research. Deepest apologies for running an intelligence operation from the rooms of the Kempinski without management's permission, but given the time constraints, it wasn't possible to make other arrangements. Habitués of Geneva probably know it would not be possible to see the fictional home of Martin Landesmann from even the upper floors of the Hôtel Métropole. It was one of many liberties I granted myself.

Louis Toscano, my dear friend and personal editor, made many improvements to the manuscript, as did my copy editor, Kathy Crosby. Obviously, responsibility for any mistakes or typographical errors that find their way into the finished book falls on my shoulders, not theirs. A special thanks to the remarkable team at Putnam, especially Ivan Held, Marilyn Ducksworth, Dick Heffernan, Leslie Gelbman, Kara Welsh, David Shanks, Meredith Phebus Dros, Kate Stark, Stephanie Sorensen, Katie McKee, Stephany Perez, Samantha Wolf, and Victoria Comella. Also, to Sloan Harris, for his grace and professionalism.

We are blessed with many friends who fill our lives with love and laughter at critical junctures during the writing year, especially Sally and Michael Oren, Angelique and Jim Bell, Joy and Jim Zorn, Nancy Dubuc and Michael Kizilbash, Elliott and Sloan Walker, Robyn and Charles Krauthammer, Elsa and Bob Woodward, Rachel and Elliott Abrams, Andrea and Tim Collins, Betsey and Andy Lack, Mirella and Dani Levinas, Derry Noyes and Greg Craig, Mariella and Michael Trager, and Susan and Terry O'Connor.

I am deeply indebted to my children, Lily and Nicholas, who spent much of last August on a research trip that stretched from the glaciers of Les Diablerets to the cliffs of Cornwall. They helped me to steal priceless works of art from Europe's finest museums, fictitiously of course, and listened patiently while I conceived and discarded several different versions of the plot, usually during yet another endless train ride. Finally, my wife, Jamie Gangel, helped me find the essence of the story when it eluded me and skillfully edited the pile of paper I euphemistically refer to as a "first draft." Were it not for her patience, attention to detail, and forbearance, *The Rembrandt Affair* would not have been completed before its deadline. My debt to her is immeasurable, as is my love.